Bedtime Stories
for CIS Males

Bedtime Stories for CIS Males

T-BOB CORVUS

JUBLIO
OKLAHOMA CITY, OK

Jublio
Oklahoma City, OK
www.jubliobooks.com

Cover artist: Zachary Schoenbaum
Book Designer: Jennifer Omner
Set in Marker Felt, BadaBoom Pro BB, and Garamond Premier Pro

PUBLISHER'S CATALOGING-IN-PUBLICATION DATA
Names: Corvus, T-Bob, author.
Title: Bedtime stories for cis males / T-Bob Corvus.
Description: Oklahoma City : Jublio, 2018.
Identifiers: LCCN 2018931368 | ISBN 978-0-9861158-6-8 (pbk.) |
    ISBN 978-0-9861158-7-5 (ebook)
Subjects: LCSH: Men—Fiction. | Man-woman relationships—
    Fiction. | Sex role—Fiction. | Short stories. | Humorous stories. |
    BISAC: FICTION / Humorous / Black Humor. |FICTION /
    Short Stories (single author) | GSAFD: Short stories. | Humorous
    fiction.
Classification: LCC PS3603.O7864 B43 2018 (print) | LCC
    PS3603.O7864 (ebook) | DDC 813/.6—dc23.

CONTENTS

THE COUILLON   1

THE FLANK STRAP   163

THE ASCENDANT   297

THE COUILLON

BY

T-BOB CORVUS

CHAPTER 1

Jack searched the insole of his shoes with a flashlight each morning. Every last shoe. He had neatly arranged each pair of three dozen Allen Edmonds shoes on a shelf in his walk-in closet, stored upside down on aromatic shoetrees. His plan of action was to frustrate the effort of ghosts, who leave sticky slimes of spiritual energy on objects that offend them. He also searched for signs of trespass by a mouse or spider.

This day, each pair seemed to plead, "Pick me." He had narrowed his choice to the 5th Avenue cap-toed oxford, but should he choose the brown? No, today it would be the oxblood.

The shirt he preferred was a tailored, paleblue pinpoint oxford with an open collar and French cuffs. Dressy perhaps, but Jack liked looking sharp. Once, he had completely lost control and nearly strangled his tailor, Achmed, over a box of new shirts. After several failed efforts, Achmed had finally succeeded in embroidering flawless monograms on the pockets and cuffs in hues that were only a thousandth of a degree in contrast to the fabric of the shirt. His best customer's initials, "JM," only appeared on the edge of one's perception. The hapless Syrian's felony was in stitching the monogram on, of all things, shirts fitted with button-down collars. "Am I a hick?" Jack shouted as he released the tailor from his choking grip. "No one but a cretin would wear a button-down collar."

Jack threw the knot in his tangerine colored cobblestone paisley bow tie perfectly. Then he pulled the knot open and retied it. He

3

probably would have liked the cut of the jib of the fit and tanned, 30-year old gentleman looking back at him from a mirror. But he avoided the damn things. His bedroom and bath had no mirror. Mirrors are unlucky.

Jack slipped a handkerchief in the breast pocket of his natural linen two-button suit and took one last look at his bedroom before leaving for the day. His Queen Ann furniture contrasted nicely with the heavy cypress beams that surrounded the doorways. Except for the width of a hand, the windows extended from ceiling to floor. *Exquisitely appointed,* he told himself. *That's what "Southern Living" magazine would say.* He tugged at a corner of the duvet bed covering and a wrinkle that the maid would have ignored disappeared. He felt satisfaction, secure in the knowledge that the knot in his tie was thrown to perfection and that a quarter would bounce off his taut bedcovers.

He stepped out of his room, right foot first for good luck, and walked on tiptoes down a dim hallway decorated with pictures of felines. He hated pictures of cats so much that he refused to use Facebook. But he stopped to adjust one that was out of level, and in doing so, he bumped into a console table. The cat figurines that littered its top clattered. His wife's sharp voice stabbed out at him from behind the door of her separate bedroom. "People are trying to sleep you know."

Jack opened a door and peeked inside. "Sorry, dear," he whispered. Jill, his wife of seven years, was still in bed, shrouded in satin pajamas. She wore a blinder to exclude the light from the windows to her soul.

Jack surveyed her bedroom.

Blech, he said to himself. *Gauche and gross.* Jill had over-decorated her boudoir. He'd forgotten how awful it was. It violated his taste, his sense of commensurateness. Jack slept in one of the spare bedrooms now. Occasionally, he regretted having asked her if her decorator was Tammy Faye Bakker. Most days he didn't.

He eased the door closed, and with his first step, another screech punctured the silence. He nearly climbed the wall. He had put his foot near one of Jill's favorite tabbies, the one that disliked him so. The primal wail of that cat always pushed him to the edge.

"Watch out for the kitties!" she yelled, adding, "you clumsy bastard."

"Sorry."

"Now get out of here. Go make my daddy and me some money, you coward."

"Golf this afternoon."

"Don't you have something better to spend your time on?"

"Business contacts, dearest."

"I need a tuxedo tonight. Some pain in the ass benefit for some kind of victims."

"Junior League?"

"Unh-hunh. Be home early."

"Yes, light of my life. Call me later."

"Whatever."

Jack held his breath as he walked past a mirror in the great room. His right hand checked his tie. He left through the kitchen and mudroom, careful to suppress any noise of heels clicking on the terrazzo floors.

In the garage, he loaded his golf bag into the trunk of his Lincoln town car. The leather bag still had that smell of new. Every club sparkled, from the woods through the irons. Even the putter looked as shiny as it had been when he unboxed it the pro shop. He had refused the floor model. It was shopworn. The staff at the country club never cleaned his sticks to his satisfaction, so he stored them at home and polished them himself.

Jack put aside thoughts about Jill while motoring east out of Lafayette in the pearly-white Lincoln, out toward the levee. He rarely drove in that direction. He hated the chills of dread that ran down his spine when he drove down the six-foot slope that marked the lowlands of the Atchafalaya basin, a decline that most travelers would never even notice.

His journey that began a dozen years ago had been the longest eight miles in the world. He was from Carencro, Louisiana, just north of Lafayette. The word meant "buzzard" in French, carrion crow. His mother gave psychic readings but her chronic, unspecific physical complaints and his dad's frequent incarcerations denied him most of the cool things his schoolmates enjoyed. He had strangled enough education out of its schools to keep himself on the football team. Jack had a talent for running at full tilt while looking back over his shoulder, and for changing directions, turning on a dime to get under a pass that fell short or sailed wide. He had his helmet outfitted with a single face bar so he would be more photogenic. His game was good enough to attract interest from the University of Louisiana Lafayette.

The recruiter wanted him to walk on, to play football without a scholarship. "We's always looking for more fresh air boys," he'd said, meaning pass catchers, who were called on less frequently to block and tackle. But on the way out of the recruiter's office, he spotted several athletic young people walking out of another office carrying megaphones. Cheerleaders. He had shown some flair for gymnastics. Without an ounce of deliberation, he walked into the office, put his glib lip and winning smile together, and talked his way into a cheer-leading scholarship. Jack spent the next four years urging the Ragin Cajuns on to V-I-C-T-O-R-Y.

Jill was three or four years older than Jack, and captain of the pom squad. The girl cheerleaders were fit, energetic, solid 9s on the index, but the pom squad was reserved for the 10s with the rich daddies. Jill shook her round, bouncy pom-poms provocatively, squatting, thrusting, grinding her body, arousing in the Cajun fans a remembrance of what football is all about. She married the president of the Sig Ep house after football season in Jack's freshman year.

He ran into her again at a country club charity function in his final semester. Jack had little interest in the plight of the downtrodden but he had attended the gala as the final gambit in a long-term project of getting between the sheets with a bespectacled sociology major from Opelousas. Her heart would melt, he was certain, if he made an uncharacteristic display of brotherly love by attending a charity event. Jill told Jack she remembered him and it might have been true. She was single again, still wearing her hair in long blonde schoolgirl tresses. She liked Jack's choice in Chardonnay, and like the wine, she had grown richer and more full-bodied with age. And available. Jack couldn't ditch the sociology major fast enough. He was glad he changed plans. Jill's astrological signs were compatible and she was a wildcat in bed. An infatuated Jack asked for her hand in marriage.

The Atchafalaya separates the eastern Creole Louisiana of Baton Rouge and New Orleans from the Cajun Louisiana bottomlands, rice fields and canebrakes on the west. Acadiana—Cajun Louisiana—had been one of the most isolated parts of the country until the Interstate highway cut through the Atchafalaya.

The basin of the Atchafalaya contains a huge freshwater wetland full of swamplands, bayous, backwater lakes, black bears, alligators, spiders and snakes that is part of the Mississippi delta system. The old women also whisper to the little ones about the most frightening denizen of the swamp, the blood-sucking wolf men, "rougarou" to the Cajuns and "Loup Garou" to the Creoles. The old crones say their once-human bodies are inhabited by spirits that have been forfeited to the devil. Why? Because the mortal souls who had inhabited their stinking flesh had mocked Lent. As their penance, the rougarou are cast into hiding, deep in the swamp, holing up in their underground dens by day. At night, they prey on the innocents, transforming themselves into animals with human bodies and heads of wolves.

Twenty years ago, fishermen discovered a pile of sun-bleached bones chained to a cypress stump in the swamp. Jurisdiction fell to the town cop of Henderson. He found the arm bones of the corpse locked in a suitcase with a suicide note pinned to the outside. "We can rule out foul play in the death of Mr. Hickey," he told reporters.

The detached skull looked up from between the skeleton's legs. The neck bones bore scars that appeared to be left by a predator's teeth, a rougarou, Jack supposed. The coroner attributed the gouges to a chainsaw, but the crack detective from Henderson found none nearby.

The Atchafalaya also figured in on his mother's death. An alligator hunter discovered her body ten feet above a lake, lying on top of an oil production platform littered with her tarot cards, in the area of a roost for crows. Her soft tissues, her eyes, had been plucked out of socket by the birds. The police didn't seem to care if the cause of her death was determined or not. The signs told Jack she had died of fright, which would be an obstacle to crossing over for her spirit. Whatever killed her left her feet pointed to the west. Jack intimated to a friend that her spirit still dwelled in the swamp.

He avoided the basin at night out of pity and fear for the spirits of the souls of his parents. He thought of them as his procreators. They left him nothing but a last name, "Hickey."

Beyond a levee, a thin strip of bait shops, bars and chandlers slouched beside a dredged-out waterway. Idle powerboats and sailboats lined the docks. Jack's Lincoln looked out of place, parked beside pickup trucks and motorcycles. He spotted his quarry seated on a restaurant deck overlooking the canal. It was his college friend, Jude Malveaux.

Jude was everything Jack was not. Slicked back and oiled, his hair glistened in sunlight as if it were rarely seen. He had no complexion. None. Jude's pencil-thin mustache looked like something that belonged under a nose. Slouching low on the bridge of his snout was a pair of mirrored aviator sunglasses, and seated behind a Bloody Mary, Jude looked like a poster boy for death-by-wooden-stake-through-the-heart if there ever had been one.

While in college, Jack wanted to change his name. He hated "Hickey" and all the nicknames it inspired, like "hick." Everyone on campus knew him as "Jack Mouton" because, once he arrived in Lafayette, he always introduced himself that way. With any luck, his new friends in Lafayette would assume his ancestor was a beloved Civil War general.

But asking to be renamed "Mouton" in Lafayette would have been like asking for a name change to "Weiner" in New York City. The courts frown on letting people change their moniker to a famous name. On Jude's advice, they travelled north to Natchitoches Parish to apply for the name change.

Jude spoke to Jack first. "Jack, old pal," he said.

"Hi ya Jude. By yourself after all?"

"Naw, man, she's in the crapper." Jude's table was strewn with debris, celery stalks, empty shot glasses, red-stained tumblers, and a mustard-smeared plate of popsicle sticks and corny dog remains.

"Oh goodness, I don't know how you put those corny dogs in your mouth." Jack removed his Christian Dior sunglasses and took a chair across the table from Jude. "Your girlfriend. She anyone I know?"

"Jill let you look at redheads?" Jude signaled 'one more' to the bartender and another Bloody Mary appeared as if by magic, before Jack could lift a finger to indicate he had a drink order, too.

"I look...I just don't grab." Jack's answer was interrupted by the roar of an approaching motor.

"Holy crap, would you look at this babe!" Jude said. A perfectly tanned, pretty girl slipped a jet ski into the dock. She had the figure of an athlete. A gentle smile spread across Jack's face.

"You know, I could have screwed her an hour ago," Jude said.

"Oh right." Jack had no idea why he was drawn to the smarmy character sitting across the table. "Why didn't you?"

"Hell, Jack, I couldn't find her!"

"You're too coarse for words," Jack scolded.

"Where's the keys?"

Jack dug in his pocket and handed a set of keys to Jude. On one end of a chain was a red-and-white fishing bobber.

"The refrigerator has some stuff in it you'll probably want to use and the bar's stocked. You're cleared with security. For chrissakes, can you clean the boat up this time? Jill had a hissy fit the way you left it a couple of months ago."

"I shoulda taught that woman a lesson when I had the chance. Biggest mistake of my life, not marrying Jill myself."

"How did you ever get so crude? Lawyers are supposed to be courtly."

"Spend six or seven years representing drunks and whores and you'll get crude too. Anyway, crude is what you like about me."

"She'd have you trained by now. Maybe a deacon in the church."

"That rich daddy of hers woulda paid through the nose to get rid of old Jude. By now I'd have a fat ass black woman feeding me my breakfast and I'd have nothin' better to do than check the Treasury rate in the Wall Street Journal."

"I want what you want."

"You'd be me if you could and you know it. And if you were me, you'd grab some of that old man's money for yourself."

Behind Jack's back, a redhead bounced out of the bar. She was about ten pounds overweight in all the right places. "Jude! Where y'at dahlin?" Her throat launched a sharp-bladed voice with an uptown accent that sounded like Brooklynese on Quaaludes. "Boo, where y'at?" She spoke in a lingo the locals called "N'awlins yat."

"There she is," Jude said. Reaching for the keys, he knocked Jack's sunglasses on the deck. "She's hot to trot. I'm outta here."

As Jack fumbled to retrieve the sunglasses, he got no better than a peek at a big head of red hair as the green door on Jude's beat-up black Camaro slammed shut.

"Call me about Mardi Gras," Jack shouted after his chum. "And clean up after!"

Looming in his field of vision was a big waiter. He needed a shave. A solution of oil and water seemed to coat his skin and he held a draught of beer with a finger inside the glass. The decal on the beer glass read "JAX" and the tattoo on the waiter's offending finger read "LOVE." Jack quickly donned his sunglasses.

"He your buddy?" the waiter asked.

"Yeah. Yes."

"Seventy-two fifty."

"One beer? Seventy-two fifty?"

The waiter handed Jack a tab and cracked his knuckles.

Julien Malveaux was another kid from the wrong side of Carencro that had enrolled at UL-Lafayette. He called himself Jude and had managed to wrangle admittance to a program called "University Studies." Unlike courses of study like "business," or "engineering," the college catalog did not list University Studies as a major. These special courses helped athletes matriculate without the burden of classroom attendance. He told people that he was a third-string quarterback, as if anyone would believe that a third-string quarterback would look like he had never seen the sun. Aside from that, his frame was slight. He rocked up off of his heels when he walked, giving him an awkward gait—he lurched forward like a gecko. He rarely attended classes. Instead, he managed a poker game that catered to the frat boys and athletes. He kept 5% of each pot for himself.

They knew one another from grade school. Jack sold magazines door-to-door and Jude stole bicycles. Jack stopped by to Jude's place often, just off-campus in Lafayette. It was the boar's den of a poker room that Jude called the "Sky Box." All his customers called the place "The Squat." The Squat had a makeshift dumbwaiter that connected it to a shack below that sold oyster po'boy sandwiches and beer. In months that did not have an "R," the place smelled of Tony C's and barbequed bologna. The building should have fallen over years ago. Jude said that the termites had been holding hands.

Jude would back the action of the worst of the dumb asses among the athletes. They settled their losses with tickets, jerseys and helmets. He protected himself with hidden cameras and sold the stuff to Jack who marked it up and sold it to his upscale friends from the fraternities. The Greeks maintained reserved seating at the poker table. Jack was GDI. He never pledged a fraternity. And he never put even a nickel at risk on Jude's felt-topped tables.

He had a begrudging admiration for his lowlife friend. To Jack, Jude was an enigma, detestable, execrable, abominable, loathsome, wretched, a train wreck. He was drawn to the skunk like a moth to the flame. Like Eve to the glib, smooth-tongued serpent. He told himself that he collected odd characters, but Jack's collection, if that is what it was, was small.

To his credit, Jude manipulated his way through life on nothing more than his wit. Jack knew his own success was built on compromise. He was happy to put on a charm offensive, exercise his golden tongue, and let other people accomplish things for him.

Jack's eyes scanned the bar tab. "Corny dogs 6, Bloody Mary III, Grand Mariner shooters III, draw IIII."

"*Grand Mariner?*"

"So you're a spelling Nazi. She was drinking it. The girl."

"That slippery bastard." Dutiful Jack peeled off five crisp twenties.

CHAPTER 2

Jack looked through the window of a vacant store bay at the backside of an outward facing sign. In reverse, he read the bold lettering. "FOR LEASE, BAYOU TECHE SHOPPING CENTER, LEASING BY JACK MOUTON, 555-8040, BAYOU TECHE MANAGEMENT ENTERPRISES, LAFAYETTE, LOUISIANA."

The interior of the bay was dusty, cluttered with the last tenant's leftover junk and the detritus of a failed general mercantile which had gone, as his father-in-law Big Leo would say, "tits up." Outside, Jack had parked his shiny Lincoln under a huge live oak tree that seemed to weep wisps of Spanish moss.

Once he was inside the storefront, he had argued with himself over whether he should move the town car. A crow had perched on the uppermost branch of the live oak after he had unlocked the door and gone inside. He mulled over a thought that the big black devil might be one of the crows who had consumed the flesh of his mother. They live for years. He despised the bird, and at the same time, he envied them for their ability to move so easily between the earth and the sky, the temporal and the spiritual.

The crow leapt from his roost and flew away. It was likely on its way to scold an owl. Or perhaps it was not content when a dingy sedan carrying two ladies pulled up near the door to the vacant bay. They were Jack's prospective tenants and he was eager to cadge a lease from them. The space had been vacant for three years and the embroidery shop they planned to open was perfect for Jack. That's what they told him they were looking for when he booked the appointment. A nice homespun shop like that was certain to draw a lot of shoppers to the property and benefit the other tenants.

Jack had the prospects pretty well sized up after looking at the sedan. It was a pale blue that coordinated with the tinted coif of the driver. Her hair swept and twisted into a bun at the back of her head. Easy pickings.

The prospects had a thousand processes to complete before removing themselves from the vehicle. The driver checked her makeup in the visor mirror, put something in her purse, then removed something else from her purse, took a sip from a tall beverage container, then put something else in the purse. Then she turned the visor over to her passenger, who repeated the same steps. The female kabuki dance, getting out of a car.

Jack opened the front door for them and flashed his broad toothy smile. "Jack Mouton, nice to meet you."

Both ladies hauled big patchwork fabric bags on long straps that hung from their shoulders. The elder one, the one with the blue tinted bun on the back of her head, extended her hand meekly. She said to Jack, "I'm Pearl." She looked older than the fifty years Jack knew she had racked up because he had ordered up her credit report before booking the appointment. "And this is my friend Lela." Lela was in her twenties, trim, but she was on a fast-track-to-dowdy, same as Pearl.

"I'm glad to see you don't rent to any beer joints," Pearl said. "And no dirty book stores. We don't want neighbors like that."

"Wouldn't even consider it," Jack said.

"Our clientele just won't put up with it," Pearl said. She and Lela rubbernecked their way to the rear of the bay. Lela, he noticed, had a nice fanny. It shook from side to side when she jiggled the back door. Locked.

Thank the stars, Jack thought. *Last thing I need is for them to see the trash in the alley.*

The Couillon

The prospects strolled back to the storefront. Jack opened folding chairs and invited the ladies to sit.

"What kind of business did you say you have?" Jack asked. He knew the answer. Jack was always prepared. But it was best to turn Pearl's mind to positive thoughts.

"Quilts. Appliqués. Stencils," Lela answered and Jack nodded approvingly, smiling. He pretended to pour over the sheaf of papers in his notebook, but his eyes were riveted on Lela. The patchwork skirt and vest she wore showed about as much leg as a burqa, but she had a nice tushie. He hoped she would test the lock on that back door a second time.

"Yeah. Quilts. A gold mine," Jack said as Lela took a seat. "You're sitting on a real gold mine."

"How much is the rent?" Pearl asked.

"Sixteen dollars, triple-net," Jack answered. *Show 'em those pearly whites.*

Lela and Pearl looked at one another stupefied.

"Sixteen dollars a foot, per year." *How dumb could these Bill Gates wannabes be?* Jack thought. He had explained this a hundred times before. His pitch was almost singsong. "That's maybe sixteen thousand. We'll measure square feet. So that's somewhere around thirteen, fourteen hundred a month."

Lela and Pearl surrendered their jaws to gravity. Their mouths dropped wide open. Their orbs opened wide.

"On top you have your heat, air, and lights. And improvements. Insurance. If the air conditioner goes out, you fix it."

The prospect's mouths were even more widely agape than before. Jack imagined an insect flying inside Lela's lips, which he observed were full and moist.

"We could never pay rent like that..." Pearl's voice trailed off in dejection.

"You know what they say. Location, location, location. You have financial statements?"

Each of the ladies shook her head "no."

"A backer?" Jack knew the answer without asking the question. He dug a business card out of his eel skin wallet and shoved it into an oversized envelope. *This lease is as good as signed,* Jack thought.

"A copy of our lease and financial requirements, and my business card. Neiman-Marcus wants to look at this space, so maybe we can..." Jack gestured with a rolling forward motion of his first two fingers. "I'll call you in a couple of days."

Lela and Pearl nodded.

Jack ushered his prime prospects out of the space, right foot first, and locked up the storefront. He left the ladies to their own devices. It might take them another hour to get in the car and get it started.

The crow had not returned to its roost, but he'd heard the hoot of an owl, so he was eager to leave. Sitting with his feet out of his shiny Lincoln, Jack wiped his hands with disinfectant and removed dust booties from his shoes.

Big Leo's strip shopping centers had been on their asses when Jack joined the firm. Economic downturn factored in their decline. The roofs leaked and the parking lots looked like a war zone. The taxes were in arrears and every day the fire insurance agent called to threaten cancellation. Big Leo had given a half interest in the shopping centers to Jill and was content to sit on his hedge fund investments, oil and gas royalties, and jumbo CDs. He chased skirts, gambled at cockfights, and went fishing. He had milked every Yankee dollar out of the property years ago and when Jack married into the family, he was more than willing to sit on his duff. He had even tried to slough them off by giving them a deed in lieu of foreclosure. The bankers smelled a rat. They supposed that Big Leo was trying to stiff them with properties full of asbestos and polluted ground water. They were afraid to be in the chain of title. It was standoff.

The Couillon

It had been a chore, but Jack was a meticulous planner and on his effort alone, he had turned the shopping centers around.

Now seven years into their marriage, Jill's interest in their marital bliss was on the ebb. The harder Jack worked, the more he subordinated his interests to her. Each time he exercised his judgment, or revealed his desires, she found something to criticize. She seemed to hold him in contempt if he showed kindness or sensitivity. Perhaps she missed Jack the scallywag. He had suppressed every inborn rogue instinct when he decided to become a real estate professional. Okay, she was stingy with the sex. But Jack would suppose that all couples experienced the same problem. Things would improve in another year, he told himself. Hell, even Jack Reacher didn't get any in the last book, and lack of nookie was the most common topic of discussion between him and the members of his golf foursome. Golf gave Jack about the only contact he had with regular people. The people at the office were all toadies to Big Leo. At home he was alone. In the solitary hours he worried about ghosts.

Someday, he would run the firm and expand into other markets. He'd fire the hangers-on that were so loyal to Big Leo. Big Leo and Jill owed Jack. They owed Jack big.

The front door to Bayou Teche Management Enterprises had been sawn from a heavy slab of old growth cypress that Jack loved. A bold logo festooned the entry with the slogan "If it's real estate you're looking for, BTME!"

He took a deep breath before entering. Inside he knew he would be barraged by clerks with stacks of pink telephone messages about leaking roofs, backed up toilets, and cantankerous air conditioners.

He wasn't disappointed but he was surprised. Harriet, the leggy receptionist, was not hidden behind a movie magazine for a change. She was chatting with a redhead in a short skirt.

"Who do we have here, Harriet?"

"Our new receivables clerk, Charma. She's been here going on two weeks."

"A belated welcome to the firm. Chaw-muh?"

"Charma. Yeah, you gotta say it in yat, Boo. Say, you a real estate agent? For true? I need to sell my condo. Me and Evangeline, thass my daughter, yeah. We been looking for like you know a better place, you know Boo?"

"Uh, Harriet? Where's the three stooges?"

Jack braced himself for the onslaught of a tsunami, the lady property managers. Each of them had the authority to address tenant complaints and none of them exercised it. They'd rather try to get Jack to do the heavy lifting. It wasn't any fun at all to have to explain to the tenants they needed to read the lease if they thought someone else would fix their air conditioner.

Each of the managers had been with the company long before Jack arrived on the scene, back when the properties were in the toilet. When Jack first came on the scene, none of them expected to have a job the next day, not a one. But slowly, Jack got the worst problems headed off. He laid careful plans and adapted them to changing conditions. Tenants moved in. Jack negotiated waivers of arrearages from the mortgage holders and managed to bring the debt to current status. Insurance was acquired and past due taxes were paid. Dead birds were swept out of the store bays and parking lots were resurfaced. Things got better. BTME started paying employee health insurance and sponsored a 401(k) plan to help the staff plan for retirement.

So, of course, the entire firm's staff vilified Jack. Behind his back they called him "that little prick from Carencro." "Nothing good from Carencro," they said. No one likes change, and Jack had changed all of Big Leo's policies. He would never earn their forgiveness for that.

Before the receptionist could answer, Jack was accosted by the three property managers. Jack had never seen any of them without a stack of pink phone messages.

Mona started. "Richards called and he has a toilet..."

She was interrupted by Laurie. "...parked in the alley that..."

And Carlie. "...drove through a plate glass window..."

"...smelling like a dead rat..."

"...and trash piled so high you can't see over it..."

"...and the roof's leaking like a sieve."

They followed him into his tidy office.

"Leave them," he said. "I'll see to them." Jack supposed that none of the property managers believed that he would address the pile of telephone messages, and for good reason.

CHAPTER 3

Alone in his office, Jack scanned each message. He needed to know what was going on in the shopping centers. Once he was done, he folded each message into a neat square and threw them one-by-one into in the trash. He made sure he missed the thirteenth toss.

He opened a newspaper and turned to the real estate section. Another staff member knocked lightly on his doorjamb.

"Mr. Mouton, would you look at these refund receipts?" It was Louise, the firm's bookkeeper. Louise was so non-descript she could probably have walked into a bank vault unnoticed. She had been with the company longer than Jack had been alive, and she held a stack of papers to her breast as if they were state secrets. Oftentimes, she brought Jack reports he asked for but would never let go of them long enough for anyone but a speed-reader to get much information from them.

"What is it?"

"Off our credit card machine. When we make refunds on credit cards."

"Screw ups?"

"You might say," she said. "It's that Charma girl."

"She's new. Let me see." Louise had called him 'Mr. Mouton.' The matter was important to Louise if she called him 'Mr. Mouton.' She usually called him 'Jack.'

Louise wouldn't release her vise-like grip on the papers.

"Am I going to have to put my foot on your chest to prise that stack of paperwork away from you?" he asked.

She finally let go. He held two slips of paper side-by-side and compared them. "Sometimes the new ones don't understand. Hmmm. Is this number what I think it is?"

"Yes, indeed Mr. Mouton."

"Thank you, Louise. That will be all."

Louise left with a self-satisfied full-body harrumph that repositioned her sagging breasts to their age and gravity defying high guardant station. Jack again compared two slips of paper side-by-side. Each had a lengthy but identical number inscribed on it. He found the same number on several more slips. He punched his phone.

"Have Charma...tell Charma I need to see her for a minute," he told the phone.

Charma bounced in Jack's office after a moment. Jack noticed that her tight-fitting outfit seemed perfectly designed to piss off her less fully-proportioned co-workers. She leaned forward, into the corner of Jack's desk, jamming that luckiest of desk corners into her crotch. She correctly supposed that Jack took notice, but she maintained plausible denial that she was using her sexuality to tempt him and color his judgment.

"Hey darling. How's your mama and them?"

"Dead."

"Sorry, Boo."

"Charma how long have you been here? Two weeks?"

"Yeah. You right."

"Can you tell me why each of these refunds have the same number on them?"

Charma's eyes travelled around the spacious room. She looked at Jack's photographs, the Mardi Gras mask collection he displayed on the wall, out the window, anywhere but at the paperwork the boss was shoving under her nose.

"Refunds is the footherest thing from my job, sugar."

"Yeah. I guess. That's why it looks so strange that each of these refunds has your credit card number on it. There must be $3,000 here..."

"For true? Darling," Charma said. Jack's eyes were on her bosom, so she plumped her girls with a quick double wrist lift. She wasn't a rocket surgeon but she knew she had a whole chest full of what Jack wanted. "I only been here a few days. These books...woof."

Charma was backing up now, away from Jack's desk, edging toward the exit. Jack took up a station between his newest clerk and the door. Her eyes raced around the room. The windows didn't offer her an exit as the firm occupied the fourth floor.

"It's not washing, Charma. You got a better story? This one sucks."

Charma's frantic orbs searched the room again. Cornered, she dove forward, shouting "Darling! Please!" She flew parallel to the floor, like Supergirl, and landed with an ooomph on her breasts and stomach, arms and legs flailing akimbo, and shouting with all the drama she could muster. "No! Please stop! No! Mister Mouton... control your passion!"

The property managers heard the kerfuffle and bumbled into Jack's office. A blizzard of pink slips filled the air as they scrambled over one another to check out the disturbance. Nothing exciting had happened at the ordinarily staid BTME since Big Leo got a soupcon of his foreskin stuck in his zipper.

Charma's collar was torn. Her bra twisted on an oblique plane and a huge amount of cleavage outspread from her blouse. Her state of disorder evidenced plenty to the three stooges.

"Mr. Mouton! How could you?" Charma remained on the floor, rolling to display her state of affairs to its best advantage.

"He just grab me...not even ax. You can't do this to me. I have a daughter anyways."

"I didn't do anything." Jack was flustered, rattled. "Charma, you take the rest of the day off. We'll sort this out tomorrow."

As Charma regained her feet, she made sure Jack got an eyeful of her tantalizing breasts and creamy thighs. Jack watched her fanny as she left of his office and beyond it, the solid cypress front door of the firm. Her bottom wiggled like two pups fighting under a blanket.

"How did she get into that skirt?" Mona asked.

"It must be like putting a marshmallow in a piggybank," Jack said. A withering glare from Mona told him he shouldn't have. He usually knew better than to speak his mind. He knew that he could trust his subordinates to take anything he said out of context.

Jack was happy to have some reason to squirm out of a date with Jill. She had recently belittled him in front of people at the Petroleum Club. He had asked for two sides of salad dressing, vinaigrette and Roquefort, and she called him "Gumby." She was doing it again. Somehow she would spin his good qualities and make them sound like a vice.

"You're indecisive," she said.

"Indecision is the key to flexibility," he told her. He found out later that it made her mad if he stuck up for himself.

He took some time to consider what he would say to make her think it was her idea to ditch him for the evening. He was less successful now than he used to be, talking himself out of a pinch with Jill. She usually saw through him.

Once she accused him of reneging at bridge, right in front of some *chieuse née* Junior Leaguers. She did it just as he put a handful of Spanish peanuts in his mouth.

"I didn't," he said. Tiny bits of half-chewed peanuts spewed from his mouth.

"Don't spit peanuts at me," she told him. Since the peanut spitting incident, she saw through every one of his fabrications. Every effort to get one over on her failed.

Jack had admired the self confident Jill from the first. She wore her emotions on her sleeve, unlike Jack, who never revealed his emotions, so much so that many people that only knew him socially described him as cold and calculating. He was a little bit jealous that she was so unrestrained in showing her intense, almost unstable emotions. She knew she was beautiful, beguiling, the most dazzling girl in town, or in the parish for that matter, and she loved herself for being so lovely. She never saw an ugly mirror. Every hour of every day was devoted to her schemes to climb to the top of Lafayette's society.

Early on, she had provided Jack material things, financial security, great sex, some affection; those things he desperately needed. But soon, Jill began to raise her voice to Jack in impatience. It became more frequent. She nagged him until he let her have her way. He had no choice if he didn't want to listen to her rants. He managed to do little more than to reinforce her scolding behavior, which became worse as time went on. Jack shrugged it off. Despite the chronic bruises to his ego, their marriage still provided Jack with financial security, and she sometimes showed him affection in public. Jack was willing to shoulder part of the blame and hoped that they might recover some measure of affection for one another.

She boasted to Jack that her design was to claw her way into New Orleans society. She planned to be King of Rex. The Krewe of Rex, the snootiest and most exclusive of the New Orleans Mardi Gras parading krewes. She would be the first woman King of Rex and after that, she would decide what her next conquest needed to be.

Instead of working shoulder-to-shoulder with Jack, Jill attended charity events, took exercise classes and met friends from the Junior League for coffee. She called her circle of friends her "Krewe" and she didn't hesitate to drop a girl that did not fall in line with her own thinking, or who couldn't keep up financially, even if her setbacks were due to a husband's finances or illness.

Jill had met with Jack and prospective tenants in their first year of marriage. She exaggerated the esteem associated with being a tenant in the shopping center in question, which a child of three could see was in a sad state of disrepair. She couldn't blow smoke as well as Jack.

She tried to make the prospects think that she had built the centers herself and asked for rents at the going rate plus a percentage of sales as a bonus. When the prospects asked about scheduled repairs, she told them that if their puny little minds couldn't picture the unique opportunity she was offering them, then they could just get in their pitiful little cars and leave the premises.

She accused Jack of being envious of her deal-making prowess when he scheduled meetings that conflicted with her schedule. She berated his willingness to listen to the viewpoints of the prospects. "You're weak," she told him.

As Jack's plans fell in place and the shopping centers improved, the once vibrant Mouton sex life ran into a ditch. He began to lose sight of where Jill left off and Jack began. He should have suspected that Jill was cheating on him, but he did not.

Then one sad day he failed a critical test. He answered the "do these slacks make my ass look fat?" question wrong. Their sexual relationship ground to a halt.

Jack messaged himself as a reminder to research the word "narcissist." He had been working on a crossword puzzle while waiting for a prospect and was unsure of its meaning. He changed plans, throwing the note away with three pink telephone messages once he was at the office. He told himself the number of messages he threw away needed to be a round number for luck, but truth he was afraid that the dictionary definition might include Jill's picture.

He should have stuck to his plan. It would have been instructional. Jill was a complete narcissist and Jack was her enabler.

Jack sat in a golf cart while the rest of his foursome putted out. Jack had played 18 holes with his pals and still hadn't mustered up the gumption to talk to Jill. He wasn't in the best mood. He'd lost concentration when he drove up alongside the body of a dead crow, half-consumed by a swarm of seething creepy-crawlies. Unable to erase the image from his mind, he lost $85 to the guy with the highest handicap in his regular foursome. *Wolf, the worst way to gamble on golf that was ever invented,* Jack thought.

He didn't call Jill first. He punched in a number, Charma's number, and when she answered, he whispered into his cell phone, "How you liking the day off?" His playing partners didn't need to know he was calling a woman.

"Oh darling," Charma said. "It's just yah know the car needing brakes. And Evangeline needs braces. What's a mother to do? Ya know, Boo? I be by work tomorrow."

"That stunt in front of the three stooges..." he started, then stopped. "Why would I let you have your job back?" It was a silly question. It wasn't where he wanted to take the conversation. He had power and she was weak. He found himself gathering the gumption to ask a question that he'd had never been able to ask another human being, a question that might have sounded natural if it came out of Jude's mouth. He didn't know his mouth could form the words, he didn't plan to ask the question, and he probably would never have asked it if he had won $85 at golf, but he was going to ask it, and as soon as it flew from his mouth, he knew he would never be able to take it back. "What's in it for me?"

"Looka your checking book, sugar. I put some back."

Jack blinked. "You don't have my account number..." All the protein ran out of Jack's goobers.

"Looka you paycheck, sugar. Your account number ain't no big secret."

"Listen, you...I might have played ball a little. I can use a few extra bucks myself, sure." His volume was getting a bit loud, so he turned his face and the phone away from his foursome. "But I can't have any of that money showing up in my account!"

"Darling. Listen. I'll sell the condo. You be a broker. You...You can list it."

"You're going to sign a note. And that comes out of the sale too."

"I'll sign, darling. I'll make it right. Don't worry, Boo. You bring yourself by my house tonight."

"Tonight. Okay. I'll be there at eight."

Jack snapped the cell phone shut and walked a brisk lap around the golf cart in frustration. He would get the firm's money back and he didn't want Charma coming back to the office. All the documents he needed were on the word processor at the office. He just needed to go to the office, add a name here, a legal description there, address, social security number, and then print them out. He knew how satisfied he would be when he carefully put the executed documents in the pocket of his alligator-skin satchel. His papers wouldn't get dog-eared or stained like they might in a standard briefcase.

He opened the phone again and mashed a button.

"Jill, yeah, it's me. Hey, I'm in a...something's come up."

"Oh ouch!' the speaker crackled. "Easy there." Jack correctly guessed that the "easy there" was Jill's directive to that muscular, tanned masseuse that worked out of Red's Gym. He heard the slurping sounds that Jill made when she drank one of those frufru drinkies that her posse of social climbers in the Junior League had been buying for her.

"You understand? I can't make it to this party tonight."

"Jack, you rat."

"I know how much you were counting on it but I really need this listing and..."

"Whatever."

"I won't be late. I hope the massage is nice."

"Mmm-mmmm."

"Honest. I'll be home early...say hello to the fatuous hypocrites for me..."

"Ooo-ooooh. Oh my GOD. I know one thing I won't be giving up for Lent."

"...honey." A creepy-crawly inched up Jack's spine. He wasn't all that observant himself but he didn't like messing around with spirits, tugging at their chains. "It really bothers me. I asked you not to mock Lent that way."

"You are so superstitious. Make sure you turn out the lights..." Then he heard her muffled voice say, "Not you, donkey boy."

Jack shut off the phone. He had never suspected Jill of unfaithfulness. He wrote himself a short reminder. "Private investigator" was all it said. Maybe Jude knew one that was good. Someone discreet. Not that he would act on it, but it might be helpful to have a better picture of the relationship between this person that thought Lent was something to joke about and the raven-haired muscleman rubbing the aches and pains out of her perfect body.

CHAPTER 4

Jack drove through a cloudburst on his way to Charma's apartment. Odd too. Jack noticed that the rain was falling but the storm was not producing thunder. Unnatural rains like this were part of the reason he preferred staying in at night.

Headlights from oncoming cars twinkled on the windshield of his Lincoln. He usually parked indoors, especially in summer, when the afternoon sky opened up in little popcorn cloudbursts just as often as not. He would have to get the town car washed tomorrow.

With the rhythmic beat of the windshield wipers, Jack remembered a steamy afternoon that he spent with Jill on a sailboat, back when they started running around together so long ago. The breeze was gentle and the sail luffed at the mast. Neither of them cared. They were lost in one another's arms. Nowadays, he was as horny as an alligator's knee all the time and any prospect of catching up on his chores with Jill seemed remote at best. The sex was rare and perfunctory. He couldn't remember the last time he and Jill had shared themselves intimately.

Charma's address lead him to a mixed industrial part of town near one of the firm's strip centers, one where the white people used to shop. Jack was out of place in his linen suit. Between Jack and Charma's door stood two hog bikes and a couple of bruisers that he suspected were their owners. A lot of doctors and dentists liked to own a hog and play the part, but neither of these two gentlemen looked like they washed their hands.

Jack locked his car door before pulling to a stop. He pretended to make telephone calls until the bikers climbed on their bikes, kicked them alive, and roared away.

Jack removed his satchel from the back seat, silently closed the door to the Lincoln and locked it with his remote key. He walked on eggshells to the door with Charma's unit number and knocked. The third time he knocked loud enough for someone to wake the dead.

Charma answered the door. "Darling. I was thinking maybe you forgot."

The condo was shabby and in a condition that would make it difficult, if not impossible, to sell. A spider web of cracks radiated from a cavity in the mirror behind the bar—it looked as if someone had tried to throw a shot glass through it—and a deep indentation in the drywall leading up to a loft looked like an impact crater. A body slam, Jack guessed. A black velvet picture that hung off kilter above the mantel depicted the Virgin Mary holding the Baby Elvis.

Charma was dressed in spandex exercise tights, low-cut on the décolletage and attention-riveting for the ruttish Jack.

"Let me look around," Jack said, surveying the premises, trying hard not to let Charma's knockers stare at his eyes. "I'll have to show it." His lip curled involuntarily as if he had just found dog crap on his shoe. "Daughter's room?"

"Yep. That room past the bar, it's hers, and that's the work shop up in the loft. Work shop! What was I thinking, darling? The master bedroom!" Charma crowded past Jack in the narrow hallway, and as she did, she rubbed her breasts against him.

Jack took a gander at the upstairs. As he descended the stairs, he held his document satchel across his eager crotch. As if. A Marc Jacobs alligator briefcase *wrapped in lead* could never hide his arousal from a girl as knowledgeable and insightful as Charma. When he arrived at the bar, he put the satchel on top and snapped it open.

"Can I call you Jack, sugar? Whatcha drink?"

"Maybe a beer if you have one. Something that's been sealed. Now about the listing contract..."

"Can a beer! For sure. Hey, I got something. Talk about good!" Charma poured a couple of fingers of Gran Marinier liqueur into each of two shot glasses, and opened a couple of cans of beer.

"Or maybe just some mineral water," as Charma handed him the brimming shot glass. "What the hell is this?"

"It's Gran Mon-Yay, baby. Suck that back and chase it down with the beer."

Jack lifted the shot glass to his lips as if it were filled with nitro-glycerine, then knocked it back slowly.

"Ain't that just to die for?"

Coughs racked Jack's body. His face turned red and he choked as if he had drawn his last breath. He struggled to open the can of beer. When he finally wrestled it open, he chased the mordant orange-flavored liqueur with beer. "Oh yeah, that's something."

It began to sink in to Jack that he was trapped, behind the bar, backed into a corner. Charma's body pinned him against a cabinet in a full press. She was loosening his tie.

"Here. That collar's too tight. Ooops." Charma feigned a turned ankle. Now she was on her knees, her head and shoulders were at his crotch level and leaning into him, pressing him toward the corner.

"Hey, this act is getting old. Let's start the signature party." Jack grabbed his satchel and twisted away, tightening his tie. Chagrined, Charma pulled herself up to the bar and took a pen that Jack offered.

He put a pile of credit card receipts to the side. "You can go through these if you want. Make sure I'm not trying to load up on you."

"I trust you, darling."

"Okay, then, here's the note, that says you're going to repay the money you took from the firm. Sign here. Right. Now the security agreement. That lists the collateral and gets filed at the courthouse.

Okay. Now the listing agreement. So I can sell this palace. Okay. Sign both places. And then there's a copy for you. We're done."

"Okay. Wouldya lighten up now, darling? Hell I seen. You was wanting it. How else you think a clerk ever gonna work up to book-keeper? You answer me that."

Jack carefully pushed Charma away, then looked her over from stem to stern. His eyes fell from her puffy little over-made-up face to below, first her neckline and then her ample bust line. She had "slut" written all over her in a way that he found ever so alluring. He could feel his heart beating faster in his neck, on his sweaty temples, and in his pants.

"I'm outta here," he said, brushing past her for the door.

"The hell you say," Charma said. She grabbed a hold of Jack's belt from behind. He put up no resistance as Charma wrestled him to the couch.

"Charma, stop that. Stop!" he told her, hoping she wouldn't. He could have easily overpowered her and gotten away. But he didn't.

In the next moment, Charma was astride him with her hand inside the fly of his hand-made natural linen trousers that had been so crisp and sharply-pressed that morning. He was in the moment and had abandoned reluctance. In those captivating moments, the roofs of the shopping centers didn't leak, the trash was carried away from the alleys, and the vacancy rate was miniscule. The world didn't have nuclear weapons, or cancer, or STDs, or child abuse. His unhappy marriage was forgotten. Ghosts were not haunting the gloomy shadows or rattling chains in the darkness of the bayous. All of the problems of the world paled into insignificance as against that white-hot plug of matter roaring through his lumbus as if it were a runaway train. His loins exploded like a volcano. Sweet release.

Slowly, Jack remembered that the world had ghosts and dark spirits, nuclear weapons, cancer, and child abuse. The roofs of the shopping centers were still leaking, the trash was piling up in the alleys and the vacancy rate was still too high. He still had an unhappy marriage.

Red with embarrassment, he fumbled to arrange his clothes. Charma cackled at him like the Wicked Witch of the West. He grabbed his satchel and busted out of the door of the condo, tripping on the threshold and falling on his face on the concrete slab outside.

A pile of falsified rent receipts were stacked on the bar in Charma's condo. In his haste, he had forgotten to take them with him.

Jude slinked like a lizard through a back patio door and into the Charma's home. His lip curled under his pencil-thin mustache in the best imitation of a healthy smile that he could muster. He pulled a tape recorder from behind the bar and clicked it off.

"Got it. Got it real good, real good. Hey, be'-be', fix me one of them shooters."

Charma wiped her hand clean and tossed a spent tissue into a trashcan before washing her hands.

"What you think you're doing?" Jude retrieved the tissue and put in a baggie.

"Eeuuww. Throw that away."

"What? Destroy evidence?" Jude rubbed his hands through his greasy hair. "That's probably two million dollars worth of DNA."

Charma fixed two shooters and put one in front of Jude.

"Oh my God," Jude said, his lizard eyes wide open as a frogs. Immediately under his nose was a pile of receipts, the paperwork proof of Charma's embezzlement. "Happy days are here again!"

"You gonna drink that shooter or what?"

"To us. Yep. We're in this together, be'-be'." Jude knocked back his shooter, then kissed Charma, deep, wet and nasty. He grabbed a handful of red hair and playfully led her to her daughter's bedroom.

In less than the time it takes to warm up the engine on a Harley knucklehead, Jude was back in the living room of the condo, reorganizing his crumpled suit. Charma emerged from the bedroom, her clothes disheveled.

"That was quick. I tell you what...," she said.

"Hey, be'-be', my time's valuable. Gotta jet. Elevenish tomorrow."

Charma waved bye-bye as Jude deposited the bagged tissue inside a ziplock and pushed the pile of receipts that Jack had forgotten into the breast pocket of his sharkskin suit. He slipped out the patio door and disappeared like a ghost in the night mist.

CHAPTER 5

Charma's father was one of those guys that had made a contract with society. He worked in a slaughterhouse, as a meat cutter. Cutting meat was one of the worst jobs a man could hold, filthy and dirty, putrid, fetid, rotten...even the air the poor bastard breathed was full of disease and infection.

"I will do this," he told himself, "and my children can stand on my shoulders." He helped bring four of them into the world and kept a roof over their heads with a woman that took in laundry to help make ends meet. He was a hero. He got out of bed, went to work every morning, and took his brood to church on Sunday. He supported what remained of Louisiana's Huey Long political machine. He voted early and often.

In that way, he had something in common with Big Leo.

Leo Foret had hitchhiked north out of Crowley, Louisiana to Shreveport. He was 16 and he figured he'd already be in Nashville if all the cotton rows he'd chopped had been laid out straight. He wore his lucky pink western-cut shirt, and carried a cardboard suitcase and a box guitar. He'd spent a back breaking week chopping cotton so he could buy the shirt, and it was the first nice thing he'd ever owned. In Shreveport, he started bussing tables in a roadhouse and earned a promotion to waiter. He stood in a few times with a rockabilly dance band that kept the patrons thirsty, and soon he was a regular. He wasn't blessed with a lot of talent, but he had a happy face and a big voice. No one objected when he stepped off the stage to dance with one of the horsey, overserved women in the crowd. He always wore a pink shirt and the band called him "Big Leo" because he was undersized.

Leo snagged a job as a floor salesman at a furniture store and his fortunes began to rise along with the band. They frequently played on a radio show called "Louisiana Hayride," and when later the show went to TV, people started recognizing him as the little guy in the pink shirt. He met Elvis Presley, Johnny Cash and Jerry Lee Lewis at the show, and loved to regal his female customers with stories of how the stars were just "folks like us."

He had a lot of sex partners, too. A great mystery of life is why so many women want to screw someone, anyone, as long as they play in the band. Leo's libido was propping up a lively market at the furniture store. On just about any day, he could trade out a quickie for a mattress and box spring set. "We're running a special on used mattresses, but we're fresh out, Sugah. The only-est thing we got ain't broke in yet. Course if they was…" If she was really good, he'd throw in a lava lamp.

Life was good for Big Leo until a promoter offered the band a road gig. He wanted the boys to tour with a Nashville act. Most of them welcomed an opportunity to tell the boss to shove it, but a road gig also meant leaving all the hangers-on willing to buy drinks and provide sexual favors. Petty jealousies broke out. Old wounds were laid bare with vile recriminations. The band never again struck a note.

Big Leo was bitterly disappointed. Stage performing lost its cachet. He took an extended vacation, back home, to Crowley, to visit his mother. The next day a working girl had to screw two salesmen to get one lousy mattress and box spring set, and to add insult to injury, she could only trade out for the twin size set. The market crashed. Without Big Leo driving the price of commodities, mattresses and trim, the market took a nose dive.

He only meant to stay a week in Crowley.

The Couillon

His mother asked him to sing and play guitar at a political fund-raiser. He bought a new pink shirt and billed himself as the star of the "Louisiana Hayride." Every pretty girl in the parish was on the front row. His guitar thumping advanced the candidacy of Edwin Hebert, a young lawyer that was making his first foray into elective office. Lots of folks in the crowd threw their grocery money into the hat. Big Leo gave $40 and spent the next day helping Hebert deliver a sack of victuals to the contributors that the candidate knew couldn't afford it. After that, his guitar playing was a fixture at Hebert's events, and on election day, Hebert asked Big Leo to hand out walking around money to black preachers. Hebert narrowly defeated his opponent and with a broad smile, took office as Crowley's newest city councilman.

His buddy pushed his pink-shirted crony to get licensed to sell insurance and real estate. Hebert was able to steer business Big Leo's way. He never returned to the furniture store in Shreveport. Hebert continued to climb the political ladder and had the clout to get Big Leo appointed to the board of the Teche-Vermilion levee district, which was in charge of most of the drunken political revelry in both Lafayette, 30 miles to the east, and the parish at large. His insurance agency flourished and his real estate portfolio began to swell. He bought a titty-pink Cadillac convertible. Big Leo learned from Hebert that money was the mother's milk of politics, but he was surprised to find out just how little it took. He and Hebert tried to screw every girl in Crowley, Lafayette, and all points between. He told Jack that "I never done nuthin but what my body required it, I find."

Charma was her father's second daughter. She had no "daddy issues" at all. She was often melancholy and boys just made her happy. She chased them on the playground and when she caught them, she kissed them on the face. She showed them her special places when adults were not on hand to make her stop, and she enjoyed the feelings that stirred in her body in Junior High when the boys touched her tittybumps. Even then, none of the teachers had a larger rack. It excited her, the power these fleshy humps gave her over boys. She could easily make their private places get hard and when that happened, they treated her really nice. The boys did not run away any longer. It was difficult for her to comprehend how their sexual arousal could be anything other than a show of love. She and all her friends heard people say it every day, the world needs more love.

But today she didn't seem to be able to keep Jude's attention. They were sitting in his tacky office and she was talking a blue streak while he scribbled on a yellow pad. Her chattering continued while they ate corny dogs at the counter of a greasy-spoon diner, before Jude left and stiffed her with the check. She babbled non-stop as they wandered around the parish courthouse. Jude stopped a janitor for directions. The man pointed toward a double-door entry. Over the entry, a sign read "LAFAYETTE PARISH LAW LIBRARY."

"I always wondered where this place was," Jude said. Inside, as Jude hit the law books, Charma's mouth continued to run until a librarian ushered her outside.

She found a vacant shoeshine stand next to the beverage vending machines. "These dogs is barking," she told a young lawyer, her legs spread wide, to massage her feet. Then he saw what appeared to be a shoelace at the end of an avenue of pale flesh, a thong. He spilled his coffee.

The puddle created a hazard. "I'll get some paper towels," Charma said.

"No, it's alright," the young lawyer said, reaching into his breast pocket. He laid several of his business cards on the floor next to the perilous liquid.

Above a long counter, a sign read "CIVIL FILINGS." Jude stood patiently a few moments, waiting with papers in hand. Ahead of him in line was an elderly nun leaning on a cane. Jude tipped a file out of her hand and a raft of papers fell to the floor. As she stooped to pick up the spilled papers, Jude cut in line to file his papers first.

In the week following, business settled into the normal routine at BTME. Jack was in a snit because the aroma candle in his office kept going out. Bad luck. The phone rang and Harriet's voice asked him, "Can you come to reception?"

Harriet had her face buried in a movie magazine when Jack arrived out front. Her boyfriend, an off duty sheriff's deputy, was pacing the room.

"Are you Mr. Mouton?"

"Hi Bob."

"Mr. Jack Mouton?"

"You know it's me. Who's suing today? Another slip-and-fall?"

"Beats me. Hey, gotta play the game," the process server said, as he handed Jack a document.

Jack held the corner of the document at arm's length as he turned toward his office.

"Come again." Jack sauntered to his office where he sat and opened the summons. In the upper left-hand corner of the form, the case was styled "IN THE MATTER OF CHARMA CHALMETTE, PLAINTIFF, VS. MOUTON AND LEO FORET AND BAYOU TECHE MANAGEMENT ENTERPRISES, DEFENDANTS." Jack scanned the document closer, his brow knitted with increased concern.

He quit reading at the second page. "Sexual harassment? Baloney! That's a lie! Baloney!" Mona, Laurie and Carlie bumbled in, having heard the shouting.

"Where's Big Leo?" he asked.

"His hunting camp. Fishing. He'll be in tomorrow. Is there a problem?

Jack tossed the papers to Mona. Laurie and Carlie, looking over her shoulder, got an eyeful too. In unison, they said, "We better call Big Leo."

"Tomorrow's soon enough," Jack told them. "I'll break it to him then. It's pure unadulterated baloney."

Alone in his office, Jack started assembling files. The documents Charma signed, the listing agreement, the receipts...where were the receipts? They weren't in his satchel. Jack ran out of the office to search his car. Nothing.

Jude's beat-up Camaro was parked, as ever, outside the Rusty Penny, a titty bar tucked between oilfield warehouses on the highway that led out of town, down the delta toward New Iberia. The parking space may as well have been reserved for Jude, he was almost always parked in the same spot. Jack jammed his Lincoln into park and stormed inside.

He found Jude tippling at the bar, filling himself with wisdom, listening to a police scanner. Strippers danced on floor-to-ceiling poles on a stage in front of him.

"Hey man, come into my office. Draw up a chair," Jude greeted him.

"Jude. I need your help."

"Sure man. Que problemo old buddy?"

"Oh man. This chick at the office. I caught her stealing. "

"Cool."

"I'm concerned. She lured me to her house."

"Cool!"

"She might have video."

"Did you screw her?"

"Not really. I mean I wanted to. Bad."

"You crack me up man."

"I mean not really. I didn't really screw her though. Oh hell, Jude, I guess she can make it look like I screwed her."

"You don't want to talk to me about this Jack. Hey, did I tell you about these twins? I had 'em both down on the floor and..."

"I lost the proof. I can't even prove she stole the money now. She's got the darned receipts. She's gonna make it look like I did it."

"Don't talk to me Jack."

"Big Leo. That miserable old reprobate. He's the problem. He won't leave the secretarial pool alone."

"Jack, read my lips. I represent Charma. Man, I've been trying to tell you. If you'd just listen."

"Jude you snake. I'm your friend. You won't sue me."

"I'm suing Big Leo, not you dude."

"Oh jeezy, Jude. Oh man. You gotta keep this conversation just between me and you."

"Doesn't work that way Jack. She's my client. I got ethics you know."

"Bullshit. You have no ethics at all. Big Leo goes ballistic every time I mention your name. Oh God. Jill's an officer."

"Jill? Cool. Something else you shouldn't have told me, Jack. You're oh for two. Haha. Hey, don't worry, man. What's a couple of million to Big Leo? Besides, they got insurance."

"You don't understand Big Leo."

"I know him better than he knows himself. Blowhards like that are their own worst enemies. Quit worrying. She's not gonna get much. Two million is a rounding error to an insurance company."

"Jill's going to kill me."

"You bring all this stuff on yourself, man. You're self-destructive."

"I'm dead. I'm worse than dead."

Jude showed Jack a pocket tape recorder inside his jacket, then clicked it off.

"Maybe I can slip a couple of bucks your way. To tide you over.

You're gonna need it if those silk-stocking insurance lawyers find out you've been talking to me."

Jude ordered a beer for the man seated beside him with his head buried in his hands. Jack gestured "no thanks" and started to leave.

"Hey man, stick around. Charma's gonna dance in a few minutes."

"Important people are waiting for me."

CHAPTER 6

No one was waiting on Jack.

He paced the floor of his office, looking over some lists the bookkeeper, Lucille, had put in the seat of his chair. He had asked her never to dump documents in his "in" basket, but like the others, she found ways to defy his wishes while following his directives to the letter. "You said...I was just following orders." All the staff at BTME was loyal to Big Leo and Jack knew that she would have already ratted out the lawsuit news to the old man.

One of the lists was a tenant roster for all the properties. Other than the grocery stores that had anchored the shopping centers since they'd come off of the drawing board, he couldn't find a single active lease in any of the centers that he hadn't personally negotiated.

Big Leo had lost interest in his real estate during the 80s. The shopping centers had happened because of him, because Hebert had thrown him a bone, an option on some land. He packaged a deal with the architects and surveyors, and negotiated leases with triple-A national tenants. He had some slugging to do, toe-to-toe with the big boys, selling off the corner properties to gas stations, and snagging good leases for the centers. He had all the prestige commercial tenants in his pocket, those with gilt-edged credit, low sensitivity to economic downturns, and good name recognition. But time marches on. Lafayette's retail shops got "malled." Neighborhoods changed. Big Leo's properties started to have a see-through look. The anchor tenants, TG&Y ("turtles, girdles and yo-yos" according to Big Leo),

Safeway, Rexall drugstores, and Otasco, one-by-one, they all bit the dust, shut down, boarded up. Following them was a rash of bank and savings and loan failures. Big Leo said, "they all shit deh bed."

When Jack joined the firm, the shopping centers had all been, in real estate parlance, "underwater." They could not be sold for enough money to pay off their mortgages. But Big Leo had fared better than most real estate operators. He still had his insurance business, and oil was discovered on a neighbor's property on a big tract he owned out in the swamp. Traces of gasoline contamination were discovered underneath almost every one of his shopping centers. He got great satisfaction in jamming those underground plumes down the throat of the big oil companies who twenty years before he had to beg to buy the corner lots of his developments.

It dawned on Jack that all Big Leo's wealth, resources, and focus seemed to be centered on the underworld. Things subterranean. To Jack it was as if Big Leo were an old dragon. An underworld kingdom of underwater shopping centers. Oil and gas from the mantle of the earth. Plumes of subsurface gasoline pollution. Even fishing at his camp in the shadowy swamp, his prey all came from below the surface, his favorite foods were harvested from the deep.

The days since Jack had taken the reins of BTME were heady, happy days for Big Leo. Fat-cat insurance companies had been put on God's green earth to pay Big Leo. And as they made him ever richer, he had come to despise them, filing phony claims on actual or imagined damages to the shopping centers, and suing and screwing his old friends in the oil companies when he could dummy up a case. He missed out on getting richer in the sub-prime mortgage feeding frenzy. He was tied up in court.

The following day, Hurricane Leo slammed into the office just before nine. The years hadn't robbed Big Leo of his big voice. He was in his eightieth year of life and dressed in his ubiquitous white suit. If it weren't for his signature pink shirt, he would have looked like a short Colonel Sanders. He was shouting in the French-Cajun patois that always got as thick as a roadhouse roux when he was angry. Jack, the bookkeeper and the three stooges could hear his rant echo out of the elevator in the lobby, and stood at attention around the receptionist when the door burst open.

"Hey thanks, Mona, for letting me break the news," Jack said. Mona shrugged.

"You bastard! What d'hell you got me in?" Big Leo liked being plaintiff but not defendant. His face was as red as a boiled lobster.

"Leo, it's a fiction. Complete fabrication. Besides. You have insurance."

"Insurance?" Big Leo's eyes opened wide and a brief smile parted his lips.

"Plenty. Anyway, these harassment claims aren't worth much. Just like a slip-and-fall."

"Insurance! What insurance?"

"D and O!"

"What you talking D and O?"

"Directors and Officers."

"Yeah. Damn glad I bought dat D and O."

"I'll call the insurance company."

"Call, yeah, I say call that D and O insurance man." Big Leo stomped across the office like a longshoreman and the floor shook. He slammed the door to his office behind him as he had a thousand times before.

It was just what Jack had expected from the miserable old reprobate. Big Leo. Big Underwater Leo. Jack had only purchased the D&O a couple of years ago, only after the cash flow could stand it. The wags at the country club gossiped like church ladies about Big Leo and the women on the payroll. The head pro told Jack that

Big Leo had invited him to come up to the office one afternoon. "Come on, Wedgie, you can help screw deh help and such."

But for today, it was better not to confront the crazy old bastard. Jack would wait until the time was right to shut the old man's yap. He was looking forward to it.

They all gathered in a conference room at BTME's office. Liz Churnow was a partner in a Baton Rouge law firm that the insurance company had hired to defend the sexual harassment claim filed by Charma. She wore a tailored jacket and matching skirt that embraced her long-limbed figure. Some women have bedroom eyes. Liz had library eyes. *Christian Louboutin shoes,* Jack thought. *Expensive.* The heels were high and spiked, the soles were a rich scarlet. They matched a purse she tossed onto the conference table as she took a seat at one end.

Big Leo sat at the far end while Jack and Jill were opposite one another midway between. Jill filed her nails as if she was sharpening them. Big Leo stretched, and slouching in his huge wing-backed chair, yawned like a lion.

"Okay, Liz, so we pay deh ten grand deductible and deh rest is on d' insurance company?" Big Leo already knew the answer.

"That's it," Liz said. "As long as the loss is under policy limits. Their case looks like a real piece of crap."

Jack sketched a picture of Liz on his notepad. In his drawing, she wore a hardhat and long white coat that was smeared with blood. She looked like a butcher. In one of her hands he drew a big gory knife. In the other, she held a couple of gore-covered testicles.

"What bunch of ambulance chasers is representing this slut?" Jill asked.

"It's some dirtbag named..." Liz flipped pages. "Julien Malveaux."

A mushroom cloud blasted skyward across the table from Jack. "Jude!"

"Jude Malveaux! Jude Malveaux!" Big Leo roared and Jack hid his face in his hands.

"I take it you know him?"

"That scumbag!" Jill was on her feet too. "This dumbass husband of mine lets him use our boat!"

"He says you like him," Jack said.

"Keep your mouth shut, Jack," Big Leo said.

"Out. Jack, get out," Jill instructed. "Daddy throw him out. Liz, throw him out."

"Not so fast. Everyone cool down," Liz said. "Everyone's an officer. We're all in this together."

"Jack's not an officer," Jill said. "Just me and daddy."

"We need an executive session," Big Leo said. "Jack. Go return some calls."

J ack stalked to his uncluttered desk. He glared out the window. He sharpened pencils. He sharpened more pencils. He sharpened sharp pencils. He drummed his fingers on the desk. The clock read 1:33. It was Friday the 13th.

He wasn't an officer. Jill was right. *Damn!* That was a fact he'd forgotten. Jill and Big Leo had been holding that carrot under his nose for years. "Next year, maybe, T-Jacques," Big Leo had said. *T-Jacques.* French for "Little Jack." That's what Big Leo called him when he wanted to put his son-in-law down, to piss on him, T-Jacques.

So the company might not be covered after all. Well, it wouldn't be difficult to come up with some documents. Might have to be backdated, but that was no big step for a big stepper. On average, the firm probably executed as many forms with a back date as it did with the correct date. Jack's left eye twitched in the way it had when his mother went missing.

But damn. Jill had already let that cat out of the bag with the

Baton Rouge lawyer. Liz would just have to play ball unless she wanted to ditch the case.

His phone was dead silent. He supposed that Harriet had been instructed to hold his calls, so he leaned back in his chair and tried to relax. In that state between being asleep and being awake, he imagined he was at a funeral. He looked down and saw that he was wearing new shoes. He startled upright when an image of a mirror crashed to the floor and shattered into a thousand pieces. He gasped at the air to recover his breath.

The clock read 4:37. The twitch in his eye had gone away. All the pencils had been ground down to a stub. Winter was over but sunset still came early. The western sky was turning pink with the resting sun.

Enough was enough. Jack took long strides to the boardroom. He swung open the door.

"Well?" he asked.

Jill was at a whiteboard. In her handwriting, a list said:

SALARY	???
INSURANCE	YES
BENEFITS	NO
CAR	NO
CELL PHONE	NO

"Jack!" Jill's voiced scolded.

"Still in session, sonny boy," Big Leo said.

Jack began to close the door but left it open a crack to listen.

"I've just about had it with the both of you, Big Leo." It was Jill's voice. The tone had that crisp, biting quality that Jack had come to hate. "Lord, what I wouldn't give to just run this company myself!"

Big Leo's voice was gruff. "We'll throw T-Jacques a hush puppy if he axe nice. He'll be on the team, at least trew de depositions."

"Sonofabitch. If you cut him off, he's gonna come to me for money.

Well he can just piss off. I'm not going to wreck my finances because you assholes think you can play winky-dinky with the hussies in the secretarial pool."

"Keep paying him," Liz told them. "The firm. Until we establish this officer mess, we can't take a chance he'll grab someone else. Sheesh."

Jack poked his head back inside the room. They all smiled back in that guilty-knowledge smile, like dogs caught sucking eggs.

"What are you talking about, 'officer mess'?" Jack asked.

"You better talk to your own lawyer about that," Liz told him.

Jack nodded. "Oh, really. I see. When you said, 'we're all in this together,' what you meant was 'Jack you better get your own lawyer'…?"

Jack's job was blowing smoke up people's ass, but that didn't mean he had to like it when someone blew smoke up his.

"In this together," Jack mumbled to himself as he stalked back to his office. "Right. Hanging Jackie out to dry, that's what they're up to. Well they're gonna pay through the nose to get rid of me. Knock on wood." He rapped the wooden top of his desk with his knuckles.

Jack unbuttoned his collar and cuffs. He loosened his tie and, in moments, every cell in his body recharged with energy. It came with the anger. He wasn't out of the woods yet, but BTME's predicament had just flipped from a team sport to an individual event. Any gratitude he had, any heavy burden of commitment to Jill and Big Leo was now off of his shoulders. Jack felt an adrenaline rush of independence in his veins.

He had to consider his options. It wasn't so much Jack vs. BTME. BTME wasn't for him but it wasn't against him either. His problem was Jude. Jude couldn't have evidence of Jack harassing Charma at the office because he did nothing to harass her. He went over the scenario a thousand times and convinced himself that even if something crazy surfaced, like a video tape of something happening at the office, and even if it were selectively edited, nothing had happened. He prayed that such a video would surface. It could do nothing but vindicate him.

But the no good skunk probably had some evidence of Jack visiting her condo, something more than Charma's testimony. It was best to assume he had evidence, anyway. If anyone was going to defend Jack, it would have to be Jack. He just didn't know why Jude had turned on him. He'd never been anything but a friend to the cockroach, buying him drinks, laughing at his raunchy jokes, and even loaning him the cabin cruiser.

Jack knew that Jude kept an office in a flea-bit old building near the jailhouse. The owners had been trying to sell it for five years. He could torch the place and send all the so-called evidence up in smoke. He could muster the nerve to do it. He knew he could. *That way I don't need to worry if I leave fingerprints. Ummm. No.* He didn't want to commit arson as a means to wiggle out of a chicken shit lawsuit. He didn't think he did anyway.

CHAPTER 7

That's it, Jack thought. *I can get a key and waltz in there like I own the place and toss the place and grab what evidence I find and be gone. Maybe not. I can't get the key without letting everyone on God's little green acre know that I've been inside.* He had seen it on TV a million times. A perfect crime committed, but for DNA. The bad guys always left fingerprints or DNA on a hair follicle, a drop of sweat, or blood...*And everyone knows that any knucklehead realtor could get a master key to the office building, easy as that. No big step for a big stepper.*

That line of thinking planted a seed and soon a scathingly brilliant plan germinated. Now Jack was a man with a plan.

The plan that was falling into place was to boldly go where everyone knew he was going. He would scout out Jude's office during the day and plenty of people would be able to testify that he had been inside and then left. And that would account for any trace evidence that might turn up later. Then he would return at night, make it look like the place was broken in. When everyone and his brother knew that T-Jacques was at home, afraid to go out. Once inside, he was certain that he could nab Jude's clandestine tape recording and whatever else kind of purloined evidence that the heel-biting dog had on the BTME case, or any of his crappy cases for that matter. Then he would destroy everything that he found and every crappy case Jude had would fall apart. Teach him to mess with Jack. Too bad for any hapless schmuck Jude happened to have as a client. He'd destroy anything he found, and if anyone wanted to point a finger, the woodwork would be full of suspects.

No one would consider accusing him of breaking and entering. He had a key. His whole purpose was to ruin Charma's lawsuit by destroying evidence of his tryst. Perception would be reality. The harassment complaint would fade into memory. Then he could reconcile with Jill and crawl back into the driver's seat at BTME.

"Is Aubrey in? Tell him it's Puddin-tane Purvis. Haha. Just kidding. It's Jack. Jack Mouton. Just teasing you." Jack cruised through downtown Lafayette, talking on his cell phone. The intersections in the oldest part of the city meet at odd angles, the streets follow the wagon ruts laid down in antiquity. "How'd you guess? Yeah, that place on Vermilion Street. I might have a tenant slash owner situation." He looked away from his reflection in the rear view mirror. "Call the maintenance man."

Jack rocked his head from side to side while waiting for the other agent to dump whatever line of horseshit was in his memory cache. "No maintenance man?" *No screaming shit,* he thought. "I'm in your neighborhood. I'll pick up a key and get it back tomorrow," he said, snapping closed his phone.

Jack picked up a key from the agent's office and drove to Jude's office address. It was an old, two-story building around the corner from the jail. The brick was crumbling after a hundred-year war with humidity and gravity. He parked in a no parking zone.

A man from the water company was reading a meter from the front of the building. "Hi there," Jack said. "I'm Jack Mouton and I'm here to look this place over. I think I have a tenant slash owner situation."

"None of my business," the water man said, walking away. He never looked up from his route book.

The lock on the front door contended against Jack's efforts for a brief moment, then opened. The interior hallway led straight through the building, shotgun style. A thief at the back door could be shot by someone at the front door. The hallway inside was littered with trash. "Hello!" Jack shouted. "Hello! It's Jack Mouton. Real estate agent. Just looking. Anyone here?"

No one answered, to Jack's chagrin. The plan called for people seeing him inside the building. He pushed a business card behind the glass pane in the door that faced the street. No prying eyes were observing him. "Surely someone is here! Hello!"

Again no answer. Jack let himself in Jude's office with the master key. A glass pane in the office door read "Julien Malveaux & Associates." Jack shook his head. What a joke. No lawyer in his right mind would associate with Jude. The glass gave the appearance of fancy. Jude had taped waxed paper over the glass to give it that expensive, frosted, Sam Spade look to the outside world. What was really under the opaque paper was safety glass, two panes of plate glass with twisted wire pressed between. Jack had seen panes of chicken-wire glass survive even after vandals had torn a place apart.

All the wood and plaster in the office was painted a dull pale green.

Jack surveyed the contents, a small desk, a steel-case file cabinet, stacks of unpaid bills. Inside the file cabinet he found a deck of naked lady playing cards, an empty bottle of Old Crow bourbon, and spider webs. Then he found a manila folder that had "CHARMA CHALMETTE VS. MOUTON" scribbled on the tab. The inside held nothing but a "stamped-filed" copy of Charma's petition.

Also inside the file cabinet, Jack found a sturdy lock box.

Jack wiped the seat of a folding chair clean and positioned himself by the window. He waited an hour, keeping an eye on his Lincoln.

Out in the street, a meter maid stopped, grabbed her ticket book off the seat, and got out of her golf cart. In the process of writing a ticket, she looked at her watch. Then she tore the ticket she'd been writing to bug bites, threw the trash on the ground, got in her cart and drove away.

Jack looked his watch. Four-thirty, quitting time. Bitch! She was supposed to ticket him so he could prove he'd been there and account for the time. After another minute, Jack left with a frown, locking the doors behind, chagrined that his plan, so carefully laid in, had not panned out completely. He was flexible. He would have to remedy the shortcomings of the plan.

The sky was dark, the street deserted. The dashboard clock said it was 1:00 a.m. A block away from Jude's office building, Jack slouched low in his Lincoln. He'd changed clothes and was now wearing black leather gloves, a black turtle-neck pullover, and black slacks and a black sock hat. He got out of his car and walked the block to his objective. He felt the outside of his thigh. Check. Keys in his right pocket, a pack of cigarettes and a lighter where he wanted them, in his left pocket.

Jack crossed himself, then right foot first, eased into the dark building for the second time that day. The outer door squeaked louder than he remembered. Jack found his way through the trash-filled hallway with a small flashlight. He beat a hole though the chicken-wire plate glass with the butt end of a standing ash tray. That would make it look as if intruders had broken through. He reached through the hole and opened the seedy office by turning a deadbolt switch.

He rummaged through desk drawers, mostly to give them a look of having been rummaged. The naked lady playing cards were where he left them with the empty bottle of Old Crow. Then he pawed through the file drawers, disturbing spider webs, methodically making way toward the lock box and the solo manila file. In the six hours since he'd been in the office, he had conjured up a fear that the box was bolted down. But it was not secured at all. "Jude, you dumb butt," he mumbled as he pulled the lock box out of the file cabinet and dropped it on the desktop.

Jack's first plan, one he had rejected early on, was to set off a blast inside the office that would obliterate any fingerprints or DNA. Without a parking ticket to prove he was there, and no one to verify his whereabouts other than the water meter man, Jack had decided that his first idea wasn't such a bad idea after all. He opened a valve on the gas heater in the corner, lit a cigarette, and wedged the butt end into a book of matches. When the cigarette burned down far enough, it would ignite the book of matches, and with the room filled with gas...

"Kaboom," Jack muttered.

In the moment he opened the gascock, his body jerked involuntarily, his neck drew into his shoulders as if he were a pancake turtle. His body reacted to percussion before his ears and brain had processed the sound that assaulted him. BANG! BANG BANG!

Jack startled again and dove to the linoleum floor under the shabby desk. Someone was pounding on Jude's office door. Jack clicked off the flashlight.

A voice in the hallway was shouting, "Malveaux! Open up. I know you're in there. Your check bounced, you turd."

Jack squatted under the particle-board canopy, his heart racing. Nothing. All quiet. Then the pounding started again, and with it a taunt. "Hey dude, you left the front door open."

Jack's mind raced. His primitive IED was burning. Time must be running short but he was paralyzed with fear. "Dammit!" Jack shouted. "You broke my door! I'm calling the cops."

The hallway was silence. Darkness. Then the voice said, "Oh the hell with you."

Jack heard the creaky front door of the office building open and close. He grabbed up the lockbox under his arm and charged toward the office door as if he was following his blocks on a well-designed flanker screen. But the doorknob snatched from his hand and the door swung open wide.

A huge beefy hand clutched the nape of his neck. "Gotcha! You skunk. Hey, who the hell are you?"

"Maintenance. Hey man, you need in there? Help yourself."

"Yo. He's got to have something in there worth something." The big hand released Jack's neck. Its owner muscled his way past Jack and into Jude's office. Now Jack was in the open field, digging for the goal line. He hadn't run so fast since high school football. He split as fast as his feet would carry him, out the front of the building, toward his car, then hesitated, gripped by indecision. He had left the big man with the vice-grip hands to a certain death when his IED lit the matchbook.

He raced back to the front door of the office building and smashed out the door's glass with the lock box. "Gas leak!" he shouted. "Get out of there! This place is gonna blow!"

The big man stepped out of the dark hall and through the busted out door. "Gas leak, my stinking ass. This place ain't had heat in years."

Jack sprinted away down an alley with the lockbox tucked under his arm. He ran like he had not run since he was headed for the goal line back when he was playing wide receiver for the Carencro Golden Bears. The last thing he wanted was to be caught with the lockbox. He needed to hide it.

His flight took him five or six blocks straight away from the tall buildings at the center of town, past an ancient Cathedral, through an open gate. Unthinking, Jack had run into the middle of a cemetery. Some of the graves contained the remains of people that died two hundred years ago, placed there when Lafayette was called Vermilionville. For most of those two hundred years, people around town had been seeing the apparition of a young woman walking the paths of this graveyard, always wearing a flowing white gown, singing hymns and rattling the ornaments that adorned the bodies of the souls interred, in search of the grave of her young lover.

The crypts were above ground, covered in plaster and painted white, streaked with black, gray and green smudges of mold. Even in the moonless night, Jack could see gaping holes in the burial chambers brought about by constant rainfall and high humidity. The broken plaster revealed the brick and mortar structures underneath.

Jack found one crumbling crypt with a hollow that might have been large enough to conceal the lockbox. It was head high. He reached inside. He felt clammy wet bones and decay. The lockbox fit, but withdrawing his hand, he felt a grip on his arm. Jack screamed in fright. He could no longer breathe.

Clinging to his forearm were the bones of a hand and arm. "Jesus Mary and Joseph," he cried, shaking the grip of bones. He tried to run but fell on his face. Lucky for him. He saw the bones on the ground, a long finger pointing to the crypt where he had secreted the lockbox. He fought his body's desire to run, crawling like a baby to the little pile of bones, picking them up. Moldering dust on the bones felt like powdered sugar. He stuffed the bones back into the crypt from which they had arisen.

The string in his legs was gone. He crawled on all-fours out of the cemetery. Only when he was outside the tall gates could he prop himself against a wall and stand.

The street in front of the Cathedral was vacant. No one saw him sneak back to his Lincoln, slip under the wheel, and drive away. He might not be able to find the crypt where he had stashed the lockbox. More than that, he might not have the stones to enter again. Leaving the lockbox to rust away to corruption like everything else in the cemetery was not an option. He would have to retrieve it.

id-afternoon of the next day found Jude berating two police detectives in his office.

The older of the two was a root-beer-brown lawman. He introduced himself as Etienne and dressed like a colorblind cowboy, boots, straw western hat and all. His French accent was as thick as gumbo. His sidekick was fresh-faced and as white as rice, dressed like a GQ fashion plate, and didn't look like he was old enough to shave. The younger lawman asked Jude to call him Detective Lily.

The place had been tossed, as a frantic real estate agent had complained to the dispatcher over the phone. The scene of the crime was not their first call of the day. Jude never made it to the office until the sun was past vertical in the sky.

Lily was interested in getting Jude's story, but Etienne eyed the occupant as if he were dogshit on his shoe. "So what's missing?" Lily asked.

"My lockbox," Jude said.

Etienne walked back and forth around the desk, putting on glasses and taking them off. The room was so small that one end of the wall was jammed against the wall. He couldn't take his eyes off of the burned up book of matches, the gray ash beside it, and the scorched circle around it.

"Contents?"

"Cash and papers. Accounting records."

"No man, you got it backwards."

"What?"

"You file for bankruptcy first," Lily said, "and *then* the thieves break in and steal your accounting records. Not before."

"Kiss my ass. There was twenty-nine thousand...I mean, eighty-nine thousand dollars in there."

"Eighty-nine thousand, right?"

Etienne whistled. "Thass a lots of dixie." He took his glasses off to take a long look at every item in the room, taking mental notes, from ceiling to the floor and around the baseboards. He spotted the wall heater, stepped over to it, brushing between Lily and Jude as if they weren't in the room, and bending at the waist to get a better look. He tipped his head back and forth looking alternately, over and through his bifocal lenses.

"You want me to put that in the report?" Lily asked. He wanted to say, "Serves you right, cockroach," but detectives had to be careful. "I mean, when something like that goes in the report, the Internal Revenue starts asking questions about where it came from."

"I won it at the casino."

"Right. A low-rent drunks and whores lawyer has eighty-nine thousand smackeroos that he won at the casino. It could happen." He scribbled on a notepad. "Course the casinos keep books on stuff like that. IRS will want to see the paperwork. Verify your story so to speak."

Jude was giving Lily the stink-eye. The detective had to pretend not to enjoy his job. Just part of the game.

"Have the handle on that valve dusted for prints," Etienne said. Then he left the crime scene to Lily and Jude.

It was almost quitting time when Jack returned late from a haircut and manicure appointment. He liked his hair razor-cut. In his office, he found Etienne and Lily. Badges hung from their breast pockets and they introduced themselves like professionals.

"So you was in the building?" Etienne was asking him.

"Yes. Certainly. Earlier. Might be a good investment. Maybe Malveaux saw me then."

"See anything suspicious?"

"I suspect they paid someone off. I'll never understand how they get an occupancy permit for that firetrap. I should talk to the Health Department. I think a water meter guy saw me. You know, I can get an affidavit."

"You should see the front door," Lily said. "Some knucklehead got in through a window then busted through a glass door to get out. Crackhead I figure."

"Any loss?" Jack asked.

"Says he lost a lockbox. A load of money the way he was talking. Bet it was empty myself. 'Turn it in' I told him. 'Report it. You want Uncle Sam up your wa-hoosey, go ahead, I'll take your complaint.'"

"He'll never file nothing. Ain't gonna happen." Etienne was staring at Jack.

"Serves that creep right. Low lifes like that always springing out these pimps and whores just makes our job harder." Lily mouthed an obscenity along with a standard middlefinger gesture.

Jack rose from his chair. "Well thanks for coming by, detectives. If I can be of any further assistance..."

Lily shook his hand. "We'll keep in touch. Thanks Mr. Mouton. Appreciate your time."

"Come on Lily. A bucket of crawfish is calling my name. They saying 'Etienne. Etienne. Eat me.'"

Lily was already out the door but Etienne stopped to eye Jack one last time. He looked him over from head to toe before slowly stepping out.

Etienne sat with his back in a corner in an open-air crawfish bar. His hat was on the seat of the chair next to him, and in front of him was a heap of empty crawfish shells. Lily had one uneaten crawfish on his plate.

Etienne peeled another crawfish and sucked the head before throwing the shell on his pile.

"Eeuuww," Lily complained. "Man you're just sucking those heads just to make my skin crawl."

"Bestest part. Where you from anyway, son?"

"Up north," Lily said. "Monroe."

Etienne snorted. "MAWn-roe? You a damn Yankee!"

"Yeah, well I been here long enough to learn to eat mud bugs. Still can't believe I'm doing that. Where you from?"

"'Round dese parts. How'd you like our little buddy back dere?"

"Mouton? He's a schmuck. Didn't get any closer talking to him. Waste of time."

"Lache pas la patate."

"What the hell?"

"Not yet, son, don't give up. Don't drop the potato."

"Scratch him off the list, Etienne. He wasn't in there."

"Course he was."

"Earlier, sure. He admitted that. Had a key."

"Hey. Lily. Lemme give you a lesson in police science. I had 400 maybe 300 suspects with affidavits. Lesson one. Every suspect with an affidavit is a perpetrator. Probably paranoid schizophrenic too, but definitely a perpetrator." Etienne devoted his attention to the remaining crawfish.

Lily screwed up his face. He pushed his lone, uneaten crawfish away and waved at the waitress for the check.

CHAPTER 8

Jack needed to retrieve the lockbox, and he needed to do it unde-tected. To do that, he had no recourse but to return to the cemetery.

He drove around the church complex. On his right, facing St. John Street, were the imposing Romanesque structure of the Cathe-dral, dozens of smaller administrative buildings, a convent and a school. It was daytime now and a gate opened into the cemetery. It was tucked behind the buildings and he decided not to press his luck a second time by trying to enter through the gate. It was locked at night, a sign told him it was anyway. How he had gotten past the gate the night before was a mystery to him. Anxiety, fear, and adrenaline clouded his memory. He might have squeezed through the bars or scaled the wall. Or maybe the sexton was grabbing some ass time and left the gate unlocked. An alternative entrance to the graveyard must be located.

Turning right on University Avenue, at the next intersection past the Cathedral complex, Jack looked for easy access over or through the fence guarding this side of the graveyard. Nothing. No problem. He was uncomfortable with the amount of traffic on University anyway and drove farther. Holding his breath while passing the cemetery, he turned right again on a narrow lane called Parkside Drive.

A deep concrete drainage ditch followed Parkside inside the church property. On either side was a chain link fence. The Parkside fence was swallowed up in a snarl of brush that obscured the back fence on the opposite side of the canal. Jack felt more at ease and quit holding his breath. A route in from Parkside offered relatively easy access but no place to leave his car. An unmanned Lincoln on Parkside would stick out like a black kid at a family reunion.

The next right turn put him on Versailles Boulevard where a short overpass crossed the drainage canal. A multi-storied office building with a big parking was on his left. It housed a bank. BTME had accounts there. A wrought iron fence on his right guarded the church complex from entry. Jack guessed the fence was no higher than his shoulders, but an ornamental fleur de lis topped each spire. Some deranged individual had designed the ornaments to make any potential intruder consider the sanctity of his ball sack before attempting to scale the fence. Beyond the fence were a soccer field, a playground filled with kids, and beyond that the graveyard.

From the office building parking lot, the cemetery was only a good driver-wedge away. Jack pulled into the bank's parking lot and drove to the rear. He had parked there a hundred times before. It would be no trick at all to climb over the chain link fence at the back of the bank lot, skid down the concrete slabbed side of the drainage ditch, and follow it under the overpass. If he walked 300 yards or so further in the ditch, he could climb up and out and be in the cemetery without detection. It was too far to hold his breath, but retrieval of the lockbox was worth the risk he would take of breathing in a malevolent spirit.

I t was night and Jack was alone in the Mouton media room watching a *Seinfeld* marathon, glad that Jill had gone to bed early, and trying to get his mind off of the foray he needed to make in the haunted cemetery. *One more episode*, he told himself, *and it will be time to go.* He watched another, then another. He had seen them all a dozen times before, but he had a thousand reasons not to get up out of his chair. He made himself click off the TV when the clock read 1:00 a.m. Jill would be dead to the world.

He had dressed again in black and navy clothes. He found an old pair of black sneakers. He was driving into the bank parking lot when it occurred to him that 1:00 a.m. was sort of like 13 o'clock. The sky was dark and overcast. Lights were on in an upper floor of the building and three cars were in the lot. He parked near the back, slid out of the car, donned black leather gloves, and slid over the fence and down to the bottom of the drainage ditch. The bottom was covered with a slick, perpetual slime that covered anything in south Louisiana that was below ground level.

He smeared his face with some sticky goo from the ditch. He had seen William Holden do that in the movies. And Robert Mitchum. And Tim Robbins. He headed down the ditch, under the overpass. Above and to his left, barbed wire crowned the chain link fence. He began counting his strides. He stumbled on. It seemed as if his heart was beating three times between each step.

As the count neared 300, he looked again to the fencing above. It was low and no longer guarded across the top with barbed wire. Jack scrambled up the concrete embankment and over the fence.

He was in the cemetery now and he was light-headed. Tiny pixels of red and yellow light were dancing across the inside of his eyelids. His blood pressure must been 200 over 150. His temples pounded; veins in his neck throbbed. He gazed into the haunted graveyard, overcome with the sense that he was a character in a movie. The camera in his brain was dollying away from him synchronized with a zoom. In one moment the far end of the hallowed grounds were two city blocks away, now background was foreground, the crypts surrounded him, they were on him, above him, and in him.

He staggered ahead, following a path of crushed oyster shells. It seemed to him as though he were running through a tunnel, but making no progress. He had the sense that mausoleums were arching over him, the cross-shaped pediments swallowing him up. On either side, crypts adorned with winged angels and moldering cherubim bordered the path. It seemed as if the somber statues were reaching out to grab hold of him. He fell and got up running. The path he was on would lead to the front gate of the cemetery.

But it didn't. It dead-ended at an iron fence. He was disoriented. Lost. Confused. His heart beat loud enough to wake the dead. His elevated blood pressure made him so dizzy he could scarcely stand up. He tried to run back to where he began but hadn't a clue of the direction to take. He was so afraid for his life that he had almost forgotten why he came. He had no idea where he was and no scheme for finding the hidden box. He careened from side to side off of the timeless tombs. He heard music, hymns, the words unhearable, and the tinny sound of thin metal, jangling, thin metal striking thin metal, music he could feel in waves that rippled over his clammy flesh.

Jack ran for his life. His legs failed him and he fell to the ground again. Crushed oyster shells flew in a spray. He tried to crawl. The hymn-singing voice was with him, behind him. He could go no farther. He was ready to surrender to the demons. He had no defense to the angel of death. He rolled over to face his doom.

What he saw was a blur, a white transparent vapor. It seemed to be holding out an arm to a cracked and battered sepulcher that was the source of the rattling sounds. It was the crypt with the gaping hole, the entry to the underworld where Jack had stashed the lockbox the night before.

Unsteady, he propped himself up against a weeping angel, then lurched across the path to the crypt, reached inside and pulled out the lockbox. It was covered with a slick and grimy dusty mold. He tucked the lockbox under his arm and fled, away from the glow of the lights of town, running as fast as his wobbly legs would carry him, crashing against the crypts, falling often, unable to keep his balance. He struggled to locate the back fence and the place of the living beyond.

Each step took him further into the gloomy night. Then he was on it. WHAM! He ran headlong into the chain link fence. He hit the cross member at chest height and he bounced back on his ass as if he had been on the receiving end of a forearm shiver from a linebacker. He groped around until his hands found the lockbox. He scrambled back over the fence and skidded down the concrete embankment on his fanny.

He retraced his steps in the greasy ditch, back toward his car. It seemed as if he'd run a mile, but now he was under and beyond the overpass. Only a few more steps and he could scramble out of the waterway. He found a place that was dark and overgrown and sure to allow him to escape the ditch without being seen. His lungs ached for air, he had a deep stitch in his side. But each attempt to scale the embankment failed. He blundered to the bottom a dozen times. The lockbox kept him from using his hands. Finally, he threw the box over the fence and pulling himself higher using an exposed tree root, managed to scramble up and over the fence guarding the ditch. His pants were shredded, but his keys were still in what remained of his trouser pocket.

He looked every way around him before slinking away from the gloom near the fence and back to his Lincoln. In a moment he was under the wheel. The big engine came to life. The doors locked. He was saved.

He drove away like a bat out of hell. The lockbox was in the seat beside him.

Even as he arrived home, his heartbeat had scarcely slowed. He hid the lockbox in his trunk and tiptoed to his room. Sleep eluded him.

Jack pushed a button and the garage door lurched into action, closing it to the night behind him. It was the next evening and his flesh was still crawling after his raid of the cemetery. He found himself falling to his knees when SCREECH! The garage door came down on Jill's favorite cat. "Damn cats!" he said. His nerves were shot.

He went to work at his tidy workbench. He put Jude's lockbox in a vise, then pounded away at the hinges with a hammer and cold chisel. A fog of dank dust enveloped him with each stroke. Finally one hinge broke and Jack was able to bend the lid away from the body of the box wide enough to insert his hand. He reached inside carefully, hoping to find video tape cassettes. If Jude had tapes, surely this is where he hid them. A thick stack of something was inside, it felt like paper. What he pulled out was a wad of paper money so thick that it would choke a horse. They were all hundreds. Jack immediately started counting.

"Holy cow! It must be 25 grand! That sonofabitch!" Something else was in the lock box. Jack reached in and pulled out a plastic sleeve full of begrimed papers. He wiped the twisted and broken lockbox clean of fingerprints, then hid it in the trunk of his car, alongside his golf clubs. He put the cash and the sheaf of papers in a garbage bag alongside the lockbox before cleaning up the workbench and returning the tools to their proper place. He, then, sprayed the air with WD-40 to mask the smell of death.

He popped his head inside the kitchen door that lead to the garage. "Honey, I'm gonna go jump in the river."

"Whatever," Jill answered back. Jack's Lincoln was already halfway outside the garage.

He drove eastward, toward the swamp, the Atchafalaya, beyond the levee. The sky was without a moon. Every place in the swamp was eerie and ghostly. He drove to a steel drawbridge that spanned a spooky, mist shrouded bayou. He remembered now that this place had a ghost story. The spirit of a mourning mother was said to haunt the bridge, or if not the bridge, one of the nearby huge, mossy live oak trees that lined the bayou. He kicked himself for not choosing a better place, one without a ghost. Jack could not count on this manifestation being as helpful as the spirit in the cemetery. He had arrived unseen and he needed to get back home. Jill would notice him being away three nights in a row, so he pressed forward.

The Couillon

He was afraid to get out of his car, so he crawled over the back seat and tried to reach the truck from inside. Fail.

He inhaled and held his breath. He had to make the lockbox disappear. He had to have the courage. He opened the trunk using a button inside the glove box, then mustered the gumption to open the door. He ran to the rear of the vehicle and retrieved the lockbox from the trunk. He heaved the twisted box as far as he could into the dark water of the bayou.

An icy cold presence behind him pressed his shoulder like a bony finger, pushing as if to topple him over the side rail. With a shriek, he raced around the car and jumped in, slamming and locking the door behind him.

His greatest dread now was that the Lincoln would not start, but his fears were not realized.

The engine started when asked. Jack jammed the shifter into gear. The tires smoked. Its trunk lid bouncing up and down, the big town car flew off of the bridge and fishtailed across the ground oyster shell road over the dry land beyond the bayou.

The Lincoln had saved his life for the second time in a week. Jack was unwilling to press his luck. He drove 50 miles out of his way to avoid crossing the haunted bridge on his way back to town.

Back home, he hung his golf clubs on their peg and rubbed them down to remove any hint of the fusty grime from the lockbox. He swept the carpet in the trunk, emptied the vacuum and washed the dust down a sink. Tomorrow was soon enough to worry about the money and check into the paperwork that he had recovered from the lockbox.

Jack was at his desk, preparing to inspect the crumbling documents that he had recovered from Jude's lockbox and brought to the office in a black plastic bag. He loosened his tie. An open collar seemed a fitting bearing for a man to assume when he examined the fruit of his grand larceny. The documents were so flimsy that they would be difficult to run through the shredder.

The newspaper account of the police investigation into the break in at Jude's office emboldened him. The article mentioned no missing cash. This might be because the police kept some facts out of the papers to trip up the burglar, but his experience was that the cops never even tried to solve the burglaries that plagued his tenant's shops. It had to be that Jude could not admit to having dirty cash. Even Big Leo had a stash of gamecock money he wouldn't want Uncle Sam to know about.

He tucked his tie in his shirt and rolled up his sleeves. "Filthy," he mumbled. The documents were covered with a blend of dust, mold, and corruption.

Most of the documents were yellow tissue copies of checks imprinted "ACME SERVICES." Jack sat back in his chair and blew a low whistle. The copies had been drawn on a BTME banking account that Jack had never seen before. He flipped through the corners. All the checks were cut in the amount of $1,000. He buzzed Louise.

"Can you run down some information for me?"

He and Louise passed one another in the hall a couple of times that morning. She bladed past, turned at a 45 degree angle with a cell phone stuck in her ear to avoid eye contact. Later in the day he walked into her office, right foot first, and closed the door behind him.

"Did you get a chance to find out something about those check numbers I gave you?"

"What was the name again?"

"Acme Services. Couple of years ago, maybe several years before that." Jack showed her a photocopy of one of the yellow sheets.

"That account's not on the books."

"That's okay. I know there's some things secret. But what is that anyway? It sounds like someone Wylie E. Coyote would buy from."

"I just do what I'm told."

"What is it, Louise? It can't be all that bad. An ex-wife maybe?"

Big Leo usually told people he'd been married five times, but on several occasions he'd told Jack it was really seven. Jack could account for the names of six, but one escaped him. Her name was never spoken, the woman who was Jill's mother.

"That's a topic we don't discuss. It's probably background checks."

"Tenants or new hires?"

"Both, I suppose. I just do what I'm told."

"You ever seen a background check on a tenant?" Jack waited for an answer.

"I've seen credit reports."

"Yeah, I've never seen background checks either."

Returning to his own office, Jack wrote the name "ACME SER-VICES" on a piece of paper. Then he wrote "BIG LEO" below. Jack studied the piece of paper then drew a line below "BIG LEO."

Jack searched 'Acme Services' on the internet. The search got 16,726 hits, but when he narrowed those results for 'Lafayette,' the computer returned 712 hits. He went to Harriet's desk and found a telephone book. Acme Services had no listing, even in the oldest phone books.

Staff had gone home by the time Jack finished his fruitless search through the 712 hits. He went to Louise's office and pawed through her file cabinets looking for 'Acme Services.' He finally found something hidden behind personal files in her desk. It was a manila file with "Acme Services' typed neatly on the tab. The file had to be old. BTME hadn't owned a typewriter since Jack was hired on and gave the last one to Goodwill. The file had dividers labeled "invoices" and "contracts." Nothing was behind the dividers but he did find two ancient unopened bank statements. He threw them in the trash.

Back at his desk, he rubbed his head and scratched his chin. "Damn!" he said. It had suddenly occurred to him that in the olden days, banks returned cancelled checks to their customers. He retrieved the bank statements from Louise's trash can.

He examined all the cancelled checks. Each envelope had less than a half-dozen checks and one of those was made out to Acme Services. With a scowl, he sat back in his chair, stumped. He looked at the check again. Nothing. He checked again, this time front-and-back. Neither of the Acme checks had been deposited. Each of them had been cashed. The endorsement was illegible. Despite his brush with death at the cemetery, Jack was glad now that he'd stolen the lockbox and retrieved it from the place of the dead.

The next morning, Jack guided his Lincoln through a lane of live oak trees. The canopy was groaning under the weight of Spanish moss. He rolled up the windows when he heard the hoot of an owl. The lane was the kind of place a sensible person would avoid at night. It led to Lafayette's most exclusive country club. Jack stopped at the bag drop and sprung the trunk with his remote control key.

A preppy young man skipped out of the pro shop and by the time Jack could get to the back of the car, was unloading Jack's clubs. "Gonna get in a round Mr. Mouton? Looks like a great day. New clubs?"

"Heya, Chip. Be careful with those. Haven't had a chance to hit them yet." Jack dug a five-dollar bill out of his wallet.

"Five bucks? Sure Mr. Mouton. You dah man."

"You're going to need it. Have you had a chance to think about that cheerleading scholarship?"

Chip smiled and shook his head. "No...not really." Jack tossed him his keys and Chip patted the trunk of the Lincoln. "I'm going to get me one of these someday," Chip said, as he jumped under the steering wheel.

"Oh wait. Forgot my cell phone," Jack said. Chip tossed him the device that he'd left on the console. Jack enjoyed seeing a broad smile spread across the boy's face as he wheeled the big Lincoln into a parking spot in the shadow of an ancient live oak.

Jack flipped open the phone and put it to his ear. His brow knitted. Curious. Something was odd. He held the instrument close to his face and punched one button after another. He checked the batteries but the phone seemed to be fully charged. Still no dial tone. Jack shook his head, shrugged, and walked toward the pro shop.

Wedgie, the club's head pro, was walking out of the shop as Jack arrived. Like every golf pro, Wedgie had big hands and big feet. He allowed the clubhouse door to close behind him. *Odd*, Jack thought. Staff at the golf course usually held doors open for the members.

"Mr. Mouton! Got a minute?"

"Hi ya, Wedgie! How's the game?"

"Been selling a lot of shirts."

"Pretty day, hunh?"

"Yeah. Pretty day all right. Say Mr. Mouton, we received a call and well you know...we're supposed to...well, your company called to see if, well, you know, to see if you couldn't play somewhere else today."

"Why would I? I have a tee time here," Jack said.

"Well, yeah, well, see, the way it is that, well, you know, your privileges got suspended."

"Suspended? Me? It's my membership!"

"Well, technically...it's a Bayou Teche membership. We checked. If it were me, you know, I'd let you play, but my hands are tied. I'm sure you'll understand."

"I'm in shock. Like a bombshell. Just give me a minute." The cell phone was still as dead as a landed carp.

"Sure. Come on in the clubhouse. We've got shirts on sale."

"Right. Like I'm gonna get kicked out of the club then carry your dumb ass logo around on my shirt."

Wedgie put his hands on his hips. "You don't have to be pissy." Chip was walking toward them with Jack's clubs over his shoulder, and Wedgie signaled to his assistant with a knobby, calloused finger. He pointed at the bag drop, and Chip turned on his heel to retrace his steps.

Jack was no longer in any mood to play golf today. He walked back to his car and let the Lincoln squeal his tires on the way back to the bag drop. He popped the trunk. No one came. He honked. No one. Jack was mortified when other club members saw him loading his own clubs.

Jack drove to a titty bar, one where he was certain he wouldn't run into any of his friends. He wanted to drink alone, do some thinking and bolster his nerve. Some said that drinking never solves anything, but Jack's dad had always said that when alcohol is suspended in a liquid, it becomes a solution.

Strippers bumped and ground, but it was still daylight and Lafayette's working men were still in the field. Customers were few and far between.

He ordered. "Glenfiddich, twelve-year-old, neat."

The bartender looked at him as if he had just landed in a spaceship from another planet. "The only thing around here that's twelve years old is the dancers."

"A beer then. A draw beer."

Jack's ass was frosted over the golf club membership and the cell phone. Over the years, he'd eaten a lot of shit from the Forets, so much that he was starting to think he'd acquired a taste for it. This "yeah, well what have you done for me lately" attitude was more than a man ought to have to take. And taking away the country club. How did they think he could run BTME without a golf membership? What was it Liz had said? Something about his own lawyer. As if he had his own lawyer. *Bitch*. She didn't want him to get a lawyer, not really.

Maybe I'd better get myself a lawyer, Jack told himself. *That'll teach 'em a lesson.* He ran down a short list of attorneys he'd used in real estate deals. He wouldn't let a single one of them represent him on a drunk driving charge. He'd find someone. Someone would help him run something uncomfortable up their asses. *If the greenie weenie is what they want, then that's what they're gonna get,* he thought.

He wished he could get some advice from Jude.

It's bullshit. Bullshit, he told himself. Suddenly he was famished. "You got anything to eat?"

"We got the Holy Trinity." The barkeep stood aside and swept his hand across the back-bar as if he were Vanna White and Jack had just bought a vowel. "Pickled sausage...pickled pig's feet...pickled eggs."

"Anything else?"

"Got some corny dogs."

Usually no...but not today. "Okay, three corny dogs." The corny dogs were decadent, fatty goodness and tastier than he would have ever imagined. When the last dab of mustard was swabbed off of the Styrofoam plate and he'd scraped off the last morsel of meat by pulling the stick through his teeth, he felt like a weight had been taken off of his shoulders. He told the bartender, "Tab me out, please." Jack pulled his credit card from his billfold and handed it to the bartender.

The barman returned moments later. "Sorry, Mr. Mouton. Declined. You got another card?"

"What? Sorry. Here. Try this one."

He returned a second time with a disappointed look on his face. Jack pulled cash out of his billfold. He'd been born at night, but not last night. This was the doings of the Forets. *I can see now that I'm going to need cash.*

The next day, Jack was sitting across a desk from his financial planner, Al Lacombe. He had his Mont Blanc fountain pen perched over a form that Lacombe had prepared for him to sign.

"You know I think you're making a big mistake here, Mr. Mouton. These 401(k)s are really building up. Why just the other day, I delivered a big fat check to a widow lady and boy was she ever happy."

"My wife wants to be a widow, too. Hey, I'll come by in a couple of days to get that check."

"Speaking of the wife, I'll need her signature, too."

"No you don't, it's my account."

"Call your Congressman. She's got an interest in your account just like you have an interest in hers."

Jack shoved the form in the direction of Lacombe and left his office without saying another word.

Jack was at his desk. He had removed his shoes and rubbed sore feet while talking on the phone. He noticed that the shoes were scuffed and that a tiny hole had worn its way into the sole. He flipped through the telephone book, and picked up the phone again.

"Classified please. I need to place an ad. A cabin cruiser. Jack. Moo. Moo. Moot..." He loved the boat. He couldn't do it. "Never mind." He gently replaced the earpiece in its cradle.

CHAPTER 9

The conference room was jam packed with suits. Men and women, ties loosened, sat seminar-style in a meeting room at a motel out by the Interstate. An easel held a placard that pronounced the course sponsors and subject, "ACADIANA BAR ASSOCIA-TION, CONTINUING LEGAL EDUCATION, TONIGHT'S TOPIC: SEXUAL HARASSMENT. DISCUSSION LEADER: BOULANGER."

The lecture leader was a guy with a receding hairline, the part that had not yet given way to shiny skin he pulled back in a ponytail. His name was Boulanger, a local lawyer, and in itself, it was an oddity for him to be the lecturer. "No prophets ariseth in Galilee" was a concept that was alive and well in Lafayette. Unless an expert was from "town," and that meant New Orleans, locals figured he was a couillon, "coo-YAWn," a dumb ass.

Jude seated himself in the back row, by himself, ready to take notes on a yellow notepad. He needed to sit where he had no distractions. His days at the squat taught him not so sit with his back to a door.

After the orator's obligatory opening joke, Boulanger cut straight to the chase. "There's a considerable amount of bad infor-mation going around about sexual harassment lawsuits, and that's my objective tonight, to clear that up. You see, sexual harassment comes in two forms. First is the 'quid pro quo' harassment. 'I will if you will.' Good old fashioned 'give me sex if you want to keep your job.' It's vicious and insidious but in terms of litigation, it's relatively easy to prove. And the workplace has been doing some pretty heavy lifting in getting rid of the worst predators, the worst offenders."

Boulanger punctuated his next statement by walking around the podium and leaning back on the dais table. He rubbed his chin for effect. "The second type of actionable harassment is 'hostile working environment.' It's harder to prove but it's where all the action is. More often than not, this is where the lawsuit arises."

Boulanger walked to the easel. "In either case, the amount of damages depends on the number of employees."

Concern etched the brow of every participant. They exchanged worried glances..."WTF?"

Boulanger pulled another pasteboard placard from behind the table and placed it on the easel without comment. This one read, "LIMIT ON DAMAGES, NUMBER OF EMPLOYEES 15–100 $50,000."

The seminar participants reacted with a cacophony of moans and involuntary utterances of horrified shock. It appeared for a moment that they would all die of oxygen depletion.

"What?!" Jude shouted. "That can't be right."

A serene smile spread across Boulanger's face. "Don't worry, friends. Calm. Let there be peace. A successful plaintiff's lawyer gets legal fees. God is still in his heaven."

The participants exhaled collectively with a great sigh. A nervous titter ran through the room. Participants high-fived one another.

At the intermission, Jude took up his yellow pad and left the conference. He'd heard enough from Boulanger to know he better make damn sure that Charma stayed on board. The amount she stood to win was considerably less than they had planned, he had promised her millions, but Jude still stood to have the biggest payday of his legal career, he had a chance to get his cash hoard built back up, and he saw no reason to put any of that at hazard.

The Couillon

Jude was in no rush as he drove to the Rusty Penny. The parking lot had chugholes that looked like razorback hog wallows. Dance music spilled out of the beer joint and into the night. He parked in his regular slot, under a tupelo tree.

A bouncer stood outside, guarding the doorway to the den of iniquity. He was tasked with collecting a cover charge but let Jude pass without payment. His principal duty was to enforce the gentlemen's club's "NO DAR DAR" policy. A sign over the door put prospective patrons on notice of the strict prohibition. The purpose of the guideline was to deny service to any and all members of a Native American clan from Houma with a well-deserved reputation for fighting.

Jude had a lifetime exemption from the cover charge. He earned free admission for life because he had given free legal advice to the club owner. Based on Jude's counsel, the owner posted the DAR DAR policy on a sign by the front door. "Public notice," he told the owner and punctuated his advice with a stern nod. "In the interest of full disclosure."

The Rusty Penny was a place for men to go to get tight and meet loose women. Inside, the joint was dark as a tomb. The bass dial on the jukebox must have been set on eleven – the reverb rattled the mirrors on the walls. Harvard or Yale could never match the ethnic diversity that manifested itself in the clientele of the Rusty Penny. The loud-mouthed Cajuns were identifiable by their footwear. They all wore Cajun Nikes, calf-high white rubber boots. Also in the concoction was a smattering of Croatians. These late arrivals from the Balkans held sway over the brackish blackwater oysterbeds. They enjoyed the floorshow side-by-side with Asians, also newcomers, who dominated the shrimp fishery in the bluewater Gulf. Oilfield trash made up the largest segment of the customer base, even that bunch was a red-and-yellow-black-and-white cocktail of Cajuns, Mexicans, Texians and Okies.

Charma was dancing at a pole. The elevated stage was lit up like a Pentecostal church. She was as naked as a jaybird except for a G-string, and she was far along in the process of bumping and grinding her way out of that. She wore ridiculously tall platform shoes with spiked, stiletto heels. Dollar bills littered the dance floor.

Jude correctly guessed that his client was almost finished with her set. A couple of months ago, he had coached her on stripping strategy. He insisted to her that she delay the strip aspect of the strip tease, saving the full frontal nudity for the end. He styled himself as somewhat of an expert on the efficacy of this particular tactic of extracting cash from patrons of gentlemen's clubs, having written a well-received paper on the subject while still an undergraduate at the University.

Jude took up his station next to the police radio and beckoned the bartender with an index finger.

"Vodka straight, Jude?"

"I'm on the wagon. Not drinking til I win this big case. What kind of coke you got?"

"Dr Pepper? Seven-Up?" In Acadiana, all soft drinks are called "coke," so Jude's order had been short on specificity.

"How about an RC. Give me a half-dozen corny dogs, too. I'm so hungry I'd eat a skunk's asshole."

"You got it." The bartender served Jude an RC cola just as Charma unleashed the last clasp that held her G-string in place. She was buck naked now, swinging the G-string around above her head. But every eyeball in the joint was riveted to her nether region, drawn there by a flash of vibrant colors, orange, yellow, dark purple and vivid white.

Charma's pubic area was shaved bald and decorated with a tattoo, the logo of LSU, a full-on snarling tiger's face. Sharp saber-like bared fangs contrasted and defined the yawning black cavity of the feline's mouth.

"Eye-EEEE! Looka dat coochie!" A white-booted Cajun, two hundred pounds of erectile tissue, launched himself out of the darkness and into the light. He was on a mission, intent on climbing onto the stage. His buddies held him back. Below Charma's feet, a blizzard of dollar bills swirled like leaves on a tempest.

Jude found Charma at a makeup table behind the curtain of the stage. She liked to call it "backstage" but it was a storage room, lit by a single naked bulb in the ceiling, and filled with cases of beer, booze, and cleaning supplies. She wore an open robe and was counting her money.

"Hot," Jude said. "Real hot, be'-be'."

Jude tried to kiss Charma, but she screwed up her face and pushed him away. "Oooo! Yuck. You smell like cola."

"Went to a class tonight. Sexual harassment. Fifty thousand."

"Fifty-thousand what?"

"Dollars. That's how much you're gonna get."

"Fifty-thousand! Fifty-thousand! Jude what kind of bullshit is this?"

"It's changed. The law. They changed the law."

Quelle horreur! Charma broke down, almost in tears. "Jude you bastard, you told me millions. Millions! You rat. How can I ever...oh shit. Dancing in a titty bar. I'm nothing but a sleazy whore."

"Fifty thousand is a lot of money honey bunny."

"Oh, I've made so many mistakes. All I ever wanted was to put this all behind me, and maybe I could send my Evangeline to a nice school."

"Ain't time to back down now."

"Oh Jude, You lied to me. Let's just drop it."

Steam was building up under Jude's collar. No one likes being called a liar, especially liars. "You lied to me. You sucked me in. So you're not backing out now."

Charma pouted. "I never lied. Not once."

Jude pulled a paper from his pocket. He was so angry he was shaking as if he were at the epicenter of an Oklahoma quakenado. "You ever hear of one...Vinnie Venevicci?"

"My ex."

"Ex my ass. You never got a divorce. Be'-be'."

"Don't mean nothing, darling."

"It doesn't mean nothing huh? Then make sure I understand, Madam Lawyer Counsel lady. The part about him being in jail doesn't mean nothing? Or the part about him being a pimp doesn't mean nothing?"

Charma pouted.

"He pimp for you?"

"No. Naw, sugar."

"This case has cost me a hundred thousand so far." The true cost of Jude's outlay was a hundred bucks. Maybe. "I came out of my hip pocket with all the costs. I made these pleadings. These statements to the court. I can lose my license. Jeez, I made you sound like Madonna."

"You've never heard me sing..."

"The Virgin Mary, you dumb bitch. Tell me you didn't tell BTME that you were single on your employment application."

"I need to get ready for my next show."

"You get back to bumpin' and grindin' that sweet ass and this idea about dropping the suit, you just put it out of that hollow head of yours. Get it? We're in this together."

Jude grabbed Charma by the hair and kissed her, wet and nasty. She resisted, tried to pull back, but then her flesh responded to his scaly touch.

"I'm sorry, Jude." She kissed him deeply in return.

CHAPTER 10

Jack always scoured the *Advertiser*, Lafayette's daily newspaper, and today he saw a notice that a lawyer named Boulanger had taught a continuing education class to the local bar on sex harassment. Jack knew who he was. He was one of the chiselers at the country club that gambled football with the oil patch crowd. He made a call and canceled appointments to fit a late afternoon opening in Boulanger's cram-packed schedule. He was told to bring a $10,000 retainer.

Boulanger's firm, Boucher, Boulanger and Chandelier, was located in the Oil Center, a sprawling complex of low-level buildings a few blocks away from downtown. "Mr. Boulanger is on the phone." The law firm's receptionist was tall and leggy and was reading a checkout-stand newspaper with a story about Brad and Angelina. It seemed like forever before she told him, "You can go back now."

"Back? Where?"

She put down her paper and delivered a withering, cold stare. "Follow that hallway."

Jack wound his way down a rabbit warren of a hallway, looking in each office. When he passed a door marked "Boulanger," he was sure he had found the right office. The gentleman seated behind a big chunk of wood asked, "Mr. Mouton?"

"It's Jack Mouton. You're Robert...?"

"Mr. Boulanger. You've brought the retainer?"

Jack extended a brown paper bag. "Ten. There's ten thousand in there."

Boulanger sat back, looking into the bag. All his side chairs had piles of files in them, so Jack had nowhere to sit but a low-back bench. He was two feet below the lawyer's eye level and separated by a desk that looked as big as an aircraft carrier. The lawyer poured himself a fresh coffee without asking Jack if he wanted a cup.

"Okay. The company. Big Bayou..."

"Bayou Teche Management Enterprises."

"...is represented by..." Boulanger flipped another page. " I-EEEE! Liz the Lizzie Churnow! Haha. I'll notice her up and get copies of pleadings. Oh man, this is going to be fun."

"I'm not guilty."

"This is a civil matter, Jackie-boy. Guilt, innocence...means nothing."

"I didn't do it."

"I'm interested in what the record says more than what you say. Perception is reality, Jackie-boy."

"Comforting."

"It's what's in the record that counts. What else?"

"Can you help me find out something about a vendor of ours? Acme Services. Just a name that popped up since this thing started. It probably means nothing...Robert..." Boulanger glared at Jack as if he was waiting for a magic word. Jack added. "Mr. Boulanger," and the lawyer scribbled, 'Acme Services' on a legal paper.

Boulanger rose out of his seat to prompt Jack that the meeting was over. "Give me a few days. I'll be in touch." Jack extended his hand to Boulanger, but too late. Boulanger had already picked up the phone and had it to his ear.

As he walked out the front door, Jack caught sight of his beautiful, lustrous Lincoln. A heavy wire rope suspended the town car from a steel arm in the back of a tow truck that was hauling it away and onto Pinhook Road.

He tried to run. If he cut across the Oil Center maze, ducked through an arbor alongside the Petroleum Club, and hurdled a low hedge, he could just catch the truck. Surely he could persuade the driver stop for enough time to get the situation, whatever it was, sorted out. Surely he could persuade the driver. People are reasonable.

Jack had to stop and catch his breath. The driver hit a green light. He had no way of keeping up.

Towed away? For a parking ticket? He looked around the lot. Hell, it was free parking. They had another reason for towing the car. Maybe he had parked in a "no parking" zone. Or a handicapped space.

No. Big Leo, or more likely Jill, just had it picked up. He couldn't even report it as stolen. It was a company car.

Damn phones. His didn't work and Boulanger couldn't get off of his, so he might have to wait for hours to snag a ride from the lawyer. Damn phones. He decided to walk home. It wasn't so far. He checked to make sure he had his keys.

Divorce was going to be costly. Boulanger would charge him the same as anyone else. If he even worked in family law. A separation would probably cost less.

Jack needed money, a lot of money. He needed it fast and he did not know where he could get it. By now, without question, BTME had taken him off of the accounts and he was willing to bet a dollar to a hole in a doughnut that the personal accounts had been drained by his ever-loving wife Jill.

Maybe he could sell the boat.

Jack had walked a mile toward home and was wearing a blister on his heel when he began to be haunted with a cold-chill. Someone was following him. Darkness was upon him and he was afraid to face whatever it was that was dogging his steps.

"Jack. Jack Mouton. Is that you? What's your hurry?"

He was relieved to know that it wasn't a spirit following him. He turned to face Detective Lily. Etienne followed close behind in their unmarked cruiser.

"You guys following me?"

"Yep," Lily said.

"What do you need?"

Lily pulled handcuffs from a holster on his belt. "You're under arrest."

"For what?"

The detective pushed Jack against a wall and clapped the cuffs on him. "You have the right to remain silent. If you choose to waive this right, anything you say can be used against you. You have a right to an attorney. If you can't afford an attorney, one will be appointed for you. Do you understand?"

"I don't understand how anyone can afford an attorney."

"Do you understand?"

"Sure. Sure. Looks like you could have picked me up before I wore a blister."

Etienne helped Jack into the back seat of the car. "Watch your head, son."

Sometime in the middle of the night, Jack was handed a large card that had the number "5" written on it. He shuffled with some scruffy characters through a narrow door and into a brightly lit room. The wall to the right was, Jack correctly supposed, a one-way mirror. The other four guys in the room with him held their number in front of their chest, so Jack followed their lead. A speaker crackled and a voice told them to turn to the right.

Jack turned right to face the mirror. He held his breath. "Number five, step forward." Jack complied.

"Give him some glasses," a voice grackled over the speaker. A cop in the room handed Jack some mirrored aviator glasses. He refused to put them on. The one-way mirror bothered him enough.

But the crow voice in the speaker insisted. When he did put them on, his body jerked away from the sight of his image repeated, from the mirror to the aviator glasses, back and forth, growing ever smaller. It disappeared into infinity. Every muscle in his body stiffened with anxiety. He held his breath and closed his eyes.

An hour later, Jack was led, still cuffed, into an airless room with three straight-backed metal chairs. Boulanger was seated, as were Etienne and Lily. Jack had to stand.

"An eye witness?" Boulanger was asking. "At night? A hundred yards or more away? You're barking at the moon, guys."

"Well work with us then," Lily said.

"I don't even know what you think you've arrested me for," Jack said, "Can someone tell me?"

"Breaking and entering." It looked like Lily was going to do all the talking. Etienne was staring a hole through Jack's chest.

"Where? When? What?"

"Jude Malveaux's office."

"I had a key! Why would I break in?"

"Jackie-boy!" Boulanger's hand was on his forearm. "Not another word."

Lily looked at his partner. "Just 'cause I haven't figgered that out yet doesn't mean we're gonna let you go," Etienne said.

"It was that bastard Jude right? That fingered me. It was him wasn't it?...Mr. Boulanger?"

"They got a tentative maybe from a bill collector," Boulanger said.

The silence was too much for Lily. "You want to talk about currency deposits in your checking account? We're here to listen."

"Well then listen to this, I've never worn mirrored glasses in my life. Why would I wear sunglasses at night?"

"Who said anything about night?" Etienne said.

Boulanger squeezed his arm a second time. "He's said everything he's going to say."

"You gotta give us something, Jack," Lily said.

Jack turned away. The cops gathered themselves and called for a jailer to take Jack to a cell.

"Give me a second with him," Boulanger said, and the cops left the room.

Once the detectives were gone, Boulanger had some pointed questions to ask. Boulanger was in Jack's face, his chief adversary now. "Big Bayou..." Boulanger was doodling on a yellow pad.

"It's Bayou Teche Management Enterprises. She set me up! Don't you see that?! Think about it!"

"So Jude and this Charma woman. They have a thing?" Boulanger asked. It was more of an observation than a question.

"I suppose they probably do. He'd screw anything."

"Okay, so a lawyer screws his client?" Boulanger pulled a quarter out of his pocket and tossed it to Jack. "Call someone that cares. Haha. Hey. You might be interested."

Boulanger picks up a file, flipping pages. "Acme Services. We represent the bank."

"What did you find out?" Boulanger was silent. He looked at Jack over his half-frame glasses. "What did you find out, Mr. Boulanger."

The lawyer liked that better. "The authorized signer, one Julien Malveaux. Of course, that doesn't tell us who owns the company..."

"Jude! You stinking bastard, I knew it!" Jack danced around the room as if he were trying to get it to rain.

"Jackie, we've exhausted the retainer."

Jack stopped dancing. "What?"

"We need more money."

Jack fell back against the wall of the holding room and blinked his eyes. "I'm just a little surprised. That's all. I mean ten thousand. I thought it would last a little longer. That's all. I mean the only thing I have so far is who Acme Services is....Mr. Boulanger."

"See if you can't bring us another ten."

"When I get out." Jack stuffed his hands in his pockets.

"Even if you don't get out, you need to make arrangements. And you might want to start planning on ten grand a month...Jackie-boy."

Boulanger reached for the door but relaxed. He turned back and backed Jack into a corner. "And if you find anyone in there that's deaf and dumb, let me know. I'll give you a discount."

Jack did not understand. "What?"

"You think you're going to run into a deaf mute in the jail house?"

"What the hell are you asking?"

"A deaf mute doesn't know anything, nothing, nada, squat. But he is able to keep his mouth shut. And knowing how to keep his mouth shut is what keeps a deaf mute out of jail. So from now on, when I tell you to shut up, it's time to shut up." Boulanger slammed the door behind him on the way out of the room.

Jack felt naked in a jail cell. He sat on the floor, back against the wall. He had no handkerchief. He tried not to touch the other dregs of humanity, who milled around, shouting at one another and no one. One of his cellmates offered him a cigarette. At first he brushed away the offer. He'd never smoked a cigarette in his life.

"You sure?"

Jack took the cigarette, put it in his mouth, and allowed his cell-mate to light it. The stinging dry smoke felt good in his lungs and he liked the tingling sensation that ran down his arms and legs.

The next morning, Jack was led into a courtroom by a bailiff. His chin sported a day's stubble. His hair was greasy. From behind the bench, a silver-haired judge asked him, "How do you plead?"

"Not guilty, your honor." It was Boulanger that spoke up. Jack startled. Boulanger stood beside him. He had not seen him when he was led into the courtroom.

"Thank you Mr. Boulanger," the judge said. "Ties to the community?"

Boulanger nodded.

"Employed?"

"Bayou Village, your honor."

Jack tried to correct Boulanger by whispering, "BTME." Whack! Boulanger had elbows like a linebacker.

"R O R?" Boulanger nodded again and the judge slammed his gavel.

"Huh?" Jack said.

"Released on own recognizance," Boulanger said. The bailiff released the handcuffs that had been protecting the citizens of the Great State of Louisiana and society at large from Jack.

Boulanger was long gone. Jack felt lower than whale shit at the bottom of the Marianna Trench. It was probably better to be charged with simple breaking and entering and not grand theft. *They have nothing on me*, Jack thought, *I can beat that rap in my sleep.* Ten grand!? Bullshit. Boulanger couldn't have spent 15 minutes finding out who had signature authority on the bank account. Boulanger had the bedside manner of a football coach. He needed to figure this guy out, find a way to smooth talk him. Until then, he did not want Boulanger to quit thinking about the harassment case. Jack had some cash, it was disappearing fast, but he really believed now that both cases would be disposed of in another month.

The blister on his heel broke open and his precious bodily fluids were draining into a filthy sock. Jack staggered a couple of miles to the company storage yard and found transportation. The firm kept an old pickup truck in the yard that came in handy for maintenance. The key had gone missing years ago. Loose connections under the dash turned over the starter when the exposed end of the red wire scraped against the blue.

Once at home, Jack was a bit surprised to find that his keys still worked in the locks. No one was home. The odor of the jail cell was still with him and the smell of food made him retch. The only thing fit to watch on TV was a movie, *Suddenly Last Summer*, which was set at a house in the Garden District of New Orleans. Miss Venable's courtyard reminded Jack of the swamp and it creeped him out.

The house was dark and spooky and he felt more alone than he had while in lockup. Did he hear something rustling in the attic? He wasn't sure.

The next day Jack took his clubs to a pawnshop. Clubs and bag, he sold them for $100. They had cost him $1,000 new just a week earlier.

He drove to one of the older shopping centers where Jill kept a bay for storage. He loaded the pickup to the sideboards with the expensive things that Jill owned, treasures that were so cute and darling, things that needed her so desperately. Most were still in their boxes.

He moved out to the strip of grass next to the street, leaned a hand-lettered sign that said "Estate Sale Today Only" on either side of the truck, where he plopped down in a lawn chair.

People stopped from time to time to kick tires, and he convinced a few that they wouldn't be able to sleep nights if they passed up buying some of the deeply discounted objects d'art he had to sell. One old fart was wearing a ball cap that said RETIRED and an I BREAK FOR GARAGE SALES T-shirt, and sandals. For protection against the chill of Acadiana's winter, he wore knee-length black socks. He had picked out a box full of small treasures, priced to sell at $10, and carried them to Jack's chair.

"I'll give you half."

"Okay," Jack said. It served Jill right to give this stuff away. "Five bucks. It's yours." Jack nodded, accepted a $5 bill from the tightwad, and then adjusted the lawn chair. The sun was moving the shadows.

Mr. Garage Sale was back within minutes with another box of precious belongings. "I'll give you half."

"It's only two bucks man."

"I'll give you half."

Jack nodded and put a $1 bill in his pocket. He put on his Dior sunglasses as Mr. Garage Sale approached him with another box of goodies.

"I'll give you half."

"Gimme a break, would ya? I'm only asking a buck for the whole box."

Mr. Garage Sale stood his ground.

"You asshole. Everything in the world I could possibly ever buy for fifty cents is in that box!"

"I like it when you talk dirty. I'll give you half."

"I'll take the 50 cents if you promise to leave," Jack said, putting ten nickels in his pocket.

CHAPTER 11

Jack awoke with a start. He'd fallen asleep on the couch after spending the day selling off Jill's favorite treasures. His shirt was soaked in sweat. Frissons, cold chills, ran up and down his spine. He had been having a vivid dream. The Saints were losing to the Ravens, and every time the defenders sacked Brees, their facemasks changed to beaks. The defenders pecked huge chunks of flesh out of the quarterback's face.

It was Jill slamming her way through the front door that awoke him. She threw herself around like a hog on ice so he knew she was angry. Jack correctly supposed that she'd been snubbed by a clerk at a store, but adding insult to her injury, she found a potato planted on her couch. Her no good husband, unshaved and greasy, slumping, quiet, defeated, drenched in sweat, smelling as if he was mildewing. She was already at Defcon 1 when she saw that Jack had stubbed out a half of a pack of cigarettes in a Waterford crystal relish dish. She was so infuriated that she skipped the opening gospel chapter and verse recitation and went straight to the Apocalypse.

"What do you think the women are thinking at the Junior League? Just tell me that!"

"Uh..."

"Who asked you? Arrested. Aaagk. Jesus Christ Jack, how could you do this to me?"

"I really...Jill...love..."

"Oh, love. Right. Well if you're thinking..." Jill made some hand gestures, bumping together her fists. "...then you've just got another think coming."

"Jill, we haven't..." Jack repeated the hand gestures that Jill had employed so eloquently. "...in a year anyway. Why do you think...?"

"Oh, you're always the one with the wise comeback. You...you. Aaagk. I could die. Just die. I'll never be able to show my face around here again."

"I didn't do anything. They can't convict me. They got no evidence." Jack lit another cigarette.

"Mardi Gras is coming up and I'm gonna have a soiree. So get out with those stinking cigarettes. I need your room. I'll have your things moved to the garage."

"Jill, I don't have money to set up house. This lawyer's breaking my back. And what's Big Leo gonna do if you kick me out while the lawsuit is going on? How's that gonna look?...lovey?"

Jill mulled over the arguments. "Okay. For Big Leo. But you're not sleeping with me. You're not sleeping in my end of the house. You can just sleep on the couch."

"I'm sleeping in my room," he said. But Jill didn't hear him. She was storming out of the room. "That went well," Jack said. He took a long, satisfying drag on the cigarette.

He'd been too busy to think while selling off Jill's treasures, and too tired to think once he returned home. He had nearly three thousand dollars, green cash, hidden in his bathroom in a shaving kit. He'd survived worse ass chewings than that, not many were that intense, but the subsequent quiet treatment was like a breath of fresh air.

He needed a plan. Boulanger was pestering him for cash. He had no idea how he was going to keep the Boulanger limousine greased. His cash reserves were dwindling faster than he could sell off used merchandise. He didn't like the feeling of vulnerability when he was sitting on a pile of cash in a crummy part of town. He needed protection.

The Couillon

Jack walked into the gun store gingerly, as if he were walking across a lily pond. The walls were covered with the finest examples of the taxidermist's craft, deer, ducks, fish, alligator heads, even a crow. When the builder laid the concrete floor of the shop, the owner had pressed alligator feet, bear's paws, and cougar prints into the moist cement. Now the footprints of the predatory beasts were in bas-relief under his feet.

He was astonished at the prices. He knew nothing about handguns, but he recognized the name "Glock" from the movies. With taxes and ammunition, a nine millimeter Glock would set him back nearly $800.

"If I still have one when you get back," the store owner told him. He answered to the name of Gunner.

"I guess you're trying that old salesman trick of making me think I need to make a decision right this minute," Jack said.

"If I still have one when you get back. Means just that. The paranoids are buying the used guns like crazy and I been having a run on Glocks. So if you're looking to stay under a thousand..."

"Okay, okay. I just wish I had a little more time. I got a boat to sell. I'd rather do that first."

"Yeah? What you got?" Gunner asked.

"Cabin cruiser. Forty-six feet." Jack showed him a picture that he carried in his wallet.

"Whatcha asking?"

"Cash."

"Yeah, but how much?"

"You a buyer for this?"

"Is the price right?"

"If I had a year...to find the right buyer, you know, polish up a knob here and there..." Jack pulled a photograph out of his billfold and showed it to Gunner. "I'd be asking two hundred fifty thousand."

"I'm good on this at a hundred fifty thousand."

Jack rubbed his chin. A hundred and fifty thousand, quick and dirty, sounded good. He didn't have a plug nickel of his own money in the rig. All the money in the boat had come from Jill. "Green money?"

"Is there any other kind?"

"I had the idea the feds were up your whoosey whatsey pretty tight on the guns."

"Gun shows, partner."

A hundred fifty thousand of long green that cost him nothing. All he had to do was sign over the title...ugh. The title. "I just thought. I got a title problem. The wife."

"Now hold on a damn minute. I ain't laying out a hundred fifty large if the paperwork ain't right."

"It's not that. We bought it over in town. My father-in-law. He knew a guy that knew a dead guy."

"I got forms that can fix that. Your old lady don't need to sign diddley squat. I'll come look at the boat tomorrow. Make sure it's everything you say it is. I'll even throw in some gun safely classes."

Jack decided to sleep over in the boat, one last time. He was not surprised by the nastiness Jude left in his wake. He had always defended the skunk. But a scumbag never changes his spots. Dirty dishes, half-eaten corn dogs, potato chip sacks, cigarette butts, and empty bottles were scattered everywhere but in the galley. Beer cans had been thrown around willy-nilly, even in the head.

Gunner would crawfish on the deal if he saw the boat looking like this, Jack was sure of it. He found some trash bags and went to work cleaning up the mess.

After an hour, his throat was parched. He mopped at his teeth with his tongue, then stumbled to the bar, licking his lips like a wino. The refrigerator was empty. Jude had left a spigot open and the water faucet was pissing dust. Jack rooted through the trash sacks, drinking the last drops of liquid from several of the bottles. His throat was as dry as a chip when he found a near-empty bottle of Gran Marnier. He looked at it quizzically. "Grand Mariner?"

Jack sniffed at the contents in the bottle. He tasted the last drops of the orange-flavored liqueur.

A wave of realization swept over him like a tsunami. "Grand Mariner!" he shouted. "GRAN-MON-YAY!" Jude was Charma's lawyer, yeah, any fool knew that. But what Jack was piecing together now was that she was the same chick that Jude had been with when he loaned Jude the boat keys. She hadn't just tripped into his office looking for a lawyer. He knew her before. The cockroach had brought her to the boat and they drank Gran Marnier shooters and he had screwed her like a tethered goat. That part was a metaphysical certainty.

"Jude, you rat bastard...you brought that redheaded bitch out here! You glorious rotten no good creep bastard! You're in it with her. You coached her. You helped set me up!"

It took some time before he believed what his eyes told him was true. Jude had entrapped him. Jack sat back on a bench seat. He socked his fist into his open palm. "I'm going to get you, and get you good. I own you, Julien Malveaux."

Jack slept like a baby in the gently rocking cabin cruiser. And when Gunner arrived, she met all of his expectations. He gave Jack $15,000 in hundreds, a 10% downstroke. Jack would pick up the rest of the cash when Gunner had fixed the boat's ownership papers and had a good title. They'd have a signing party. Jack would have enough cash to ride out the lawsuit with a Glock in a concealed holster.

Jack finalized the purchase of a quart of Gran Marnier at a local grocery store. "You deliver, right?" The cashier nodded. "Here's the address. I want to enclose a card."

Jack signed a sympathy card, adding a note, "SORRY ABOUT YOUR FUTURE DISBARMENT, YOUR OLD BUDDY."

Jack returned to the gun shop later that week. He'd scoured his closet to find dark shoes, slacks and a pullover long sleeved shirt. His only motive was to avoid looking conspicuous, but he didn't own a stitch of camouflage gear.

Gunner came out of the restroom under the stuffed crow, shaking moisture from his hands. He took up his station behind the counter. "Sorry man. You didn't clear the background check. Maybe another time."

"I just got charged," Jack said. "I'm not guilty."

"It ain't up to me, man." Gunner locked the pistol in the glass showcase under their noses.

"Gimme the money back then."

"Sorry. You bought this discount on a Mardi Gras coupon." Gunner pointed to yellowed sign that said "NO RETURNS ON HOLIDAY MERCHANDISE." "It's company policy."

"Dammit. Then give me my eight hundred back."

"That thing ought to clear up in another five or six days. A couple or three months, maybe. Hey, we'll have some of those cop killer bullets in Friday. Makes a guy get hard just looking at them. Did you bring the papers on the boat?"

"You think you can screw me over on the Glock, well you can just stick the boat up your ass, Gunner."

Jack had already wheeled away from the counter and was outside the shop when he heard Gunner yelling after him, "I'm coming after you, Jack. You give me my money back. You'll be sorry, you son of a bitch. I've got friends. I'm not a man to be trifled with."

Jack sat at the railing along the elevated stage at his new favorite place, a titty bar. He was drinking alone, smoking a cigarette.

A stripper approached him and rubbed his thigh. He enjoyed it yesterday and even more today. He stuffed a dollar down the front of the stripper's G-string and was slow to withdraw his hand, looking at the floor, as if to blush. "Are you married?"

"Just a boyfriend."

Jack pulled back the dollar before she could grab it. "Boyfriend! What do you think I am?"

The stripper yowled, "Hey you bastard!"

Jack laughed and pushed the dollar into the stripper's bra. So many slobs to take advantage of, so little time. She stilted away on high platformed shoes. Jack laid his head down on the bar and groaned.

A shaft of light poured into the bar as a Cajun gentleman entered, flush with cash from payday, yelling "Laissez les bon temps rouler. It's Mardi Gras."

"Hey! People are trying to sleep you know." Jack ordered another drink. He had already had one too many, but it was happy hour, 2-for-1, but for Jack, happy hour was starting to mean 14-for-7. "And hey. Could you call me up one of them yellow cars?" Jack was digging in his pockets for cash. "I got an appointment downtown."

Jack stumbled into the offices of BTME, drunk as a lord. He knew he was in the right place when he saw two Harriets reading two movie magazines. Mardi Gras decor festooned the lobby. Harriet ignored Jack. He bounced back and forth between the walls on his way to Big Leo's office.

Big Leo was telling him "Jill and Liz called. They both stuck in the Mardi Gras traffic."

"Figgers," Jack said." Hey, call 'em up. Get 'em on the phone. My time's valuable."

"No big hurry, son. Their lawyers sent over questions. In-toe-rag-atories."

"Have you got anything around here to drink?"

"I can see you ain't gonna be much help. I always figgered you for a stinking drunk."

"Hey, at least I don't let a stinking drunk know my secrets."

Big Leo looked at Jack as if he'd never seen him before. He'd certainly never seen him sticking up for himself. "Why don't you go splash a dab of cold water on your face?"

"Why don't you and Acme Services kiss my ass?"

Big Leo's countenance fell. "You don't know..."

"I know plenty," Jack said. He was bluffing. "I know what Jude knows." Now he was lying.

A low grumble built in Big Leo's throat, but gritting his teeth, he held it back.

"So let's just start with you taking back that little shot about me being a stinking drunk."

"You're right. I take it back. Every word."

"How about that car? You sold it yet? I sure miss having wheels."

"Maybe we could get you to drive it for us. At least until we sell it, eh?"

"Perfect. And talk to me before you entertain any offers. And the cell phone. I need that turned back on."

"Eye-eee, Jack if you'd just said. I can't imagine what that Liz lawyer woman was thinking."

"Before I leave this evening, Big Leo. Get me those keys. I'll need it if I decide to take Jill to the Mardi Gras Banquet this evening."

Big Leo hustled out of the room. Jack sat in Big Leo's chair and it felt nice. He put his feet up on the desk and lit a cigarette. The ashtray was empty.

When Liz arrived, several cigarettes butts stood at attention in the ashtray. Liz, Jill and Big Leo entered the boardroom in single file.

Jill threw her purse on the table. It landed with a heavy metallic thunk. The purse opened enough so that Jack could see the muzzle of a pistol. It seemed to stare at him while Liz rattled off a sonorous discussion of facts and rules and precedents.

Jack was getting sleepy and ignored Liz' diatribe. BTME's defense was not his problem. He had written some of his thoughts on a yellow tablet in front of him. Across the top, it said:

SECRETS I COULD TELL OLD LIZZIE and below that a list:

1. ACME SERVICES BLACKMAILING COMPANY (OVER WHAT??)
2. JUDE AND CHARMA LOVERS,
3. COMPANY COERCING ME

He figured to let Liz finish her dog-and-pony show, and then tell them all about how the cow was going to eat the cabbage.

"After my own investigation, I determined that BTME does not now nor has it ever fostered a climate of sexual harassment. We prepared papers today. So. What about damages? Title 7 entitles sexual harassment victims to collect back pay, lost wages," Liz was rattling off this spiel, her eyes fluttering as if she were reading the text off of the inside of her eyelids. "Sometimes reinstatement. No pain and suffering. Sex harassment victims can recover compensatory damages and get a jury trial. These damages can be future pecuniary losses, emotional pain, suffering, inconvenience, mental anguish, loss of enjoyment of life, and other non-pecuniary losses. Plaintiffs can also collect punitive damages, if they can demonstrate that an employer acted with malice or with reckless or callous indifference. The legislation, however, limits the sum of compensatory and punitive damages according to the number of employees..."

Afterwards, she showed them the answer that she had prepared for BTME to file in the lawsuit. All allegations denied, Big Leo was a deacon in the church, a pillar of the community, yada yada yada. Liz swore that the facts stated were true to the best of her knowledge and belief. Everyone agreed.

After looking over the answer, Jack drew a line through each topic.

Another plan was starting to foment in his brain. His plans changed. He was flexible. He would keep his powder dry until a more opportune time.

Liz punched some keys on her laptop and an electronic bundle of legal papers blasted off on the information superhighway. "It's filed," Liz said.

Jack eased into the seat of the Lincoln with a relaxed sigh. He had almost forgotten how comfortable the seats were. It seemed like a year since he had sunk into the cushy seats. The booze was wearing off and he shut his eyes. Sleep overtook him in a moment, sitting behind the wheel, the car still in the parking garage.

He awoke to the sound of thunder. It was Jill, pounding on his window. He pressed the button and the electric window dropped halfway. Jill was clearly on one of her rampages.

"Jesus Christ, Jack. Couldn't you at least pay attention when Liz is asking you questions?" She cast her eyes to the heavens. "Dear Lord above, why did I ever marry this goofball?"

"I don't pay attention 'cause there's nothing in it for me."

"I see you have transportation again. What did you tell him? Did you threaten him?"

"Big Leo has a secret or two, Jill. He's negotiable now."

"What? Tell me."

"Oh, I'm not sure that's so wise. It's better you didn't know. Hey, you gotta have your deposition taken, so I'm doing you a favor."

Jill reached through the partially-open window and tried to get a strangle hold on his neck. She would have tried to recreate his birth by pulling him through, but he leaned away and avoided her grasp. "Jack, you better tell me. What did you find out?"

"I worked for the son of a bitch. If you think I spent ten years just fluffing my nuts, you're wrong. Think I never learned anything?"

"Something at the office then."

"I've said enough. I've gone as far as I'm going. Wow. The more sober I get...I'm so drowsy. I'm gonna catch a cat nap." He yawned and rolled up the window.

"Jack, you'd better tell me." Her face was as red as a baboon's butt, but she could read his lips.

"Wake me when I get home." Jack let his eyelids droop, and at the same time, with a turn of the key, the big Lincoln roared to life. He drove to the exit ramp pretending to have fallen asleep.

Jack watched Jill through a squint. She stomped away to her Porsche and opened the door. Before getting in, she put her hand on her hip and patted her foot. She slammed the car door and headed back toward the office.

Jack waited a few moments, thinking, then decided to follow her back into the offices of BTME. He took a camera kit with him that he had stored in his trunk.

CHAPTER 12

During Jack's nap, the parking garage had filled with Mardi Gras revelers, laughing, shouting, all in the wildest array of colorful costumes. Jill shoved her way through the tangle of crazily-attired bodies, entered the building and pushed a button for the elevator.

The offices on the fourth floor were dark. Laughter and shouting filtered in from the revelers in the street below. Jill held a flashlight in her mouth and dug into a bank of file cabinets. Nothing interested her in the first drawer. The files she withdrew were thick and dusty. She grew frustrated in no time. She removed the flashlight from her mouth and made a spitting sound.

"Maybe Big Leo's office..." Jill tiptoed down the hallway. As she passed an alcove, a dark form jumped out and grabbed her from behind. Her attacker held his hand over her mouth. Jill struggled to cry out for help.

"Quiet. It's me. Jack," he whispered. "It's me. Be quiet. Will you be quiet? There's someone else here. Quiet."

Jill relaxed. In the dim light, Jack motioned for her to follow him as he walked in the direction of Big Leo's office. Light was coming from under Big Leo's door, and with it, rowdy noises.

BANG BANG BANG!

Jill startled. She was at the point of panic.

"It's just firecrackers," Jack said. "Outside. Calm down."

As they tiptoed closer to the light under the door, again...

BANG BANG BANG!

Jack jumped on Jill and held his hand over her mouth.

"Security! Anyone in there?"

"Quiet, Jill. You'll get us both shot."

Jill was as stiff as a board until they heard the security guard trudge away, whistling on down the hall. They dropped to their knees and crawled to the door of Big Leo's office.

Jack produced a digital camera with a long snake lens. A flexible cable connected the lens, no bigger around than a pencil, to the business end of the camera. He turned on the camera and slipped the lens through the crack under Big Leo's door. He twisted the gooseneck mounting until it pointed in the direction of Big Leo's chair. Nothing. He twisted it back in the opposite direction to reveal action at the other end of the office.

CRACK! CRACK! CRACK! "Bro Hoof. Bro Hoof. Bro Hoof."

A scene emerged on the tiny LED screen of the camera. Big Leo, it looked like Big Leo anyway, was wearing what appeared to be a pink blue body stocking and a multi-colored wig. He whinnied like a horse. Each vocalization seemed to say "more" to Big Leo's...guests. Two people were with him. Perhaps a whip, or something like it, was cracking over his head.

"Daddy!" Jill whispered.

"Quiet. Let's get a couple of minutes of this on tape and get the hell out of here."

"That thing have a microphone?"

"Jeez, Jill, aren't you expecting just a little too much?" Jack and Jill let the camera run, their eyes fixed to the little LED screen straining for a peek at the action. Finally, Jack shut the camera off.

"That's enough. Let's get out of here. We have a banquet to go to."

"The banquet. I almost forgot," Jill whispered.

They slinked away as noiselessly as possible, undetected, alert to avoid security. They drove home in their separate cars.

The Couillon

Jill dressed in a Catwoman costume while Jack downloaded the video onto a computer. Her outfit was as tight as the hide and Jack enjoyed watching her put it on. It fit and exaggerated every curve. While the computer processed the file, Jack unwrapped a costume that Jill had bought for him. It was a shaggy red overall with big footies and a hoodie. When he was finished dressing, he shook his head. She could not have selected a better costume, if her goal was to heap ridicule on her husband. She wanted him to attend the Mardi Gras banquet as Clifford the Big Red Dog. But he didn't care anymore.

When the computer finished its processes, Jack directed the program to send the finished product to a big high definition screen, then hit the PLAY button. "We ought to be able to see better in HD...here."

Jack and Jill watched spellbound as Big Leo hopped and skipped around his room in what looked like a pink onesie pajama. On his head was a shock of hair-hat in reds, greens, and yellows, and on his forehead, a rainbow-hued cone made to look like the horn of a unicorn. "He's a bronie!" Jack said. Big Leo was taking a series of noisy swats and bitch slaps from two leather-clad dominatrixes.

"I wish I could see a face," Jill said. "Oh daddy, how could you?"

"Oh jeez, I love this," Jack said.

"Look. There's one. She's there again. Come on bitch. Turn. Face the camera. That's right. Mooooore...Louise! Jack! It's Louise the bookkeeper!"

Jack fell off of the couch and onto the floor convulsed in laughter. His sides were splitting. "That's your bookkeeper not mine."

"Wait...here's the other one. Oh...my...gawd...it's Liz! It's Liz! Jack, it's our own lawyer."

"That's your lawyer, not mine, honey baby."

"What's so funny? If anyone knew this...I mean if...if..."

"They already answered those interrogatories. Turned 'em in. She told them Big Leo was pure as the driven snow. A deacon in the church. But the truth is Big Leo's had his peter in the payroll for years. They've committed perjury. Big Leo and the lawyer, both of em. He's gonna get slammed and she's gonna get disbarred."

"Big Leo would die if...he could lose the company...lose the company..."

"He'd lose it to you, Jill. Oh my oh my oh my. I can't believe my eyes. Big Leo. A bronie.""

"To me? To me! I'm his only heir."

Jack sat up on the floor with a serious face. "No need for me to keep my secrets now."

"Tell me."

"Jude has been blackmailing Big Leo for years. I just figured it out. And if you ever get a chance, check out Acme Services. That's Jude, and with what I have on him, he and that Charma girl are going down with Big Leo, big time."

"Oh Jack. Jack! Jack! You did it. It's my company now. For me, you did it!" Jill jumped on Jack and ripped at his fruity dog costume as well as her own. She had power now, she was going to New Orleans, she would accept a bid to join the Krewe of Rex, and her sexual desire for a man's body was now as hot as the hubs of hell. "Come on, Jack, get that silly thing off."

Jack busied himself trying to extrude his torso and Jill's complete body from their costumes at the same time. His task was hopeless. He was stuck in the Clifford costume. She was now buck naked and on him and together they rolled to the floor. The red overalls wouldn't release their grip, even as Jack and Jill wrestled into a position unimagined even by the authors of the Kama Sutra.

"Wait." Jill reached for her Catwoman mask and put it on. Then she redoubled her efforts to take out her sexual frustrations on this hunk of man flesh that was by coincidence her husband. She flipped and was now astride him, each fist full of red fabric from the front of his costume in her vise-like grip.

The Couillon

"Oh Jack, we're in this together after all. Oh, Jack..." Her pelvis was pounding against his like a jackhammer. In a moment, the beautiful blonde alumni president of Delta Delta Delta Can I Help Yah Help Yah Help Yah surrendered to the oncoming ecstasy. With each driving thrust, she pulled and pushed at the neck of his costume. Eyes like saucers, his head slammed into the hard terrazzo floor with each athletic lunge. Jack could hear her shouts "Bayou...Teche... Management...Jill...Mouton...PRES..I..DENT!" Then he heard a wail. It sounded like the depraved howl of a rougarou echoing out of the basin. Consciousness departed him.

CHAPTER 13

Jack woke up, shaking his head. He couldn't focus his eyes. His brain processes were slowed like a boat in a round turn. Perhaps he had heard the sound of a door slamming shut, he was not sure. And maybe at the edge of his perception he had heard an engine. What he knew was he could hear the distinctive raspy exhaust of a Porsche Carrera and squealing tires. He was still stuck in the goofy Clifford the Dog costume.

He stumbled to the garage. Jill's car was gone.

Let her go, he thought. But she was driving as if she were on a mission. She wasn't going to a costume party. She wouldn't speed away to soiree. She was drunk on power. She was probably going to confront Big Leo. She didn't know how to keep her mouth shut and whatever advantage Jack had over Big Leo wouldn't be worth a cold bucket of piss if she shot off her mouth now.

If he could catch up to her, he could make her tell him what she had in mind, head her off perhaps...Then he saw it. A note pad beside the landline in the kitchen. He could see a faint impression on the pad. He found a pencil and rubbed the lead sideways across the notepad. A white image of the last thing written on the pad emerged in relief. A phone number. An address. Jude's phone number and address. She was going to confront Jude.

Jack ran down the narrowing options in his mind. He might yet be able to catch her. He could persuade her to leave Jude alone. Liz would not be happy at all if she knew Jill had contacted the plaintiff's lawyer directly. To hell with Liz, Jill might squeeze Jude just so she could throw Jack under the bus. Whatever she had in mind, she was a loose cannon, and Jack knew nothing good was going to come out of her confronting Jude.

He jumped in his Lincoln, backed out of the garage and onto the street, and sped away, hot on Jill's tail. For a moment, her taillights flashed in the distance, but she easily outdistanced him. He could not keep up. What could he do to help derail whatever it was that was on Jill's mind? Confusion. Right. He needed chaos. Charma. Perfect. He wrestled his cell phone out of his pocket and mashed in a number.

"Information? Give me a number for the Rusty Penny...Rusty... Penny. Penny. It's a titty bar, dammit."

Jack punched the number information gave him into the phone. "Charma. Lemme talk to Charma. It's urgent. I got to talk to Charma." An eternity passed. Jill's taillights were nowhere to be seen, but the address was etched in his brain. He sped at breakneck speed toward Jude's humble abode.

"Charma, this is Jack. Jack. Yeah. That Jack. Charma, you and I have a situation here. I think my wife is having an affair with Jude Malveaux." A screeching scream blasted the cell phone away from Jack's ear. "Yeah. You better help me 'cause he's selling you out. You better get over to Jude's place quick."

He was ready to snap the phone shut, but he had one last thing he wanted to tell Charma.

Jill's car pulled into the driveway behind Jude's car. She knew she was in the right place. The vanity tag on the beat-up green-on-black Camaro read "SO SUE ME." A couple of blocks away, down the street, a neon RUSTY PENNY sign assailed the night sky. Jude had selected his living quarters so that the Rusty Penny was within convenient walking distance.

Jill crawled out of her Porsche. She was still clad in the skin-tight Catwoman costume. In three long strides, she was at the front door, pushing her way in.

Jude had heard a car skid to a stop outside and had gone to the front window. He was peeking through the blinds when Jill blasted into the room. No one was more surprised than Jude. But his expression changed as he looked her over from head to toe. He smiled a creepy smile. In the revealing costume, Jill looked hotter than a guinea hen in a red pepper patch.

"Hey, be'-be'. Gettin' crazy!"

"You cockroach, we're gonna settle this mess once and for all."

"What?"

"The lawsuit. This lawsuit with my husband. This lawsuit with my company."

"Your company? It's your company now?"

"As far as it makes any difference to you, it's my company. We're gonna do what I say and I'm gonna do it my way. And you can just forget about Acme Services from now on too."

Acme Services. She knew about Acme Services, the only good thing Jude had going for himself. He couldn't let it just fade away. He bristled. He was speechless.

"So what's it gonna take, Jude? Let's put all this behind us. What's it gonna take?"

Jude froze, he had no words. Not Acme Services. He depended on that money. Bile rose in his gullet, but before his eyes, an alluring smile emerged from Jill's lips. Behind the Catwoman mask, her eye grew smoky. She slowly unzipped the front of the skin-tight costume. "You always wanted some of this. So what's it gonna take, big man?"

Jude's courtroom eloquence returned. "You must think I'm pretty stupid. Just 'cause that schmuck husband of yours can't control himself doesn't mean I can't." His argument was foolproof.

"Fix us a drink, Jude."

As Jack coasted to a stop past Jude's house, his cell phone was still to his ear. "One last thing, Charma! You got a gun?" And after a pregnant pause, he added, without affect, "I sure would if I were you."

He watched as, down the street, Charma exploded out the door of the Rusty Penny. She was wearing her show wardrobe, sexy underwear, net stockings, and crazy-tall spiked heels. She looked slutty, just the way men like women to dress. She ran as if on stilts, straightaway toward Jude's house, striding forward in fits and lurches, each step hampered by her fuck-me shoes, an inferior choice of footwear for a tête-à-tête with a rival mistress.

Jude pulled away from Jill and swaggered to the bar. He became, in that moment, something he had never been before, suave. He was the most interesting man in the world. He was Hugh Hefner without the captain's hat and pajamas. He was James Bond. He stepped behind the bar, poured two Gran Marnier shooters and opened two beers. Jill followed him. She pasted herself to his torso, a leg bent around his. She rubbed against him as if she were a feline.

They exchanged loathsome smiles. "Knock that shooter back, Jill be'-be,' then chase it with the beer." Jill complied and so did Jude. Neither took an eye off the other. Her embrace enfolded him like Saran Wrap.

The front door of the house burst open again. In the mirror behind the bar, Jude saw Charma hobbling toward him on her 6-inch heels, yelling, "Jude, you low life cheating bastard!"

"Hey Charma, just in time," Jude said. While he was in Jill's arms, he was powerless to drop the pose. He was still in character, the most interesting man in the world. "Come join us. Three's company."

"You rat!"

"Talk nice now. This is the defendant. We're talking about me getting a subscription to the Wall Street Journal. And she's got a fat ass black woman that I been thinking about hiring, too."

"Even the Grand Mon-Yay!" Hell hath no fury like a woman cuckolded. Charma fumbled in her purse and withdrew a pistol.

"Naw now, be'-be'."

"You selling us out, me and Evangeline, her school. But I'm ready to put all this behind me now!"

Jude stepped away, out of Jill's clutches. "Give me that. You're not..." Out of the corner of Jude's eye, he saw a black cat-like arm flashing for the pistol, and BANG! The gun discharged, but Jude never heard it. A tiny lump of lead was bouncing around inside his skull before the perception of sound could fire his synapses. He reeled away and fell into a Laz-y-boy chair, with a round, red-black hole square in the middle of his forehead.

Jill and Charma looked at one another, their eyes nearly bulging out of their sockets. Each of them was splattered with Jude's blood and gore.

"Aw no!" Charma cried. "Oh darling, I shot you dead you dirty rotten filthy bastard." Still howling, still holding the gun, Charma wailed, and backing up, the shag in Jude's carpet snagged the stiletto heel of her tall fuck-me shoe. She tripped backwards and the back of her head slammed into the corner of a coffee table littered with skin books. Charma moaned and her lights went out.

The next moment, having heard the shot, Jack charged through the door. He was still dressed in the Clifford the Dog costume. He quickly surveyed the scenario. Jude's hole in the head was oozing blood, and the stripper was sprawled on the floor.

"Jill! What's happened? What have you done?" he asked. He knelt on the floor, over Charma, feeling for her pulse.

"Oh, Jack! What have I done? She just burst in...I grabbed...Jude's head...eeuuww!"

"She's dead."

"Eeuuww. What's on me?"

"Blood. It's all over you."

"What was she doing here anyway?"

"We'll never know. Jude's dead too. Both of them."

"Jack! I've got to get out of here. The Junior League...The Krewe of Rex..."

"Hell with the Junior League and Rex. You better worry about the cops."

"They'll suspect me."

"No kidding. I suspect you."

"I didn't do it. I'm innocent Jack. Help! Please! I'll do anything!"

Jack tried to rub his hands through his hair to help him think, but he was still wearing his dumb ass Clifford costume.

"Anyone see you when you got here?"

"No..."

"Then get naked." Jack started undressing himself.

"Jack...rrrRRRrr.... sexy."

"Get that bloody costume off, dammit."

Improbably, Jill did what she was told. She got naked. She helped Jack squirm out of the grip of the Clifford costume. He shoved the red costume into her trembling hands. "You're putting this on."

Jill looked at the tiny Catwoman costume. "You'll never fit..."

"It's covered with blood! Put the red thing on and get out of here."

"What if someone sees me?"

"I know what I'm doing, Jill. I saw this on Pulp Fiction. I'm doing the best I can. So you split. Get out of here. I'll do what I can to clean up."

Jill looked at him with a puzzled frown.

"Evidence, Jill. Or would you rather try to explain it yourself?" Jill was shaking like a leaf. "No? I didn't think so. Now get going."

"Thanks, Jack. I'll never forget this." Jill was gone and Jack was alone.

Now in his underwear and socks, Jack assessed the scene. The gun was still in Charma's hand. Good. It had prints. He spotted two sets of glasses. One pair had lipstick on the rim. He wiped those clean, and then rolled each of them through Charma's limp fingers, and one through Jude's.

He needed to forget Jill and think about himself. He stepped into the bedroom and soon had himself dressed in one of Jude's suits, dark and slick. He looked in the mirror for the first time in years and startled when the man looking back at him returned an ice cold, Mafioso stare.

He knelt again over Charma. To his great relief, she was still breathing. "I've been wishing you'd die. For once I'm praying you live, you whore."

He wiped both sides of the doorknob and started to leave, giving thanks to the powers of the night that his wife was so damn gullible. He stopped. He picked up the bloodied Catwoman costume and folded it neatly. He grabbed a plastic bag from the coffee table and emptied it of its skin books. The Catwoman costume slid inside.

Jack leaned back against the door to admire his work. A smile broke across his face. "Jill, I own you now. I own your soul. You will be my slave in the afterlife." *Damn, that sounded good*, he told himself, all the while knowing it wasn't true.

He closed the door and slipped away into the night.

CHAPTER 14

Etienne and Lily surveyed the wreckage of Jude's apartment. Chalk outlines indicated the places where the bodies had been found.

Lily had plenty to talk about. "The way I have it," he said, "is that the woman...she showed up, super-sleaze there let her in, they had some drinks, they argue..." Lily stood in about the same place Charma stood. He held an imaginary gun out in front of him. "...and bang! Blasted away. One shot. Between the eyes. Surprised her. She fell back. Hit her head."

"I don't know," the praline-brown, senior lawman said.

Lily rubbed his chin, walking around the room for the hundredth time. "Should be fingerprints on those glasses. Should be residue on her hands."

"Not much police work to do here..." Etienne said. "We hear anything from the hospital?"

"He might make it."

"It's a cryin' shame."

"He's still on the table. She's banged up bad. Should live though."

"I don't like it. Let's go see if deh neighbors saw anything unusual."

Etienne ambled out of the residence, casually, as if he was going to get a shaved ice.

Jack and Jill were the only citizens of Acadiana that took any interest in Jude's well being. He'd been hauled to the hospital in an ambulance, given heroic medical treatment, and was now lying in a hospital bed. A one-inch wide bald strip ran across his scalp, back to front. A machine drew each breath for him and blew air down his throat. Jack and Jill were watching a television news report when a lady doctor walked into his hospital room to share Jude's prognosis.

"There's complete paralysis..." Her attention was distracted by a report on the TV. A newscast of Jude's shooting was just then being aired.

A television crew had found an elderly couple that was willing to talk, they had some information to share, and the reporter had shoved a microphone in their faces. The old dear had a sweet face. Her sidekick wore a ball cap emblazoned with an eagle, ball and anchor. The missus was doing the talking. "I heard a commotion going on over there so I looked out and said to my husband Carl, I said, 'Carl, would you get over here and look.' And then we seen this... this here...well I can only tell you what she looked like to me and she looked to me like a...she was dressed like...a...Carl?"

"A [BLEEP]." A mechanical beep overtoned the old man's voice but anyone with eyes in Lafayette Parish could read that his lips had mouthed the word "whore."

"...Yes. And this, whatever she was, that's just what she looked like to me, and she just walks in like *she owns the place?* And then this here red dog showed up. I'm sure of that. And then I thought I heard a gunshot. I said, 'Carl, I heard a gunshot.' But Carl, he's my husband, he said...well he said...uh...Carl?"

BLEEP! Carl mouth says "bullshit" but the audio had him bleeped out.

"...Yes. And then that red dog leaves and then, oh that poor Mr. Malveaux. We never seen that...me and Carl, he's my husband, we never seen that...the one that looked to me like...that was dressed like...a...Carl?"

BLEEP! Carl mouthed the word "whore."

"No...we never seen her again. Thank God. I think she shot him dead."

The Couillon

The doctor punched a remote control to turn the TV off. "As I was saying, there's complete paralysis. The damage was so extensive."

A nurse attended the patient. She was African-American and she had a big, fat ass, a prodigious amount of junk in her trunk. She was on the business end of a syringe that was large enough to feed a horse, two feet long, at least. It was filled with gruel. Each push on the business end pushed a calculated volume of boiled and crushed grain down Jude's throat. She plunged the syringe again and some surplus gruel surged out of Jude's lips and down his chin.

"Poor fellow seems to be aware, too," the doctor said. "No chance whatever of improving on what he has now."

"At least he doesn't have to worry about what to give up for Lent," Jill said.

"Jill..." Jack said. "That's not funny."

"A lawyer you say?" the doctor asked.

Jack nodded. The doctor shrugged one of those "he probably got what he deserved" shrugs and left the room. A loud, evil laugh, "Mwuhahaha," filtered into the room from the hallway outside.

The nurse was kind and gentle with her charge. "Taste good? I know it does. That's nice." She removed the syringe and wiped Jude's face clean, plumped his pillow and tucked him in. She turned the television set back on. "He likes to watch. Anyway, I like to think he likes to watch."

The TV announcer was wrapping up the newscast. "...and finally, the ten-year Treasury bond rose three basis points to yield one point eight seven five percent. The ten-year bond is frequently cited as the best indicator of interest rate movement generally. This report a service of the Wall Street Journal...In other news..."

The carcass of the cockroach from Carencro stared at the television screen, ogling, frozen, silent, aware, trying to scream. He was unable.

As her first ministerial act as president of BTME, Jill called a meeting with Big Leo, Liz, Jack and Louise. Everyone but Jack was afraid of her now. No one doubted that she would test her authority, both practical and titular.

"Big Leo, you're out. You too, Jack. Neither of you will be welcome at BTME. And Liz, you convince the insurance company to settle for two million, not a penny less."

"What about Louise?" Jack asked. "She was never loyal to me, but I think she does a good job."

"Okay, Louise, you're on strict probation."

Jack chauffeured Jill to Boulanger's office for a signing party. Jill insisted that the documents were important enough to be squired to the signing in a Lincoln, not a Porsche. Jill was in her Junior-League-finest tailored suit. The receptionist ushered them to a conference room that was filled with spring blooms, where they were greeted by Boulanger and Liz Churnow.

"Thank you-all so much for the accommodation," Jill said.

"No problem at all," Boulanger said. "We had a snag. Turns out Miss Chalmette was a married woman. So it's better to get these documents signed as soon as possible. Okay. If you'd sign here..."

Jill signed every page that was marked with a red tag as Boulanger droned on, "...and here...and here...and these are your copies."

"Thank you so much, Robert," Jill said. "Didn't she have a house?"

"Witness these please, Janie," Boulanger said, handing the documents to his clerk. Jack noticed that the young woman was well put together. "She did have a house. A condo. A bit rough. Bad neighborhood."

"It ought to be worth something," Jill said.

"If it is, you owe that Jackie-boy a debt of gratitude. BTME is holding some papers on the house, so the company stands to get all its money back. Be made whole."

"Even a blind hog stumbles over an acorn every now and then," Jill said.

"You're lucky she's alive."

Jill bristled. "What do you mean by that?"

"If she died, her husband would get it. Louisiana law lets the spouse have the house. If he occupies it, it's his. No one can kick him out."

"I never knew that."

"Code of Napoleon. Carryover from old French common law. Trouble is, he's in prison. A real can or worms."

"Jack is lucky."

Boulanger nodded. "Luckiest guy in the world. Thank you, Mrs. Mouton. These papers will make one little girl very happy." Turning to Liz, he told her "Okay, Churnow, turn over the check."

"Now Bobby," Jill said to Boulanger, "you make sure that Evangeline is well cared for, now, you hear?"

"We're going to put this money in a trust for little Evangeline and there's plenty to see to it that she'll go to an excellent preparatory school and a fine university. And BTME comes out whole."

"This is the kind of solution that's possible when some people don't think with their baloney ponies. Thank you, Robert," Jill said.

Boulanger shook Jill's hand and reached across to shake hands with Liz. She gave him the stink-eye and stormed out of the conference room.

Now Jill was Scarlett O'Hara. "And what of the mother? Do you have any news about the child's mother?"

Boulanger shook his head sadly. "Mentality of a two-year-old. Sad. Terrible waste."

"Any prognosis...for recovery?"

"Afraid not. It's all behind her now. She probably remembers nothing, but who knows?"

Jill took Boulanger's arm familiarly. "Thank you again, Bobby, for all your good help. And tell your mama I said hello."

"You know I will."

As everyone headed toward the exit, Jack tugged at Boulanger's elbow. "Can I have a second? Mr. Boulanger?"

"What is it Jackie-boy?"

"The charges...are they dismissed yet?"

"In the process."

"How long then? Before it's off my record?"

"No hurry."

"No hurry for you, but I need to get on with my life. I can't make plans. I need a clean record."

"Probably this week. Call me. Maybe end of the month...or two. I don't know."

Jill was dressed for the office. She had selected a tailored pin-stripe suit. She would turn heads when she walked across the lobby carrying her leather briefcase. She snapped red suspenders in the mirror and adjusted a yellow tie. Gone were the long blonde schoolgirl tresses. Jill sported a severe new hairdo that tied back in a bun. Her oeuvre shouted "all business." She looked a lot like Liz.

Jack watched her from the veranda. Flowers were set on a breakfast table, alongside bowls filled with fresh fruit and stubbed out cigarette butts. The landscaping in the yard was exquisite. Spanish moss hung like wispy sheets of glassine paper from the long low branches of live oaks.

Jack was dressed in black, wearing sunglasses. He looked like Christopher Moltisanti in "The Sopranos." He grinned a disgusting, lecherous sneer at the maid and when she saw him, she scurried away.

He was alone all day. He found a book he had always meant to read in a place he had not left it. It was about warding off spirits. *Nothing better to do*, he told himself, and read it from cover to cover.

An hour before he expected Jill home from the office, three black-draped Goth girls appeared on his doorstep. They used the ornamental knocker rather than the doorbell. The hammering blows echoed in every room of the big, empty house.

Each one of the deadheads had skin that was as pasty white as a corpse. Their pale flesh might not have been so noticeable but for the tattoos that littered their legs, arms and necks. They told Jack they were seeking relics from an unmarked Confederate graveyard that they thought had once occupied the area. He told them if they didn't get the hell off his property he would sic the dog on them. As if he would let a crotch-sniffer in the house. Of course the Goths didn't know that he disliked dogs. They left in a huff. Jack didn't want them to return, so he poured out a box of salt on his front porch in the shape of a cross.

He decided to spend the rest of the afternoon researching the claim of his ashen visitors. He got on the internet and googled terms like "ghost haunt Louisiana Confederate graveyard" dozens of times. Most hits returned stories about slaves and people finding hidden rooms filled with the skeletons of children. He stopped searching the net when the anguished face of a woman flashed across his monitor. It happened a second and third time, the image flashed before his eyes faster than he could perceive it when he clicked from one site to another. He thought he saw the same ghoulishly white feminine visage in the sheer fabric of his bedroom window treatments. She had cavernous eye sockets and something chubby thrust out of her horrific face. *It must be true,* he told himself. He found nothing conclusive, but the idea that was planted in his brain by the pallid Goth girls began to take root. A lot of the odd things that had happened recently could very well be because he was living on top of an abandoned Confederate cemetery.

CHAPTER 15

Jill blasted into the BTME office like a whirlwind. Under her arm, she had a boxful of personal knickknacks and pictures of cats. The three stooges scurried to attend to her whims.

She told Mona, "Get me a rent roll on all the properties," and Laurie, "Get me a copy of the most recent financial statements," and Carlie, "Get me coffee. And none of that Sunday School coffee, either. I want decaf latte."

"Anything else? Jill?" Mona asked.

Jill removed a screwdriver from her purse and jammed it under a plastic BIG LEO FORET sign on the door. When she applied pressure, the sign splintered into a thousand pieces. "That's Mizz Mouton from now on. Get someone to replace that sign. I don't want plastic and put my name on it in bigger letters. And I want to see my husband's cell phone bills for last month."

Jill slammed the door closed behind her.

Jill sat at her desk, looking at Jack's cell phone bill. The bill listed "RUSTY PENNY TITTY BAR" on the fateful evening of Mardi Gras.

"That bastard called her."

The next day, Jack was late for a command performance. Jill insisted he meet her for lunch at an open-air oyster bar. She had a briefcase at her feet and Jack supposed she was carrying her pistol. The other patrons stared at them, curiosity scrunched their noses. They must have wondered why such an elegant woman would break bread with a gangster, let alone engage a thug in intimate conversation.

"I've replayed that night over and over again in my head. I don't know how many times," she said.

"I don't know how you have time to think of anything but the firm. Heavy is the head that bears the crown. This wife of mine, what a trouper!"

Like any narcissist, Jill was suspicious of anyone she classified in her mind as a subordinate. "I had so much smoke blown up my ass I feel like I've had a tobacco enema," she said.

"We can discuss it at home, Jill."

"I feel safer here. I'd like the Catwoman costume back."

"Quit fustigating. It's over. I've seen to it."

"You told me she was dead."

Jack leaned forward and whispered. "What do I know? I thought she was dead. I've never seen a dead person. Not up close."

"It's just the grace of God that...Jack, if she clicks on, we'll be in deep...up to our clavicles."

"You're in a little deeper than me."

"What were you thinking when you called that Charma person?"

How did she know I did that? Jack thought. *Cell phone records.* He leaned back in his chair. "Calm down, Jill, we're in this together."

"In it together. Good. Then give me the Catwoman costume. That will calm me down."

"I burned it. Out in the swamp."

"Bullshit. You're afraid of the swamp. Why would you tell me such an obvious lie?"

My oh my, Jack thought. *She really wants the Catwoman costume.* The conversation ended. A server brought a tray of oysters on the half-shell, and it was April, the last springtime month with an "R." "Have an oyster, while they last, be'-be'," Jack said. He doctored up a large, plump bivalve with a squirt of hot sauce and slurped it from the shell, but he never quit staring at his wife. *Maybe I do own her. She wants it really bad.*

Jack tried to put himself in Jill's shoes on the way home. She had told him that all she did was try to push the gun away. If Jack had learned anything at all from watching *Law & Order*, Jill probably wouldn't be charged with a crime, if the truth came out. She probably lacked the requisite legal intent, plus her daddy had clout. But once the cat was out of the bag, people would find out that Jill had been in Jude's house, alone, that she knew Jude. Jude the low life lawyer. Jude the low-rent cockroach. The scum that she had been standing next to, standing close enough to have been in an embrace because she would never have been able to grab a gun that was pointed in his face if she had been at the Mardi Gras soiree like all the other upwardly mobiles. Close enough to him that his brains were splattered on her Catwoman costume.

No, if anyone in polite society knew that she had driven her own car to Jude's house in that crappy part of town to confront him, she could forget about being the doyenne of society in Lafayette and Acadiana. No matter how rich she got, she would never be accepted in the cloistered circles of New Orleans society. She could forget about joining an exclusive Mardi Gras krewe. She could forget about being the first woman to be crowned King of Rex.

So the way Jack sorted it out, she needed Jack on her side and she needed Jack to keep his mouth shut. If she wanted to run the show at the office, nothing could make him happier. He was tired of chasing prospects, chasing his tail, chasing rainbows, spitting peanuts. He could see himself branching out into minerals management, landman work, working in the oil patch. He wasn't too old to learn. He had several friends that plied that trade and none of them was half as glib or persuasive as he was.

And Jill would take over Big Leo's office and if she wanted to hide her light under a bushel, those beautiful long blonde tresses, with that uncompromising, austere, forbidding bun, he could live with that. Perhaps they would have lunch together. Jack even imagined them working together as a team again, he sharing his expertise, giving her advice, introducing her to his contacts, sleeves rolled up, meetings with architects and engineers, bankers, ordering in Chinese when the days were long.

Surely she would change and appreciate him more. They could spend time together, buddy around sometimes. Perhaps their friendship could be salvaged, and if one thing led to another, maybe they would become intimate again, fall back in love. If one thing were going to lead to another, Jack could see that he needed to keep the Catwoman costume in his possession. No way would he let it out of his hands, no way he would destroy it.

In May, Jack stopped by the office once a week to pick up mail. Today his office door was chained shut. Jill watched him rattle the chains, smiling.

"What's this?" he said.

"Just what it looks like," she said.

"Let's talk," Jack said.

"My office."

Jack followed Jill in the direction of the boss's office. Jill closed the door behind her subordinate.

"What is it you want?" Jack said.

"Acme Services. What the hell is it?"

"You tell me." Jill was fuming.

"Okay. It's some mail drop Big Leo sent money to," Jack told her.

"Starting when?"

"Twenty years or so back. So what?" Jill was still giving him the stink-eye. "I don't know what it means, just that it's important."

"Okay. Now give me the Catwoman costume."

"I told you. I burned it."

"Let's see some scraps."

"It's ashes. Any scraps are out in the swamp."

"You're terminated."

"You can't."

Jill grabbed a handful of Jack's shiny suit and pulled him across the desk, telling him under her breath, "I'm going to own everything worth owning in Lafayette, and then I'm going to New Orleans and I'm going to be the first female Rex."

"And?"

"And I can't be true to BTME's mission if someone is on my payroll that's under indictment."

She's recording this, Jack thought. He didn't need to be a genius to figure that out. She wasn't practiced, not like Jude had been. Jack's eyes searched the room high and low, looking for a microphone. He wanted to make sure his voice was clear. "Hey. Me tampering with evidence, that's just a slap on the wrist." Jack spotted nothing but still trusted his instincts. A recorder was hidden somewhere. He continued talking, loud and clear. "I only did it for my loving wife. Understandable. You know what's funny? I don't think the ten years for attempted murder even bothers you. That's nothing compared to the Junior League."

"You louse. This Parish isn't big enough for the both of us."

"The Junior League. Ha! They won't hate you for shooting her, but they will hate you for not killing her."

"You leave me no choice...but divorce."

"I'd happily go to jail," Jack shouted with sobs in his voice, "if it meant we could keep our little family together." Under his breath he added, "Big Leo may have started this company, but I made it make money. So think about how that's gonna shake out in the divorce, be'-be'."

"Okay. Okay. But you're off salary. I don't want to see you around here. Not even your shadow."

"Don't worry. I'm branching out. I'm doing what I want for a change. I'm starting my own business."

"You don't have the capital to compete with me. I'll break your back..."

"I don't need much capital. In fact, you leased me everything I need. The space. Gave me a real great lease. And cheap. A real long-term cheap lease."

Smiling, Jack pulled a photocopy of a lease form from his breast pocket. His signature appeared twice, both as tenant and as agent for the landlord. He dropped it on Jill's desk. Then he left.

CHAPTER 16

Jack stood in the middle of the parking lot, watching a crew install a sign that said "JACK'S GENTLEMAN'S CLUB, LIVE NUDE GIRLS" across the entrance to Lafayette's newest titty bar. He was dressed like a mobster and all puff-chested smiley when a frumpy lady approached him. She seemed familiar.

"Is that you? Mr. Mouton, you promised. You can't open a strip club. Not here. Our lease! Think about our customers, please." It was Pearl, the tenant with the appliqué shop.

"Got a problem? Talk to management. Jill Mouton is in charge. Here's her number. And let her have an earful about that trash in the alley." Jack sneered and flicked a business card in Pearl's general direction. It fluttered to the ground.

Jill peeped in Jack's bedroom door. It was the middle of the night, his bed was unmade and unoccupied. Again. She looked in the garage and confirmed, his car was gone.

She started in on his roomy walk-in closet. She was on a mission. She would find the Catwoman costume and destroy it herself. She checked every stitch of clothing on every hanger. She opened every drawer and turned out its contents on the floor. A lacquered box held charms and talismans. She threw it against the wall and it exploded in a thousand pieces. She knocked all the storage boxes off of the shelves and broke open every lock on every piece of luggage. She found an empty pistol case and half a box of ammunition. Otherwise, nothing.

She turned out all the drawers in his dresser and wardrobes. She ripped the bedclothes off of his bed. She threw off the mattresses. Nothing. She looked under the bed. YOWL! She was looking down the barrel of a pistol at a big black cat. Instinctively, she had withdrawn her pistol from the holster under her arm. It was a miracle that she had not emptied the clip into the feline.

Jill emptied all of Jack's toolboxes onto the garage floor. She turned over every drawer in each of his tool chests, cleared every shelf, and looked in every nook and cranny. A pull-down ladder gave her access to an attic. Nothing.

Jack returned home at 5:00 a.m. The sky over the swamp was brightening. He hated being away from a safe place when it was dark. He found his tools spread everywhere in the garage and his bedroom tossed.

"I burned it, dearest," he shouted at the microphone that he supposed was recording his actions. "Or did I forget to tell you?" Jack was bemused. A small, self-satisfied grin was on his face. He was getting under Jill's skin. In his bedroom, he picked his charms out of a pile of splinters. He started to clean up the rest of the mess, to put things back in their place, but then he shrugged. He would leave it for the maid. Disorder didn't bother him any longer.

At 5:00 a.m. the next day, Jack exited the bar and walked to his car with a bank bag under his arm. It was bulging with the night's receipts.

His Lincoln was the last car left in the lot, as his patrons had taken his advice. "You don't have to go home, but you can't stay here."

The Couillon

Out of nowhere, a sedan sped toward him. Its driver's dark face was obscured by a floppy hat. He faked right, and drove to the left, narrowly avoiding the fender and certain death. The car sped away. He was unable to get the license tag number. He didn't know if the driver was a man or a woman.

He suspected the driver was Gunner. The gun store owner said that he would settle accounts. And Big Leo had a grudge. But he was surprised by the prescience of the words that came out of his trembling lips. "Jill, you bitch, I never thought you'd stoop to this."

Jack regained his feet, shaken, dusting off his sharkskin suit. He was alone. The streets were empty. He had no witnesses to the first attempt on his life, and not a scrap of evidence to implicate Jill. She needed his help if he was alive, but she was far better off with him dead.

A week later, driving home in the dawn hours, he tapped the brake and the pedal went all the way to the floor. His leg pumped, hammering the pedal up and down like a sick robin's ass. Nothing at all. Ahead of him, cars whizzed across an intersection. He swerved left, involuntarily, across empty lanes of traffic, up and over a curb. The heavy town car crashed into thick underbrush. The big Lincoln slowed to a stop. Jack exhaled. He was pitched precariously over the bank of the steep-sided Vermilion River.

Jack scrambled out of the car and back through the brush. His ears were filled with the sound of branches cracking and vines snapping. The Lincoln was sliding forward from its perch. Jack stumbled out of the jungle and fell on the grass along the roadway. He passed out.

Police investigated the accident. Yellow plastic ribbon surrounded the site. The rear end of Jack's Lincoln was standing out of the water. Steam belched up from the submerged engine. Jack sat on a curb, dabbing at his face with a handkerchief, his body trembling and his nerves rattled. He was having difficulty focusing his eyes.

A sour scowl came over his face. Two men were approaching him, the detectives, Etienne and Lily. "Good morning there Mr. Mouton," Lily said.

"They sending homicide detectives out to investigate automobile accidents nowadays?"

"The investigating officer, he's my pal."

"Who said homicide? You sure been in a couple of scrapes here lately, son," Etienne said.

"That breaking and entering thing was bogus. The charges were dropped."

"Yeah," Lily said. "That's what I heard. Curious though. A guy never has a run in with the law. Then he's on the scene of a breaking and entering. Strange deposits show up in his checking account. One of his employees tries to kill someone. Then this guy's nearly killed in a wreck and the brake line's cut."

"You have anything you want to tell us?" Etienne said.

"Could you call me a cab? I need to go get an aspirin."

Etienne signaled Lily with a thumb. "Say goodbye, Lily."

The detectives strolled away from Jack, rubbing their chins. "Dropped the charges. That bust was righteous, man," Lily grumbled.

"Lily, lesson number two in police science. You can't learn nothin' while you're talking."

"What's that supposed to mean? Just trying to put him at ease."

"It means cut the chit-chat. Tuat t'en grosse bueche. Big mouth. This guy's gonna give his own self up."

Lily stopped but Etienne continued to walk toward their cruiser.

CHAPTER 17

It was mid-afternoon and Jack left the house headed for Gentleman Jack's titty bar. He had taken the company's old pickup truck while the Lincoln was in the body shop, which was fine with Jill as long as he didn't leave it in the driveway or the street where people could see it. The insurance company was dragging its feet but in the end, the town car was going to be classified a total loss. It was obvious. He was sure he would never be able to bamboozle Jill into replacing his wheels with something nice.

He slammed the door of the pickup closed and it bounced back open. He held the handle in its open position and closed the door gently. The lock engaged and Jack backed out of the garage.

On the way to work, Jack noticed a chicken coop in the side yard of a shack. A hen stood on top of a fence post, crowing like a rooster. *This can't be a good sign,* he thought.

As he drove into the parking lot, BANG BANG! The sound of a gun rang out. Jack slammed on the brakes, the door flew open, and he dove out of the cab and to the ground. He crossed himself as he crawled between parked cars. No more than two shots had been fired. He called 911 on his cell phone. He was afraid to move.

The detectives that arrived to investigate were Etienne and Lily.

When they arrived, rain was pouring straight down. They found Jack, soaked to the bone and shivering, still crouched between cars. He was holding a pistol and his body shook like a dog trying to pass a peach pit.

"Come on out from there," Lily told him.

"Son, ain't no one's gonna shoot at you with us here," Etienne said, extending the offer of a beefy, nut-brown hand. Jack took it, and as his head raised over the tops of the cars, he looked over his shoulder, right then left, then behind.

"Man we don't need to solve crimes," Lily said. "We can just follow you around. They'll happen right in front of us. Our statistics are gonna be great this year. You're a godsend."

"I'm glad you think it's funny that someone's trying to kill me."

"I got time to listen," Etienne said.

"Pretty soon you'll fill us in on what's happening," Lily said. If you're smart. Hey man, you look like you need a drink."

"You nervous as a cut cat, son," his partner said.

"What do you mean 'cut cat'?" Jack asked.

"Don't mean nothing. Just an old expression," Etienne said.

"Does that bother you? You allergic to cats?" Lily said.

"I need a drink." Jack walked away from the cops and into the bar.

Jill walked off of the driving range at the country club and returned to her cart. Her golden blond locks were twisted in a tight bun and held in place by a visor. With every article of clothing bearing a logo, she looked like she had just stepped out of an ad in a golf magazine. Her clubs had knitted cat headcovers. She found Jack sitting in the passenger's seat, wearing dark glasses and a shiny suit. He was out of place. Most of the golfers around the links of the country club made wardrobe decisions that excluded sharkskin.

He had been having trouble sleeping days and he had no intention of letting Jill kill him when she found it convenient. His plan was to make her angry. Create confusion. Get her to do something stupid. He would fight but he was determined to choose the ground to fight on.

"Nice to see you picking up the game," Jack said. "You have the perfect physique. What with that fat ass."

"It's business," Jill said with eyes like daggers. "Contacts."

She pushed her foot to the floor and the cart sped away. Just as she got to top speed, she drove over a curb and onto the first tee box. She got out of the cart and selected her driver.

She teed up the ball and took a mighty swing. It dribbled forward twenty yards. "Merde," she said. She slid under the wheel of the cart and drove it off the tee box in the direction of her ball. She slammed on the brakes and gouged deep skid marks into the turf.

She got out of the cart and selected another club. She teed up the ball in the fairway and tried to hit it again. It dribbled forward. "Merde!"

"Keep your head down," Jack said.

"Why don't you just leave?"

Jack pulled a white hanky from his pocket and waived it. "Let's call a truce. I'm tired of you trying to kill me."

"If I thought I could get away with it."

"Well you can't. If you kill me, you'll go to jail."

Jill only had to take a step or two forward to attempt to hit her ball again. She teed it up again. Swing and a miss. "Merde!"

"Left arm straight. You had it right all along. You're a crackerjack all right. But don't worry. The Catwoman costume is safe. Someplace you can't get your hands on it."

Jill boarded the cart, slammed on the accelerator for 20 yards, and then hit the brakes hard. The cart skidded to a stop, tearing into the turf again. She got out, selected a club from her bag, and teed up her ball.

"I'm a worrier. I said to myself, 'Jack' I said, 'ol' Jill, she might be angry enough to risk it. Cause the costume really doesn't prove anything.'"

Jill took a swing at her ball. The ball bounced a dozen yards. "Merde!"

"Keep your knees bent."

Jill walked forward to her ball while Jack prattled away. "It doesn't prove anything, does it? Just raises a suspicion. So if you look at it my way, I may as well have nothing. What I need is insurance."

"You are such a bastard."

Jack heard a shout. Behind them, a foursome of golfers was on the first tee. Jill teed up her ball.

"Hey! Speed it up! Playing through."

His hand hidden from Jill by the cart, Jack shot the finger at the duffers. "Strange you should mention the word bastard. You find out where the Acme Services money was going?"

"Jude Malveaux."

"You figure out why?"

Jill stared icicles at Jack before swinging wildly at her ball. "Merde!"

"Hit against your left side."

Jill boarded the cart, clobbered the accelerator, then the brake. She left another ten yards of torn turf in her path.

"Well since you seem to have overlooked the obvious, let me give you some information. To cement our truce. Have Jude over for Easter. It's a time for family. He's your half-brother." Jack had no proof at all but perception sometimes trumps reality.

"No! You're lying! You couldn't...."

"You think Jude was blackmailing Big Leo when he was 10 years old? No. Jude's mother was."

"I can't...Jack...The thought has occurred to me...but not Jude..."

Jill was never this gullible. She was falling all over herself to believe Jack's calumny. "Let's consider the future. Big Leo dies. His loving daughter Jill and his bastard son Jude inherit his money, share and share alike, it's the law."

Jill got out of the cart and selected another club.

CHAPTER 18

The clouds had opened and rain was falling straight down when Jack arrived home on Sunday morning. He was dead tired. A case of Jack had gone missing, so he fired the bartender and tended the bar himself. And careful not to turn away a single new customer, he had yet to adopt the "NO DAR DAR" policy that was so ubiquitous in the delta titty bars. The Saturday night show had been plagued with fist fights.

He had stewed it over in his mind all night and now he was certain that Big Leo was not trying to kill him. Cutting a brake line just wasn't his style. He would pretend to believe Big Leo was guilty, at least for today, maybe he could panic the old fart into siding with him. In the unlikely event that Jill was innocent, he didn't see how it would move the ball in his end of the field for Big Leo and Jill to kiss and make up. He was elated that she had that seed of doubt in her mind about Big Leo. She stole BTME from him. They needed to be at odds.

In spite of the rain, Jill was radiant, skipping across the lawn in a yellow raincoat. Her hair was coiffed in that damn bun under the hood. She stepped into the filthy cab of the pickup and curled up a lip. "We could take my car." Then she caught a whiff of Jack and changed her mind. She didn't want her Porsche smelling like an ashtray in a titty bar.

"Forget I said that. Let's get this over with before I catch a disease. Yuck."

"Sorry I'm late."

"I'm hungry. You have anything to eat?"

Jack had several corny dogs in a Styrofoam go-box, leftovers from the snack warmer on the back-bar at Gentleman Jack's. He took one for himself. "Take one. Not bad."

"Corn dogs? Eeuuww."

"They aren't that bad. Try one."

"Eee-yuck. I changed my mind. Those things are nasty. Jack you're nasty. This truck is nasty. I'm not going." She struggled to open the door of the truck.

"Let go of the door." He hadn't been with Jill two minutes and she was already on his last nerve. "We're going. And you're going to eat the goddamn corny dog."

"Not on my life." The door wouldn't budge.

"I said eat one."

"I'd rather die. You are such a hick."

"Don't you dare call me a hick."

"Hick. Hick. Hick. What you going to do about it, hick?"

Jack leaned across the cab and jammed his corny dog in Jill's mouth. He loathed Jill in this moment, she and her sneering, hate-filled arrogance. He would teach her not to call him hick.

Jill was surprised by his aggression and tried to yell. She only accomplished the task of opening her mouth wider. As Jack pushed harder, the corny dog slipped further down her throat. "Winning the company just wasn't enough. You had to kill me too. Well guess what, Jill? You need to show some respect."

Jack was unable to relax until he was certain that Jill was dead. He eased back into his seat on the driver's side. This was not what he had planned. He didn't remember even considering snuffing Jill. Murder wasn't on the operations menu. Killing another human being, even Jill, was not the method of self-defense that he preferred. He was trembling from fear, adrenaline, and the cold and damp. But since the windows of the truck were fogged over, Jack figured that he was not at risk of neighbors observing his deed. He had the luxury of time to think.

By the time his body quit shaking, he knew what he had to do. He went into the house through the mudroom and gathered up a black leather Ghurka garment bag from Jill's closet. She had spent more for the bag than most guys pay in alimony.

He pulled the truck inside the garage and put Jill's body in the garment bag. The bag fit her like a glove and she slipped in without a struggle. No one could have seen him bagging the body behind the closed garage door.

He drove toward the Atchafalaya with Jill's body stuffed into the black leather garment bag at his side. He parked in the lot of the marina where they kept their cabin cruiser. He was prepared to wait until nightfall, but the docks were vacant. The garment bag was easy to pick up and load in the boat. He found a couple of broken pieces of concrete and loaded them in the boat as well. He snagged Jill's purse and also brought a fabric duffle bag from behind the seat of the truck. He powered up the boat and slid away from the dock into the waterway that led to the swamp. He left the pickup truck unlocked. He never had a key.

He motored perhaps ten miles, north and east he imagined, without seeing another boat. Adrift in a backwater passage that he was certain was infested with alligators, Jack placed the concrete chunks in the garment bag, closed it, and eased the black bag and all its contents over the gunwales. It disappeared into the black deep. He was in near shock from fright and cold.

He cruised back in the direction he came from, circling back toward the levee. He turned south on a channel that led to the coast. He followed it all afternoon, past Cypress Island and through the Wax Lake Outlet, on beyond the Intracoastal Waterway and into the coastal plain. In his mind, Big Leo's fishing camp was across the bog to the west.

When he was certain that no one else was within miles, he powered down the engine and swung the boat into a dredged-out canal that led to an oilwell production platform. Then he turned hard into the shore, lurching off-balance as the cruiser grounded on the muddy bottom.

Jack pulled the Catwoman costume out of his duffle bag. It was in a plastic sack that he wiped clean. He stowed the bagged costume under a bench at the stern along with Jill's purse. He wiped the steering wheel clean of prints. He didn't know why he did that, it just seemed like the thing to do. His didn't want to deny having been on the cabin cruiser. But no prints would broaden the number of options he would have for explaining his actions later.

Then he jumped from the grounded boat and onto the soggy shore, hoping to leave a boat situated so that it would evidence that its owner left in a panic. He disappeared into the grassy marsh as rain washed the boat clean of any prints or stains he might have overlooked.

Night fell hard. Jack had steered the motorboat out of the forested cypress and tupelo swamp and into a perpetually flooded prairie, closer to the Gulf, where the passageways were broken with island-like clumps of vegetation. Low shrubs and clumps of oyster grass choked together above the brackish water. The muddy bottom was covered with a half foot of water. It seemed as cold as ice. Before he had taken three steps, the muck swallowed up his Alan Edmonds wingtips. He was barefoot.

Points of the compass have little meaning in the coastal area of Louisiana, but he reckoned that he must be somewhere south and east of Lafayette. He would navigate in the direction he guessed the sun must have set in the cloud-shrouded sky. He would find a roadway. He was able to make some progress by stepping on the clumpy rootballs of the oyster grass. He stumbled toward the faint smudges of gray on the horizon that hinted that a town or a shopping center might lay below.

The Couillon

Under attack by insects, he smeared his skin with fetid mud that washed away when he swam across narrow channels that were as cold to him as ice water. When he was atop one of the thousands of tiny islands, making way was so difficult he wished he was in the water. And when he was in the water, he was fearful of freezing, of lurking alligators, snapping turtles, cottonmouth water moccasins, and spirits of the dead. Insects swarmed his head and face when his body was safe underwater. They choked his mouth and nose. He could scarcely breathe, and his earnest prayer was to be back on top of the marsh grass. He feared his heart would explode in his chest.

But more than that, behind him, howls began to rise from the swamp. *Rougarou,* he thought. Creatures sent from hell to punish the believers that had ignored Lent, the half-man half-wolf, the blood-sucker, the beast, the scourge of the swamp, the man-killer rougarou. Jack's slogging getaway from the basin had turned into a frantic escape. He was too afraid to look back, afraid even to cast his eyes on the creature of gigantic proportion and the head of a wolf that pursued him. A thing covered in long hair matted with mud and swamp grass, garish saber-like teeth bared, eager to be sunk into the flesh of a sinner. Jack's body continued to run, his flesh knew his brain would surrender if his eyes were allowed to face the rougarou. He ran on beyond the limits of human endurance. He confessed his transgressions to the Almighty. He swore he would never ignore Lent again.

The rougarou seemed near him now, just an arm's length away. In another moment he would feel its hot breath on his neck. But then before him, directly across his path, was the Intracoastal Waterway. He dove in, exhausted, every stroke was torture, yet he needed to swim. The temperature of the water was arctic. Day and night, the 200-foot wide waterway was choppy and always crowded with ship and barge traffic. He could easily be run over and drowned. Each time he rolled on his side to breathe, wakes of muddy brackish water washed over him. He'd swallowed a gallon of icy drek by the time he reached the far shore.

The rougarou must have had difficulty crossing the waterway. Bone-numbing tremors wracked his body. Each exhausted breath tore out of his lungs with a shriek for help. Jack ran on through the waterlogged grassland. The howls of the rougarou had drawn close fast, but Jack had been faster. The rougarou had not caught up with him.

As the tomb-dark sky gave way to rays of dreary morning, the channels of cold dark water were fewer and further between. In the dark, Jack waded across the waterways. Now they were shallow. The tide was ebbing. He was thirstier than he had ever been and his muscles ached with exhaustion.

A mile ahead, he saw a string of stilted shacks near an abandoned sugar mill.

CHAPTER 19

Etienne and Lily grilled Jack in the emergency room of the hospital. An EMS crew had taken him there after he was found at the old sugar mill. His face sported two or three day's growth of beard. Mud covered him from head to toe. Insect bites welted up every inch of his pasty flesh. He told his story as fast as his mouth could form the words.

"We were going to meet her father at his fishing camp. Business. And these Croatian oystermen tried to ram us. Must have thought they could rob us. They chased us for miles. I was lost. I dodged. The water was getting shallow. The passageways more narrow. The boat grounded in the mud. They boarded the boat and were screaming bloody murder. I couldn't understand them. I jumped into the marsh grass and beat it the hell out of there. I was hoping Jill would get away but I'm not sure..."

"You pretty brave them being riffraffs and all," Etienne said.

"Embrasse moi cul," Jack said.

"Speak English," Lily said.

"Kiss my ass. I woulda stayed but I was outnumbered. Three to one."

Etienne never blinked. Jack was practiced at bullshiting his way through anything but he could see that Etienne wasn't a buyer. He had nothing to gain from lying anyway.

"Aw hell, I'm lying," Jack said.

"Tell us the truth," Lily said.

"Truth is, I wasn't staying. No way. I was outta there, man. I didn't look back. She was trying to kill me. Why would I risk my life for her?"

"What?!"

"It was Jill that tried to run me down in the parking lot. And the river. She cut my brake line. Shot at me. She admitted it. She was doing her best to kill me, so you think I'm gonna risk my life to save her?"

"Go on," Lily told him.

"She knew I suspected her in that shooting. You know. Malveaux and the redhead. I think she was a witness. Maybe more than a witness. Has she showed up?"

Etienne sat back in his chair. Lily started to ask, "Are you wanting to file a police..." But he read Etienne's cold glare and decided it was best to shut the hell up. Together, they stared at Jack.

Several police boats swarmed the waterway. Scuba divers burbled, partly submerged, searching the bottom. Lily boarded a launch from the marshy grass-covered bank. He was muddy from head to toe. He held wad of mud over his head that was a big as a loaf of bread. It was a shoe.

Etienne watched him, clean as a whistle, sitting in a deck chair.

"Never ever find a body out there, never." Lily brushed at mire on his jacket but only managed to smear it around.

"Gators. Tide comes. No tracks," Etienne said, picking up the bagged Catwoman costume.

"Well at least we got something to run tests on," Lily said. "It'll be interesting to find out if these splatters are blood."

"It's blood."

"Taking bets on whose it is?"

Etienne sniffed at the bag. "Smells like skunk. Jude Malveaux."

"What's the bet?"

"If that don't test out to be Jude Malveaux's blood, I'll kiss your ass, on the fifty-yard line of the LSU-Notre Dame football game, during the half-time show."

CHAPTER 20

Big Leo resumed control of BTME in Jill's absence. Technically, she was a missing person. Big Leo was the only named beneficiary in her will, but until her remains were found, the disposition of her property was in limbo. Whether she was alive or dead, Jack could stay in the house under the peculiar laws of succession in Louisiana, but he had to scrape each month for enough cash to pay the utilities and the maid. Her didn't have a plan for paying insurance and taxes when they came due.

During the day, Jack had nothing to do. Sleep eluded him. He sat around the house in pajamas. His body smelled of mildew. The house was so lonely. He only went outside to travel to the titty bar and only returned when it closed. He traveled everywhere by taxicab, since Big Leo had sent a couple of bruisers to take possession of the pickup truck. Jack was isolated. A noisy murder of crows roosted in a live oak tree behind the house and constantly interrupted his sleep if he was lucky enough to drift off.

Alone, he obsessed about the weather, the weather the day he k... the day Jill d...disappeared. The sky that day had been raining but he was unable to remember the thunder. He fretted that he had not planned ahead. He should have eased her body into the swamp with her feet pointed east for good luck. He wished he had removed her body from the pickup truck feet first. The mirrors of the pickup truck had trapped her soul, he feared. He should have covered them. He was glad that Big Leo took the truck away.

At his most solitary moments, he prowled the house. He started finding Jill's personal items in places they did not belong. He found some of his own items in odd places as if they had been hidden. Had he heard a muffled giggling from Jill's room? He sensed that he was being pushed inside her boudoir. A stuffed toy cat was on the bed, covered with dust as if it had been in the attic. Her room smelled of perfume. All the rooms of the house began to smell of her fragrance. He fired the maid.

When he did nod off to sleep, he often heard footfalls in the attic or the sound of a chair moving. Curtains seemed to stir. He captured Jill's cats. They had been hissing at him, so he dropped them off at the humane society.

The crows were growing more bold, roosting now on his windowsill at dusk, tapping at the glass with their bills. When he went outside to shoo them away, he saw a ghost drifting out of his yard and into the tangled brush coulee that drained his courtyard. It seemed feminine and self-aware, with a dark, brooding aura. Her hair was pulled up behind her head in a bun. He found a handprint on the window that he believed had been left by the ghost.

Messages left on his answering machine were nothing but mechanical hums. The device seemed to be coated in a thin film of mucous. On the recordings, a faraway agency echoed as if it were coming from deep down a tunnel. He played it over and over. Was the voice saying "red-rum" or was it just moaning? He was not sure. An electric sound crackled when he turned on his television. "Jack did it," this manifestation seemed to say.

He set up motion-sensitive cameras to catch images of the spirit that was haunting him. Some exposures showed blurs, or opaque, swirling vortexes of mist. Perhaps one revealed the image of a Confederate officer with a curved knife, his bloody sleeves rolled up to the elbow. He printed the pictures for a closer look, and his hands shook as he tore those to bug bites.

The Couillon

It was midday and Jack had not slept well for three days. He called a cab and gave the cabbie an address on a rundown, dead-end lane in the nearby town of Breaux Bridge. He held his breath as the cab drove into the Atchafalaya Basin and again when they drove past a cemetery. The cab turned down a long lane of crushed oyster shell. Live oak overhead choked out the sun. A sandwich board sign told them when they found the right place. "READINGS WITH MADAME LICENTIA" was written inside the oversized silhouette of a palm. Mystic zodiac symbols served as foretokens of the secrets that the Madame promised to reveal to the believer.

The sandwich board was outside a slouching travel trailer. The tires were flat, and vines threatened to consume the rusty shell.

Madame Licentia answered the third time Jack knocked. "Sorry, I was in the back. You here for a reading?"

"Yes, well, more in the way of counseling. Advice."

"Welcome. Come in."

"You are younger..." *Rather pretty, too,* Jack noticed. Her hair was done up in a cobalt and purple dew rag. A heavy eyebrow sheltered large, coal black eyes and lush red lips. Linked rings hung from the lobes of her ears.

Jack seated himself across a table anchored by a crystal ball. Flimsy many-colored scarves dropped from the ceiling and strings of show-me-your-tits plastic beads dangled from the head jambs of doorways.

"So. What will it be?" Madame Licentia lit a candle with a long match.

"I've been seeing...I'm plagued with ghosts. I think the house is haunted."

"Go on."

"Faces in the mirrors. Personal things hidden. Moving chairs. That sort of stuff."

"Are you like afraid of the dark?"

"I am now. I see them everywhere."

"Wow. What do they look like?"

"Come on. You know what ghosts look like."

"Well...spiritual energies. They can take like many forms. Mostly they are just consciousnesses that haven't yet, you know, crossed over. That have, like, you know, patterned ways, playing out some life tragedy, you know?"

"So...?"

"You must be very sensitive if you are like seeing them all the time."

"My mother was a sensitive."

"You've definitely got the gift. How cool is this? Have you ever, like, thought about taking up the craft? Yourself?"

"Readings? Me? I don't think so."

"I could, like, sponsor you."

"I'm not sure..."

"Yeah. See, if I recruit you, and that puts you like, on my down line, you know. And you recruit people and they go on your down line. We're associates, you know? And you make money and I get a piece. And your downline makes money and you get a piece and I get a piece of your piece. Plus all the stuff, the merchandise. You get it wholesale. It's a gold mine."

"Maybe some other time."

"Man, if you got ghosts, you need to strike while the fire's hot, you know."

Jack rose to leave. "Maybe you can give me a call."

"Like what's your number?"

"You're the psychic. Figure it out."

Jack had the cab drop him at Gentleman Jack's. He was angry. Angry that he couldn't find a professional spiritualist to counsel him. Things weren't like they used to be, not like when his mother practiced the craft. Back in the day, spiritualists were practiced, experienced, honest. Not a bunch of multi-level marketers and quacks. Another daytime wasted. Soon night would be on him. Swindlers. Charlatans. To hell with Madam Licentia, to hell with all of the fakers.

It was two hours too early to open, but he was frightened of the spirits in his house and he was desperate for a Bloody Mary. When he saw himself in the mirror of the back bar, he startled. The figure staring back at him wore mirrored glasses, a pencil-thin mustache and greased-back hair. For a moment, the image was Jude. The shakes returned to his hands. Perhaps he heard a noise from the storeroom. Something shuffling? Perhaps not.

He focused on the task of fixing his drink. Lots of vodka and light on the tomato juice. He slopped about as much on the bar as made its way into the glass. He was unable to get the tumbler to his lips without spilling the drink, so put it down. He bent over, his face to the glass, and slurped the potion like a dog.

Again, he heard a resonance, a rustling from the storeroom. It sounded like a newspaper unfolding, a rustling fabric, or a dirty vinyl raincoat. He hadn't noticed before but a dim light shone underneath the storeroom door. The whispering sound gripped him, surrounded, and swallowed him in fear. *It must be Jill*, he thought, returned from her watery grave in the world of the dead to exact vengeance.

"Jill?" he said. "Jill?" He tiptoed quietly to the storeroom door. "Jill? Is that you?"

He pushed the door open and stepped back. The figure of a woman faced him. Behind her, a glaring bulb hung from the ceiling on a single strand of electrical cord. It swung back and forth. His eyes were wounded by the bright light. He couldn't see the face but he could see that her hair was pulled back severely and bound behind her head. Above her, in a two-handed grip, the apparition brandished a heavy butcher knife.

"Jill! Don't kill me. I'm so sorry. Jill!" He fell to his knees, frozen. He was powerless to defend himself but it made no difference, he had already given up, surrendered to his fate. As the light bulb swung its macabre path, back and forth, the backlit presence stabbed down and into Jack's neck. Again and again. He did not resist.

Each mirrored lens of his sunglasses reflected an identical image of the phantom. Blood ran like water down the floor drain of the storeroom. The titty bar was silent.

A sad Pearl sat at a repurposed dinette table in the appliqué store next to Gentleman Jack's. The police detectives were with her. Lily wore blue jeans and boots like Etienne.

"He's dead." Pearl sobbed into a embroidered hanky.

"I know that, Pearl," Lily said. "He was a bad man."

"Evil," Etienne added.

"Just a horrid man," she said.

"He deserved to die," Lily said. "Just what I know about him. He deserved to die. Terrible that he'd do that."

Etienne reached out. His soft hand cradled Pearl's. "He did it to someone's mother."

It was the thing in her life that made her most proud. Motherhood. Nothing meant as much. Etienne's kind expression of its worth tipped Pearl over the edge.

"All my money. Gone. I couldn't pay the rent. I killed him." Etienne handed Pearl a tissue. She blew her nose. "After that disgusting bar opened, the ladies just quit coming..."

An interment ceremony convened at the cemetery near the Cathedral. The only attendees arrived together in a limousine. Big Leo brought six women. They were all dressed like prostitutes, all perched on tall stiletto heeled shoes. A boombox played "Saint James Infirmary," a mournful Dixieland tune.

Etienne and Lily leaned against a crypt, keeping a respectful distance. The cops were dressed in their darkest blue jeans and boots, and out of respect, Etienne and Lily removed their straw cowboy hats and placed them on top of the crypt.

Big Leo held a shiny brass urn. He nodded at the girl who had been designated Director of Music for the rites, cueing her to cut the volume. He stood over a round hole in the earth that the graveyard's sexton had drilled with a post-hole digger. Because of the shallow water table, the bottom of the hole had filed with mud before the sexton reached the necessary depth.

Big Leo lifted the urn to the sky, mumbled "Ashes to ashes, dust to dust," and released the urn from his grip. It sailed down from the little man's hand and into the hole without touching the sides. A resonant GALLUMP! reverberated across the graveyard. The sound it made was that of a turd dropping into a cistern. A fountain of muddy water six feet high shot up from Jack's final resting place.

As the ladies left the gravesite, the Director of Music toggled the boombox back to life. Now it played a triumphant, happy Dixieland tune. Big Leo fondled each girl's fanny as she bent over to load in the limousine.

"Laissez les bons temps rouler," Etienne said. He and Lily donned their hats and sauntered back to their car. Behind them, the door of the limo slammed and the music faded away.

"An old lady," Lily said. "With a butcher knife at that."

"Who'd a thunk it?" Etienne shivered.

The detectives walked side by side in silence.

"Where you come from, Etienne? Down around Saint Martinsville?"

"Martinville. No 's.' Yeah." Etienne stopped. "Lily, will you do me a favor?"

"Sure, Etienne, anything."

"I hereby appoint you to be in charge of the whores and such at my funeral. Jiss round 'em up. Keep them in the back wit you. Missus Etienne don't need something like that."

"Sure, man, anything. Just ask," Lily said, and added with a shake of his head, "What a waste. When all he had to do was tell the truth. Somewhere."

"Well, no man works so hard as a man dat marries for money," Etienne said. Together in silence, they loaded into their squad car.

"Lily, I'm starving. A bucket of crawfish is calling my name. Dey saying 'Etienne. Etienne. Eat me.'"

"Okay. I'm down with that. Maybe I can get something low-cal."

"Son, it ain't deh seafood dat make you fat, it's deh batta, I find," Etienne said.

THE END

THE FLANK STRAP

BY

T-BOB CORVUS

CHAPTER 1

My given name is Earl Ray Bird and don't get any wise ideas because there's more than a couple of guys that's come to regret pretty quick that they had a germinal idea to call me "Early Bird." So if you get it in your mind to call me Early Bird your ownself, just keep your trap closed. I can't remember the first time I heard it. It's not original. It's not funny. It's boring.

Aside from people trying to make a joke of my name, I have real issues. My spinkter is in a kink. I'm twisted up as tight as Dick's hat band.

I went and got myself shit-canned from the best job a thirty-year-old guy with a lousy education could ever hope to get and that's why I'm pissed. It's my goal to get that job back. I pride myself on being a stand-up guy, but since I lost that job, I've been in retreat from my problems. I can't figure out why, I don't like it. I've learned my lesson. By God, no more running away. I'm going to put the reins in my teeth and go in, both barrels blazing. Nothing is going to stand in my way from this time forward.

When I was on the bubble as to whether or not I had a future with the company, this prissy HR guy told me to start writing a daily journal and get anger management counseling. Like a dang fool, I told him to take his anger management counseling and put it where the sun don't shine. Those guys in HR are nothing but a bunch of nest builders and I bet he was getting a kickback on anger manage-ment kits from some salesman buddy.

The theory behind a daily anger journal is that if a guy can figure out what makes him go balsamic, he can learn to act a little bit more like a normal human being. But I was in the know about the anger management scam he was running, because he ran that same rigmarole on one guy that was caught drinking on the job. When all you have is a hammer, every problem looks like a nail.

I honestly don't think I have an anger problem. But now that I'm just another vital statistic in the ranks of the unemployed, I can see that until I can make a good showing of fence-mending my sorry attitude, I might never get a decent job again. I need to do something, even if it's wrong, if I'm ever going to get hired back on. My suppositories are usually reliable, and it's my current thinking that I have a dang good chance of getting put on the payroll again, especially since when I go back with my hat in my hand, I can show them that I did get some anger management after all, even if I didn't need it, and I did it on my own violation.

My problem is that events have conspired to keep me out of the workforce for a couple of years now and some days I just sit here fluffing my nuts. I probably have the fluffiest nuts in Beckham County, Oklahoma.

I'm having a hard time getting started with this journal because most days now, nothing gets my blood pressure up. I have a nagging cough, but other than that, nothing at all. I don't even scream at the whack jobs on Jerry Springer. I just go over stuff that already happened, again and again, trying to figure out what I could have done different. It's the past that's driving me crazy. Those bygones are what would be the easiest thing for me to get put down in my journal. But what I'm supposed to put down in an anger management journal is the stuff that makes me go crazy day-by-day.

I stewed this over, this problematic, for a week or more. It was a real obstacle to me getting started until I realized that no one was going to be reading my anger management journal anyway. No one was going to tell me, "Earl, you did it wrong. Start over." All they are interested in is seeing that I did something along the lines of navel gazing and also that I have some tangible proof in the way of something written that looks like a journal. That ought to be enough to move the ball in my end of the rehabilitation field. So I am going to put down the things that my metal will let me put down. I'm going to take it serious, even if I have to fudge the rules a bit.

The first thing I think about when I try to peel back the artichoke leaves in my brain is that I never really settled down anywhere. That probably contributes a lot to me fustigating over the past. When I was a kid, my parents were on the move all the time. If the rent was due, the old man was looking for another place, another town. I think I played on at least a dozen different football teams from 7th grade through graduation. We lived from pillar to post in every little settlement in Beckham County, Western Oklahoma, and sometimes down in the City, which is what folks out here call Oklahoma City.

In fact, we lived in the City when I poobered out. Our house was on ITIO Boulevard. I can remember thinking that was pretty cool because the initials "ITIO" stands for "Indian Territory Illuminating Oil Company," the outfit that brought in the Oklahoma City oilfield. The street is a sorry excuse for a boulevard and it's only a block long. But for some reason, ITIO is an image that always comes to mind when I start thinking about my inauguration with the oil-patch. That's also where I lived when I got my growth sprout and started learning about members of the fairer sex, which just be clear, is women. Good lord, I heard that a college back east gives the kids sixteen different boxes to choose from when the form asks about "SEX." For me, good old M and F is plenty, they suit me just fine.

A stint in the navy almost ruined my ability to talk like a normal human being. If you're in the mess hall and you want the salt, the navy teaches you that you're wasting your time to say, "Please pass the salt." That won't get you a single solitary grain of salt. If you want the salt, you have to say, "Pass the f***ing salt" and even then, you got to say it with authority if you want the salt. I'm just sharing that little inside information because as another part of my self-implemented rehabilitation, I'm trying to eliminate some of the coarse language that gives other people the green light to think I'm a dumb ass. Damn and hell, they will have to wait for another day, but I think I can seem a little bit more educated if I can eradicate f*** and c*** and that other c*** from my language. I'm trying to quit using them.

I have other flaws and experiences that I regret, but I can say, that after fifteen years of dealing with members of the opposite sex in all manners, I never did anything really despicable unless my body required it of me.

So anyway, I was running pretty steady with this sweet-hearted blonde by the name of Chloe Reece. This was a couple of years ago. I'm going to withhold mentioning her last name for reasons that I suspect will become more clear when a few more artichoke leaves get peeled back. She had a nice job in a bank in Sayre, and was hearing wedding bells. I didn't have the good sense to shut off her chit chat when she cozied up to the notion that we might have it pretty good if we put our pensions together.

My one-eyed ex-cousin-in-law Peavine had bought this big Dodge Ram truck, brand new, straight out of the dealership. He was making payments to the bank. Had it all decked out with fancy tires and doo-dads and kept showing up late for work. So they shit-canned him and all of a sudden he was upside down on the truck. He loved that truck. So to make a long story short, he pulled the engine and hid it out in his neighbor's barn and let the bank repo the truck with no engine.

I bought the truck from the bank cheap with his money and then flipped the rig back to Peavine. I met Chloe Reece in the process. She never said nothing repository about me being in league with my one-eyed ex-cousin-in-law Peavine, even though she's as smart as a tree full of owls. Next thing you know, we were hooked up together pretty steady.

I trace back all my problems to a prospect we were drilling out in the Granite Wash. By "we," I mean Prometheus Drilling Company and the "Granite Wash" is this red-hot area that's making the old geologists look like fools and dirt farmers as rich as six feet up a bull's ass. Imagine a gigantic box of huge Legos getting spilled out across the landscape, except that the Legos are blocks of granite and they are two miles deep in the direction of the mantel of the earth. That's the Granite Wash, and especially a trend called the "Hogshooter." The geologists all agreed for years that as far as oil and gas was concerned, the structure was as dry as a popcorn fart.

I had worked my way up to pusher, which meant I was in charge of all the hands on the rig and that I was in charge of keeping about $40 million worth of equipment working on making hole. Like always, when we were drilling, we worked three tours, which the Yankees would call "shifts," and which is pronounced "towers" in the oilpatch. Anyone stupid enough to say "too-ers" has marked his ownself as a greenhorn which is almost as bad as being tagged a Yankee.

We were drilling on this place and calling the prospect the Westerfield #1-10. What that means is that this was the first well and it was located in section 10 and that the minerals were owned by someone named Westerfield. It's not this way in east Texas, but out west here, they surveyed out the land a long time ago and the "legal" map looks like a checkerboard. Each county is laid out in ranges, and each range is laid out in square townships, and each township is laid out in 36 sections, each a square mile.

This Westerfield was also the surface owner. I guess that in other places, it's unusual for the mineral owner not to be the surface owner, but back in the Dust Bowl times, lots of land owners out here sold off their minerals just to put grub in their kids bellies.

So another oddball thing is that if we were to make a well out of this prospect, ³⁄₁₆ of the money would go to Westerfield if the well produced oil. ³⁄₁₆ths is a sort of standard royalty for paying the mineral owner for his share. The fly in the oinkment is that some of the neighbors are entitled to a share if it came in a gas well. The regulators figure an oilwell out here drains 40 acres, sometimes more, but that a gas well drains 640 acres. Westerfield owned three quarters of Section 10—480 acres—and his neighbor Vorhees owned 160.

Vorhees had a daughter that was so pretty that every time I looked at her, I thought I heard angels playing music. She had dark hair and smoky eyes with a smile that glowed like a sunrise. Wynona. A sweet fanny too, a really sweet fanny. I guess from riding ponies her whole life.

So if Prometheus made a gas well, Vorhees would get ¼ of ³⁄₁₆ths of the money. Prometheus was a contractor, and we were working for Black Kettle Energy, one of the big players on the Granite Wash. But the point is, Black Kettle didn't give a rat's ass who got the royalty money, whether it all went to one person or if they had to split up the pie a hundred ways.

We were making hole at a pretty good clip when I learned from Chloe Reece that Westerfield held a mortgage on his neighbor's property and that he was trying to foreclose on poor old Vorhees, the dirt farmer with the daughter with the nice fanny. Westerfield was already on my bad side. He was always coming around complaining. Every day it was something. The heavy equipment was damaging his roads. His fences. His cattle. His ponds. Even his wind. The wind? Yeah, he said we were messing up his opportunity to sell a wind lease for a big windmill. He would have been complaining about us screwing up his trees, but except for mesquite, cactus, and sagebrush, the place was as bald as a cue ball. Mean old coot was just throwing shit up on the wall to see what would stick. He thought he could squeeze Prometheus for cash. Old bastard. His deal was with Black Kettle, not Prometheus. He should have known he was farting at a whirlwind.

It was Black Kettle that paid Westerfield for the lease, and it was the lease that gave them the right to drill. Five years ago, he had nothing but a pair of filthy overalls, a 10-dollar bill, and never changed either one of them. Now he was rich and thought that meant he had the obligation to try to make everyone else eat a shit sandwich.

My crews were all needing a bottom-hole bonus, and the company stood to make more profit if the well came in early. On top of that, it sure didn't set right with me to think about a guy like Westerfield foreclosing on his neighbor whose family had probably been scratching out a living on that hard scrabble old place since statehood. I figured it would throw a monkey wrench in his plans if the well came in a couple of weeks ahead of time because that would give Vorhees a chance to stall off the foreclosure. If it made a gas well, so much the better. Old Vorhees could probably borrow from the bank and pay Westerfield off.

I decided that I would thin out the mud in the #1-10 and bring the well in under the wire.

So that needs a little explaining. A driller puts this chemical mud in the hole he's boring. It's made by mixing an extra-heavy crushed stone into water to make a slurry. When it's in the well bore, it's so heavy that it holds back any bubbles of gas that want to burp out of the earth. And when it's thin, it lubricates less and that lets the driller grind out the hole faster.

I was way under balance—the mud was really thin—and I'll be damned if I know why the home office wasn't on me like ugly on an ape. They got all kinds of microscopes and sensors located all over the rig that bounce their readings off of satellites to the home office. The idea is to let the company know if a pusher is letting his crew grab too much ass time by spinning the bit in the ground.

We were making hole at a record clip. And when we wore the bit out and had to trip the drill pipe out of the hole to replace it, we pulled thribbles, which means three joints at a time. The mast was holding a rack of drill pipe 90 feet in the air.

I didn't return some phone calls and someone else was asleep at the switch. That's all it took. As bad luck would have it, we hit a high pressure gas pocket and it blew out the well. By all indications, the drill pipe was wadded up like spaghetti somewhere downhole that we couldn't get to, and a bubble of gas was trying to get to the surface where it was sure to catch fire and burn $40 million worth of surface equipment.

I knew as far as it had to do with my job, the shit was going to hit the fan, but it was on a delay fuse. The big shots from Prometheus were on the way to Beckham County in their Lincolns with a view to crawl up my ass because the company man from Black Kettle was crawling up theirs. I had at most a day.

For a few hours there, me and my crew were all eyeballs and elbows. To get the whore under control, we had to fill the wellbore with cement. The cement job needed a lot of water, so I bought it from Vorhees. He and Westerfield both had ponds, but Vorhees' water was easier to get. Before the sun sunk in the west, we got the cement pumped downhole and the blowout killed. And I got shit-canned from my job. The chance of me getting hired by another drilling company was nil. Gossip travels in the oilpatch at the speed of light.

Only one thing that came out of that fiasco that was for the good. I heard it from Chloe Reece. I guess old Vorhees got a few dollars from selling water to the blowout, and that let him stall off the foreclosure.

I think that Chloe Reece would always throw me a biscuit if I was hungry, but she was stand-offish now because I had no prospects to be earning the kind of money that I had before. Vorhees was still poor as a church mouse, but he was a good guy. He let me use a rundown old bunkhouse as a place to lay my head.

That bunkhouse is where I came into contact with Old Wynona. If I started writing that part down now, I'd be getting ahead of myself.

CHAPTER 2

S o I was sitting around that broke down old bunkhouse with nothing to do but swat flies and worry about what color my unemployment check was going to be. I had no hope of getting back my dream job with Prometheus, which had taken possession of my company truck. I hot-wired that old pickup truck, the one me and my one-eyed ex-cousin-in-law Peavine had cabbaged off of the bank. It was pretty bruised and battered by now, but Peavine was able to use his wife's car as she was in custody. I guess I could have gone fishing to waste away the time but I didn't have any gear. It was well into summer and noodling season was past.

I had some bonus money coming from Prometheus, but they had an office building full of number crunchers who were plenty capable of pencil-whipping me out of most of it.

I was sitting on the tailgate of the truck, feeling sorry for myself, still pissed off that I'd stuck my neck out for an old dirt dobber, even if he was good enough to let me use his bunkhouse. I saw Wynona and a friend down by the corral, kicking up dust. Wynona had a colt on a leader and was just sort of leading it around. I guess that's the way they get trained.

So I thought I'd go down and watch the girls. I had guessed Wynona was wearing real tight blue jeans and my suppository was right. They both looked pretty. I had taken an observatism one time when I was drinking beer that when there's two or more girls in a group, coveyed up like quail so to speak, that they all look better than they would if they were off by themselves as singles. So the covey factor probably contributed to the look of the other girl, who on closer inspection was more cute than pretty. She had a scrunched up nose and reddish-blonde hair, and she had that way that makes a guy want to call her some stupid cutesy name.

Both of them were way too young for me, just barely out of high school. So by dead reckoning, I'd say that was a dozen years of difference, or ten, rounded off. Now don't get me wrong, I've had my share of girls that were too young for me. But I shied away from entanglements. Experience told me that being with young girls can get old fast.

"Hey, Wynona."

Wynona nodded. "You know my friend? Junie Westerfield."

"Hey, Junie. You related to that cranky old bastard next door?"

She gave me a shitty stare. "I'm his daughter."

My big mouth gets me in hot water all the time. "Hey, nice to meet you, Junie." *Change the subject*, I told myself. "Good looking colt, Wynona."

"Thanks, Earl Ray. Hey, Junie...you think he'd do it?"

Junie just gave me another stink eye. Just because her old man was mad at me, I figured.

"Who told you my name is Earl Ray?'

"What else would it be?" She was right. I'd never met an Earl Wayne or Earl Darrell. "Glad you came down. I been meaning to ask you for a favor. You have plans Saturday?"

"Well I was thinking about going to town." That was one of the bigger lies I'd told recently. If I made it to town, I'm not sure I could afford gas to get back.

"We got a ranch rodeo team. We need you to ride for our brand."

Well Mrs. Byrd didn't raise no fool. I had a pretty good idea in my mind what a ranch rodeo was. Ranch rodeos are events for working cowboys to show off their everyday cowboying skills. The events are different than the TV rodeos. Roping, horsemanship, ground work like penning up steers and such. No bull riding or bull dogging. The equipment and tack used the same as what's used on a working ranch. And everyone competes on a team, and to get on a team you have to really live on a ranch. Which I did.

So anyway, I was thinking about how much fun it would be to ride a bucking bronco and imaging myself whooping it up and spurring the cranky old bastard on. "Well if you let me snag a couple of gallons of gas from your old man's tank, you can count me in," I said.

Saturday came and I met Wynona and Junie at the fairgrounds in Sayre. Each of them had to haul their favorite horses by trailer because they were entered in some horsemanship and cattle penning competitions.

Junie and Wynona were also entered in an event they called "team doctoring." The idea is to cut a calf out of a bunch, rope it at head and heels, jump off the horses, get him on the ground, cinch up his front feet and back feet, then mark a big X on his side with a piece of chalk. Trying to symbolize giving the steer some medicine. Wynona had her rope on his neck real good, then Junie came up from behind and threw hers at his heels. She just caught one leg. The horses backed up and took all the slack out of the rope, and the steer couldn't run any more. But he was still three-legged. Junie grabbed him by the tail and pulled him over. Then she and Wynona were on him, grabbing those legs and cinching them in a half hitch. Wynona pulled a big hunk of soft chalk out of her vest pocket and marked a big X on his side. They stood over him, jubilating, raising their fists in triumph like Rocky.

Damn I was proud of them. Soon enough the steer kicked out of his bonds and was trotting back to his nutless buddies.

"You all was on him like ducks on a june bug...Hell, you tugged on that tail like a floor hand slinging chain, June Bug," I said.

"She's not going to be happy—you calling her June Bug," Wynona said.

"Hell, that's a compliment. It ain't every man-jack that can make a good hand in the oilpatch."

"Don't compare cowboying to the kind of rape you and your kind are putting on the earth," Wynona said.

I'd met a gillion do-gooders in my life that believed all that Hollywood crap about the environment. Of course, I thought it was a pretty stupid way of thinking, and it came as a shock to me that Wynona was twisted that way. But I was into cowboying today, not politics. I took a selfie of Team Vorhees—Prometheus didn't take away my cell phone, I bought that myself—the three of us, cheek-to-cheek, smiling ear-to-ear.

When the times came in, Wynona and Junie placed second in the doctoring, so all of us were pretty excited. We had a chance at winning a trophy. The next event was the bronco riding. I was an eager beaver.

Next thing I knew I was on top of a rank old stud who was made into an extra nasty piece of horseflesh by a flankstrap cribbed up around his cods. It didn't hurt him, but it made him mad enough to buck. When I thought I was ready, I gave the hands a nod, and that old bastard hit the sky. I was off on the first kick. Flipped over, head over heels, and landed flat on my back. I was seeing double for five minutes. I knew I was going to feel it in my bones the next day.

So if Team Vorhees was going to have any success in the rodeo, it was going to come in the wild cow milking competition.

We were just one of six teams. We all lined up together. When the horn blasted, Wynona and Junie and all the riders raced across the arena to cut a cow out of a bunch. I was on foot. They chased this old cow down and threw ropes around her neck and I hobbled to catch up. I was still kind of wrenched up from the bronco ride. When Wynona and Junie had her lassoed, they cinched their ropes around their saddlehorns and their horses backed up to keep a strain on the line. Then they scrambled off their ponies and looped more rope around the cow's neck, mugging her, backing away to hold her so dumb ass old Earl Ray could scramble in under her and squeeze off a cup or so of milk into a coke bottle.

The Flank Strap

Now, if in your mind's eye you're thinking about one of those big black and white Holstein cows in the Chic-Fil-ay commercials, or one with brown eyes and a great big old floppy udder, you got another think coming. This was a big old rangy red cow, rawboned and mean, with gouging horns and sharp hooves. Her hip bones and shoulders stuck out and she reminded me of one of those warthog tank killer warplanes. She didn't like the ropes around her neck. She didn't like me fondling that wrinkled scrap of skin that passed for an udder and she didn't like me squeezing her tits, even though I was considered by many of my oilfield trash pals to be a highly accomplished petitioner of the craft. And, hey, I'm sorry if you don't like my choice of words for describing the female anomaly. I grew up in the oilpatch, it's a place where you never hear the term "boobs." Regular sized tits is referred to as tits. If they're on the small size, it's titties. Big tits are big old tits. We don't even call guys from New York City or Los Angeles boobs. They're damn Yankees or assholes. But back to the matter at hand, my intention was to milk that rank old range cow for the team. For Wynona. Wynona with the nice little bubble butt.

In fact I was probably thinking about her butt when it happened. I've sort of blacked out on some of the details. I do know that out of nowhere, a hoof sizzled through the firmament and glanced off my skull over my ear. I don't think Nadia Comeneci was limber enough to pull the move that cow did, even on her speediest and most agile day. That old range cow must have contorted her body like a pretzel.

I also remember sailing across that rodeo arena like a dried up cow patty. When I could halfway focus my eyes, I was laying on the dirt floor of that arena and my shirt and jeans were covered with spilled milk and cow shit. The coke bottle was broken. Every last drop gone. Other milkers were racing toward the finish line with bottles full. A horn blew. Team Vorhees came in dead last.

Needless to say, Junie wasn't very happy about that. "Damn, Early Bird, what the hell happened to you? We was winning! You cost us a trophy."

I saw two Junies side-by-side and wasn't sure which one to answer. "I'm sorry, June Bug. Maybe next time."

"June Bug! I should kick your ass for that."

Later we had a hot dog or something, I'm not sure. I was still woozy and decided I better make up to Junie as I might need help getting home. "You know, June Bug, I'm sure sorry that we didn't bring that well in on your place."

"I don't know what's come over you, gambling like that. Taking all those risks. My daddy said you act crazy. Someone needs to put a flankstrap on you."

"Well I was thinking of old man Vorhees. And Wynona. He needed a break."

"I hope you didn't do that on my account," Wynona said.

I decided to talk to the Wynona, who I was seeing out of my right eye, which was the one on my left. "I had it on good information that old man Westerfield was the one with the flankstrap and that he had it on your daddy and that you all was going to lose your home place."

"Well, that's all put off six months now, anyway. And it's none of your business. Whatever, it's nothing I'd want to see you fracking up the landscape for or polluting the ground water. It's Mother Earth, after all. We have to live on this planet."

Not having complete command of my debating skills at the moment, I decided to let sleeping dogs. The girls didn't seem to blink when I drove away from the fairgrounds holding one hand over my left eye. The sky was kind of blustering up and what had been wispy clouds in the northwest showed dark against the horizon now, giving signs underneath of blowing up into a high prairie thunderstorm.

Sheets of rain were coming down like a cow pissing on a flat rock by the time I made it back to the Vorhees place. Lightning was flashing and the peals of thunder sounded so near I had the feeling it was all just missing me. That old truck hit every bone-jarring pot hole and rock on the road back to the bunkhouse. The windshield wipers slammed back and forth, still it was almost impossible to see the trail. I slid to a stop on the slick mud and scooted under an eave.

Inside, the bunkhouse was pitch black. I suspicioned that the electricity was off, but the light came on in the refrigerator. Inside was a half eaten can of beanie weenies. Not even one can of beer. The light switch on the wall didn't work, I flipped it on and off a couple of times. Whenever a light was off, I always hit the switch several times. No idea why. That trick never works but I still did it. The definition of insanity they say. The bunkhouse must have blown a fuse and it was too dark for a man with double vision to bump around in the dark to find out how to fix it.

It wasn't a problem to find the bed. I stripped to my skivvies and flopped down on the mattress. Every muscle in my body started remembering the trauma of getting bucked off that bronco. I was hoping a good night's sleep would just ease the throbbing where that rangy old cow had clipped me with her hoof. I knew there wasn't an aspirin in the place.

I dozed off an hour or so. I figured an hour because the rain had stopped when a cramped muscle woke me. It never rains in this country for more than an hour. Comes a toad strangler and lightning strikes and the wind beats everything up, then it's gone. Lightning was flashing far off in the east. The thunder grumbled now, low and far away. I waggled the light switch a few times and still nothing. No light in the room except for a strange glow coming out from underneath a door. It was half blocked by a bunk, but I could see the dim light trying to crawl out the crack at the bottom. I wasn't seeing double any more.

I figured the doorway must open a closet and that I'd find a fuse box inside. I didn't want to turn on the lights but I suppose I'd had a better feeling knowing they'd come on if I needed them to, and the idea of the fuse box causing that glow was enough reason to investigate. So I pulled the bunk back enough so the door would swing open, but it seemed to be stuck. I yanked and shoved. I thought I'd pull the doorknob out. The door was wedged in and didn't give up its place without a struggle. I felt a little movement, then more, and with a scratchy scrape, the door yielded to an opening just wide enough for me to squeeze through.

I had not realized that the bunkhouse had an adjoining room, but that's just what that door opened into. The room was lit by one dim bulb under a shade that directed it down to a desktop. Beyond that, in the shadows, I could see the outline of a figure. A person? I didn't know. It took me awhile for my eyes to adjust to the light, dim though it was. The office was tired. All the furniture looked worn out and dog-eared.

What was seated across the room, planted in a worn out, over-stuffed chair, was this old woman. She looked to be about 70 or more, old-maid-sad and weary. She was wearing a polyester pantsuit and from the large number of snags in the fabric, I thought she must have been run backwards through a briar patch. Her hair looked like a fright wig. She had that look of someone that had been waiting way too long.

And there was me, standing in the doorway like a dumb ass, in my skivvies, asking "Who the hell are you?"

"I'm Wynona," she said. "The boss man's daughter. You remember me. Earl Ray."

Needless to say, I blinked. I found a blanket thrown over a chair and wrapped it around my waist. Don't know if I was hiding my nakedness or cold. It just seemed like the right thing to do. I watched her as she loaded up her lip with a pinch of snuff.

"No one calls me Earl Ray. Except Wynona."

"Yeah. I know. It's me all right. Plus fifty years. Fifty pounds, too! That door there's some kind of a time thing or another. Fifty years later on this side."

I stepped over to a window and looked out. It was still raining a bit which I could only see when the lightning strobed. Outside I saw the same old broke down barns and corrals. But a ragged trailer house stood in place of the farmhouse.

"Well I'll be dipped in shit. Hell yeah," I said. For some reason, when I was younger, I thought it made me seem smart to say "hell yeah" pretty much the same way Jed Clampett said "well doggies." It was habit now. "I heard tell of these time things."

"Been looking forward to seeing you again, Earl Ray."

Lightning struck again, closer than before, and I got another look at the Vorhees home place. "This old farm never promised nothing so I don't guess you're much disappointed."

"Nope. It sure ain't much to write home about."

"A good hand could have made this place something, I reckon."

"I never found me one of them," Old Wynona said. "I was pretty particular, if you remember. Always on the lookout for a top hand, just never found him."

"You're happy though," I said, not knowing whether she was happy or not.

"Humph."

"You sure was a pretty thing."

"For all the good it done me." Old Wynona squirted a black stream of snuff spit into a cup.

"Turned everyone's head." I must have wrapped myself in a horse blanket. It was chaffing my nipples. I looked outside again.

Old Wynona arose from the overstuffed chair to look out the window with me. She had been sitting on a little inner tube. My one-eyed ex-cousin-in-law Peavine had one like that once when his asshole declared war on his body. "I wish I had it to do over."

"Hell yeah. There's plenty of beds over there. Hey, come on over."

"That door don't work for me. Won't let me go back. God knows I tried."

KABOOM! More lightening struck nearby. Another cell of the storm could be following the one that had passed.

"Just look at this sorry old run down place," I said.

"Yeah, I have looked. And believe you me, I deserve better than this."

"You sure was a pretty thing." I couldn't think of anything else to say.

Old Wynona swung a foot and kicked me in the ass playfully. "Earl Ray, we ought to be able figure some way out of this rut. God. I don't want to die broke on this old hard scrabble hill."

"Yep. A couple of smart ones like us'uns. I don't have nothing coming in but an unemployment check." I didn't want to admit I was going to get screwed out of my bonus.

"Why don't you make me some money? Put in a savings for me."

"Why sure. Anything you say. What can I get you? A million? Five million? Unemployment pays real generous."

"What will it take? What do you want?" she asked.

I had to ask myself if she was really serious. "Hell. It don't take nothing much to make me happy. Only thing I want is my old job back. I might like a little kiss from Wynona, too."

"I bet you could use more money," she said. "I could."

I reached in my billfold. I had six ones and handed them over to Old Wynona. "Here, take it. Money's bad luck for me. You take it. You can have it."

Old Wynona looked the money over good and hard, then handed it back. "It ain't no good to me."

"Take it," I said. "May as well be a horse collar around my neck. It's yours."

"That cash won't do me no good. No good at all. They changed the money. I couldn't spend that if I wanted to."

That sure as hell caught me off guard. I slumped into a chair, wondering what else changed in those fifty years.

"Put it in the bank. Open me up a savings with my name on it."

"With six dollars? Hell yeah. That ought to work."

"Six dollars? Is that all you have?"

The Flank Strap

I remembered a $100 bill tucked into the back of the billfold where I kept my lucky rubber. It had come in handy once or twice when I had to bail out a drunk derrick hand. The money, not the rubber. "Well, I got a hundred. You can have that. I'll put it in the bank tomorrow." Then, as sort of an afterthought, I said, "But you got to get me a kiss from Wynona as part of the deal." My thinking is it's a bad idea to take a deal offered without some negotiating.

"Okay, it's a deal. And I'm going to help you get your job back."

"Aw, hell, Wynona. You're wasting your time. Why, she don't know I'm alive. And as far as Prometheus is concerned, you're farting at a whirlwind."

"Oh hell, I think you're as hunky as they come. Always have. Kinda sweet on you if the truth was told."

I had myself one of those Hallmark card moments there and then. This feeling rushed over me of how it was that I'd never had anything like a real home and hearth and how I brought that all on myself for the simple reason of trying to screw every woman that came in my line of sight. Red and yellow, black and white, they were just trophies in my sight. The good, the bad and the ugly. Didn't make any difference how shallow, the dumber the better. I was afraid if I looked down right that minute, that I'd see a great big hole in my heart. I had feelings for Wynona in that moment that I knew weren't the best. She was a hot number, but no matter how good she looked, I figured she was trouble for someone down the line.

"She has a strange way of showing her interest." I didn't like saying that. It's the best I could do.

"Earl Ray, the kiss. It's been taken care of."

"Right."

"Don't believe me? Go get your phone."

"I sure like it, you calling me Earl Ray."

"Go get your phone, I said." So I did.

"Scroll over to that picture you took today."

"Well I'll be jiggered." In the selfie picture I took up at the fairgrounds, there was Wynona, giving me a great big smooch on the cheek.

"Okay, Peckerneck, time for me to go." Old Wynona reached out, touched my hand as tenderly as it had ever been touched. She left the bunkhouse office through an outside door.

"I'll be dipped in shit," I said. In reality, I was thinking *Maybe she does think I'm cute. Or hunky.* It occurred to me that when my bonus came through, I might add some money to the $100. But I could decide that later. Right now I was tired and needed some sleep, so I engaged all my sore muscles to push myself through the narrow inner doorway that led back into the bunkroom.

CHAPTER 3

The next day was the Lord's Day and I slept through most of it. It was a luxury to me. When we were on location, drilling, I never had Sundays off.

Monday, the sun was shining and nothing came in the mail. I found the burned out fuse. It was one of the old fashioned kind. I screwed a penny in behind it and the lights came on. It wasn't the smartest or the safest thing to do, but I had a reputation for recklessness to uphold. Truth is, I couldn't find any modern day fuses in the bunkhouse and I'd have to drive to town to buy some.

Back and forth to town was a habit I didn't want or need. I had coffee, a couple of cans of peaches, a box of Cheerios and a crust of bread. I'd wait to go to town. A day. Or two. I needed groceries, but gasoline was expensive. I'd wait for the unemployment check.

It came after noon on Friday, $386, so I fired up the truck and drove into town. The fuses cost three dollars and I figured my bill of groceries was going to set me back $40 and a tank of gas another $40. So counting the hundred dollar bill that was safely tucked in my rubber compartment, I had a little more than $400.

I filled up with gas and decided to do my banking next. I didn't want to leave my groceries sitting around. Chloe Reece looked mighty nice. I'd parked down the block by the beer joint because I didn't want her to see the pickup truck I was driving now. She had an inquiring mind. The bank had her in charge of new accounts that day. It gave her a good opportunity to study, she was taking classes at the community college.

So I cashed my unemployment check and moseyed over to her desk. I chatted her up to be nice then handed her the musty hundred dollar bill. "I want to open a savings account."

"Someone call the newspaper," she said. "We haven't had a new customer in a month." She grabbed a form out of her desk and talked out loud while she filled it in. "Earl Ray Bird."

"No, wait," I said. "It's not for me. It's for Wynona Vorhees."

She pushed her glasses onto her head and leaned back in the chair. "Wynona Vorhees?"

"Yeah. You know her?" Like I said before, me and Chloe Reece had been sort of an item on and off, so I knew when she acted like she didn't hear right that the conversation was headed away from high finance and off in a personal direction.

"Well, yes." She gave sort of a snorting sound and snapped her head down. Her glasses slid from her forehead back to her nose. She grabbed more forms and scribbled on them. She didn't look up, but told me under her breath, "You know, she's going to just have sex with you so she can steal all your stuff."

My first reaction was to smart off something about yeah, that same trick had been tried on me before to varying degrees of success. But I decided "better not." I didn't want Chloe Reece to think I was accusing her because she was one of the handful that hadn't tried that particular trick. "Well I figure I'm fully protected from that sensuality because I don't have a pot to piss in or a window to throw it out of. I don't have stuff."

"Men." She scribbled some more. "What's her social?"

"Her social what?"

"Her social security. Her number."

"How the hell would I know?"

Up went the glasses again as Chloe Reece eased back in the chair. "I can't open an account without a social."

"Oh come on, you're just trying to be difficult."

"Nuh uh. It's rules. Which I follow. Which I don't put my job on the line to break." Women. They can be a pain in the ass. You can quote me on that. Chloe Reece was hiding behind some rule just because she was jealous, I'm pretty sure of that.

She handed me a form for Wynona to sign. No way around it. I was willing to try to help Old Wynona get what she wanted. So to do that I would have to get Chloe Reece what she wanted. The last thing I wanted to do was tell young Wynona some of what was going on because then she would only think that I was just trying to get in those tight jeans, which was a thinking point that I have to admit I had on the front burner. I should have been able to work that out if...

If.

I always try to avoid the "if" game when I can. But the day would have gone different if I hadn't parked the truck down by the beer joint which I did just because I didn't like parking it near the bank. They took a big write off on it and people out west here don't like to flaunt their mischief like they do down in the City. If it wasn't for feeling like I had to play peek-a-boo with the truck. If. If my aunt had balls, she'd be my uncle.

So anyway, I was striding down this sidewalk, within spitting distance of my truck, minding my own business. It was parked in front of a place called "The Paddock." My tongue was as dry as a cow chip and I was swabbing it around, trying to wet my lips. I rubbed my mouth with my hand. That's when, like I say, minding my own business, a voice rang out from that den of iniquity. "Hey, Early! Whatcha doing, pal?"

I recognized the voice of a buddy and answered, "Hey, Verl Lee."

Then another friendly greeting reached my ears. "Hey, Pearlie-boy! Get in here quick!" It was Teddy Jack, another old pal. His mother came from up around Tulsa and he got his name from her favorite TV personality. He and Verl Lee were reliable daylight beer joint customers. They usually worked the midnight tour.

So I didn't think it would be polite to stay outside, even if I had been minding my own business. Inside, the Paddock was as dark as a tomb. People occupied places at the bar. Some of the regulars were slapping dominoes under a cone of light on the table near the crapper. I couldn't tell who was who until my eyes adjusted to the light.

"I wanta hear about that bronco ride," Teddy Jack said.

"Teddy Jack. Hey, Hoss."

"Hey!" Hoss yelled. "You just the cowhand I been looking for, Squirrely. You sure looking thirsty. Buy you one?"

I felt my way to the bar and seated myself atop a barstool.

"Get this good old boy an icy cold beverage, Jim," Hoss said.

So that first beer was gone before I finished retelling all the details of my one-second bronco ride, and having accepted Hoss's offer, it was incontinent on me to buy him and me another one. We talked some football and after a couple more, someone got out the dice.

I never have seen anyone so lucky with the bones. I hit my number every time I was shooter. I was hotter than the hubs of hell. I was up probably $200. I had loose bills hanging out of every pocket. Them dumb butts were out of money and bawling and making excuses about going home to see Mama. I had a hot hand and a full tank of gas and hey, you got to make hay when the sun shines. The nearest casino was that Cheyenne Arapahoe place over to Clinton, the Lucky Star, 45 minutes away.

I kept winning, playing the Oklahoma Indian form of craps, which is ridiculous when you think about it. First of all they make a guy chuck in fifty cents. They call it an ante, but that's deceivious. You don't get it back if you win. It's supposed to go to some fund for Indian kids but even gamblers aren't stupid enough to believe that. If you're a good enough craps player, you can cut the house odds to maybe 3%, but with this dumb ass ante, if you're betting $5, you lose 10% before you ever throw the dice. And don't get me started. They don't even play craps with dice. They have numbered cards turned upside down. The shooter rubs his chin and says something like "A, G." And the stickman turns over the cards in the A and G boxes, and

The Flank Strap

WHAW-LAW, if the numbered cards are a 2 and a 6, the point is 8. Which you try to hit by calling out more letters of the alphabet.

Oklahoma Indian craps is so stupid. I was up probably $1,500 at 3:00 a.m. and cashed out for $3,200 at 7:00 a.m. I had two hours to get to a cockfight in Chickasha.

This arena was built inside a corrugated steel barn. The pit was surrounded by bleachers, probably eight rows high. The lowest three rows were molded plywood stadium seats with arm rests, and the upper rows wooden planks. The seats and aisles were full of cowboys, Mexicans, Chinese, Native Americans, and African-Americans, folks of both sexes, and aged from little kids on up to ancients who were getting around the arena on walkers.

Two men, two angry roosters, and a referee occupied the ring. The crowd was cheering, then as the handler let loose of their roosters, the noise died, and the arena fell as quiet as a whisper.

"Pit," shouted the referee, and the handlers let the cocks fly into one another, their feet high and in front of them, kicking down at their enemy.

They did that by nature. They have an upside down claw on their heels that the cockfighters replace with a needle-sharp gaff. With feathers flying and wings flapping, the crowd exploded, cheering them on. In just moments, it was as if the tongue of the crowd had split in two. Half the spectators shouted "yes," and the other half shouted "Aw shit." Then the noise dropped to a dull rumble. All the spectators were offering unsolicited commentary to one another, talking like they knew what happened. It was like watching Sports Center on ESPN. Then the betting started again.

All the gambling business was handled public outcry. Some of the spectators with big voices shouted out what bets they were willing to make, and the bet was set with a wink or a nod. After the first fight, a Chinese man in an ill-fitting suit peeled $200 off of a wad of bills that would choke a horse and handed it to me as two men, each cradling a rooster under his arm, entered the ring for the next bout. One chicken was red and one was yellow. The handlers strapped steel gaffs to the legs of their cocks.

I was on my feet. "Lay two hundred! Lay two hundred!"

"Hell man, ain't no one gonna bet with you. You're hotter than a fresh f***ed guinea in a red pepper patch." It was a rancher from Beckham County that I'd seen around town. He said one of those words that I am trying to explunge from my language. But he was right. My luck was running hot.

"Lay two hundred, one eighty!" I still had no takers. "Lay two hundred, one sixty! Where's the action on this fight?"

Across the ring, I spotted Westerfield. He took the bet by pointing a grubby index finger at me. "You're on."

The wager was set. I was betting $200 and Westerfield was only betting $160. Since I was betting more, I had the pick of the cocks. "Yeller then, Wes. I got the yeller chicken."

"Pit!" the referee shouted, and the handlers loosed their fighting cocks. Each bird jumped high and toward the other in an explosion of colored feathers. It was over almost as soon as it began.

"Yeeeeeeeeessss!"

"Aw shit." Only this time it was me saying "aw shit." Westerfield was a Jonah.

But two more chicken wranglers entered the ring with a couple of fresh roosters and like a dumb ass, I hollered over to Westerfield, "Hey, Westerfield! Lay double or nothing."

"Hell yeah."

"Then I got the gray."

I would have quit but I didn't have to. I ran out of money. I left before the derby was over and I drove home. When I banged down the ranch road to the bunkhouse, the truck's gas tank told me I had less than a quarter of a tank of gas. I didn't have any groceries, but my hundred dollar bill was still safe. I hadn't put it on the line and it was still secure alongside my lucky rubber.

So my Sunday was a bust.

L ater in the afternoon, I heard a dog barking, and went out to see what was going on. Down at the barn and house, Wynona and Junie messing around the outbuildings. Thinking maybe there was something to see, I sauntered down to see.

They were looking at the nest of a paper wasps under the eave of the barn. The dog was barking and yelping, I figured he must have got himself stung. I felt his pain.

I saw some piglets in the stockyard and decided to break the ice. "I guess that old sow had her pigs."

"Yeah," Wynona said. "A few days ago. We didn't know she had 'em."

"How many?" I asked. "Eight? Nine?"

"Can't you count?" Junie said.

"Hard to get real precise nose count, Junebug. They're running every which way."

"It can't be that hard."

"Hell, why don't you count 'em?"

"I think I will," Junie said.

The barn had a low shin-high door. "I'll help," I said. "I'll go in the barn and run 'em out that hog door." I went inside the barn and Junie stationed herself by the low narrow door. The mama pig was in a stall with several of her piglets.

"Shoo pig," I hollered. "Shoo. Shoo. Aw shit. No!"

Junie stooped over to peer into the barn. I saw her face peeking through the low hog door. "What's the problem now?"

"Shoo pig." I jabbed the old sow in the fanny with a stick. She shot out of that stall like she'd been fired out of a canon and sprinted toward the hog door.

Junie saw her coming but froze. The sow hit her at the knee and bowled Junie over. She fell on her belly, onto the sow's back, head facing the rear, holding on for dear life. The sow ran about three laps around the lot at breakneck speed, and skidding to a stop at the edge of a muddy wallow, bucked Junie head over heels into the sludge.

I ran out of the barn in time to see it. I wished I had video tape. "Eight seconds!" I yelled. "If that ain't a record ride, I never seen one."

"You bastard." Junie was soaked in hog shit.

Wynona was choking back a laugh, standing right next to me, I guess wondering what I'd do next. My best plan was to act innocent. So I said, "Someone ought to clean this place up. It's an ecological nightmare."

That jab went over like a turd in a punchbowl. "Kiss my ass, Earl," Wynona said. "You're mean." She didn't call me "Earl Ray." For a moment, I thought maybe we were going to have a global cooling episode.

"I had nothing to do with that."

"I don't believe you."

"Hell, it was just a joke."

"Apologize."

The prank was all over almost before I knew it was happening. If I'd strategized a trick like that for a year, it wouldn't have come off that smooth. But in those days after I lost my job, I didn't have the usual quantity of starch in my civvies, so I did apologize.

When I look back now, I kick myself for not realizing that for Junie, the sow was only phase one. After a dinner of Cheerios and water, I started feeling the need for a constitutional, so I grabbed an old magazine from a stack in the corner and headed to the backhouse. The cover showed some Nazis torturing a blonde whose big old tits were hanging nearly out of her blouse, so my literary expectorations were high, even if those pulpy advertising pages at the back part of the magazine were destined to be used to wipe my ass.

I was enjoying the feature story about a hard-boiled private investigator. Some bad guys from eastern Europe had pistol whipped him in the first couple of pages of course, but I had got far enough into the read to where he was ready to slap around an Asian girl with pouty breasts. That's when I felt something unusual kind of flitting around my best friend and worst enemies which were hanging at a lower altitude than the outhouse shelf my butt was perched on.

Those old fashioned outhouses have a low door at the back, and sometimes chickens get inside and feast on the bugs and other easy pickings in the outhouse basement. For some reason, a chicken that picks through shit for his meal is nowadays called "free range." So my first thought, when I felt something tickling at my cods, was that it was some of those free range chickens.

"Hey, you damn chickens, get the hell out of here. Git I said. Git now." That was usually enough to send any old range hen to scurrying off. But the sensation of a breeze malingered on my backside and something was still nudging at my nut sack.

My pants were bunched around my ankles, but I got up to see what the rumpus was all about.

So what I saw was a paint can swinging on the tine of a pitchfork. And what I heard was Junie laughing. The paint can sprung open and the outhouse filled with wasps. She must have captured that nest of paper wasps from under the eave of the barn and had incarcerated them inside that paint can. I'll be haunted the rest of my days by Junie's evil laugh when she slammed the hatch door shut.

I was tugging at my drawers and slapping at wasps and I guess Junie ran around the outhouse and pinned the door closed with the pitchfork. Anyway, that's what my forensic investigation disclosed after I managed to tip the outhouse over by rocking it back and forth sideways. I took another hard lick on the head.

I must have been stung a dozen places. I chewed the paper from that stroke book into poultice wads and dobbed them on my stings. That seemed to soothe the pain a bit.

I woke in the middle of the night wondering if I could ease the pain with some new paper wads. That glowing light was under the inner doorway again, so I pushed my way through. Old Wynona was sitting across the room, half lit by a single bulb hanging from the ceiling. I slumped into a chair.

"What happened to you?" she asked.

"Paper wasps."

"I'm talking about the money."

"Some old boys got me drunk."

I wasn't in any mood to take an ass chewing and I guess she could see it. She coughed out a laugh. "Men. Explains why I never got me one, I guess. You didn't need no help from them old barflies. You got drunk all by your ownself."

"I told you money was bad luck to me."

Old Wynona slapped her hands on her knees, stood, and moseyed over to me with her hands on her hips. She was fleshy and moved about as graceful as a sack of doorknobs. I didn't know if she was going to slap me or what. I guarded myself though, because I didn't want to get bumped on a wasp sting. Instead, Old Wynona just gave me a hug. A big hug, sustained. She held my head in between her breasts and kissed me on top of the head.

"You rascal. When you ever gonna learn?"

I extracted myself from the embrace, guarding against low thoughts about what those sagging old tits might look like. My cheeks were burning, so I must have been blushing bright red.

"Come on now, Wynona. That's kind of personal."

"Ha! Got something to show you," she said. "Look at that picture again."

The Flank Strap

I opened my cell phone and scrolled to the picture I'd taken at the ranch rodeo. In the picture, I was kissing Wynona, but now she'd turned her lips to mine and was kissing me back.

I wasn't ready for that, I looked at Old Wynona and she smiled.

"I figured she was going to write me off. That rough stuff with Junie and all."

"I like your gumption. You're a breath of fresh air. You need to get that savings in and then take me dancing."

"By the way, I ran into a snag with the savings. I got some papers for you to sign."

She signed and told me, "Okay. Make a date to go dancing. I set my mind on twirling around the light fantastic with you."

"Oh, come on. I can't dance. And Wynona don't know I'm alive, always got that Junebug hanging around."

"Aw, c'mon. Junie's my best friend. You know how to line dance, don't you?"

"Hell no! That's for them...uh funny boys."

"I'm telling you, Earl Ray. You ought to learn it."

"It'll be a cold day in July..."

It did turn off cold that day. I'd collected another unemployment check so I drove into town on fumes, did some checking around and found out that a dance hall in Clinton was giving lessons that very night. Forty-five minutes later I had my dumb ass parked in a chair on the front row of a big barny place that called itself "The Western Oklahoma Ballet."

The teacher was kind of ephemeral, he wore pink cowboy boots and a hat. His shirt was covered with rhinestones. He wasn't no spring chicken.

He had eight students, all girls except for yours truly. And line dancing was the topic of discussion. I had been known to do a little rock and roll dancing, and was above average at two-step, which was critical care for cowboy dancing, which going further to explain, is mostly about dancing and drinking beer.

But Phillip was learning us line dancing tonight. "So it's one, two, scoot your boot, turn, kick, seven, eight. You try it."

We all lined up and stepped out what Phillip showed us. It was a little stiff because he didn't play any music. "One, two, scoot your boot, turn, kick, seven, eight."

I don't have music in my soul as a backup. I stumbled through the steps.

"Early, just what in the world was that?"

"I'm trying hard, Phillip. Honest."

Phillip positioned himself behind me and grabbed me by the hips. All the girls giggled and I bet I turned six shades of red. Everyone knew that Phillip had alternate ornamentation.

I don't want anyone to get the wrong idea that I'm a Neanderthal or nothing. I like girls and I know there's some guys that don't. If they want to take themselves out of the game, that just means more playing time for me. There's even some girls that like girls, hell, I like girls. I can't begrudge them for that. It's their business.

"Now! One, two, scoot your boot, turn, kick, seven eight. Again. One, two, scoot your boot, turn, kick, seven eight. Do you feel it Early? Do you feel it now?"

"I feel something, all right, and I'm getting the inuendo that it's you, Phillip. Damn it, Phillip, if you got some Brokeback Mountain ideas germinating out of that head of yours, you just knock it off."

Well, that's about all having to do with the dance lessons that I'm prepared to share, other than to say, I kept my temper and actually learned a line dance or two.

CHAPTER 4

So the next day I was driving past the training paddock. I saw Wynona out there. She had a colt on a leader, so I slowed to a stop and backed up. I leaned out the window.

"Hey there, Wynona. What's going on?"

"Hey, Earl Ray. Daddy's gone into town."

"I'm not wanting your daddy. I been looking to talk to you." I eased out of the truck and sauntered over to the corral.

"Watch you don't spook him now."

Just then, Junie carried a bale of hay out of the barn and into the paddock. "Hey Early Bird." That damn Junie seemed to be ubicoitus and was getting on my nerves.

"Junebug. You hire on out here?"

"'Naw. Wynona and me both got colts."

"You guys doing a real good job with them. Real good."

"This 'un here's gonna run them barrels without breaking stride," Junie said.

"Hey, Junebug. Why don't you go put that sow in the barn?" I made a "get the hell outta here" gesture to Junie with my thumb. Junie stuck her tongue out at me.

The only privacy I was going to get was by talking low. "They got a big dancehall over to Elk City now, you hear?" I said to Wynona.

"Yeah," Wynona said. She was intense on watching that colt trot in circles. I didn't think she was getting my drift.

"You been?"

"I have," Junie said. I was getting the idea that Junie was a big blowhard. Claiming she'd been someplace she hadn't. Shoot.

"Sure enough? Well you don't have any interest then."

"I been meaning to go is what I meant to say," Junie said.

"I bet Wynona hasn't been. You want to go?" I asked her.

"Un-huh."

"You will?" I asked.

"What?" Wynona shot back.

"Go dancing, girl. With me." In my experience, girls like to act like they don't have a clue what you're talking about. The purpose of this is to keep a guy from talking roundabout. Make him be explicit, which of course, is a language skill they sure as hell avoid at all costs.

Wynona forgot her colt for a second and did a quick double-take back-and-forth between Junie and me.

"With you? I mean uh. You want to take me dancing?" she asked me.

"Why shore. I been learning."

"Uh. I got to uh. Junie help me."

"He's wanting to practice on you, Wynona."

"Oh. I mean, uh, if it was like sort of a test drive or something. Just part of your lessons, right?"

"Anything you say. Saturday night."

"Well then why the hell not. Sure Earl Ray. We'll go dancing with you."

"You're on. I'll gitcha after supper."

I got in the pickup truck and thought about what she meant "we'll go dancing" while the starter cranked. The Queen of England talks about herself as "we" so I just shrugged it off.

"You could take a girl to a restaurant," Junie was saying. As I drove off, I turned up the music to drown out that voice which was getting to be like fingernails on the chalkboard. I put two and two together and came up with sixteen. My Queen of England explanation was bunk. Junie was planning on tagging along.

The Flank Strap

It doesn't take a rocket surgeon to figure out what happened next. Junie was all decked out in her fancy duds and jumped in the pickup first when I drove by the home place to pick up Wynona. People call that a fifth wheel. I have puzzled that finger of speech over and have never been able to make sense of it. Once I had this Superduty and it had this hitch in the bed so that the trailer's weight got evenly distributed over the axles. That's a fifth wheel. It makes the pickup ride smoother when it's hauling a load and keeps the trailer from swaying. I will go to my grave mystified over why they call a stag girl a fifth wheel, especially Junie, because she sure as hell didn't smooth out the ride. Every time I looked over at Wynona, Junie just stuck out her tongue at me.

On the way into town, a police car blasted past us going the other way. He was at top speed, siren blaring, lights flashing.

"Whew! I thought maybe I had a busted tail light or something," I said.

Another police car whizzed by with siren and lights ablaze, and then a third. They were all headed in the opposite direction.

"Something big must be going on," Wynona said.

That dancehall was dark as a tomb. Only the bar and the dance floor had lights. We bought a pitcher and started looking for a place to sit. A couple of pairs were two-stepping up a storm to the music from the jukebox.

I'll be danged if we didn't sit down right next to Chloe Reece and some pecker-necked guy that was wearing a tie and a business suit.

"Hi, Chloe Reece," I said, tipping my cowboy hat to her. I'm glad I treated her nice. She was dressed in the kind of suit she'd wear to work and her hands were shaking like a leaf when she tried to drink her beer. She was sucking them back hard and chain smoking.

"Better slow down with that, Chloe Reece," the suited guy said.

"Earl this is Bobby. We work together."

"Nice to meet you Bobby," I said, shaking his spindly hand. He had golfer's calluses.

her. She was surprised, I guess, especially when I told her, "I was thinking maybe you'd give me a little smooch."

"Earl Ray! How much you had to drink?"

"Just a couple of beers." Like everyone knows, "a couple of beers" means at least two quarts, and therefore, it was a pretty close approximation of the correct amount of beer I'd consummated.

"Come on, Wynona. Just a little one."

"No!"

"Aw, come on. Why not?"

"You're old enough to be my daddy. Well almost. And that disgusting snuff you dip. Look. You got a juice stain on your chin."

Wynona let herself out of the pickup truck and ran up to the back door of the house. "You can try again some other time. But I wish you'd get rid of the snuff." She slipped into the house and the porch light went dark.

When I got back to the bunkhouse, I rummaged around and found a bottle of Jack that was half empty. The alcohol evaporates out of a bottle that has been opened, so I determined that the best policy was to head off disaster and finish it off.

As I neared the bottom of the Jack, the glow was under the doorway again, so I decided I better check in. Old Wynona was sitting in her overstuffed chair on that danged inner tube.

"So?" she asked.

"I'm on cloud nine. Never knew a man could feel this way."

"Earl Ray. That's the nicest thing you ever said."

"A thought keeps crossing my mind about maybe running around some with ol' Wynona."

"I ain't a gonna go be your party girl, son. You ain't got two nickels to rub together."

"Well I'm not saying it's a sure thing, but if I wanted to, I'm pretty sure you'd come around to my way of thinking. Hell, there ain't no one else but me."

"You are a born romantic."

"Looks to me like...well the clues I get from looking at you now, you're gonna die an old maid, so I don't see what it would hurt."

Old Wynona frowned and shifted her weight on the inner tube. "Marriage doesn't mean anything. It's money that matters. My daddy died broke. It looks like that's what's laid out for me, too. God. Dying broke."

"Money ain't everything."

"Hey. Dang it, you been fiddle farting around and dancing up a storm, and I got nothing to show for it. Nada."

"I done just what you said."

"Hell. You ain't done a damn thing for me. Just for you. You was gonna open me up a savings, remember? Have you done that?"

"Yes, I did. And I only got a few bucks left. That dancing don't come cheap."

"Have you ever thought of taking a girl out to supper?"

"What the hell for? Who'd fix your old man his supper?"

"Listen, a few bucks ain't enough for me. I need to see some good faith, Earl Ray, or I'm gonna lay off helping you out."

"Hey, Wynona, banks ain't all that safe. What about them desperados? Cleaned out First State, you know."

"Cleaned out. Bullshit. Hell, mostly all they got was just checks."

"Yeah?"

"And if I remember right, the bank put up a bigger reward than the money they got off with."

"Twenty-five hundred reward. Real desperados, though. Chloe Reece was a bundle of nerves."

"Like Chloe Reece needs an excuse to drink tequila. Weren't no desperados, neither. Just a bunch of kids from over to Medicine Lodge."

"Yeah? Where's their hideout? Maybe I could put in for that reward."

"Why would I tell you?"

"Hell, Wynona, I'll make it right by you. You can trust me."

"I wouldn't trust you any farther than I could throw you."

"Okay. I'll do this one on halves. I swear to God, Wynona."

Old Wynona paced the room, stilted, like she had cob up her butt. I think she was having a hard time making up her mind. "Okay. Against my better judgment, but okay. They're laid up in that old dugout down there on the back of Sonny Culpepper's place."

I could almost feel twenty-five crispy hundred dollar bills in my fingers. "Twenty-five hundred. And all I gotta do is claim it."

"Put half in my savings. You promised, now, you hear?"

CHAPTER 5

I figured it was best to go straight to the sheriff's office the next morning. I wasn't about to try to corral a bunch of desperadoes even if they were kids. That's why they give the sheriff the big money.

It wasn't but a few years ago he was just a Sayre town cop, which puts the best face on it. He was the night cop. Forney DeFore. Just hired to prowl around town making sure the kids didn't tear the place down. One night after a football game, he stopped in the city park to take a leak and stumbled into a drug deal in the process of going bad. One guy was already as dead as a carp and the other one pretty much smashed out of his brain on his own goods. Forney comprehended the one that was still alive and gathered up enough evidence to charge the guy, get him convicted and sent to "Big Mac." It's not a hamburger for chrissakes, it's the state prison down to McAlester. The arrest and conviction made him a superstar in Beckham County, so next election, he ran for sheriff.

"4-ney d-4 4 Sheriff." He had signs all over Sayre, the county seat, but he needed to carry Elk City, a town five times as big, 15 miles away. The only other community was out west in Erick, which was famous the world over for being the town where Roger Miller grew up. You remember him. "King of the Road," "Chug-a-Lug"...really hit it big back in the day.

Hell, I voted for old Forney and within a year I wished I had my vote back. They used to have a titty bar outside Elk City which had been outside Forney's jurisdiction as long as he was a town cop in Sayre. That changed when he became sheriff. He did a lot of undercover work, he claimed it took him year to build his case. He finally brought a bunch of the girls up on charges for dancing buck naked. The titty bar couldn't find replacements so that pretty much shuttered the place. The good people of Beckham County slept snug in their beds after that, secure in the knowledge that they laid their heads in one place where By God hardened criminals would think twice before committing a murder or showing their pussy.

Forney had a cramped little office in the basement of the Sayre courthouse which wasn't much bigger than what would accommodate his bulging belly.

"Yeah. Yeah, Sheriff," I told him. "They're laid up down there on the back of Sonny Culpepper's place. In that old dugout. I'm sure you've seen it."

"When did you see 'em, Early?"

"T' other day. After lunch."

"What you doin' back there on Sonny's place? That place is posted. No trespassing."

I don't have any idea why this old fartknocker was being so dad-gum inquisitive when bank robbers was on the loose. Sure, I'd been tipped off, but I didn't think I'd be helping my case to tell him about Old Wynona. I hadn't told anyone about her yet. Probably wouldn't, either. The porthole in time was nobody else's business.

"I weren't right back there. I mean. I seen 'em. Back there. Way to the back."

"Why don't you empty out your pockets on that table there, Early."

Son of a bitch. I emptied my pockets. Didn't have nothing but a few coins, tin of snuff, a billfold and a pocketknife. "I'm wanting that twenty-five hundred reward."

"Let's just see what you got there."

"You can have the snuff. I quit it. Listen, I ain't done nothing, Sheriff."

He was stirring my valuables with the end of a pencil. "Then you got nothing to be afraid of."

"Okay. I was scouting out a place to hunt turkey. Is that all right with you? Come on, Sheriff. We can go down there and catch them old desperados. Hell, I'll help out."

"Early, you're a pretty good old boy. Never in much trouble. But I still ain't buying your story. Sonny don't let no one hunt on his place. You know that."

I turned my toe into the concrete floor of the sheriff's office. "Okay, Sheriff. You got me. Hell. I was driving home drunk as hell on moonshine liquor and I had a headlight out and I had me this underage whore. We just kinda ran off down there with our contraband."

"Oh," he said. His bottom lip was sort of rolled out. "Well hell, why didn't you tell me earlier? Shit. Didn't know you had a good excuse. A damn good excuse. Hell, that makes all the sense in the world."

"You gonna be proud you believed me on this one Sheriff."

Next thing you know, we were roaring down this trail back of the Culpepper place, lights twirling and sirens blaring to beat the band. This place was pretty brushy, not like that rocky knob the Vorhees place was perched on. The Sheriff's car skidded to a stop near Culpepper's dugout.

The Sheriff and I got out and so did I. We took up a station behind his cruiser. The dugout was a half underground shanty, the roof was sodded over with buffalo grass. A late model Chevy was near the door, and smoke curled from the chimney. Those desperadoes must have had something cooking.

"There they is Sheriff. Laid up inside, just like I said."

"Yeah maybe."

"Maybe nothing. That's them."

"I'm calling for backup."

I could see my reward money slipping through my fingers, sure as hell. I could smell it evaporating. "Hell, Forney, that's gonna take hours. They'll get away and I won't get my twenty-five hundred reward."

"Just good police procedure, Early."

"To hell with that. This ain't nothing but a bunch of kids. I'll go roust 'em out myself." I was stomping toward that dugout door before the Sheriff had a chance to grab me.

"Early! Get back here. Early!"

So anyway, I strolled up to the door of that dugout liked I owned the place, grabbed the latch with one hand and pounded on the door with the other. "Hey, dammit. What the hell you kids think you're doing? You damn kids, git the hell outside here."

K-BOOM! A shotgun blasted the front door off of its hinges. I was standing there like a dumbass holding nothing but that doorknob. For all the good it was doing me, I may as well have been holding my dick. I let out a yelp. "Shit the bed!"

I ran across the clearing on a serpentine route, dragging that door. My hand wouldn't let loose of that doorknob no matter how hard I tried. Froze tight. Since shotguns were blasting behind me, throwing up bits of dirt and debris ahead of me, I didn't spend a lot of concentration on letting go of the door. Buckshot pelted the sheriff's cruiser, and just as I was diving behind it for cover, I took a load of buckshot in the ass. I began then to square up my logic about police procedures and rules of engagement. "Sheriff!" I yelled. "Call in for backup!"

I looked up and that fat ass Forney was all assholes and elbows, hooking it down the trail we rode in on, on foot. And he had his damn car keys in his pocket, it was reasonable for me to hypothecate.

"You want us, you're going to have to come in and take us, lawman." Shit.

Shit shit shit.

I psychoanalyzed the situation. I was sore-assed but not demobilized, and them being a headcount of at least three meant that I was a goner for sure if I didn't seize the offense. I run off into the brush and circled behind where I could step up on the roof of the dugout without them seeing me. I pulled up a clump of prairie grass and stuffed it down the chimney.

Next thing you know they were hollering and shooting shotguns. Smoke poured out of the door of the dugout. One after the other, three desperadoes stumbled out, choking, eyes blinded by the smoke. Lickity split, I was whacking them over the head with a two-by-four. By the time the sheriff came back, I'd found handcuffs in the cruiser and had them all hooked up together and in my custody. These guys didn't look like a bunch of schoolboys to me, they were hardened killers, covered with tattoos of skulls and dripping knife blades, and cussing like sailors.

So when we got back to town, a group of townspeople gathered around to hear my virgin of what happened, which squared pretty much with what the Sheriff told except for the part of him hooking ass out of there like a turpentined cat. Damn coward. Junie was in the crowd and she poked me in the butt which was sore as a boil. The seat of my drawers was shredded and spotted with bloodstains.

Junie thought it was funny, at least I think so. She was rolling on the ground, laughing.

One of the townsfolk that was gathering around handed me a business card. I'd seen the guy around from time to time. He was a little bitty fart and as old as dirt. The card told me his name was Raiferd Haffley and that he was an attorney at law. "I ain't guilty of nothing," I told him.

"Son, that shot up ass is worth a quarter of a million dollars of pain and suffering. You got here just in time. Oh, the pain. OH, the suffering."

I took his business card and put it in my billfold.

So the next day I was full of piss and vinegar. I didn't even scrape the cowshit off my boots before striding into the bank, but I did have on a different pair of jeans. Bob the bank manager was on hand for pictures, but I told him I wanted Chloe Reece to count out my reward money.

"Twenty-three, twenty-four, twenty-five. Yep. That's it. Sure nice doing business with you, Mr. Bird."

"I want you to take half and open up a savings for me, and put the other half in a savings for Wynona." I handed over the signature card that Old Wynona had signed. I put my address on the card so Wynona wouldn't get any mail. Not for the time being, anyway.

I pretended to two-step out of the bank, but my ass was still sore.

I drank until I couldn't hardly stand at the Paddock, and didn't have to buy a one. They were all compliments of one friend or another. So I was wasted when I got back to the bunkhouse and fell asleep in my clothes.

After midnight, I rolled over on my back and the pain in my sore ass woke me up. That door showed a glow underneath, so I pushed through to find Old Wynona. She was sitting on her inner tube as usual, but the room was spiffed up. It looked like someone had cleaned and dusted. Even the furnishings looked better, perhaps some of them were new. Still not elegant, but it was a damn sight nicer room than it had been before.

I don't think I would have recognized Old Wynona if I ran into her on the street. She was still an old lady, but she looked like maybe she had been to the beauty shop. Her hair was combed and set and she wasn't wearing that tattered old polyester thing I'd seen her wear before. I had her bank book, so I took it from my breast pocket and tossed it to her.

"I put some back for my own."

"Smart thinking for once," she said. Clack. She had a way of clicking her dental appliances when she wanted to make a point. "I been thinking. Working out a business plan. You're gonna make me a pile of loot."

"Why would I help you?" I asked, and I was as serious as a heart attack. "I got an ass full of buckshot from them desperados. You said they was kids."

"Memory plays tricks. I guess I got it confused." She pulled her legs up under herself in the chair. "Big shot bronc rider. Ha. Crying about a few little pin pricks in his butt."

"I ain't crying."

"You're gonna get a big insurance because of me." Funny how she pronounced it. "IN-shore-ince."

"Hell yeah, you're a regular damn guardian angel."

"And if it wasn't for me pushing, I still wouldn't have no savings."

"Maybe you're right." I didn't have the will to fight. I was starting to get lonesome for Wynona.

"Something's bothering you."

"I'm getting an ache for Wynona. I'm afraid I'm getting kind of sweet on that pretty thing."

"Still wanting to run around some?"

"Just tell me what I need to do."

"For starters, get them teeth fixed, and shave off that seedy mustache."

I loved my mustache. "Hell, I'm attached to this old thing."

"It looks like broomcorn."

"This is what got me thrown out of school."

"You grew a mustache in eighth grade?"

"Hell yeah." Jed Clampett again.

"Well lose it. Then get you some fancy new duds, and a new pickup truck."

"Huh?" I asked. "What for? That old pickup has plenty of good miles left. And I don't like making payments. Even if I had a job."

Old Wynona looked out a window. "Come here and look."

My mouth dropped so wide open it would have cost $100 to get me a shave. As my eyes adjusted to the dark night, I could see the corrals and outbuildings of the Vorhees place but they were better kept up than before. "Someone's been busting his ass cleaning this old place up."

"Funny what a little extra money can do."

Then that old hag patted me in a familiar way on the cheek of my ass. I was still sensitive and jumped like I did when I got shot. "I wish Wynona was as proud of me as you are."

"Hey. Just remember, we're both better off today than we was yesterday."

I did a quick survey of the room. Almost everything had been replaced except for Old Wynona's butt inner tube. "We got lots in common. We both got a sore ass."

"I always hated vegetables."

The new couch had a glossy black leatherette covering. "I sure do like that couch," I said.

"Pure naugahyde."

"Bet that set you back a bundle." I cautiously eased my tender butt down on the couch, rubbing the surface with my hand. It felt like that Corinthian leather that Ricardo Montalban had on the bucket seats of his Chrysler.

Old Wynona placed her inner tube on the couch and sidled down beside me. She was uncomfortably close for my taste. Inside my space. And then to add insult to injury, she leaned across me in a rubbing sort of intimate way.

"See what's in my pocket," she told me. I'd seen my one-eyed ex-cousin-in-law Peavine try to pull that trick plenty of times, so I was wary. She put her hand up to the area of her body where I reckon her knockers used to reside so as to hint that what she wanted me to look at was in that shirt pocket. Something sticking out looked like maybe it was a playing card. I was real careful to desist from letting my hand contact any flesh, even the flesh that was covered with the shirt. I pinched the card between my pointer finger and my middle finger and eased it out slow. It was a photograph. It was of me and a youthful Wynona, standing in a bass boat. I was holding up a big stringer of fat bass.

The Flank Strap

"Well I swan to goodness. Look at them large mouth," I said. I must have been smiling ear-to-ear, because Old Wynona was grinning back at me. That started me to thinking maybe other things had changed. I got up and went to the window to look out at the ranch again. Even though it was dark, I could see the neatly painted outbuildings and corrals.

"Got this old place looking right smart. If I get the heavy hint, you're trying to tell me that she's going to fall in love with me."

Wynona's face fell. She must have been thinking I was a real dumb ass, which point wasn't in contention. "It ain't no HER, Earl Ray, it's ME we're talking about."

I gave Old Wynona a long once over, then studied the photo. I could tell from the heat that my cheeks were bright red. Hell, her feelings weren't bruised at all. She was play acting, having fun with me, trying hard to make me embarrassed, and I decided that I could have fun with her.

"She might be a little light for the kind of work I do."

Old Wynona fired back, "Look at you. You sure as hell ain't no prize." But I could tell she enjoyed me messing with her.

CHAPTER 6

I can't figure out why I'm writing this next stuff down. I had some notes and I can't now decide just why I thought exposing myself with them would liberate me. Maybe I'm just putting off writing about some events that really make me mad. I don't know for sure. I will have to make another note to figure out later on why I jotted these notes down in my voyage of discovery.

So after throwing down to both of the Wynonas that by God I wasn't going to no dentist, I made an appointment. I sometimes bluff and bravado around, but in the long run I usually compromise. A circuit riding dentist came to town every week or so since Beckham County didn't have enough mouths to keep a full-time dentist in business. Now here's another thing that pisses me off. Every time you go to get any kind of doctoring done, you have to go through a fat, ugly lady that's sitting behind a computer monitor, that talks to you like you're four years old. She's like a gatekeeper. A guy could be bleeding to death from the mouth, but until the fat lady behind the monitor gets done with her thing, you don't have a chance of seeing a doctor.

"Can you spell your name for us?" This Queen Elizabeth sound-alike must have thought I was a second grader. "Of course I can," I said. "Do I look like an idiot?"

It was good of her not to answer. She had more forms for me to fill out than Jimmy Carter had little liver pills. I was on the verge of telling her she could fill them out herself if she needed them so damn bad.

"What's this for?" I asked.

"Hippa. It's a law."

My law-breaking days were over, so finding out that I might have to stand up tall against the law, I changed my mind about the forms. Then she came up with another condition. She wouldn't let the dentist take a look at my mouth on credit so I had to chuck over $150. Upfront. She let me in once the forms were done and the cash was on the barrelhead.

Dammit if they didn't need to run an X-ray on my mouth. I actually have some familiarity with X-rays, they run downhole X-ray tests on oilwells to find out about the rock in the pay zone and I didn't see what rocks had in common with my head. So I put up a mild protest. I just wanted a good cleaning. They wasn't in much of a mood to explain, and besides they already had my $150. The actual part of taking the pictures wasn't so bad.

For the cleaning part, I had it in my mind that maybe they had a little thing that would sandblast the crust off my teeth, but what he had was a more like a rotary grinder, only not so brittle. The doctor had one of his helpers actually doing the work which was fine by me. She was pretty and had a sunny temperance. She poked around in my mouth with a hook and that's when I first discovered that a man's body has a nerve that runs straight from the jawbone to the nuts. She'd dig at it, swab it, polish some, have me spit, and dig and polish some more. She even offered to show me how to brush my teeth. So like the ignorant dummass I am, I said "hell yeah" like Jed Clampett, because I didn't see how she was going to brush my teeth without a little more of that tender young body of hers rubbing up against me, which was an experience that was quite pleasant.

What a letdown. She just sat down and showed me using her own mouth. She added $35 to my bill for "brushing instruction" and turned me back to the fat lady behind the computer monitor. It was a tag team operation. The one that rubbed up against me applied the flank strap and the fat lady cinched it up. I forked over the extra cash.

The Flank Strap

The barber across the street didn't try to run a trap-scam on me like that daggone dentist did. He had a look on his face like a grade school hall monitor when I told him I needed to disappear the mustache. He knew I was doing it for a woman, and he knew I couldn't face shaving it off myself. I felt foolish. I felt small. I felt spineless. He knew.

The barber was like the dentist. No credit. I had to give him a twenty for the cut and shave and tip.

They had a shiny red Silverado at the truck dealership that had all the options I wanted. I hated to see that old beater go, but I had the title folded up in my pocket.

"I'm unemployed."

"Hell, it don't matter. Talk to the F-n-I guy."

"My eyes are okay. It's my ass that's sore. Maybe I can talk to the F-n-ass guy."

"F-n-I...finance and insurance."

They squired me into this little bitty room to talk to this bonehead that wouldn't have it any other way than me leaving the place with that Silverado. It had every option you could think of, some I thought were superbluous, but it was all a one-price package. He offered me a no-money-down deal with low interest and e-z payments.

"You realize I'm an unemployment statistic."

"GM. Government Motors. The government thinks it's smart to put you behind the wheel of that truck."

So it didn't take much to put me in that brand spanking new red Silverado, I had credit with Government Motors. I borrowed a tow-bar and drove away, pulling my old beater behind. I couldn't part ways with that old pickup. It had been good to me when I needed it most. My cash funds were depleted and all that did was just make me wish the dentist and the barber were as clever with money as Uncle Sam. They'd each be doing land office business if they sold on credit like the government. And I'd have more walking around money at my disposal if they weren't so pigheaded parsimonious.

It goes without saying that Wynona and Junie swarmed all over me and that red truck when I drove up to the bunkhouse. Oooh-ing and aah-ing and mashing every button on the dash. They turned on the air conditioner and in no time the cab was cold enough to hang meat. Kids, I had fun just watching them.

"You need to take us for a drive," Wynona said. She never had a thought of just where in the blue-eyed wide world I was going to get the money to keep up payments. I sure didn't.

"Why Early Bird, just look at you." It was Junie what was chiming in with the Early Bird scenario again. "Look at him, Wynona, he's lost his mustache."

"Earl Ray! Don't you look handsome. I never noticed what a well-favored smile you have," Wynona said.

I hemmed and hawed around for awhile, mostly hoping Junie would get the picture and maybe trot off. Not a chance. I was wanting to take Wynona out for a hamburger or something. I guess I could say I wanted to while my teeth were clean and my lip skinned off like a baby's butt but in truth I wanted to go while the inside of that truck still had that new car smell that they put in there for an afro-desiac. The Navy put saltpeter in the food to keep us sailors from getting sexually rustled up, and Government Motors uses that new car smell to get women's hormones stirred up. America is messed up sometimes.

I'm pretty sure that Junie knew what I was planning. She probably smelled an onion burger sizzling on the grill in my brain. Anyway, she started popping off.

"Hey, Early Bird, don't you think you ought to take a girl out for supper in that fancy new pickup truck?"

"Yeah, I really do. Wynona? What do you say? You like to...I mean you think you could get away for a little supper? You want to go?"

"Shoot yes, Earl Ray," she said. "We both do."

Quicker than Jody, Junie was in the truck. Folks say Jody was so fast, he could turn off the light and be in bed before the room was dark. That was Junie, riding spang in the middle of the seat which meant Wynona was on the outside pressing her tender little bottom against the passenger side door instead of me. Not what I had in mind at all.

We made it over to Erick on the back roads. Not that much farther than Sayre, really, and worth the all the extra jaw-jacking from Junie because we were headed to Cal's Country Cooking with one bill of fare on my mind. The restaurant was out by the highway in a sort of log cabin looking place. They made the world's best chicken fried steak.

The waitress Dottie put on a non-stop floor show. She talked a blue streak from the minute we got there. "Howdy, girls, Earl. Just seat yourself wherever you want. Earl, when you going to move into town?" She handed me three menus. "My mom-an-them got a cute little bungalow, just right for you. Over by the church. Ginny-an-them lived there for a time. Til she had the twins. That boy is a caution. Just like his daddy I told my mama I wanted to..."

From down at the cigarette smoking end of the cafe, a voice hollered out, "Hey Dottie, I need a refill."

So that thought about the twins or wherever it was going sort of trailed off with Dottie grabbing a pot of coffee as she went. We found a booth, Wynona slid in and Junie right behind her. Any thought that might have entered my mind about snuggling up to Wynona just went out the window. We hadn't really had much of a chance to look at the menu, but I was getting the chicken fry no matter how tender my teeth were.

"And the next thing you know, here come the police. And the fire department. The poor old lady was shut in that house and they hauled her out on a gurney just like what you see on the TV. You folks had a chance to figure out what you want?"

"I'm having the chicken fry," Junie said. "With plenty of gravy. And a piece of pie. You got strawberry pie? Peach?"

"We got peach, honey. How about you, Missy?"

"Bring me two bowls of chili and extra crackers," Wynona said. "Hold the beans. You bring me some hot sauce too?"

"And the chicken fry for me," I said.

"Took her straight to the hospital and what I heard was they sent in a helicopter from the City and flew her out like a sack of potatoes. And that old so-and-so she been living with. Standing there looking. Just looking. My daddy said 'Leo, you got insurance don't you?' and Leo said 'Aw hell, it's a hospital, they got to take her.' So then my cousin that's married to my other cousin..."

"Dottie!"

"...she had to run back to Amarillo to get..."

I lost track now of what she had to get in Amarillo but whatever it was it was mission critical, I'm certain.

"You can order some okra or corn or something, Wynona," I told her. "Just get it on the side."

"Nah. I don't like vegetables. Never touch 'em."

It was starting to get darker outside and it was damn pleasant just to sit there across the booth from Wynona, watching the lights from the trucks passing by, flickering in her eyes. Her smile was as pretty as one of those gals on an old Coca-cola sign.

That danged Junie was hopping around, back and forth across Wynona trying to get this jukebox thing to operate. It was on the wall in the booth. The tunes on the playlist were all classical music. Elvis. Jerry Lee Lewis. Ray Charles. Someone must have installed it in the 60s and it looked like it must have been years since it worked.

"Early Bird, give me a quarter," Junie said.

"That thing don't work, June Bug. Hell, I never seen it work."

"Quit being such a tight ass, Early Bird."

"...them boys had been out in the deer stand twelve straight hours and it didn't look like they were going to even get off a shot and then my red-headed uncle's brother heard some kind of huffing sound from off to where they left the truck. Okay, two chicken frys and one bowl of chili, extra crackers."

"And the hot sauce."

Dottie wore a pocketed apron and pulled out a bottle of that red sauce like they splosh on raw oysters down in Louisiana. "Anything else I can get you?"

"The pie," Junie said, and Dottie nodded.

"Well wouldn't you know it, these two bucks were back in some brush behind the blind and they..." As Dottie walked away and her voice trailed off, Wynona took that hot sauce and opened the top. She must have poured, oh hell, I don't know how much of that red liquid fire into her chili, but when she stopped the bowl wouldn't have held another drop.

"Good Lord, Wynona, did you get all you wanted?"

"What's the problem?"

"That stuff's hot. Your food eating habits are a little unconventional, that's all I'm saying." I was thinking about poor Old Wynona, so uncomfortable all the time, sitting sore-ass on that inner tube, which is to say, my heart was in the right place. I thought that I could make a meaningful contribution of advice which would help the old dear kiss her hemorrhoids goodbye.

"Anything else you want to say?"

"Well it ain't like it's my business but I sure as hell wouldn't want to be your asshole tomorrow."

"Early Bird," Junie said. "You're the asshole."

"Enjoy your chicken fry, June Bug," I said.

The only conversation I heard from that point on came from Dottie. The temperature in that truck stop cafe must have dropped about 25 degrees. I didn't hear another word spoken even when we got back home.

CHAPTER 7

I was pretty disappointed with that escapade of taking the girls to supper and was happy to have held some icy-cold adult beverages on reserve in the ice box of my man-cave at the bunkhouse. A game was on the TV. I can't remember even what sport it was, just that the beer tasted good, washing down the last morsels of taste on my tongue from that chicken fry.

The parts of my body below my belt buckle were beginning to talk to me about their needs, so I cogitated on maybe patching things up with Chloe Reece, pondering on what I might do to downplay the shitty way I had treated her. She was bound to think I dumped her in a cold-hearted way.

I shouldn't feel guilty but I did. I had always been up front with Chloe Reece that marriage was never going to be an option on the Earl Bird menu.

In the first place, I really didn't know how to be a good husband or God forbid a father. I didn't get a real good demonstration from my own father who wasn't what you'd call a family man. We had some times when he wasn't around. And when he was, he spent most of his evenings at the beer joint.

My one-eyed ex-cousin-in law Peavine had what seemed like a regular marriage most of the time, but his deal didn't hold any attraction for me. Peavine's wife had a habit of passing bad checks, so every once in awhile, she had to spend a few months in a corrections facility. It didn't bother Peavine. He took the position that marriage vows weren't binding during those times when one spouse was incarcerated.

In the second place, marriage seemed to me like a piss poor preposition. Like having to ante in the Indian craps game. A sucker bet. A guy has to be careful as hell to make sure a girl doesn't get in a family way even when they aren't married. Plenty of the guys I knew were paying child support to women they didn't really know for children they never got to see. Every spare nickel. So it's real easy for a careless dad to wind up living in his mother's basement.

Kids need a dad and it strikes me as a healthy idea for society to come up with a way for single moms to have a pool of prospects that have a few dollars to spend. Divorced men aren't much better than a pack of broke-dick dogs.

It only gets worse once a guy is married. She can get herself in a family way in the same fashion as a single woman, but once the ink dries on that old marriage license, a guy is on the hook for all her bills too, not just the kid's. A married woman has half the money and all the hoohah. And on top of that, if a fellow gets a good job, he might have to choke up alimony if they decide to split up. Like I said, it's a sucker bet. It's like playing craps and betting you'll make your point the hard way. You'd have to be drunk.

And thirdly, single women don't even seem to guard the prize. I heard tell from the old timers that women were picky about who they laid under in the good old days. That was then. This is now. So why buy a cow when milk's so cheap?

I drifted off to sleep while pondering over such matters.

When I woke up it was pitch black outside. The TV was making this static, scratchy sound and the screen was specks of white and black and gray jumping every which way.

And the greenish light was glowing again under that doorway. I pushed through to find Old Wynona sitting on the rubber inner tube on one end of that black fake leather couch. Her face was drawn and I noticed she winced every time she shifted her weight.

"I tried my best to get you lay off the hot sauce and jalapenos," I told her.

"Why don't I just put you in charge of music around here. When I need advice from you, I'll whistle." She shifted her weight from one bulky cheek to the other.

"It's not advice. I'm just observing the obvious."

"I plan to cut back. Laying off the hot foods is actually pretty high on my agenda," she said. "But I'm devoting every waking moment to getting my finances squared away. What about you? Far as I can see, you spent the last couple of months just fiddle-fucking and farting around."

She was right. I had no defense. It was like I'd just been spinning the bit in the ground. "Yeah. I can't seem to get anything going."

"I think you'll like the solution I worked out."

"The stock market. You're gonna pick me some stocks. That's it, right? I knew it."

"You must think I'm pretty dumb not to have thought that idea up already."

"Jot some names down and I can buy a few shares and I'll be in tall cotton in no time."

"Listen redneck, there ain't no 'I' in 'team.' This is something 'we' are going to do. For us. And no, it ain't stocks. Where do you think I can get stock prices from fifty years ago?"

"I don't see how a guy could go wrong with Apple."

"Penny ante."

"Google?"

"Out of business."

"Wal-Mart?"

"Tits up. Nope."

I had stood in line for hours at Wal-Mart, trying to get them to take my money, so finding out that some day they would shutter the place, well, no one should be surprised.

"We're going in the oil business," Old Wynona said.

"That takes capital, Wynona. Something I'm short on the supply of."

"Get with that lawyer of yours...old whatchamadoodle."

"Haffley? Raifferd Haffley?"

"Yeah. He'll help you get the paperwork set up. I'm gonna turn you into a leasehound. I want you to get with old Groendyke. Know him?"

Groendyke was a farmer, just a couple of miles over. I nodded.

"Take a fifth of whiskey. Have a drink or two. Get a lease on his minerals."

"I can barely afford the whiskey. Where in the hell you think I'm gonna get the money for the lease?"

"You give him a draft. It's like a check, only he can't cash it."

"My one-eyed ex-cousin-in-law Peavine's wife did ninety days for that."

"This is all on the up and up. He can't cash the draft for thirty days. And that gives you thirty days to get to the city and peddle the lease off to some high roller." Old Wynona clicked her teeth. "Ought to be able to turn a quick twenty grand."

A yellow sticky note on his shingle told me Haffley was in court which they had placed conveniently just across the street. Damned if the little old fart wasn't front and center, pounding on the pulpit when I popped into the first courtroom.

"It's not right, Your Honor. If I can't give a client the best representation possible, then I ought to be permitted to withdraw from the case. We outlawed slavery in this country a hundred and fifty years ago."

The Flank Strap

The judge leaned forward and looked Haffley's client square in the eye. "Stand up, Miss Higgins. What do you have to say about that? Do you want him to stay on as your lawyer?"

When she took to her feet, I realized that Haffley's client was one of those strippers that Forney DeFore had arrested over at the titty bar in Elk City. She looked pretty normal with her clothes on, but I knew she was a stripper. I had witnessed her performances on numerous occasions.

"Your Honor, the only reason he wants to fire me is because I quit sleeping with him."

Well what few folks was in the gallery bust out laughing at that, but the judge was red as a beet. He slammed his hammer down again and again like he was killing rats. "If I hear another outburst like that, I'll clear the courtroom."

But no one hushed up any at all until Haffley started yelling and waving his arms. "Your Honor, I'm 83 years old. I don't know whether to deny that allegation or go out in the hall and brag about it."

Long and short, Haffley got dismissed off the defense of the stripper. He was looking back at me, wearing one of those bashful grins, like a possum caught eating shit. I carried his satchel over to his office for him. I explained what I needed.

So with a file folder full of documents Haffley worked up for me, I set off to find old Groendyke. I stopped by the Dollar General to get some reading glasses. I noticed that I had some difficulty focusing on the documents at Haffley's office.

Groendyke was an old German farmer that scratched out a living on a place his grandpa homesteaded. I think he only gave $8 for a haircut. $2 a side. His place was a couple of miles west of the Vorhees place. I showed up after lunch. I figured it was best to drop by unannounced. If he was going to tell me to get gefickt he'd have to do it man to man.

Groendyke's wife had hoisted an old wicker basket to her hip and was carrying it out of the house. It was full of wet clothes. I offered and she let me carry them to a sagging clothesline for her. Groendyke came out next, wiping his hands on the bib of his overalls. He returned my "howdy" and walked toward my truck. I think he wanted to give it the once over.

"Whoo-eee. She's a pretty rig you got there, Earl."

I spread out my paperwork on the fender and put on my new glasses. "I got a proposition for you, Groendyke," I said.

He put on his readers, too, and started looking over the first document I handed him. Over his shoulder, near the house, his woman finished hanging the clothes. The line drooped low and threatened to let the clean clothes touch the ground but after she hung the last shirt, she propped the line up with a long pole to keep the laundry out of the dirt. Groendyke still had his nose buried in the paperwork as the old woman walked stiff-legged back toward the house. She looked plum tuckered out. She pushed on her back with one hand the way my uncle did when he complained of his sciatica. When she got to the house, she turned on a water spigot and filled a tub and wringer washing machine with water from a garden hose.

"How much an acre? I want four hundred."

"Well, Groendyke, that's a lot of money but I think it's fair." I wrote "$400" into a blank space on the lease document. "So while you're signing...here...Mrs. Groendyke? Could you help us?"

As Groendyke signed, his woman hobbled over to the pickup. She signed beside her husband's signature.

"Here's your copy. And here's your draft. Sixty-four thousand dollars."

"Draft? You never said nothing about a draft."

"Why sure. That's the way this here business is done. The lawyer typed this stuff up for me, so I know it's on the square."

"I want my money."

"You'll get your money. Sixty-four thousand," I lied, sort of. I didn't have sixty-four thousand, and if I wasn't able to flip the lease, Groendyke didn't either. "Sixty-four thousand and a three-sixteenths royalty when this old honeyhole comes gushing in."

Groendyke looked around his place. Scattered at random around the barns, he had parked several pieces of tired old worn out farm equipment. A broken down tractor, a moldboard plow here, and old spring tooth harrow there. All grown up to weeds. His equipment looked like scrap iron. His house hadn't seen a drop of paint in ages. I might have seen a tear when he looked at his wife wrestling wet clothes through a wringer. He wiped at the corner of his eye with a handkerchief.

"I sure been hankering for one of them air conditioned tractors," Groendyke said.

"Just take that draft to the bank and it's good in thirty days. If it ain't, you call me."

He folded the draft and stuck it in a pocket in the bib of his overalls. "If it ain't, I'll be looking for you all right."

I didn't waste any time getting to the City. I made a stop at a western store to outfit myself right. The exploration folks in these oil companies have a certain inspection about what a leasehound was supposed to look like and I wanted to make sure I blended in. I bought a new Stetson hat, a camelhair jacket, and a yellow silk shirt. And a 10 carat fake nugget necklace that would probably turn black, but not before I put on my dog and pony show. My ragged blue jeans and scuffed up cowboy boots provided the right contrast.

The first stop I made was to Texola Energy. A leggy secretary ushered me into a conference room on the top floor of a high rise. Ceiling-high windows let the occupants look out over the dusty, sprawling metropolis.

A bearded guy in a plaid shirt and heavy-rimmed glasses walked in first. No doubt a geologist. He had several rolled maps under his arm and didn't offer to shake hands. He unrolled a map on the big table and started trying to locate the Groendyke property. We were joined by a guy who never took his eyes off of his own shoes. I pegged him as an engineer. Together the geologist and engineer pored over the map.

"You fellers go ahead and kick this old prospect around if you want. Hell, don't make any difference to me. No hurry."

"Well, I don't know, eh," the geologist said. "The trend there might just run oat to the south." A Canadian.

"Of course if it doesn't..." the engineer said.

"Then there's always a chance of a fault, eh. Lot of faulting in this township. Or an anticline. We need to see some more science on this, eh," the geologist said.

"Yeah. The geologist I got working on this. Well, he just won't commit neither," I told them. "That's my cross to bear, I guess, it's what I get for hiring the most conservative geologist in the state of Oklahoma." From what I'd seen in the past, everyone with a lease to peddle was required to claim he hired the most conservative geologist in the state. So this was just noise. They didn't believe it, but they would think I was an amateur if I didn't at least claim it for fact. Which it wasn't.

"If you got geology on this, I want to see it," the geologist said. He straightened his glasses and tugged at his short beard. That was his tell. He wanted the lease. He was hooked. I just needed to reel him in.

"Hell yeah. You'd be crazy not to. Maybe I can get it back from Matthews."

"You got Matthews—Mike Matthews—looking at this?"

I didn't want to outright lie. "You ain't the only oil company in town, you know."

The geologist and engineer put their heads together for a brief private conversation. The geologist was tucking that plaid shirt under his belt. He was nervous as a cut cat.

"What's your sign?" the geologist asked me.

The Flank Strap

"Huh?"

"Your sign. Your horoscope. What's your birthday?"

"September. September 9."

"Virgo! I knew it." The geologist nodded approval to the engineer.

"What you wanting for this?" the engineer asked.

"I'm wanting seven hundred an acre and a sixteenth override."

"Six hundred and a thirty-second and it's a deal."

"Okay. You bring this well in and us guys will be doing a lot of business up home there."

"Yeah. Bring us some more leases out there," the engineer said. "We like this play and never had any luck getting prospects. Damn Germans."

The conference room had a bar and refrigerator, so I just acted like I owned the place. I poked around and found a bottle of Jack. "Water? Coke? Seven-up? Name your poison, boys." I reached into a bin full of ice cubes and tossed some into three tumblers.

The engineer said, "I hope your hands are clean."

"Well there ain't been nothing on my hand but my pecker, and there ain't been nothing on my pecker but my hand."

The Jack went down smooth as buttermilk, which is generally the case when someone else buys the bottle.

The deal went down just like the Jack. Smooth. Texola Energy inspected Groendyke's title and didn't find any glitches, so they cut me a big fat check. I turned $32,000 quick cash for myself on top of what it took to cover Groendyke's draft and also earned myself a sweetheart override. I'd get one-thirty-second of the oil and gas that the lease produced, when and if it did, which would be a nice kicker. The profit was in my pocket. That was the main thing. Hell, it didn't even make a difference if the oil company ever drilled a well. I had mine, and the oil company wanted me to bring them more deals. So I was cock of the walk.

CHAPTER 8

I couldn't get that check to the bank fast enough. $96,000 is a lot of money. I put $16,000 in Wynona's account and $80,000 in mine. After Groendyke's draft cleared, that left $16,000 for me. I waited for Chloe Reece to help me get the money in the right places. She was helping another customer, but so far, she'd been good luck for me and I didn't have anything urgent that would make me want to break in another cashier to my way of doing business.

I had never heard things moving as fast as what they did but in a couple of months, Prometheus Drilling, my old outfit, had a rig on the lease making hole. The noise was deafening. I'd almost forgotten how much I loved drilling. Pushed up piles of sagebrush and mesquite formed a perimeter around the drilling site.

I met Texola's Canadian geologist and engineer over there at Groendyke's well site one day to kick clods and taste the drilling mud. We nodded heads and had to shout at one another to talk over the screaming engines and generators. Out beside the road, I saw Wynona, Junie, and a group of farmers standing beside a concession stand that some enterprising guy had set up net the drilling site. They were all scarfing down ice cream cones, snow cones, popcorn, and cotton candy. Rubes. So naive, they all expected the well to come in a gusher, darkening the sky, which I have to admit was an idea they got from me. I had really packed them full of shit.

I kept myself busy as a one-legged man in an ass kicking contest, busting my hump to get some more leases to flip.

Westerfield was pissed off at me all over again. He had this twisted notion that the only way Good Fortune could ever land on another man's porch was if Westerfield got screwed out of something that was his. In his feeble brain, Groendyke's well was going to drain some pool of black gold that was percolating under his farm. Bullshit. That just ain't the way it works. Crazy old fart wanted me to lease his minerals, too, which was a non-starter. They were tied up for a few more months by the lease I'd been drilling when the well blew out.

Chloe Reece wouldn't return my calls, so I asked Wynona to go dancing again. She was still maintaining an arm's length, and yeah, we had to take Junie with us. Wynona ordered some nachos with jalapenos, and some jalapenos on the side. Then she doused the whole mess with hot sauce. I think she was wanting to prove something to me.

At the dance hall, we ran into a lady that I recognized from somewhere. She was at the next table. I couldn't place her, she was probably eight or ten years older than me, but she had a face that was buried in a wrinkle of my memory. One of her girlfriends had just graduated from an income tax class and they came to the dance hall to party. They all called her Roxie, a name that didn't give me a clue. She kept sneaking looks at me and smiling, so I was pretty sure she knew who I was. My face had been in the paper for nabbing the desperadoes. She and her friends all had happy feet.

After a line dance, we were all laughing and when she grabbed on to me and I sort of swung her around. The band struck up one of those old Righteous Brothers tunes and next thing you know she had herself pasted onto me like saran wrap and I didn't mind at all. Roxie was wearing a blouse that was struggling to justify its existence—she had a whole chest full of tits and they were threatening to make their escape. She was the only one in her bunch that knew the schottische, so when the band struck one of them up next, she said "One more dance, Earl Ray."

I had no defense. She called me "Earl Ray." She could have walked off with my billfold right in that moment and I wouldn't have been able to kick up a fuss. I couldn't figure out where she knew me from. "You know me from somewhere," I told her. "Do I know you?"

She gave me a twisted smile. "Can't you come up with a line that's a little bit more original than that?" I could tell she meant to stay mum. That's another great mystery. When a guy wants to know something, a woman clams up. And when he wants to watch a ball game, she won't shut up. I looked over to our table and could see that Wynona was getting over-served pretty quick, so I decided to put my investigation into Roxie's background on hold.

If Wynona had a problem of me dancing with other women, it wasn't my fault. The dance hall had a definite gender imbalance that night. It was ten women for each man, so I had extra obligations. The women were counting on me.

When I sat for a spell to wet my whistle, Wynona seemed to think I wasn't paying enough attention to her. She kept rolling her eyes like everything I said was ignorant, laughed at everything Junie said, and turned away when I tried to talk to her. So when I'd just about had my fill of that old shit, I asked her to step outside a minute. "We could both use some fresh air."

Well that's when I decided I would tell her that I'd put some money back for her. When I think back, I have no idea why I thought that it would improve things between us, her being half drunk and all. I should have planned it better. But I didn't.

"I'm working on a business plan," I told her. I don't know what she thought, whether she thought I was just hiding money from my creditors or trying to fiddle the unemployment people who were still sending me a weekly check. She seemed confused, she smiled, and she blushed. Even in the dark, I could see that.

The next thing that come about didn't happen under my nose so I have to rely on someone's virgin of what went down. And who it was that told me was Roxie, the gal with the chest full of tits that I couldn't remember. She was the one that told me. How she came to know is that all the women went to the head at the same time. They do that for a reason I don't understand. Now if it was me, I'd rather use the facilities all by myself and hell, back when I was drilling wells, one of my favorite gags was to pretend to scold the floor hands when they went to the porta-pot. "Just one at a time in there, you hear me?"

So my suppository is that when they all go off like that, it's not to take a piss. Anyways, Roxie told me that Wynona told me out on giving her some money and that Junie took it up and blew it all out of correspondence. She told me Wynona said, "Why Earl Ray, I just don't see how you could possibly be interested in little old me." But the topper, or so says Roxie, Wynona said that I said "You're my everything, Wynona. My lonesome old heart aches when you ain't with me. Hell, I'd die for you."

And then this gaggle of geese made a collective swooning sound, according to my snitch Roxie. I promise that I never said what Roxie said Wynona said I said.

Then Junie tells them all, "He's stashed away a bundle for Wynona already. I bet it's half a million. The old pervert." That would have been a sight to see. Must have been a stereophrenic intellectual pretzel contortion for Junie to say something nice about me without saying something nice about me. She would never polish my apple.

So anyway, when they all came back, Wynona told me she wanted to show all the girls my new truck. "Why sure," I said.

"It's locked up," she said.

So while I dug my keys out of my pocket, she wrote something on a bar napkin and pressed it in my hand. I didn't bring my readers, so the best I could do was tuck the message away in my shirt pocket.

The girls left the joint in a covey, and a few minutes later, when they came back, Wynona and Junie weren't with them.

"Did you run them off?" I asked.

"I guess we did," Roxie said. "They jumped in the truck and roared out of that parking lot like scared jackrabbits."

If they wanted to take the truck for a spin, I didn't have a big problem. So I asked the guest of honor for a dance, Dora Ruth, the one that wanted to be an income tax man lady. Roxie had bedroom eyes. Dora Ruth had library eyes. The band was on break and the jukebox was playing a funky Jimmy Buffet song, "Carnival World."

> *But talk is cheap*
> *It takes money to buy your freedom*
> *And the tax man's knocking at your door.*

"Earl, have you thought about what that money is going to do to your income taxes?" Because of Jimmy Buffet, that's just exactly what I had been thinking about and all of a sudden, I wasn't none too happy.

So when the dance was over, I ordered another pitcher of beer. I stewed about taxes until that was gone, thinking all the time that Wynona and Junie were just taking the truck for a joy ride. After about an hour, I pulled that bar napkin out of my pocket and asked Roxie to tell me what it said. Hell, she was too drunk to read it, so she gave it to Dora Ruth.

"We'll see you back at the ranch. We need to start seeing others."

So there it was. Wynona shot me the finger right there in front of about eight drama queens and one future tax man lady that I hardly knew. Some of them commenced to bawling about love gone wrong and some was falling on the floor laughing. I was choking back the desire to upchuck while each of them laid in plans to tell everyone in town about me getting jilted by Wynona after giving her a bundle of cash, which Wynona probably figured was a measley $1,000 or so, and Junie was trying make out to be a half a million, all the while doing her best to make a half a million sound like chump change and make me out to be a cheapskate pervert.

So before you know it, the band was calling last round, telling us "you don't have to go home, but you can't stay here." One by one, Roxie's pals said their adieus, but Roxie was plastered.

"You ain't fit to drive." I said the obvious.

"Take me home," she said, I think. At least, she didn't pull back any when I helped her get to her feet. She was mumbling something that sounded like an address but then started sounding like "metabolize." She slurred her words like she had a mouthful of peanut butter. She turned into my arms and put my right hand on her breast. I mention that it was my right hand because I have always found my right hand to be much luckier than my left.

I mashed the button on her key fob and lights flashed. It was a titty-pink Cadillac, not brand new, but pretty nice anyway. It was difficult to drive, as she was hanging all over me.

In my defense, what with all that getting fired and being broke and getting myself up and around and starting my own business and squiring Wynona around, I had been neglecting my bodily needs and the soft touch of a woman seemed awful nice to me right then. That was especially so since Wynona had just ripped my heart out of my chest and thrown it down on the ground and used her heel to grind it into the beer-soaked sawdust on the floor of that dance hall right there in front of the biggest bunch of drama queens in Beckham County.

So anyway, to be a good citizen and friend, I agreed to drive Roxie home. I probably wouldn't meet all the technical requirements to be a designated driver because I'd had a few beers myself. It was difficult to get a fix on what town she lived in, let alone what her address was. And if I'm to be criticized for having moved my right hand onto Roxie's snatch, I want to say in my defense that it seemed to me like a less dangerous position for my limbs to be in while trying to operate a powerful motor vehicle. Also, she seemed to like it, and besides, if there's any blame to be laid, I think that ought to be offset some because I was only doing it at that moment in time because my body required it of me.

About a half a block ahead, this barrier came down across the road. Lights were flashing at me from swinging arms. A train was going to cross ahead of us. It wasn't at the crossing yet, and I guess I probably could have driven around the crossbar. Even though the roads were empty, pulling off a slalom trick like that one-handed isn't smart. So I eased the titty-pink Cadillac up to the barrier and stopped. It was a slow freight train. Even in my slightly impaired state, I could read all the graffiti on the cars as they passed.

Then, ker-WHAM. My head bounced off of the steering wheel. "What the hell?" I yelled. Another vehicle was busily bashing into us from behind. I looked around just in time to see lights back off and then dart forward again. Ker-WHAM. That titty-pink Cadillac slammed through the wooden crossbar. I slammed my foot to the floor as hard as I could, but ker-WHAM, we were hit again. The nose of the titty-pink Cadillac hit the train and the air bag blew up in my face.

Of course, Roxie was bellowing like a cow that stepped on its tit and I was pumping the brake and I took my hand off of her snatch to try to get the titty-pink Cadillac's transmission into reverse gear with my face full of airbag. I couldn't see nothing, the air bag blocked my sight of anything ahead. I got it into what seemed like it had to be reverse and slammed on the accelerator. Ker-WHAM. I ran into whatever was behind. Ker-WHAM. It backed off and slammed me into the train again.

It seemed like it took forever but finally the train was gone. We must have been pushed into the train thirty times, and then of course I backed into whatever it was bashing us from the rear another 30 times. I heard squealing tires behind me and before I could untangle myself from the air bag and drag myself out of the titty-pink Cadillac, whoever it was behind me was gone.

"What happened?" Roxie was still inside the titty-pink Cadillac, which was far enough away from the tracks that it wouldn't get hit by the next train. She was unharmed but the titty-pink Cadillac wasn't going nowhere. Roxie proved the rule that it's almost impossible to get hurt when you're drunk. It seems like that's because a drunk rolls with the punches. It's not worth trying to find out for sure.

The railroad crossing was dark now. I needed to assess my situation.

The cops would sure as hell get a report from the train that they'd hit something. They'd be rolling to the scene soon. They'd want to take me captive for driving drunk. If I hit the trail, they'd arrest Roxie, charge her for driving drunk when she was innocent of the charge. I didn't like that option.

I reached into the titty-pink Cadillac and pulled the keys out of the ignition. I threw the key fob as far as I could. It landed in a thicket of Johnson grass in the bar ditch. Good. The key was unlikely to ever be found.

That's the best solution I could come up with on short notice while impaired. I left the scene on foot, headed across country in the general direction of the Vorhees place.

First, I figured that Roxie was better off the way I handled it. The cops couldn't charge her with driving drunk because she was just a passenger in the titty-pink Cadillac and she didn't have a key. She was passed out so they weren't even able to charge her with walking drunk. Even drunk I knew the titty-pink Cadillac was a total loss. An insurance company would have screwed her like a tethered goat if they knew some asshole had been driving it drunk. So she was better off with me out of the picture.

If anyone was going to find out who pushed that titty-pink Cadillac into the side of a moving train, it would have to be me. Even though the back end of the titty-pink Cadillac was bashed in, the cops would never suspect anything or try to start an investigation.

I trudged ten miles through cactus, sagebrush, and mesquite to get back to the bunkhouse. It gave me some time to think which I hadn't done for months. Halfway back to the bunkhouse, I was pondering over the how, why, and wherefore of me being in the position of getting a titty-pink Cadillac smashed like a beer can while I had my hand on the snatch of its owner that could say "metabolize" but not her name. As I neared the bunkhouse, my mind turned to churning over about how I was going to owe a big bill of income tax on the money I put aside for Wynona.

Sunrise couldn't have been too far away when I stumbled into bed. My head was splitting with a headache from the beers and banging against the steering wheel after getting rear-ended in the titty-pink Cadillac, and stumbling like a fool over ten miles of mesquite, sagebrush and cactus. But that glowing line of light was showing out underneath the door, so I got up and pushed my way in. I had plenty to get off my chest.

"I got a bone to pick with you, Wynona. We never talked about income taxes."

"Everybody has to pay taxes, Earl Ray."

"An income tax man lady says I got a tax problem."

"What the hell does she know about it?"

"She's going to take up doing income tax refunds. She says they're charging me a tax on my money and yours both. Jeezy wheezy, all we done was just plow up a snake."

"Somebody's gotta pay it."

"If I gotta pay mine and yours both, there ain't nothing left over for me. That ain't fair."

"You have a plan?"

"Hell yeah. I'm quitting. Flat giving her up. This money sure as hell ain't worth getting killed over which by the way someone tried to kill me and this gal Roxie this very night."

"Lucky that didn't happen. You'd have to find yourself another brilliant tax man lady to get these brilliant insights. Hell, she's just trying to scare you so you'll hire her."

Wynona clattered her false teeth. "You think this Roxie person would be interested in you if you didn't have no big shot oil deals? If you was a floor hand or bussing tables at a truck stop?"

I didn't have an answer for that.

"You think she'd be interested in you without that brand new red pickup truck? Or if you still had that seedy mustache or yellow teeth?"

I walked over to the window.

"Look. You just put a third in my account and keep the rest for yourself from now on."

"I'll run that by the tax man lady," I said.

"I seem to remember Roxie. She's kinda broad in the beam. Don't you think?"

"I never noticed." Actually, I was a little surprised that Old Wynona knew who Roxie was.

"Yeahm, I do remember her. Has a big lard ass."

"She's pretty as a picture."

"Wears them old pushy-up brassieres."

"And she's plenty damn smart, too."

"Ruined her brain with all that tequila. Now listen up. I got another prospect for you."

I leaned on the windowsill. I was tired and my brain was spinning. I looked outside and in the early rays of daylight, I saw a substantial brick house standing in the place where the old Vorhees shack had been. Beyond it, the outbuildings looked better than I'd ever seen them.

"I been thinking maybe this relationship me and you have needs to be more business-like. More professional."

"Get over there and get a lease on the old Westerfield place." I could tell by the edge on her voice that she was miffed.

"Westerfield's? It's under lease."

"Get a top lease. It kicks in when the old lease expires. "

"Junie will queer that for sure."

"Give it a try. Just try."

"Yeah. I'll think on it."

CHAPTER 9

Yeah. So while this Groendyke well was being drilled, I started having more run ins with Old Westerfield. I think he thought I'd made a nasty crack about Junie and he still had a bug up his butt about the #1-10 blowing out. His big mouth was making my new business venture difficult. He was telling all over that I was cold drafting, which I was, but he made it sound like an unethical business practice when the true facts are that everyone does it. I put off going to see him. I was sick of the old bastard.

I finally got Chloe Reece on the phone and we decided to see one another the next Saturday afternoon. Her boss Bob wanted her to get a physical inspection on a herd of cattle on a ranch north of town. I stopped to fill the gas tanks on the pickup and Old Westerfield came out of the store munching on a candy bar. "You!" he hollered and starting running toward me.

I should have stood my ground right there and duked it out with the old fart. But he was one of those rawboned old scoundrels and I didn't see a good place to get a submission hold on him. Plus, I wasn't sure he didn't have a gun. So I kind of ran around to the other side of the truck. He came right after me. So after a couple of laps, I headed out for downtown. I was sure I could either outrun him or shake him off of my trail.

I don't know if you ever tried to run in cowboy boots but it's a hell of a lot harder than it looks like in the movies. The collar around the ankle jams up and you got no flex and no mobility. I was running like in mud. I thought about sitting down long enough to pull them off, but Westerfield was gaining on me and I didn't want to take his full assault with my ass on the ground. So I kept running.

Pretty soon, I was running down a sidewalk in downtown Sayre. I saw an alleyway and I darted in. I found a stair leading up the side of a building. I was at the top in no time, taking two steps at a time. Westerfield was at the bottom and still charging like a bull elephant. A door at the top wouldn't give, so I jumped a rail and landed on the roof of another building. I ran across a flat roof and found a place I could jump into the bed of a parked pickup truck. Then I was on the street again. BAM. Behind me, I heard Westerfield land in the bed of the truck. Looking back, all I saw was his blood-shot eyeballs and a blur of legs. I couldn't shake the son-of-a-bitch.

Katty-cornered across the intersection, I saw the doors of the Baptist Church standing open wide, so I cut a bee-line in that direction. Up the stairs and into the vestibule. KA-LUMP KA-LUMP. Westerfield was still breathing down my neck, clomping after me, both of us in slow motion, him in his old hob-nailed brogans and me in my cowboy boots.

I shot into the sanctuary and it was chock full of folks all gussied up. Must have been a wedding. I had to scamper around the bride and her daddy to get down the aisle, hurdled over a rail covered with flowers, and clambered into a baptistery behind the pulpit. Thank goodness, the dip chute was as dry as a chip. I was out of the tub fast as I could and blasted through a back door to the church and into another alley.

Half a block away, I saw a grain elevator. Surely I could shake the old fart in there. As I ran, I gulped for air like a landed carp. Stitches ripped at my ribs. My lungs ached. Still I ran. I followed an incline into a lean to that covered the receiving pits of the elevator. I found the man-lift and stepped on. The tread was no bigger than a business envelope, but the mechanism lifted me up and away. I was gliding up a narrow tunnel and into the top of the elevator.

Up top, the elevator was crowded with bins and conveyors. Dust a foot thick covered every ledge and rail. My allergies attacked me with a vengeance. I coughed and sneezed and my eyes filled with tears. I looked below and could see that Westerfield was on the man-lift and headed up. He would arrive up top soon. Nothing good was going to come out of me trying to share that cramped space with him, especially with him in a foul mood and me having a coughing fit. I crawled higher, up and into the dumping bin. And that's where I found the opening to a chute. I dove in, headfirst.

Not a beam of sunlight entered the chute, I spiraled down fast. In a few moments I saw the end of the tunnel. I shot out like bushels of grain and into a boxcar filled with grain.

"You bastard...you better...you treat my Junie like a lady. You hear me?" I heard that echoing out from the mouth of the chute, the voice heaving for breath. Only thing I could figure is that Westerfield wouldn't fit in the chute. Otherwise, he'd be on top of me half covered in grain.

I was wet with sweat and the dust from the top of the elevator had me covered head to toe. The wheat in the boxcar was filthy, too, the air so choked with dust I couldn't see the other end of the boxcar. Choking for every breath, I crawled out the narrow slit that gave the grain chute access to the innards of that boxcar.

When I made it back to the truck stop and Chloe Reece, she told me I was so filthy I looked like a tarbaby. She always did have a good sense of humor.

I guess he had good cause to be angry with me about Junie.

My chilly bond with his daughter Junie seemed to get worse every stinking day. One night when the three of us was headed over to the dance hall, can't remember just exactly when it was, but it was wintertime and colder than a well digger's ass in the Klondike. My truck had one of those long cabs and Junie was in the back seat. I stopped at a Git-N-Go to pick up my one-eyed ex-cousin-in-law Peavine. His wife was back in stir so he was temporarily single. I thought maybe Junie would like some company.

"What in the hell you think you're doing stopping here, Early Bird?"

"Well I thought maybe we could make up a foursome." Peavine came quick-stepping it out of the store, zipping up a pillowy down-filled coat, chawing on a plug of beef jerky. Like I said, it was cold. "Scoot over, make room for Peavine, June Bug."

"I ain't gonna budge. Not one damn inch. Dammit Early Bird, he's a married man. I ain't going out with a married man."

Peavine danced around to the passenger side. The truck didn't have a separate door for the jump seat, so Wynona opened her door for Peavine and pulled the seat forward.

So Peavine stepped up on the running board and tried to squeeze in behind Wynona. He's a pretty big boy, and he was wearing this big heavy down-filled coat, so it was going to take some squeezing to get his fat ass in. What seemed to work best was for him to go in ass first. You should have heard Junie squawk.

"Get your stinking ass out of my face, damn you. Earl! Wynona!"

"I'm stuck," Peavine yelled, and damned if he wasn't. He was yelling like a steer in a squeeze chute. So was Junie. I don't know which one had it worse. Probably Junie. Peavine had been stuck in tight places before, but as far as I know, this was the first time Junie ever had a fat man's ass rubbed in her face. She finally came to her senses and slud over to the driver's side like I'd asked her to. Peavine was still jammed in. He couldn't shit or get off the pot neither.

Damn it was cold, but oilfield hands pride themselves in coming up with practical solutions to difficult problems. I got out of the truck and went around to reconnoiter.

Looked to me like all Peavine needed was a good push. "Exhale you big tub of guts," I told him. "I'm gonna shove you right on through." So I reached in and found some hand grips that seemed solid. I pushed with my legs and pulled with my arms, and Peavine fired through that slot like he'd been shot out of a gun.

Trouble was that the firm grip I found was his back pockets. When Peavine squirted through the breach, his drawers stayed put. He fell back on Junie bare ass naked from the waist to the knees. I know now what is meant by the phrase, "the past is prologue." I only thought the squalling was bad before. Junie yelled out like a banshee. It didn't last long, because the next event of importance is that she sunk every tooth in her head into Peavine's hairy gooseflesh.

He let out a scream and jumped across inside the cab to the passenger side, plopping his bare ass down on the icy-cold chrome metal seat buckle. I thought he was going up and over the front seat.

The long and the short of that was that Peavine finally managed to propel himself back through the breach. He hit the ground like a ton of bricks, his moon shining like a beacon in the bitter cold night for anyone twisted enough to want to look at it.

No one wanted to go dancing after that. On my drive back to the ranch, I wished I could trade places with Peavine's wife for a few days.

I went by the store the next day. I checked with the clerk to see if maybe if a surveillance camera recorded the event. By that time the video had looped over itself and the episode was lost to prosperity. Dang.

CHAPTER 10

During the time I was dodging Old Westerfield, the well over on Groendyke's place was nearing total depth. When they get as deep as the geologists and engineers say it ought to go, they stop drilling and log the hole. Then they drop measuring devices on a wireline into the bottom of the hole and then pull it out real slow. Some of the tools fire off electricity into the rocks. Some of them shoot X-rays. The idea is to find out whether they found hydrocarbons or not, and also gather up other information, like how porous the rocks are, which helps them figure out how to produce the well.

Those guys that run those tests are real science guys. The device on the end of that wireline will stretch the line when it's dropped a couple of miles down a hole in the mantle of the earth. So when they make the charts, they even jigger their drawings to account for the stretch in the wireline.

The log showed a pretty good blip in the zones they drilled to. That was the scuttlebutt anyway. The Groendyke well was a tight hole. No one was talking. Keeping all their cards close to their vest. That's a good sign usually, meaning the company wants to get some more leases bought up while keeping it all hush-hush about how good the well was they completed.

The drilling contractor ran some casing, cemented it in place, and started the process of getting moved off the location and onto another. Some other company would get hired to complete the well. All the things it takes to make the well produce get handled by a smaller, less expensive rig. And they do it all for little old me. Well, not really ALL for me. I had a ⅟₃₂ interest in whatever the well produced and it didn't make any difference how much it cost to drill or put in production or operate later. I had an override, which means I had a free ride on expenses. Old Wynona might have thought part of it was hers, I don't know, we never talked about it. We would have to dicker it out later.

So the completion rig came and went. They installed a stack of valves called a christmas tree. No above-ground storage tanks, which tells you it's a gas well. Even though I had a 32nd override, all I heard was the sound of one hand clapping. Nothing happened. The well just sat there like a bump on a stump.

What should have been happening was that some pipeliners should have been out there installing an underground line to collect the gas, to run it out across country to tie into a bigger line, which then would run off across country to tie into an even bigger line. The pipeliners didn't show. The Groendyke well was shut in, and if Groedyke didn't buy his air conditioned tractor with his lease bonus, then I guess he'd just have to wait a few months. I was back to fluffing my nuts.

I decided not to share this poop about the delay with Old Wynona. The way I looked at it, a couple of years didn't mean anything to her. Fifty years in the future to me was fifty years in the past to her. I had the watch but she had the time. She got her share of the money out of the flip. Except for snagging another couple of leases and sharing a third with Wynona, the ball wasn't moving at all in my end of the field.

She didn't even seem all that interested in my business. All she wanted to talk about was young Wynona. She pecked at me like an old turkey hen, pushing me to make a peace with her younger self.

"The only way I'd be interested in having anything to do with her would be to make her jealous. That would be fun," I said. "Seeing as how she made me look like a fool in front of God and everybody."

"Oh hell, forget that. The mortgage is coming due. I need your help to cover that nut again."

"I ain't accusing, but she could have been the one that bashed Chloe's Reece's titty-pink Cadillac into the train. I wouldn't put it past her."

"Oh fiddle faddle. I wouldn't never have had the balls to try something like that. I swear, it wasn't me."

"Who was it then?"

"Don't have a clue. I got something here someplace I want to show you."

While she was rummaging around in her desk, I took the opportunity to look out the window. I got another shock. The light from the moon was dim, but what I saw was that the old place looked all spiffed up, even better than before. The ranch looked like a doctor or someone with more money than good sense owned it.

"Ah. Here it is. Take a look at that." She stood to hand me a photograph which I couldn't even look at. I hadn't really taken a good look at her until now, and just the sight of the way she had gussied herself up just blew me away. She was wearing blue jeans, cowboy boots, and a snappy western-cut blouse with mother-of-pearl buttons. Not a stitch of polyester. She wasn't clacking her teeth anymore. Even her hair. I hadn't noticed before then, but it wasn't that mousy gray like it had been. Now it was silver and it looked to me like she'd been to a beauty parlor at least. It was done up stylish and all the stringiness was gone. She'd lost a lot of weight.

"I doubt you'll even recognize her."

The eyes were drawn and sad, but the round, dimpled cheeks told me who it was. "That's Chloe Reece. When did you take this?"

"A few days ago. Just to show you. She don't have nothing on me."

The years hadn't been kind to Chloe Reece. She looked like a plop of cow shit in a wagon rut, truth be said. "Well, how nice," I said. I didn't know for sure why she was showing the picture to me but I sure as hell wasn't going to say anything good or bad about Chloe Reece until I figured out her invective plan.

"This here is the reason you need to quit it off with Chloe Reece and get back to chasing me." She slapped herself on the side of the fanny and nodded her head.

"She's a sweet gal and a pretty darn good friend. I enjoy her company."

"You need to quit her."

"Oh, better not." Who I spent my time with wasn't anyone's business but mine.

"The more time you waste with her, the longer it's going to be before I marry you."

"Marry me?" That caught me off guard. I didn't know how her mouth could even form those words. "You won't even talk to me. And what makes you think I want to marry you?"

"You can lie to you but you can't lie to me. You want me. I know it."

"Well yeah, I thought about a relationship a time or two, but not for long." Relationship is a word that I learned to say in the place of what my old man would have called screwing. "It's pretty far-fetched to think she'd make up with me."

She was staring at me with her brow kind of low and with a tiny grin. "That part's not so hard. You need to apologize first…"

"Apologize for what?"

"Hell I don't know. You can apologize for causing lung cancer. You just got to apologize for something. Anything. Here's the key point. You got to apologize in front of my friends."

"Who? June Bug?"

"And others."

"What the hell for?"

"It's just the way it works. I can't help falling head over heels for you if strip yourself of every ounce of dignity and do it where all my girlfriends can see you. Now that's true love."

"Lord, Wynona, that's a lot to ask."

"I really want you, Earl Ray."

In my heart, I suspected she was telling the truth. So far in my pitiful shitty love-starved life, what always gave me the worst cases of the horned colic was when a woman let me know she wanted me. This fifty-year differential in our ages was a wild card, but I knew that if I could awaken that desire in the twenty-year-old Wynona, we could make beautiful music. I was never able to get that idea out of my feeble brain after that. And that was the moment when Old Wynona sowed the idea in my brain. I admit that at one time I had been infatuated with young Wynona, but it was the seed Old Wynona planted right then that awakened the roots that would sprout and blossom in my heart, the origin of what would become love.

"We have another matter on the agenda. I want you to get my daddy to give you a mineral lease."

"On this place?"

"Yep," she said. "That note that old Westerfield has been dangling over his head is about to come due again."

"Why hell yeah, if you think he'd lease. I always figured he was bit by the same tree-hugger bug as you...her."

"He'd listen. He'd lease if the money was right, if he thought the lease was..."

"Was what?"

"A wedding present."

I sat in a stunned silence, watching her put that picture of Chloe Reece back in the scrapbook binder. I saw some other stuff too. Yellowed newspaper clippings, pressed wildflowers, ribbons. I thought it might be smart to look through the scrapbook someday, but from the look of the sky outside, daybreak wasn't so far away. I didn't know what would happen to me if I let the sun rise on my dumb ass fifty years into the future and I didn't want to find out.

CHAPTER 11

For days after that, my waking hours were absorbed in thoughts of making up with Wynona. I tried to figure out how to get my agenda accomplished without an excuse. I thought I could make up something but I didn't want a public apology to be the first step in the sequence of shit I was putting myself through. I conjured up all kinds of crazy ideas. I even tried to think of a way that I could horn-swoggle old man Vorhees into signing a lease and then next marry Wynona, and only after we was hitched would I have to make up with her. That's how desperate I was to avoid prostating myself in front of a bunch of post-high-school-girl drama queens.

I thought about maybe just calling her on the phone, or talking to her out there by the corral, but Old Wynona told me to make sure I did it in front of all her friends. She insisted that part was mission-critical. So the telephone and the corral were out of the picture. The trouble was, there just weren't many places in Beckham County where people clustered up. A movie theater? No way to guarantee all the girlfriends would be there. A high school football game? Wynona had already graduated and so had most of her friends. I just couldn't think of any better place than that old dance hall.

I also needed to mastermind a gathering of a gaggle of her girl-friends. I puzzled on that detail for a couple of weeks. I suppose a lesser man would have asked Junie for a little help. That wasn't in the cards. Junie seemed to think I was the devil incipient and she had shown herself to be dialectically opposed to anything I said. When that fact finally sunk in my feeble mind, it helped me hatch a brain-child that was simple and foolproof.

I cornered Junie out by the corral one day. We exchanged an insult or two. I think I told her I wanted to put some dough on her face and then bake it into a gorilla cookie. Then I let on to her that I was still raw-assed about them two cutting out on me at the dance hall and stealing my truck.

"Payback is a bitch, June Bug." Haha, calling her "June Bug" was inspired. That nickname galded her ass every time. "That's all I'm saying."

I told her if I ever ran into Wynona, I probably wasn't going to hold back. I was at Defcon 2. Thermonuclear was enemant. I also told her I was meeting Chloe Reece at the dance hall Saturday night and I'd appreciate it if she and her posse just met up somewhere else.

So of course Junie and Wynona and a whole passel of her friends showed up at the dance hall. I waited outside. If Junie met my expec-torations, she would have the geese perched on the front row, waiting for the floor show. I had throwed a few bucks at the bouncer and he gave me the hi sign when the covey of drama queens reached critical mass, which I estimated was twenty.

Junie snared me at the door. "Where's Chloe Reece?" she asked.

"She's going to wash her hair and get a headache," I told her.

I headed straightaway for Wynona. I stepped onto the dance floor and hollered at the band and ask them to lay off playing just for a minute. I stepped in front of Wynona and dropped down on my knees.

"Wynona," I said, "I can't stand myself anymore. I'm sorry. I'm as sorry as I can be. Can you forgive me? Darling?"

"I'm not letting you off that easy, Earl Ray."

I got my face closer to the ground than my asshole, as if I was going to kiss her feet. Just holding myself in that juxtposition was enough, I could see, to melt the pretty thing's cold heart. That little flourish of putting my face closer to the ground than my asshole was a trick

I learned from my old man. In fact, that was the only thing worthwhile that my old man ever passed on to me. With his finely tuned power of sharp observation, he had noticed that my mother always smiled when she saw him put his face closer to the ground than his asshole. Lighting pilot lights, fixing flats.

Someday the government will commission a study, I suppose, but this little known fact about how to make women happy—putting your face closer to the ground than your asshole—is a great technique for anybody willing to find it and write about it and explain it. That explains why I was groveling on the floor.

"I missed our anniversary and that's unforgivable. How in the hell could I have done that? I'll never forgive myself. Can you forgive me?"

The gaggle was all abuzz. "He's crawling on all fours...ass in the air. Begging. Bawling like a baby," they were saying. If they saw tears, that was all the better for me. But I was not crying, I want everyone to know that.

"He's faking," Junie said.

"Promise you'll never do it again," Wynona said.

"With all my heart I promise this to you, Wynona Vorhees. I'll never forget. My love." I was up on my knees now.

"Oh, Earl Ray. You old rascal." All the girlfriends were digging in their purses for tissues.

"Marry me. Be mine. Will you marry me, Wynona? Please?" I plunged my face toward the sawdust again and screwed my ass up even higher than it was before.

A collective swoon seeped out of the gaggle.

"Yes, Earl Ray," Wynona said. "Yes yes yes."

"I'll make you the proudest woman in Beckham County. Hell in the whole state. There won't be a woman that can hold a candle to you."

"Talk to daddy."

Junie was pissed. She was the one that pulled together the floor show. She was puckered up so tight you wouldn't have been able to drive a pin up her ass with a sledgehammer.

Next day, I found old man Vorhees on his back underneath a pickup truck. Only his legs stuck out. We exchanged howdies.

"Transmission. Real delicate, real delicate," he said.

"I asked Wynona to marry me."

"Give me a couple of feet of baling wire, would you?"

The bed of the truck had several pieces of wire all twisted into rat's nests. I found a piece long enough and handed it to the old man.

"That ought to get it. Hell Earl, she never showed no interest in anything but horses."

"She said 'yes' so now I'm asking you."

"Can you find a pair of pliers?"

Of course I could.

"There any WD-40 up there?"

"Right by the duct tape."

I handed the oil to Vorhees and heard him spray his work. He slid out from under the truck.

"If that don't fix her, nothing will." He wiped his forehead with a red handkerchief.

Vorhees had a cooler in the bed of the truck. I looked inside and found some cold beers. I pulled a tab on one and handed it to the old man.

I thought he was going to suck it back in one gulp. "Who's going to fix me my supper?"

"Hell, Vorhees, I guess Wynona will. I'm planning on moving in."

We set a date and Wynona started planning. A dress, flowers, bridesmaids, a rehearsal dinner. She even planned a honeymoon. She booked rooms in Oklahoma City.

"I got the bridal suite," she told me.

"Bridle? Kink-ee." Junie gave me a shot in the ribs to set me right. In my fertile mind, my first idea of what she was talking about was along the lines of handcuffs.

She picked out a baby blue tux for me and set that off with a ruffled shirt.

As the day grew nearer, Wynona's old man saw me at the truck stop and came over to share a cup of coffee.

"You know I don't have a pot to piss in or a window to throw it out of," Vorhees said. "I'd sure like to give you young'uns something nice."

"You could do me a hell of a favor if you let me lease those minerals," I said.

"It don't set right with me...this old rock pile don't promise much but she's been like a sister to me. Wynona will shit a brick. She don't cotton much to anything she thinks would hurt the...Gaia she calls it, Mother Earth. She's against anything that's progress. Drilling, fracking, vaccines, gynecological modified foods, global warming, you name it. She's against it."

"She don't need to know. You sign a lease, that's our wedding present. I'll give you a draft and everybody is happy."

That's pretty much what happened, too. It didn't take but a phone call. I flipped that lease to Texola so fast it would make your head spin. They were still sitting on the Westerfield lease because they knew it would make a well. I think they were planning on maybe setting a wedge deep in the old blowout hole. Those wedges deflect a diamond coated drill bit so it drills a window in the old casing and lets them punch a new hole alongside the old one. That's called a whipstock. It saves the operator a ton of money because most of the hole has already been drilled.

Whatever it was they planned, Vorhees got his money and I banked a third of my profit in Wynona's bank account. The cash money I turned came in handy and I also carved out a 32nd override for myself.

Wynona wanted to enlist every girl in the county as an attendant in the wedding. Maids of honor, flower girls, cake cutters and guest book wranglers. I don't even know what all sorts of necessary work she had planned out for each one of them. The number of bodies she had lined up inflicted the number of men I was supposed to round up to carry my cup.

The short list of guys I came up with was headed by my one-eyed ex-cousin-in-law Peavine. Most of my closest friends were working dark til dawn or had pulled up stakes and left for the Dakotas or south to the Eagle Ford play. Among the locals, I thought maybe Peavine would stand up with me. Maybe, too, Verl Lee and a few of other guys I knew from the Paddock. Maybe Red, Slick or Buzz. Wynona vetted them carefully and crossed them all off the list.

"Don't you know anyone that doesn't have a nickname? Oh my God, not Peavine."

"He's my ex-cousin. In law."

"His wife is in prison," she said. I didn't like the way one of her eyebrows turned down.

"Again?" Not again.

My idea of maybe some of her girlfriends dressing up like men was shouted down. I figured it was a bad step to start off a marriage with a disagreement, so I looked for a reasonable compromise. Like they say, I will if you will. *Quid pro quo*. I agreed to let her have her way if—and only if—she'd quit crying. She had some male cousins who would stand up with me.

We congregated over to the Church of Christ where they don't like instrumental music in their services. The rehearsal was for the girls. The guys don't have much to do, really. Wynona was all giggles. I think she maybe have been one of the first girls in her crowd to get married.

Junie kept popping off about how she was going to squawk when the preacher said "if anyone has just cause for throwing the brake on this wedding, speak now or forever hold your peace."

The Flank Strap

After that we all gathered at a bowling alley for kind of a dinner to celebrate the rehearsal came off...what? Without a shooting? I never understood why anyone would celebrate a rehearsal. I just did what Wynona told me to do.

They served two big pots of chili. Hot with beans and hot without beans. We interlocked our arms and fed a twinkie to one another for a picture. Wynona smeared that filling all over my face.

The next item on the agenda was some dancing. Vorhees was wearing new duds. I wouldn't have recognized him. He paired himself off with an old widow woman and they were dancing the Cotton-Eyed Joe when I went to the restroom to wash the twinkie cream off my face. When I came back, old Vorhees was sitting on his ass on the floor, leaning against a pool table. All the folks crowded around him. His face was pale and drawn and I knew that he was in a lot of pain. Someone called an ambulance and all we could do was wring our hands and wait.

We put off the nuptials which were scheduled for the next day. We buried the old man in a raggedy ass cemetery on Tuesday. Someone with the cemetery outfit had tried to kill off the mesquite and sage but that project had a ways to go yet. The graveyard was as flat as a griddle and the name on an arch over the entrance—"Mount Pleasant"—must have been put there by a comedian. A sextet of elderly hymnists sang a nasal "When We All Get To Heaven."

> *When we all (when we all)*
> *Get to heaven*
> *What a day of rejoicing that will be*
> *When we all (when we all)*
> *See Jesus, we'll sing and shout the victory.*

That outfit had nothing on George Strait. That was the sorriest most punyest singing group I'd heard in a lifetime. They sure as hell fell short on that promise of rejoicing with songs and shouts of victory. The Baptists have it all over the Church of Christ in singing in my estimation. Both outfits would benefit by dialing down on the false advertising but at least the songs come off better at the Baptist Church.

The singing was so bad that I couldn't help but let my mind wander. I wondered who had named that place "Mount Pleasant." Another piece of false advertising. It wasn't a mountain and it was about as unpleasant as it could be. I reckon that a town's Chamber of Commerce must come up with names like "Mount Pleasant." Up in west Kansas, they got a town named "Garden City" and another one named "Liberal." They need to pass a law to put a halt to folks handing out names such as that. It's false advertising.

We decided to put the wedding on hold for awhile. I liked the old man, he had been generous with me, giving me a place to live and all, but I didn't think honeymooning with his only daughter was a proper way to show respect while he wasn't even cold in the ground.

CHAPTER 12

Wynona didn't have a clue of what to do about the business of dealing with her father's death. We looked high and low for a will and never found anything at all. I suggested we sit down and figure out just where she was.

She was the only heir to the home place which was on a 160 acre tract. A square, a half mile north to south, and a half mile east to west.

She really gave me the stink-eye when I showed her Vorhees' copy of the mineral lease and some paperwork that showed that he had signed the draft and put it up for collection at the bank.

"I never agreed to let anyone rape this land," she said.

"Your old man did," I said. That put a chill on the conversation. It was like at one of those movies where all of a sudden, the room gets so cold that you can see the vapor come out of the actor's mouths when they exhale. "You'll be getting a big fat check any day now."

"I won't cash it."

"They're going to drill whether you cash it or not."

She also had about a dozen horses and some rusty old broken down equipment. She was going to have to pay a lawyer to drag the land through probate. We didn't know for sure at the time, but it was my suppository that she'd have to get the judge to sprinkle some holy water on the oil lease money as well.

The stinker was that Westerfield still held that mortgage on the place. Best I remember there was about $80,000 owed and the note would go in default if Westerfield didn't get paid somewhere in the neighborhood of $12,000 every year. The next payment was due in a couple of months. I don't understand why the old fart just sat there collecting social security and not going to the bank to borrow some money to pay Westerfield off. Maybe he had bad credit. Maybe owing the devil next door was better than owing a heartless bank. It just looked to me like he could have got enough on the place to get Westerfield paid off and out of his life plus have some left over to buy a few head of cattle. A quarter section won't support but a half dozen cow-calf pairs in Beckham County.

I knew better than to say anything to Wynona about selling the horses. She had money in the bank that I'd put there, I guess she thought it was peanuts, but right then it had maybe $40,000. The thought had never even crossed her mind that I'd put back enough to be worth walking across the street for, or that she could get enough cash from that account to grease old Westerfield. If it did, she didn't show it.

I came away from that sit down with bruises. Wynona just didn't know how to face hard realities. She was brokenhearted about old Vorhees, I can understand that. But when I said, "you got to get a lawyer" she was all in my grill with "why me? Why is this happening to me?" Like losing a loved one never happened to anyone else, ever.

"When that check comes in you're going to have to run that through probate, too."

"Why me? Why me?"

Shit. She was real pleasant when I told her the social security was no mas and that she'd probably have to get a J-O-B. At least until we married. "Why can't I just train horses? That's what I want to do. Why me?" Jeezy wheezy.

I decided to go see Westerfield by myself. I wasn't all that sure that my embroidery of the mortgage terms was correct and we needed to set our plans based on true facts, not suppositories. I was uneasy the same way I would be if I was putting my hand down in a rattlesnake den.

The Flank Strap

I drove around a corner and saw old Westerfield heading down a ravine with an armful of empty fertilizer sacks. He threw the bags on a trash pile.

He caught sight of me and gave me the evil eye. Then he struck a match and threw it on the trash pile, then pushed the fertilizer sacks into the little flame.

KA-BOOO-OOM. A bright flash of light almost blinded me. A mushroom cloud of smoke and flames shot skyward out of the trash pile.

Those fertilizer sacks had exploded like a bomb. Old Westerfield must have sloshed some diesel fuel on the bags. I'm sure that's what he was thinking as he sailed backwards about twenty feet and landed like a ten-pound turd, flat on his ass.

Fire spread into the buffalo grass, sage and mesquite. It caught a gust of wind and the flames grew as tall as my head. In another minute, the fire could be out of control and burn down everything in the county. I ran down the ravine to the trash pile and commenced stomping fire like a maniac. Took me a couple of minutes, but I got her put out. I was black as tar from the soot and ash when I went over to see about Westerfield.

"Thanks, Earl," he said, shaking his head as if he was confused. "What you doing here?"

"Hey, Westerfield, I need to talk business, and I ain't interested in none of your monkeyshines."

"I appreciate you putting out that fire." The skin on his arms and face was flecked with little tiny cuts where he'd been hit by flying gravel. Looked like he'd fought a circle saw. The hair on his head and forearms was singed and still smoldering. But he was as nice and friendly as he could be. "Thank the heavens you was here to put out that fire," he said. We were like two old pals. Old school week.

I got his keys and pulled his pickup alongside to give him something to lean back on in the shade. We chitchatted a bit about how good looking his daughter was and I lied to make him happy. I didn't think I'd have another opportunity, so I told him, "You know, Wes, we ought to try to top lease these old minerals."

"Oh?"

"Yeah. Just in case Black Kettle lets it go back, you got another fish on the line."

"Oh, I don't know. That don't get me top dollar."

"Listen Wes, if Black Kettle shows up with a rig tomorrow, you won't get another dime. And even if they do, hell, we made a good well over on Groendyke's place and as of today, there ain't been no one seen a plug nickel. I don't know. Maybe you'll live forever. I doubt it. If you ever want to see a dime for yourself, you need to make things happen. You can't wait it out."

"I need to think it over."

I snagged my briefcase from my truck. I filled the damn lease papers out in longhand. Strike while the iron is hot. That's my motto. If he said "yes," I didn't want him to get any second ideas.

So that's what gave me the occasion to put my readers on out there in the prairie beside that ravine, leaning on Westerfield's truck. Without my peepers, I would have never seen something on the bumper of his truck that confirmed a suppository of mine that I didn't think I would ever be able to prove as an eye witness: pink flecks of paint, more pacifically, pink paint in the titty-pink hue. That was proof positive to me that it was Westerfield's truck that had tried to push Roxie's titty-pink Cadillac into the train that night that I was driving it. That would mean the usual suspects would be Westerfield or his daughter Junie. I inclined to think it was Westerfield himself because that night, more likely than not, Junie was out in some pasture cutting cat's asses with Wynona in my pickup.

While Westerfield fiddle-farted around dabbing at his wounds and jack-jawing the top lease, I sat down beside him and rubbed my chin. I put my papers and the draft back in my Haliburton briefcase.

"Wes, you don't know how it pains me," I said, "to point out that there's titty-pink paint chips on the bumper of this old truck."

The old fart started mumbling and I could see that we could be out there all day backwashing the story if I let him do it.

"It don't make a damn to me whether it was you or Junie. Probably makes a difference to the sheriff."

"What can I do to make it right?"

"I need for you to let me top lease this place and then sell me the Vorhees mortgage," I said. Westerfield owned three quarter-sections of land, three times as much as Vorhees, and I'd make enough money off of flipping the lease to pay him for the mortgage and still set aside a third for old Wynona.

I got that all done—the lease flipped and the mortgage bought—while Wynona was still wringing her hands about winding up her old man's affairs. My intention was to tell her that I'd paid it off and burn the mortgage, well I hadn't really decided when exactly. I wanted to do it to sometime real dramatic. I dreamed up this fantasy of whipping out the paperwork and setting it afire in front of a crowd and then they'd all cheer and everyone would drink beer and be happy as pigs in a wallow. Events conspired and I just never got around to telling her.

One of those events that kept all the balls up in the air was that the opportunity came up to sell a lot of clay from the Vorhees place. That geologist from Texola was the guy what made me wise. The place had a freak deposit of clay which was in short supply around Beckham County and west, out in Texas. The oilpatch liked to put it on pads where they drilled wells. It helped stabilize the location so that the heavy equipment didn't leave giant ruts. Homebuilders liked to put it down on building sites.

I knew Wynona was kind of a tree-hugger but I was still caught by surprise by her negative reaction, when I breached her on the subject. She went into a rant. I thought she was going to throw herself on the floor and have a tantrum. "I won't leave a scar on Mother Earth," she shouted.

I talked and talked and convinced her to slow down long enough to realize that we could get them to dam the mine and make it into a pond. A big one too. That would be good for the horses and deer and ducks and jackrabbits and coyotes and who knows what all.

It would also make her a healthy royalty.

CHAPTER 13

I t was damn sure a big day when they spudded in the well on the Vorhees place. A few days before, a dozer had cleared an acre of its mesquite, pushing it all back in piles.

We'd already got hitched, I'd moved out of the bunkhouse and into the house. It was nice to be able to put my civvies in a chester-drawers and take a constitutional indoors for a change.

Trucks were coming and going from lights to lights. It was so busy, you'd think the place was the Grand Central Station up there in Oklahoma City. Big belly dumpers carrying loads of clay meeting other belly dumpers coming back empty to get another load. And the oversize flatbed trailers hauling in pieces of the drilling mast, substructure, pits, pumps and generators for the drilling rig. Sure as hell was a lot of commotion.

I yearned to be part of some big enterprise like that again. The part I played of getting the place leased didn't seem like much compared to the effort that was put in by the lowest roustabout on the crew.

As I said, me and Wynona had tied the knot by this time. According to Peavine, it's good to marry them when they are young, that way you can train them up right. He should know. I spent more hours trying to get mine trained than I would care to count.

Money wasn't an object any more. I never told her I bought the mortgage papers. The clay mine was paying off like a slot machine and I still stumbled over an oil lease that I could flip every so often.

Wynona enrolled in classes at a junior college over in Elk City. I bought her a labtop computer and a new truck to drive so the commute wasn't a big deal.

I don't know just what classes she was taking, psychology and sociology I guess, but every now and then she'd spout off some crap about how America was the cause of all the problems in the world. That didn't set right with me, and I'll be damned if I can figure out what that has to do with psychology. Whenever that old shit got started, I always stuck up for the good old red, white, and blue. Not that it did me any good.

I noticed, too, that her mail from the college came addressed to "Wynona Vorhees." She never even thought about enrolling until we married, so my suppository was that she intended to keep her maiden name. I wasn't so sure I liked that. It seems like something we could have talked about.

This next situation probably went on for a couple of months before I even noticed it. It was something that became a habit of hers. When I realized it, I let it get under my skin. That's an understatement. I thought her habit was going to drive me to jacking off.

She would be talking, then without any warning, her voice would raise up like she was asking a question. Right in the middle of a sentence. "Earl Ray, let's go into town? For a bowl of chili." "Earl Ray, I'll be in the barn? To exercise that filly." Before long almost every sentence she spoke ended in the middle, sort of like a question, as often as not, whatever she said ended up like a question too. "Earl Ray, I think it might rain? Tonight?"

Someone told me once that Tom Cruise's teeth are set in his mouth sort of antigogglin. Those main teeth of his right in the center of his face are off center. He does have two teeth there, but only one is plumb. Off center, not under his nose. Maybe it's my oilfield training, but anything that's not set at a 90 degree angle looks like it was put together by a bunch of half-wits, and my brain automatically squares everything up. Once I saw that one tooth of Tom Cruise's set right smack straight under his nose, I have never been able to unsee it. I got to where I couldn't unhear a question right spang in the middle of whatever in the hell Wynona had to say.

Only thing I could figure was that this way Wynona was talking was something she picked up from those college professors. "Earl Ray, bring me a spoon? For my chili?" I mean every damn sentence came out that way. We didn't talk much.

When we did talk, seemed like she was always on a kick, faunching about the rain forests or Indians and how we'd screwed them so good and hard. Maybe so. Well it wasn't just that, which I'd heard dozens of times before, she was also talking about how spiritual the Indians were and how our religion wasn't any better than theirs and that "white folks had sprinkled smallpox? On blankets? Just to kill them off?" Just a load of crap like that. Doesn't seem like what a person wants to go to college to learn.

On the score of religion, she was up in my grill about creation. "I don't know what it is with you Baptists? And Noah and the Ark? You have to be kidding."

"Listen, Sugarbaby, if I believed the world was six thousand years old, I wouldn't last long in my business. Those sediments were laid down millions of years ago."

She just rolled her eyes like I was an idiot. At least she didn't ask herself a question.

She also got enrolled in some philosophy class that loaded her up with even more BS. I called it "America = bad 101." She'd bring up what they was spoon feeding her just for the entertainment value of watching me go all Ted Nugent on her. Hell, I was proud to serve the country, even if no one shot at me, and I'm damn proud to be an American, too. I don't care what her professors tells her. This here is the best country on the face of the earth, even if they only let kids think one way on campus.

She must have been taking some class having to do with earth science too, because she was all bent out of shape now about fracking oil wells and groundwater and solar panels and the rising oceans. What a crock of shit.

We still had some mesquite trees tangled in hedgerow piles that the drilling company had pushed up when they built the pad to drill the oilwell on. She invited her professor and a bunch of students out to our place for a weenie roast. I think it was the earth science class because they were all interested in the oilwell. I thought I'd never have a better opportunity to burn those mortgage papers, so for a time, I just drank beer and minded my own business watching her professor snarf down the free weenies. He was wearing a floppy Indianapolis Jones hat on his head and some lime green plastic slip-ons for shoes, and he gobbled those weenies down like a con-victed man. I bet he smoked up a couple of joints of that whacky tobaccy on the way to the ranch.

I noticed that the kids were starting to cluster up around me and that they were whispering to one another with grins on their faces.

Next the professor came sidling up. "I showed the students a film the other day," he said. He had mustard on his droopy mustache.

"Sounds like you got a pretty sweet deal," I said. "They got any more jobs like that over to the college, showing movies? I think I'd be good at that." That's my way of trying to be friends, joshing around some.

"I showed a film that documented a man and his family that lived near hydraulic fracking." No sense of humor. "They could set his tap water on fire."

"You don't say."

"His tap water was burning all because of fracking," he said.

"Uh huh." Sometimes I say "uh huh" like that but the professor knew my meaning was that I thought he was as full of shit as a Christmas goose.

I think my meaning went over the heads of them kids. They were giggling and chucking one another in the ribs with their elbows.

Wynona hung her head and shook it side to side. "He's disgraceful," she said.

"What do you have to say about that?" the professor asked.

"Why don't you tell them? What you think? Go ahead," Wynona said.

"Okay. Yeah, what I think. Well one thing's sure," I said. "That's horseshit of the first caliber. They don't put stuff in frack water that will burn. And it's not something you see every day, but lots of groundwater has methane in it..."

That's all I had to say. The professor and Wynona and all the students were yapping and shrieking. I couldn't have got another word out even if I had a magnaphone. I wanted to tell them that it's only receptacle kids and pinko college professors and lawyers that believes that baloney. Baloney, that's all it is, pure unadulterated baloney.

That's because the well water around these parts, if someone is lucky enough to make a water well, gets pumped up from maybe 300 feet. The oilwells are mostly all producing from two miles down. That's two miles of iron pipe and inside that, two miles of tubing inside it, all cemented in the hole to keep fluids from getting out. Leaks could never worm their way into water-bearing rock when the well bore gives it a low-pressure path straight to the surface. I told this to Wynona a hundred times.

"Anytime you want to listen, we can conversate," I told them.

"I'll listen as long as what you have to say is in the consensus range of acceptable opinion," the professor said. "We don't want to destroy you. We want to change you."

"Listen Doc, I may not have a PDF behind my name but you're full of shit. Have another weenie. It's on me."

That's the way I remember it anyway but maybe it didn't all get out. They were jumping up and down and squalling, the professor and students alike. Like monkeys in the zoo. At least they weren't throwing turds. But they got my point even if they didn't hear it. I understand that maybe someone doesn't give a hoot in a holler about how an oilwell works, but I don't get why anyone, especially my wife, would rather let some tweedy goofball finger-sniffer run a trap on me just to amuse a bunch of pimple-faced college kids that had no job prospects other than holding down a couch in their mom's basement. I forgot about burning the mortgage.

That might not have been so bad but next term, when Wynona had to take a history class, I figured out that she didn't even know the North fought the South in the Civil War. She didn't have a clue about what made them fight. She voted in American Idol but she wouldn't vote in regular elections, not even for the guy I was backing who was running against Forney DeFore.

The sex life we had as husband and wife started off with a bang, but by the time the drilling crew was starting to look like they were nearing total depth, the physical part of the romance had pretty much fizzled. I didn't know what to do. I hated to see Wynona unsatisfied with that part of our marriage and I was getting pretty sick of being sexually flusterated all the time myself. I felt like an old broke-dick dog. I got so concerned, I pulled out some of those pamphlets the Church of Christ preacher gave us when he was putting on a show about whether or not he'd help us tie the knot. For all the good they done me.

I dragged a chair and a case of beer out there by the pond and read those handouts over in private while the logging crew was doing their thing. I had a tickle in my throat like a cold was coming on, so I gave the beer to the logging crew. It didn't hurt me none to stay in their good graces, even if the story going around about me was that I wasn't fit to be a pusher on a merry-go-round.

When the Texola engineer and geologist showed up on location, I knew that it was time to read the logs. No one objected when I walked into the Texola trailer house where the company man had been living for a couple of months, watching over this well.

The Flank Strap

The head man on the logging crew had forgotten more about reading logs than the engineer or company man ever knew. They stood aside and let him tell them what they said. The log was a sketchy zig zag across a strip of paper that was maybe six inches wide. The paper broke in neat folds and was stacked as deep as a book. The oil men ignored all but the last few pages. The log man had a colored pencil and filled in some of the spikes on the graph with red. He turned a couple of more folds to what I guessed was uphole and started filling in a wide swath. His markings went through the fold and back further up the page. "Hogshooter," he said. "Two hundred and twelve feet."

All I knew was we were damn sure going to make a hell of a good well. I made a mad dash into town and got there just before they rolled up the sidewalks. The package store was just ready to close. I bought a magnum of champagne and headed back to El Rancho Grande.

First place I went was to the old bunkhouse. That greenish light was glowing under the door, so I pushed and shoved my way through. The hinges squawked just to let me know it had been awhile since I'd been in. Sitting on her inner tube on a couch across the room was Old Wynona, looking pretty darn spiffy for a woman seventy plus years of age.

"You ain't never gonna believe it!" I said.

"The well come in?"

"Did she ever! Two hundred feet of pay in the Hogshooter! I-EEEeeeeeee!!" That rebel yell didn't do my raw throat a bit of good.

I grabbed that old gal's hands and we danced around in a circle, jumping and screaming like schoolgirls. Hell I guess I must have tripped on a shingle nail. Next thing I knew I had Old Wynona on her back on that overstuffed couch with me on top, big as Dallas. She kissed me and I kissed her. Hard. Hungry. Deep and familiar, passionately, right on the mouth. She had her tongue probing my mouth, reciprocating. My flesh was hungry and my loins filled with lust. Wanton, willing. I didn't even reprehend that I was doing it, but when I understood what my body was doing, you can believe me, I pulled back, unnerved. My intention was to be true to Wynona, my wife Wynona, and I had more than a little bit of guilt over sucking face with her older self, even if it was herself. It still didn't seem right.

Old Wynona smiled at me and laughed. Those flaccid pools that had glimmered in the headlights of the semi trucks on I-40 were now bloodshot and jaundiced. I guess she thought me blushing was some kind of amusement. I struggled to regain my feet.

"Someone needs to drive that shingle nail back in place," I said.

"Here. Let me fix you some of that champagne," she said, and I was damn glad of it. I needed something to brace me after taking a shock to my system like that and truth be told, I wasn't sure how to get the damn bottle opened anyway.

"Find some cups," she said, popping the cork.

I scuffled around and found some paper cups and let Old Wynona pour us a couple.

"I ain't never had none of this champagne." I was taking tiny sips to cut my sore throat some slack. But she sucked the first cup back and was already reloading.

"Pretty good stuff," she said. "Thanks for thinking about me." She held out her cup and I refilled it again.

"Hell yeah."

"Here's something you might enjoy." Old Wynona rummaged around in a drawer and withdrew another picture. It was a younger Wynona, standing on a seaside dock with a long fishing pole. A large billfish hung by her side.

"Well I swan to goodness."

"Look over there." A big stuffed billfish hung on the wall of the office. I hadn't noticed it before now, so I surveyed the room, to see what else I had overlooked. Someone had given the old place another makeover. It was all fitted out in oilfield décor, a mix of oilfield memorabilia and horse stuff.

When I looked back at Wynona, she was bottoms up again. She filled her cup and drained it again. I was just swilling mine when my curiosity got the best of me and I looked out the window. The full moon lit the place up like a Christmas tree.

The Vorhees place looked fantastic. A big modern brick house stood in the place of the ragged old shack.

"I guess the stock's doing real good," I said.

"Horses always look better when they eat grass in the shade of an oil well," she said.

I nodded and sipped a bit more. I wasn't sure I liked champagne.

Old Wynona caught her image in a mirror and sauntered over to get a better full-length look. This outfit she had on was stylish as it could be. She stroked the fabric with her hand, pressing out the wrinkles where just minutes ago my hands had been groping.

"Do you think I look fat in this?"

"Maybe."

"So now you think I'm fat."

"A little. All right?"

"I guess that just because I'm fat you think you can just take advantage of me."

"What the hell are you talking about?"

"You just drag in here any old time you want. Where the hell were you earlier?"

"Me and the company man…"

"Jesus Christ, Earl. When you gonna learn to speak English?"

"Can't you save it for later?"

"You been slacking off a lot lately."

"Now I know how it feels to be nibbled to death by a duck."

I think she knew I was right and that was probably why she broke off from continuing to squabble. She sat back in her chair and swirled her champagne. "I've been thinking about race horses. Did you check that picture out? The one in the iron frame?"

She pointed to a photograph in a horseshoe decorated frame that hung on the wall. In it, young Wynona was standing beside a quarter horse and smiling at a jockey, who was decked out in racing silks. I squinted to see. I took the frame off the wall and held it at arm's length.

"He's something special."

"The jockey?"

"No, dumb butt, the colt."

"Who's the jockey?" I handed the picture and frame to Wynona, wishing I had my glasses.

"It's the jockey and trainer both."

"Just tell me. Who is the son of a bitch?"

"It's not a he. It's Junie, and she owns an interest in the colt."

"Oh. Yeah, Junebug. I reckon two or three percent would be a pretty big piece for a trainer."

"She had half."

"Half of 3 percent?"

"Half the colt."

"Junebug owns half? That little squirt?"

"I don't think it's constructive to refer to our partner as a little squirt."

Some reason, the idea of being in partners with Junie riled me up. "Partner now. Hell yeah. Let me see that picture again."

Old Wynona handed me the photo. I looked more closely, still couldn't make out the faces. I threw that picture, frame and all, all the way across the room. It struck the wall and shattered into a thousand pieces.

"I should have run that little bitch off years ago."

"What the hell difference does it make to you?"

"I wear the pants around here, if it's okay with you."

"Some man. Do you have any idea how unfulfilled I've been?"

"I don't know what the hell you're talking about."

"I'm talking about sex! Do I have to spell it out? God, how thick headed can you be?"

Just the mention of sex made me wince. I liked doing it alright, but I never was comfortable talking about it with women. Just the mention of it and I lost my upper hand over the old gal. "Lay off talking about that. You know I don't like it."

"Don't like sex? No wonder you're so bad at it."

"I don't like talking about it. Hell, you talk like you was in the damn pool hall. Ain't no one ought to be talking like that to a woman. Just to other men."

"Just listen to yourself. You think I'd ever have kids with you? Forget about it."

"What more do you want from me? I gave you everything I could."

"Maybe you ought to spend more time in the field. Watch the bulls cover the cows. You might learn something." Then the crazy old thing grabbed my hand and wrote something on the palm with an inkpen. Big enough I could read it. It said "THE JOY OF SEX."

"What's that supposed to tell me?"

"It's the name of a book. You ever read a book?"

"I can read just fine."

"You ever bought a book? They got stores full of 'em."

"You don't have to be a smart ass."

"Get the damn book. You probably can't find it in Sayre. But I bet they got it in the Wal-Mart over to Clinton."

"And?"

"And READ IT damn you!"

I don't mind telling that my feelings were a little bruised after that little face-to-face.

Futrell's Store had farm and ranch goods, and a tack shop. I hesitated to go in the place because I was feeling a cold coming on.

Seed and feed always had a way of kicking up my allergies and I didn't want to compound my discomfort. But it was the only place in town that had any books, so the next day, that's where I started my quest. Old Man Futrell had a rack full of reading material but as my fingers started doing the walking, I came to realize that mostly all he had was brochures, plus some farm and ranch magazines.

"Looking for something pacific there, Early?" Futrell was a bony old guy. He was wearing the same straw cowboy hat he wore in the 1950s. I don't think he ever took it off, even indoors. I don't think a real cowboy would wear a hat indoors. The tack shop was a jumble of stuff no one could find anything in except him.

"Sort of...just looking..." I said. I was shy about revealing the nature of my quest. If I was to tell him I was looking for *Joy of Sex* he'd jump to the conclusion I was trying to buy a stroke book. "I don't think you got what I'm looking for."

"I can order. Anything I can help you with? Whatcha looking for? Got a real good article here on a new seed wheat."

"Nah. I'm uh...sort of...maybe..."

"Something on protein supplements?"

"Un uh."

"Got some schiz-matics on a new stubble mulcher."

"Hmmm."

"Early, dang it, what the hell you looking for, son?"

My mouth couldn't form the words, so I opened my palm and let him read the words Old Wynona had scribbled. Soon as I did, I regretted it. It was written in the palm of my right hand, so even a dope would know that someone else had written it.

Even Futrell. "Ahhh," he said. I saw those beady old eyes dart back and forth while the right vs. left information penetrated his skull. "AaahhHHHhhh."

"It's called 'The Joy of whatcha-callit.'"

"Yeaaaaah. I kinda mis-con-screwed your intentions there. Maybe they got some of them Joy of whatchacallit books....did you check over there at Ilene's Superette?"

"Jeez, Futrell, I know them women clerks over there. I can't go buying something like this from gals I know."

"You try the lie-berry?"

"Library?" I pulled out my hanky and blew my nose. Damn dust.

"Yeah. That's what I figured. What we need is some expert consolation. Hey, Mrs. Futrell?"

Futrell shuffled into a back room. Thank the Lord, I didn't want to discuss delicate matters like this in front of an old woman. Mostly I was whispering anyway to save my voice which I was worried about losing. I could see him bumping his fists on top of one another. I figured he couldn't mention the subject to his woman either.

He returned to the book rack. "The missus says try the Wal-Mart."

"Wal-Mart!?"

"That's where the Methodist women's book club gets books."

"Hell the closest Wal-Mart is 30 miles." That wasn't quite true. I'd have to drive past two Wal-Marts to get to one where I wouldn't be embarrassed to buy a book about sex.

Futrell shrugged his shoulders. "Hell, Early, those bastards been trying to run me out of business. I don't refer many customers to them. Don't what-cha-ma-call-it then. I'm getting flusterated, just trying to help."

"Well tell Mrs. Futrell thanks anyway, Futrell. Be seeing you."

"You can tell her yourself," he said, but I was already out the door, coughing and wheezing, on my way to Clinton, thirty miles to the east, where no one knew me.

CHAPTER 14

Over to Clinton, the Wal-Mart is as big as a football field. They had a pretty big rack of books and lots of them seemed to be about romance, considering that most of them had a picture of a man's midsection which was all riffled up with a six-pack. I told myself that it was odd that the muscle-bound figures were all men. No women. I guess that big man muscles must sell a lot of books to women. I wondered why someone didn't put one of those wiggle-pictures on the cover to give the book a bit more sizzle. I might have bought one.

It goes without saying that I couldn't find the book that I was on a mission to get. I looked and looked, squeezing my nose with the hopes in mind of choking back a sneeze.

"Can I help you find something?" A woman's voice. I jumped like I'd been shot. A clerk sneaked up behind me when I was distracted by my quest and allergies. I was still thinking about those wiggle-pictures, but my thinking had evolved to thoughts about a wiggle-picture of a bare-breasted woman.

I closed my eyes for courage. "Would you have a book called *The Joy of Sex*?" It came out in a whisper, partly because my throat was raw and partly because I was scared shitless that the clerk was going to be some pretty young thing like my Wynona and that I'd get all tongue-tied and start stuttering. It took an effort for me to exhale, open my eyes, and turn to meet the clerk.

"Earl Bird, is that you? Earl Bird, why I swan to goodness, it is you."

The clerk was that lady, Roxie, the same one that I had run out on after getting smashed up in her titty-pink Cadillac.

"Well I'll be dipped in shit. Roxie. I've been looking all over for you." Of course, I was lying through my teeth.

"Was that you? You know, with me, when my car got smashed up?"

I couldn't deny it. "Yeah. It was me." Having to fess up to that made me feel lower than whale shit in the bottom of the Marianna Trench. If she'd taken a lamp off the shelf and to whack me over the head, I probably would have let her.

"I thought it was. I was drunk as a skunk."

"Yes you were."

"I shouldn't have been driving." That was music to my ears. I always thought the identity of the driver was a secret I'd carry to my grave. "I appreciate you doing what you did," she said.

I thought she was saying that to get me off guard. "It wasn't my finest hour."

"Oh no," she said. "They couldn't prove it was me driving. So my insurance took care of the car. Thank the heavens. The transmission had been acting up and I was behind on payments. Getting out from underneath that Cadillac was the best thing that could have happened to me."

"You got to be shitting."

"Nope. You finding what you're looking for?"

"Well what I'm looking for is a book."

"Yes...title? I couldn't hear you the first time."

"It's *The Joy*...The Joy of...of..." Ahem, I cleared my throat.

"*Joy of Cooking*? Or Sex?"

"That second thing you said. Have you got it?"

"Well Wal-Mart doesn't...but I do."

"I need to get one for my one-eyed ex-cousin-in-law."

"I'm off work here pretty soon. Follow me home and I'll lend your one-eyed ex-cousin-in-law my copy."

She evidently misconscrewed my meaning of "one-eyed ex-cousin-in-law" and I should have been tipped off to the manner of her thinking by her knowing smile.

"You think you might have some cough drops?"

So there I was in her house, sneezing and hacking, and she was freshening up and putting on something more comfortable which means she was taking off her clothes and my mind was screaming at me "no, no, no." But that voice seemed to get shouted down pretty easily by a wall of sound from down below where my beltbuckle had been just minutes ago.

We worked ourselves through *The Joy of Sex* with dogged determination. It seemed like to me an odd way to approach it but I think Roxie was consulting the index and proceeding alphabetically. She was meticulous, careful to test all the variations. If we skipped a technique, Roxie insisted that we come back to it. I think she wanted to be thorough because she was going to post a review of the book on Amazon.

Now it's my experience from sitting around oilpatch doghouses shooting the shit and drinking beer with oldtime whore-hounds that the rules of the game are that it is okay to exaggerate elements of a story, particularly those that can be stretched without changing the overall story so as to make it unrecognizable. What you don't want to do is tell some magnificent stemwinder about how the pusher got caught screwing a nanny goat, and then maybe a couple of years later, have some asshole ask you to tell that one about how *you* screwed a nanny goat. Almost always a guy will recycle a good story and claim the glory parts happened to him, especially if he's a damn Yankee that has never done nothing that trespasses the boundary of decency, so he has to steal stories to build himself up. And even money says that if he wants to hear it again it's because he's forgot the best parts. And if he forgot the best parts, it's certain he only remembered the worst parts, and probably he's been telling around a virgin of the story that puts me at the tail end of a nanny goat humping away. That's how rumors get started.

So that is my explanation for why I am being especially careful to be precise when I tell that Roxie had sex with me from the time she punched out from the Wal-Mart until before midnight, when I fell exhausted into a blob of trembling flesh. I had a sharp pain in my side brought on by my allergies and the exertion. It wouldn't go away. I thought maybe I'd broke a rib or ripped cartilage or tore a muscle.

I was exhausted, at death's door, and fell into a deep sleep before she could turn off the light on the nightstand. My head was dizzy with images. In a dream-like state, my pecker turned into a railroad train, a cloud of steam blasted around me as the engine plunged into a tunnel.

The screech of the whistle pierced my eardrums. I startled awake and pain stabbed me again. I didn't know where I was. I clapped my hands over my ears. "What the hell is that? Where am I? What the hell time is it?" I couldn't catch my breath.

"Three o'clock." And Roxie was on me again, snatching and grabbing for my vital parts, trying to find something that would come alive. She'd set the alarm. Set the alarm! She had me pinned and evidently wanted to practice some of the difficult material we had glossed over in the middle ranges of the alphabet.

I was huffing and puffing so much I started to cough. Roxie must have thought I was choking. She grabbed me from behind and pulled hard. It was the Heimblick remover and I felt something snap. She tugged and pulled at my belly until I yelled out in pain. I was breathing more natural again. But she was on me with renewed vinegar, intense on making up for lost time.

The sun was up when I made my escape out of her bedroom. I was afraid to wake her. I crawled out of her boudoir on hands and knees. My throat was dry and I still had that hacking cough. Each time I convulsed it exasperated the stabbing pain in my side. I worried that I might be dehydrated. Every muscle in my body ached. I thought I'd been run over by a truck.

A pile of mail was on the floor under a mail slot through the front door. I couldn't help but look. All the envelopes were addressed to Roxie Wickersham. The name "Wickersham" etched itself in my memory.

Thank the Lord, the sun was at my back as I drove to the homeplace. I don't think I could have seen the road with the sun in my eyes. My cough wouldn't go away. Each time I wheezed a sharp pain shot through my old bones. Tears filled my eyes.

I hoped it was the pain and not the growing sense of remorse that overwhelmed me. A cough would go away, some day. Not the remorse.

I hadn't really wanted to go with Roxie to her house and yet I did. And when one thing led to another, I never shut it down. I should have nipped it in the butt. I let my little head do the thinking for my big head.

That name "Wickersham" kept haunting me, too. I thought about it in between coughing attacks and each time seemed to provoke another spell. I was afraid I'd bust another rib if the coughing didn't pass soon. I imagined my thorax and the cartilage between the bones, just like the skeleton we had in the biology class in high school. That's where I learned what metabolism is, and thorax too.

So that's when I started putting two and two together and the result was sixteen. I realized who she was. Roxie Wickersham was the same person that I knew a few years back as Miss Mildred Wickersham who had taught me biology in 10th grade.

So I slinked back to the homeplace, feeling like I was slithering on my belly like a snake. I had to pull the truck over a time or two when tears filled my eyes so bad I couldn't see. I put my head down on the steering wheel and sobbed like a baby. Pain shot through my sorry old bones like an electric shock when I sucked in air.

I snuck into the house and crawled between the sheets in a spare bedroom under a tsunami of thoughts that washed over me every minute about how I'd smashed up a titty-pink Cadillac that belonged to my high school biology teacher whose snatch had felt so nice in my hand. I started coughing again. Maybe I had tuberculosis. Or a collapsed lung.

I had followed my pecker into plenty of places in the past that I would be afraid to go into armed with an AK-47. But that was before I was married. Things were supposed to change. I gave my sacred promise to Wynona and I broke it. I swore to be faithful and I cheated on her.

To my credit, some of the stuff me and Roxie did probably doesn't rise to level of actual two-timing. As one-time President of the United States of America William Jefferson Clinton told us, eating ain't cheating. Even if some of the stuff wasn't cheating on a technicality, I had adultery in my heart at least four times with Roxie. Even if some of the extra stuff wasn't over-the-line immoral, I still think I let Wynona down and I let myself down as well. I hated me and what I'd become. I wondered if I should rat myself out to Wynona. I knew I would. It wouldn't be pretty.

I fell out of bed late in the afternoon. I was still having these coughing attacks which I guess I shouldn't be complaining about. Coughing was about the only exercise I'd been able to get since marrying up with Wynona. Lord, it hurt bad. I ran my sorry old sack of bones under the shower. I would sometimes just stand there and let the water run down my body as if I was a giant rock in a gentle stream. Not today. I jumped like I'd been shot when that hot water dribbled down over my privates. The skin in my crotch burned like I was on fire.

First thing, I thought it was a rash, but on closer inspection, I discovered that it was an abrasion.

I poked around in the medicine cabinet long enough to find a twisted up tube of oinkment. I smeared it on and it helped quieten the fires. Every joint in my body hurt. I think I was almost crippled, but nothing hurt as bad as the overwhelming remorse I felt for giving myself over to my animal desires with Roxie Wickersham.

I found Wynona lounging by the swimming pool which we had recently installed. She was so easy on the eye when she was scandally clad. After we built a new house, we tore down the old frame farm-house and dug out the basement for the pool. The oilwell and the clay mine and the rodeo stock had been good businesses for us and let us build a brand new house.

Wynona spent money like it was water and we ended up with a show house that was too ostenspacious for my taste. I told Wynona I wanted to put in an office in the bunkhouse. She told the bulldozer operator to clear it off but I jumped in to save it. She insisted until I told her I was fond of historic preservation. I was afraid of losing my porthole in time.

Wynona looked as pretty as a speckled pup in that swimming suit. She looked like a model in a picture at the checkout counter of the grocery store. But my batteries were drained and she didn't arouse my lower nature.

My body was telling me that I was hungry not horny, but not for what Wynona was chowing on. She was snacking on tortilla chips and a green chile sauce that was so hot it burned my eyes to look at it. I had another fit of coughing. I thought I was going to cough up a raw oyster. My appetite disappeared.

"Could you cover your mouth?" she said. She was reading a mag-azine about thoroughbred horses. "You know, I've been thinking maybe we ought to dump the rodeo stock."

I couldn't choke back another cough and doubled over in pain.

"Rodeo seems so inhumane," she said.

"It's a good business," I said, trying to straighten myself up. "Those rank old studs just love to buck. Have you ever watched them throw a cowboy? If a horse could smile..."

"This Lexus looks like it was made for me." When I tried to look at the picture, she barked at me again. "Oh stop! Please. You'll spill the chile sauce."

It didn't seem like she had the time to listen to me tell her what a rotten unfaithful bastard I had been, so I went back to the house. Perhaps if I was healthy. Perhaps when she was less preoccupied. I told myself I'd do it tomorrow. But I knew that she would be preoccupied tomorrow. And the next day too. We hadn't talked in a long time. Maybe not forever. I couldn't remember.

I would talk to Old Wynona.

CHAPTER 15

A line of thunderstorms blew into Beckham County that evening. Tornado warnings were out.

In better times, I'd sit around a beer joint with some good old boys and watch the storms on TV radar. We had a game. If the weather man said "hook echo" or "wall cloud" or "Doppler radar," we all drank a beer, but we had to drink two if he said "tornado on the ground" or "baseball-sized hail." We all drank four if he said "Beckham County." A year or two ago, just the smell of whiskey or a woman's muff would drive me crazy. But on this night, I think the smell of either one would have made me upchuck.

When the worst of the storm was past, I threw a slicker over my shoulders, left the house, and headed down to the bunkhouse.

I would have been surprised if the glow under the connecting doorway was dark. I pushed through the way I had on a dozen occasions.

Old Wynona was sitting on that vinyl leather couch propped up by the butt pillow of hers. "Slipping around on me, huh?"

I should have known she'd know. I think I should have known. It struck me as odd that she'd be up in my grill about it. She knew what was going to happen. Why would she only get pissy now?

"What do you care?" I've come up with better lines than that lots of times. She just caught me flat footed.

"Did you ever think of disease? What if you got some slut pregnant? Jesus, you take stupid risks."

"Stupid, huh? You think I'm stupid?"

"You take stupid risks. Clean out your ears."

"You never complained none before." Another chestnut of wisdom. I came down to the bunkhouse to get some advice on how to make amends for my error of having the morals of an alley cat, and all she wanted to do was chew my ass.

"You're nothing. Nothing."

She didn't have to say that. That's when I had a sudden flash of insight. In recent memory, I'd pulled her sorry old bones out of abject poverty, and each and every time I did, I got into a pickle. Worse than that, when I did run into a snag, I found myself running from the trouble. I really didn't like myself not one bit. In that moment, I grew a pair and decided I wasn't going to take another ounce of shit from the old crone.

"I had every intention of being true to you. And another thing, I'm good enough to work my ass off for you. And I'm good enough to get shot at."

"You're talking crazy."

"If I talked sense, you wouldn't understand it. Crazy is sending a dumb ass off to get shot at. Why would you do that?" I didn't need her to answer. It was all becoming clear. "Cause you didn't care if I was dead or alive, that's why."

"You'd be nothing if it weren't for me. Just a shitkicker. A shitty old shitkicker."

"That's enough."

"Shitty shitkicker. Shitty shitkicker. You and them damned old shitty oilwells. If I ever wanted to go somewhere nice, I had to get Junie to go with me."

"My heart ain't enough. You ate that up like an old coyote. A flesh eating old wolf bitch that don't care for nothing but her own self."

"I gave it all up for you. Everything. I could have had any man in the county. Now what do I have?"

That right there was a real good question. "You got half royalty on that oilwell you hear pumping."

"Half! That royalty's mine, shitkicker!"

"Oh..." She was right. She owned the minerals. I just had an override. Other things were becoming clear, too. "Well, I'll be damned. I can't believe I never seen it before now."

"Mine. You hear? Not yours."

"You was surprised they found oil under this place." I acted like this was a fact, but it was just a guess.

"I always knew it was there," she said.

She "knew" it was there. Bull. Shit. She didn't know, no one did, not until some greasy young men punched a hole to the mantle of the earth. And based on the look of the place when I first stumbled in that bunkhouse, no one would have ever made a well on the Vorhees place if it hadn't been for me.

"That ain't right. You was as poor as a snake when I ran on you."

"Okay. So what?" I was right.

"You tricked me again. I put every dime I ever had in this old well."

"And you're making a killing."

"No thanks to you. Just like when you sent me off to catch them desperados. You knew it wasn't just kids."

"You'll get over it."

"How come you got no pictures of old Earl Ray? Answer me that. Why hell, you knew if I went looking for that book, that I'd run into Roxie Wickersham." Another guess.

"You give me too much credit." Right again.

"Yeah, well I haven't had a lifetime to figure out how that doorway works so maybe you did spring a trap. Maybe you didn't. Fact is you had a flank strap on me all the time and I never even knowed it." I sort of reared back. "Why I ought to..." I'm sure she was reading whatever signals my body was sending off. She thought that I wanted to smack the holy hell out of her, but I didn't. Instead, I took out my anger on a framed photo that was propped on her desk. It flew across the room when I took a big swipe at it.

Old Wynona ran to the shattered frame and crouched to pick it up. Clutching the yellowed photo to her bosom, she shrunk back from me in fear. The photo had become a picture of Wynona and Junie standing with rods and reels beside a big billfish that was hanging by its tail.

"Don't you even think about hitting me," she said, wiping a tear from her eye.

"Maybe I ought to, but frankly, my dear, I just don't give a shit."

I had no interest in hitting her. I never had. In that moment, she and I both knew I had no interest in her at all.

Tears rolled down her cheeks as big as horse turds. "You don't love me anymore!" she bawled. "You'd whack me one if you did. Junie told me all along. You bastard. After everything I've done for you."

I pulled the door between the rooms closed behind me. I would never open it again. Never.

Rain was still falling as I slogged back to the house. With the heavy, humid air, each time I inhaled, pain tortured my chest. I was heaving, out of breath. I hollered out "Wynona!" when I walked into the kitchen. I searched the house and never got an answer. "Wynona! Wynona! Where the hell are you?"

I looked in the living room and den, then looked out the window. Wynona's car was in the shed. Junie's car was alongside.

I looked in every room until I came to our bedroom. I walked in and found Wynona in an embrace with Junie. A loving embrace.

"What the hell is this?" I asked. No one needed to answer. I could see now what was true. What I could never see before.

Junie smarted off first. "Don't tell me you're that stupid. That you never suspected."

"I was pretty stupid. But no mas. I ain't no one's fool anymore."

The Flank Strap

Wynona asked me, "Where you going?"

"I'm hitting the dusty trail."

"Earl Ray," she said.

I was afraid she'd do that, to say "Earl Ray" the way she did just to weaken my constitution. It didn't work this time. My constitution was already shot to hell.

"Wait, Earl Ray. Don't do anything rash."

Damn she looked sexy. But I had possession of my cojones for a change. "You ain't got nothing over me no more." I had another spell of uncontrollable coughing, but I was able to find a few pieces of my gear and threw them in a carpet bag. Some clean shirts. Work boots. Civvies. The essentials.

"Let him go, Wynona. Don't stand in the way." That was probably the first time I ever agreed with Junie about anything.

"You aren't getting anything from me. Not a plug nickel. You hear?"

"I don't want nothing from you. I got my overrides. I got part of that well out there. And I still got my shot in the ass money." Gasping for air, I slung the carpet bag over my shoulder and hit the door.

"Earl Ray! Stop!" The front line of the Dallas Cowboys couldn't have held me back. I had no intention of stopping.

I looked back over my shoulder to see Wynona peering outside through a window. Junie eased to her side, renewing her gentle embrace. Wynona's face struck me as emotionless, no tears, no remorse, no regrets. I saw her open her arms and take Junie to her side. I honestly hoped they would find happiness.

I drove away through the rain in my old pickup truck, out toward the county road. The farm road was bracketed by tall fences. Leaving was like looking out a chute leading away into an open rodeo arena. Fingers of lightning danced across the night sky.

So that's how it all came down.

I'm going to renew my efforts to get hired on drilling oilwells.

That's what I really like doing, and I think if I can get put back on as a floorhand, and if I watch my Ps and Qs, I can work myself back up to pusher. Like I said before, I'm putting the reins in my teeth and going in with both guns blazing.

I might look up Chloe Reece. She was just as nice as she could be, pleasing to the eye and she also seemed to have the ability to overlook my flaws.

I even thought I might stop in for a visit with Roxie if I ever get my health back.

THE END

THE ASCENDANT

BY

T-BOB CORVUS

CHAPTER 1

ONE-WAY TICKET TO NICEVILLE

The morning air was as thick as cane syrup. Droplets of water hung in a cold vapor that coalesced into little rivers; they ran down the windows of the bus like snot. I held a one-way ticket to Niceville.

The cretins who joined me on the journey obviously took no effort to look presentable. Their personal grooming made me think they could have been characters in a Victorian penny dreadful. *"Throwbacks,"* I thought, my lip curled in a sneer. *"The kind of low-lifes that knuckle under to authority. They get treated like cattle so they act like cattle."*

Only one taxi was standing at the curb outside the bus station. Leaning on the fender, a gone-to-seed cabbie played air guitar, singing, "I shot that woman 'cause she made me sore, I thought I was her daddy but she had five more."

His voice was raspy, a garbage disposal jammed full of composite roof shingles. At first, I thought he was Danny Bonaduce, only this guy seemed really unhinged.

His eye spotted my golf carry-bag, and with a salute, he jumped behind the wheel and pulled alongside. The golfer inside me recoiled. I paid plenty for the nice leather overnight grip, and the hard carry case with the "Callaway" logo and the clubs inside it were almost new.

I didn't want to look him in the eye. I averted my gaze and noticed, no more than a little 9-iron away, a Rastafarian tramp holding a battered cardboard, hand-lettered sign. "I SMOKE MARIJUANA EVERY DAY." His skin looked as coarse as shoe leather.

Several rolls of toilet paper rode shotgun on the front seat of the cab. I would have jumped out but we were away in traffic. "The FPC, right?" The cabbie's voice boomed as if he thought I was deaf.

"F P C?"

"Federal Prison Camp."

"Just visiting," I winced.

"Yeah right. Just visiting. I stand on the cab line here at ten forty in the A. M. every day just to pick up bus riders visiting the FPC with golf clubs."

"Maybe I need to work on my short game."

The driver hit the brake and as I lurched forward, he shouted, "Hold the phone." Now he had his head out the window; screaming like a washerwoman, "Hey, Spock!"

The cab skidded to a stop alongside the Rastafarian panhandler. His hair was as white as snow and hung in snarled dreadlocks, his wardrobe layered and filthy. The mint juleps at Churchill Downs come in tumblers with bottoms nowhere near as thick as the lenses of his dark eyeglasses.

From the floorboard of the cab, the driver pulled up a plastic bag full of fruit and produce. He topped the sack off with a couple of rolls of toilet paper. Handing the kit out the window to the beggar, he yelled, "Them's all organic. So, don't go trading for no dope. I'd let you have more paper but I'm running low."

The Rastafarian named Spock didn't say hello or thanks.

My eyes locked with the bespectacled beggar. He glared at me as if he was trying to plumb the well of my soul. Goosebumps rose up on my neck. He mumbled something at me but his words were incoherent. He pressed the scrawled, stained cardboard sign to the window. "I SMOKE MARIJUANA EVERY DAY."

"Turn up the heater, would you?" I asked. The driver slammed on the accelerator and launched us into traffic again.

Mindless to the traffic, the driver turned his head to shout at me. "If you got any drugs or weed, you better leave it here. You take a hundred bucks for them Callaways?"

"I don't do drugs," I said, "And the golf clubs aren't for sale."

"Haha. You must be one of those guys that never inhaled. Hahaha."

"Never tried."

"Never tried, my fanny. Have it your way, buddy boy. We don't have a lot of time. There's some stuff you need to know. Now the FPC, that's the federal prison camp, it's right next to an air force base. Yeah, they got an oversized alligator nest just outside the gates that they call a golf course. Built by Al Capone. Which don't make any difference, sunshine, 'cause you ain't getting them golf clubs inside a federal prison."

"I got a lawyer...he says..."

"Yeah, you right. Probably top of his class." Between his teeth, the cabbie sizzled a few bars of a riff from his song. "Since I quit cussing, no one would guess, but I was in there myself once. An inmate. Yeah. So, to me, it ain't nothing to be ashamed of. I put my time to good use, too. So, in a way, it was worth it. The FPC, that's where I got my ascendancy over women."

"Ascendancy over...?" It was a question that wasn't worth asking. "What were you in for?"

The cabbie whistled another little bit, then cut himself short. "It ain't even eleven o'clock yet. You want to take the scenic route? They ain't expecting you 'til two. What do you say? I'll give you a hundred twenty-five for them Callaways, so looking at it my way, the cab ride's coming out of my pocket."

He had me nailed, as if he'd been reading my mail. I was early, and if this fartknocker wanted to drive me around town, I might as well just let him do it.

"Call me Putz," he said. "The place you're going to don't have a fence, just a yellow stripe. On the other side of the yellow it's Eglin Air Force Base. That's where I met old Spock back there. He wasn't my bunkie, but someone has to look out for him. He just up and walked away one day."

The cabbie proceeded to reel off some of his "big house" stories, tales about the life of an inmate, inside, and hell, I can't explain it, because he was the last person in the world that anyone would call eloquent, but vivid images of the things he was describing pushed into my mind. Maybe I was tired. Maybe I just wanted to forget my problems and was willing to suspend disbelief. I can't explain it, but pictures popped in my mind as he unwound his tales and the images were sharp. The yarns seemed practiced, but as intense as if they had happened just yesterday.

CHAPTER 2

BIG HOUSE

What Putz shared was a story about the first time he walked into the inmate's TV lounge. It was a tired place, the whole FPC was, too. Everything painted federal green. The carpeting was threadbare; the hollow-core doors may as well have been made of Styrofoam. The drywall looked like Florida drywall always looks, imbibed in sweat. An ageless aroma hung in the air, the odor like a wet dog or an Uncle Wally fart. But the signal feature of the shabby FPC was sound. Noise echoed inside the '70s structure built by the lowest bidder.

A dozen or more inmates loitered in the lounge, milling in and out. Some shot pool on a decaying table, its felt timeworn and as cobwebby as cheesecloth. None of the cues had tips. Other jailbirds sprawled across Naugahyde couches, most dressed in nylon gym clothes or gray sweats. Two-thirds of them were Latinos, the rest of them reposed on some other corner of the white/black spectrum.

Putz moseyed around the room and was drawn to a wild-haired inmate that sat at a desk behind a stack of law books, scribbling notes on a legal pad as if there were no tomorrow, highlighting, transcribing, killing rats, bent close to his notepad, peering out of green-tinted eyeglasses. Through the thick lenses, his orbs looked like piss holes in the snow. At his back sat an ancient television set. The picture rolled every couple of seconds and the sound was scratchy. The show was probably a soap opera but the audio was garbled and the screen flipped too often to read the actor's lips. It didn't look to Putz like the TV was contributing anything but noise. No one was watching.

"Minimum security is almost the same as pre-release. You find all kind of guys in a federal prison camp. Drug dealers. Bank robbers. Mafia dons. Doctors and lawyers. Contrary to the popular suppository, most of the population is Latinos. It don't make no difference what you done as long as you're not violent. If you lose control, it's bingo bango bongo, man, you're off to lockdown quick as Jody."

Putz approached the TV set. It was bolted to the wall, high in a corner. He looked around again and once he'd convinced himself no one was watching, he reached up for the channel knob.

"Don't touch that dial," the wild-haired crazy man shouted.

How did he see Putz? The crazy man didn't have eyes in the back of his head. Maybe he was talking to someone else. Putz double-checked. No one was watching the TV. "You're not watching."

"Go ahead, then. Let one of these missing links work you over. You masochist. At least I won't be the only one in here on his deathbed."

"Didn't know it was life or death." Putz drew back from the TV. Even if the channel had been tuned to something good like Jerry Springer, the reception was too lousy to make the effort worthwhile.

"That guy Spock back there...the panhandler, he was an inmate. Just walked out one day. That's a sure-fire way to get sent to maximum security. You can run, but you can't hide. The man will find you sooner or later. When I first met old Spock, he ran the prison library. One of the drug dealers named him Spock because he used to be a rocket scientist or something."

"I heard about you. They call you Spock. You trying to get yourself sprung from this joint, Spock?"

"Not me, I'm working out a case for one of the black kids. Holy cosmos, fifteen years on a trumped-up assault on an Indian reservation charge. Can you believe that?"

Putz shrugged. "I can believe that, yeah."

"That wasn't a rhetorical question."

"I got my own problems," Putz said.

"So smug you are, you lactose tolerant types. You never think about anyone else but yourself, do you?"

"I have always been a dukes up guy and I didn't like the tone this Spock character was coming at me with."

"I think about my BabyDoll. I'd rather die than let her be alone at Christmas."

"You might think differently if you'd spent half your life on the toilet stool, purging boiling water from a spastic bowel. Some phony god you dreamed up curses this pitiful world with cancers and... erectile dysfunction...and all you worry about is whether you can sink a three-foot putt. You freaking putz."

"Once the word got around of what Spock said, there wasn't no way I was going to get called anything but Putz. I've been called worse. Of course, Spock didn't say 'freaking putz,' but now days I talk with a PG rating, 'cause like I told you, I decided to quit cussing. Anyhow, Spock got reduced sentences for lots of the black kids. Too bad for him. His own sentence was righteous."

Putz grabbed a magazine. It was five years old. Another exercise in futility. All that afternoon, a steady stream of black inmates brought tribute to Spock. A carton of cigarettes, tins of canned mackerel, sacks of M&M candies.

As suppertime approached, Spock gave his hoard of canned mackerel to a Latino with a jagged scar across his face. The others called him Rojo and he had cigarettes to trade for the canned fish.

"I thought I might introduce myself to this Rojo guy, but before I could say anything, he told me, 'Chinga tu madre, puta.' That there was one angry Latino. He had bad attitude written all over his scowling face, and heck, everyone knows what 'madre' means.

I figured I was better off not knowing what he meant by the rest of what he called me."

I considered telling Putz that I'd take a rain check on the cook's tour of Niceville. I could do without a taxicab travelogue. But then I changed my mind. It might not be a bad idea to get the lay of the land. What would it hurt? A package deal, some good and some bad. Even when you hit a hole in one, you have to charge yourself a stroke, right? Before I had a chance to speak up, Putz was yakking his head off again. He must have had the volume knob turned to eleven.

"So anyway, Spock sprung so many black kids out of prison that they fired him from the library and put him to work in the repair store with me and my first bunkie, Dickdock. The repair store is just off base, too. A place where the airmen can borrow chainsaws and rototillers and crap like that. Self-help. Every air base in the country has one. At Eglin, they run the repair store with inmates from the prison camp. And when you're on a work detail, you have to wear a uniform."

A handful of khaki-clad inmates grabbed some ass time on the loading dock behind the repair store. An overhead door opened into a dark warehouse, and the men lounged in the opening, unguarded. They wouldn't be in minimum security if they posed a runaway risk.

Spock hunched over an electric motor as if modern civilization would collapse if he failed to bring the device back to life. A black inmate in his twenties, the others called him Beale Street, sat with his back against a frosty stack of boxes marked "frozen pork chops." Dickdock was pacing, licking his lips as if he needed a drink, and tapping a pencil on a clipboard. Putz leaned on a push broom. They clustered in the shadow of the depot, where the open warehouse door drew a gentle cooling air current into the storehouse.

"Oh no," Dickdock said. His voice seemed set in a constant whine.

"Beale Street. We still owe the Mexicans. Why does this always happen to me?"

"Listen, Dickdock, it's three hundred to the kitchen," Beale Street said. "The Mexicans get a hundred sixty-five macks, the brothers get forty-two cartons. Don't they teach you nothing in medical school?"

Dickdock still had his head in the numbers when an Air Force car drove up, slammed on the brakes, then backed up to the dock. The driver stepped out. He was well known to the inmates. Major Slaughter was his name, one scary dude, Rambo on steroids, not much older than thirty. He was outfitted in camo with large black helicopter-shaped pins on his collar. He swaggered to the back of his car, and as he opened the trunk, he shoved a paper into Putz' chest. An equipment order.

"The general's wife will be by to pick this stuff up," he told Putz. Then his eyes turned to Beale Street. "Hey you, convict! Throw a case of those pork chops in the turtle-hull." Beale Street slid off the dock and grabbed a case of the chops. He dumped it into Major Slaughter's trunk.

"Why do we have to honey these guys up?" Dickdock's fists were clenched. "We don't answer to them."

"Building 141," Beale Street whispered. "Special operations. Black helicopters." Major Slaughter drove away without offering thanks. The air was more breathable now. The inmates exhaled a sigh of relief.

"Someone is always trying to muscle in on our juice," Dickdock whined. "We'll never get this project to balance."

Major Slaughter had tried to imbed the shop order onto Putz' chest. He peeled it off. A step ladder and a door mirror. No problem. The items were easy to find in the storehouse and he brought them to the loading platform where Dickdock still fussed about balancing his books.

"It's still short."

"Don't worry," Beale Street told him. "Butterfly can throw in some generic virginia. It's distribution."

Dickdock glared at Putz. "What's that stuff, Putz?"

"I just filled an order."

Beale Street tapped his temple. "Quit helping, man. You'll get us busted. What you doing?"

"Two and a half years."

Wheels began to turn in Spock's head. "Two and a half years, huh? Let's see that's three sixty-five times two point five. That's uh..."

"Nine hundred thirteen days," Beale Street said.

"Three to two you can't get in the drug and alcohol program," Dickdock said. Putz had his bunkie Dickdock pegged for a drinker and his comment was another tell. His bunkie liked to gamble.

"I'm going to wiggle out of that drug and alcohol dog and pony show as soon as I can figure out who has my file. Cause heck, I ain't no drunk. I hardly ever even drink a beer."

"Don't be an idiot, Putz. Drug and alcohol treatment knocks off a year," Spock said. His hands pushed and pulled side-to-side is if he was operating a slide rule. "Subtract another fifteen percent good time and you're out uh..."

Beale Street shook his head. "You'll get your walking papers next December twenty-third. You bozos act like you can't do arithmetic."

"I can get that file of yours to say you're a woman if you want," Dickdock said.

"December 23rd. Wow. That's a relief. If alcohol treatment gets me home by Christmas, then I drink like a fish," Putz told them. "Now, what's this crappola about a bus ticket?"

An Air Force blue SUV backed into the bay and the discussion stalled. The driver was a female and she slid from the seat and traipsed, yes traipsed, to the rear of the vehicle. She was a total knockout and the inmates enjoyed looking at the package, every bit, every inch, front and back. She was not young, forties probably, but she was drop-dead gorgeous, trim and athletic, strolling sloo-oo-oow on red, spike-heeled shoes. The eyes of the inmates followed up each leg as if they were watching a rocket taking off at Cape Kennedy. Up past a muscular calf, above thighs as smooth as caramel, she wore a short tennis skirt that was slit on the side higher than the cheeks of her fanny.

"Holy cripes," Beale Street said, clearing a wad of nothing in his craw. "Look at the tits on that child."

"Does someone have a mirror for me?" she asked. Her voice was thickened by an eastern European accent.

Loading the mirror in the SUV was secondary to getting a closer look at this, the most divine of God's creations. Spock grabbed the mirror away from Putz. With a come-hither smile, the wench indicated that she wanted Spock to hold the looking-glass still. She gave herself a once-over; the inmates gave her a dozen-over. They panted like a pack of winded foxhounds.

Spock's effort to hold the mirror still was overkill. This goddess had the raw power to hold the mirror's gaze. "Dahlia," Spock slobbered.

"Charmed. How did you know my name?" She checked her makeup and applied more lipstick. It was easy for Putz to figure out that she'd never seen an ugly mirror. She opened the back door of the SUV once she was satisfied that her makeup was perfect.

"I hope we have room," she said. Her throaty Slovene pronunciation of "room" sounded like "womb." Spock eased the mirror to the ground, jumped from the dock, missed his footing, and skidded across the driveway on his belly.

"Knock it off, Spock," Beale Street said. "Someone's gonna see you, man."

"What can they do, put him in jail?" Putz said.

"All the Air Force women like to tease the prisoners. I figure they get their hots thinking about some poor schmuck back in his cell and working off some fantasy. Even the officer's wives do it."

Dahlia hesitated. She reached out with a bronze arm to help Spock to his feet. For a long moment, she held him in her arms. She smiled. Right in his face. She massaged his muscles and his eyes nearly popped out of his head. Sweat squirted from every pore on Spock's brow and ran in rivers over his thick green glasses.

"Goodness," she said. "Aren't you the powerhouse?"

Spock's body stiffened, and as the blood ran out of his face, his complexion bleached. He was an alabaster statue.

Dahlia arranged a place for the mirror in the back of the SUV, bending over to push and shove at loose packages in the back. The hem of her skirt...something as short as that garment shouldn't really be called a skirt...whatever it was called, it worked its way up and over a world-class round tushie. Lime-colored panties peeked out at Spock. The sinew on his neck stood out like wire rope. Bodily fluids soaked his uniform and puddled at his feet.

She glanced back at him, her eyes twinkling. She seemed to delight in the knowledge that Spock got a real good peek. "Do you think we can get it in?" she asked. She had smoky eyes and a knowing allure, like Greta Garbo, but she also had that get-your-ass-over-here-you-stinking-bootlicker smile of Barbara Stanwyck. The tiniest smile. At the edge of perception. She hadn't had this much fun in days.

"Yeah, we'll get it in," Spock's voice cracked and gained an octave. "Don't you worry about that."

Head count. Five minutes."

A daily ritual. The inmates were supposed to line up and count off in front of Boss Hack, a world-weary civil servant with long fingernails. She stood about four feet tall and could tell you on a moment's notice exactly how many days she had to go to retirement. All the inmates knew she wouldn't hesitate to write up a disciplinary referral on them for infractions, especially the rules that were the most meaningless and arbitrary. She screamed out again and her practiced yell carried over the roar of the noisy room.

"Head count. Five minutes."

Spock jumped up to stand beside Rojo and the nose count was taken: "one, two, three four..." Every inmate accounted for. Spock handed over a dozen tins of canned mackerel to Rojo. In exchange,

Rojo gave him a pair of lady's panties, a sheer fabric printed with kitty-cats on a field of yellow.

Spock exploded. "What the hell you trying to pull? We had a deal." He was up in the scarred face of the Latino, fists clenched, teeth bared. It looked like a fight was going to break out. A slippery slope to maximum security for both inmates. The tension broke when the Latino laughed.

"Here you go, El Spocko, just what you ordered." He pulled a pair of lime-green panties out of his shirt and tossed them in Spock's face.

Spock shuddered, inhaling deeply through the lingerie that hung over his nose. "D...D...Dahlia," he murmured. He stuffed the panties in his pocket.

Dahlia Balyew. She's kind of long in the tooth, but she has a body that's as strong as lye soap. A real tease. Lots of the pilots had wives that were big prick teasers, too. While the old man gets his jollies doing barrel rolls in an F sixteen, their wives get off thinking they turned an inmate to stone. Some of them ain't even that good looking, but they have a lot of fun teasing.

As Putz told it, a few days later found Spock hiding out in the storeroom of the repair shop. He had staked out more secret places to sleep than anyone. That day, he needed quiet time to plan his finances and he didn't like the picture he saw. With his access to the library cut off, his revenue had dropped off the table. The only income he had was the eleven cents an hour he earned working, or some would say, screwing off, in the repair store.

A noise startled him. He followed the sound that led him between the ceiling-high shelves loaded down with plumbing fittings.

At the end of the shadowy aisle, a boxed bathtub stood on end. And peeking out from behind the tall container he found a young lady, a captain's wife. She signaled Spock to approach her, giving him the come-on, beckoning him forward with a smile and a curling finger. She dodged behind the tall carton.

Spock looked back over his shoulder. No one was coming. The

storehouse was quiet. He stepped behind the box and found the captain's wife bent over a bench, looking back at him with a drop-your-drawers smile, pulling up the hem of her dress.

Spock sputtered. "So where is this going?"

"Say 'what do you want from me, Catherine?'" she told him. "Say just exactly that. 'What do you want from me, Catherine?'"

"Wha...wha...what the freak do you want from me, Catherine?" Spock mumbled.

She pulled her hem higher. Spock's tongue dropped out of his mouth. He hoped to release his junk similarly; he tugged frantically at his belt buckle. With a final yank, the young lady exposed her butt, now only concealed by...white panties.

"White!" Spock shouted out as if he'd been shot. "White...ite... ite!" echoed to the far corners of the warehouse. Spock slumped back against a box of plumbing fittings on the other side of the aisle. An avalanche of PVC cascaded over him. All the starch in his erectile tissues turned to mush. White panties didn't do the trick; worse than that, they turned him off. They did less than nothing for him. He needed lime-green. Without lime-green, this woman that called herself Catherine was just wasting his time. He tightened his belt, a tear welled in the corner of his eye. "Sorry, lady. Employees only back here."

For weeks after that, in the evenings, Spock sat alone in the inmate's lounge, hang-dog, brooding in a corner. Most inmates hung out in the lounge to snag some R&R, watch TV, shoot pool or play cards. Several black inmates set a perimeter to keep the riff-raff from intruding on Spock's space. He mumbled to himself, agonizing over his personal problems. He had no income. He had needs. Wants. His body had unrequited desires, but made demands he couldn't carry out. He mumbled to himself, "What is the law? Not to spill blood. Not to chase other men. Not to go on all fours. Not to eat flesh. This is the law. Are we not men?"

CHAPTER 3

ARE WE NOT MEN?

"So, this general's wife threw Spock into a funk, and finally, one day, he just walked away. Put on street clothes and just walked over the yellow line and he was gone. You can run but you can't hide. It don't take them no time to find a guy that walks out. When they nabbed him, they sent him straight to lock down which is the same as what you people in the free world call hard time. No more minimum security. All his good time, just pfffft out the window.

"They should have put him to some kind of decent job. They must have a hundred science labs on an Air Force base. But the Warden's got a rule. You can't do nothing that uses the tools or skills you used in your trade on the outside. Cooks don't cook and bricklayers don't lay bricks. Not that the Air Force officers give a rat's patoot for what the Warden says. Especially the General. It's his darned Air Force base, and Eglin is the biggest one on the face of the solar system. And if the General ain't powerful enough, he's got this place called Building 141 that's full of assassins so bad they eat Navy seals for lunch. I never seen one of them black helicopters, they're invisible, but at Eglin, they got them.

"As long as he had his lawyering business, Spock had it pretty good inside, plenty of boodle, with the added plus that he had the blacks protecting him. The most important thing about being in prison is that you got to make money off of some scam or another because they only pay you eleven cents an hour. That's seven bucks a week."

A blue-painted used-to-be school bus drove into the FPC lot. From the highway outside the camp, no one would think the minimum-security facility was anything other than a gone-to-seed motel. A young black male sobbed when he saw the prison camp just outside his window. The new arrival might not have been twenty, and he sagged back into the seat. He was dirty, hungry, and shivered feverishly. "Home sweet home," he told the vacant seat beside him.

"But when it came to earning his way, Spock couldn't hold a candle to Butterfly. No one could. Even when his scam was hitting it on the downstroke. Butterfly got back to the FPC just in time for pork chop night, which was a scam run by Beale Street and my first bunkie Dickdock. Beale Street was a real bona fide criminal but he had experience in distribution. Dickdock was a medical doctor, a urologist. He just had a gambling problem."

For the evening, the inmates all shucked the uniforms they were required to wear in the daytime. A line of men dressed in gray sweats shuffled past a steam table in the dining hall. Putz, Spock, and Butterfly lead the line past Dickdock and Beale Street, who heaped gravy-smothered pork chops and other hearty foodstuffs on the square trays presented by passing inmates.

"You shoulda seen it in the good old days, when the Senator was here," Dickdock said.

Butterfly crammed food into his mouth like Joey Chestnut. He hadn't had food in his stomach in days.

Sitting apart from the chop-gobbling inmates was a group of skull-capped convicts, blacks and whites, Muslims and Jews. They chowed on a muddy gruel, and Spock chose to park his carcass at their table.

"You ought to try fish oils," Spock told them. "Unparalleled efficacy with triglycerides. Now that's not to say they can't be overdone. Got to watch it. Fish oil supplementation increases LDL, studies prove it."

Beale Street wasn't so magnanimous. He snarled at the Jewish and Muslim inmates. It pissed him off that anyone would turn up their nose at his cooking. "They're ready to break," he told his serving partner. "They'll be in line soon."

"A carton of smokes says they stand their ground," Dickdock said.

"You're on," Beale Street said. "Hey assholes," he shouted over the din of the dining hall. "Hey, there's good food here. Kids are starving in China."

"Dude, that's undue influence," Dickdock complained.

"We're going to throw this out!" Beale Street shouted. The gruel-eaters dropped their spoons.

"Don't listen to him," Dickdock begged. "Concentrate. Ask yourself 'what would Mohammed do?'"

"This pork chop is begging you. 'Ab dooooool. Eat me, Abdul.'" Two Muslim inmates pocketed their headgear and jostled into the serving line.

"Hallelujah, brothers, you're in the bosom of Abraham now. Thank you. GEE-sus!"

Butterfly elbowed his way back into line ahead of Wang, an Asian male FPC staffer outfitted in a waist-length white physician's assistant's jacket.

"Butter-fry you sorry buzzard you stay outta my face you horse's patootey you not gonna get nothing from me by gosh not even a gall-danged band-aid you buzzard you."

The bones of half a pig already lay decomposing on Butterfly's tray, but he wasn't shy about snagging another helping. Even as he moved down the line, he packed it away as if he'd never eaten before. "Oh, my soul, this tastes good."

Butterfly was a repeat offender. Dickdock and Beale Street knew him. He'd been an inmate at the FPC before. It was Spock's

legal genius that put him back on the street in the first place. I was really surprised to realize just how effeminate he was."

"Do you realize what kind of crap you're ingesting?" Spock shouted at him. "Good god, man, think of your fundamental aperture."

"A soon as he recovered his health, ol' Butterfly got off of his ass and back on his back til he was back on his feet."

The pork chop night story lost its way. Now Putz was telling me about Butterfly and his work assignment. The way I saw him was with the blush of health on his cheeks, in his khaki prison uniform, with a clear plastic bag slung over his shoulder. He patrolled a beach where hundreds of airmen collected to catch the sun and enjoy the sand and surf.

"They assigned him to trash patrol. Basically, that's the road crew, but he spent most of his days on what us gringos call Pecker Beach."

Young and old, red and yellow, black and white, Butterfly smiled demurely at all the swim-suited airmen. At first, he stuffed a sock in the crotch of his uniform trousers, but as his revenue stream grew stronger, he began using a roll of currency, which grew in size commensurate with his earnings. The airmen took notice. At any rate, a few of them did. Butterfly only needed a few.

"Some green money makes its way inside, but it's contraband. Cigarettes is the main unit of exchange, but the Mexicans, if you want to deal with them, you better have canned mackerel."

Putz shifted gears again. His story staggered off in another direction. Next, he was telling me about the FPC barracks. It was a long, narrow room that held two dozen metal bunk beds, half on either side of a central aisle. Tall, narrow school lockers against the walls separated the bunks. The sleeping quarters were just as noisy as the common area.

The bed that had been assigned to Putz was the upper berth against a back wall. Some long-forgotten inmate had carved the words "THE WATERFRONT" in the spongy wallboard above his bed.

At the foot of his bed was the crapper. The jamb over the door said "LATRINE."

From the bowels of the toilet facility, a voice shouted "Judas Priest, would you flush the darned thing once in a while?" A commode discharged its contents. The water must have dropped into the pot under high pressure. KA-WOOSH! The noises reverberated inside the shithouse and ricocheted off of the tile walls and into the open barracks.

Butterfly opened a locker; it was full to overflowing with canned mackerel and cartons of cigarettes. He picked out a small sack of M&M candies.

"Hey dang it, there's nothing here to wipe on. Who used all the shit tickets?" The sound of another blast of water slamming through a toilet echoed out of the latrine.

Butterfly sat on his bunk and dabbed the red candy on his lips as if it were lipstick.

"Unless you want to work your buns off, which 'A', no one wants to do, and number two, is going to make your buddies look bad, you better start off the day collecting your props. The road crews get pickup trucks, and as long as they get back for head count, there ain't nothing to keep them from driving into town."

At a convenience store in Niceville, two khaki-clad inmates crawled into a trash dumpster. They filled their plastic bags with trash and handed them to Butterfly, who tied them off and hoisted them into the back of the truck. On the theory that the best place to hide a pebble is on a beach, the inmates filled the truck's bed full of bagged trash, and once garnished with weedeaters, no one would ever question the diligence of the crew that set off to grab some ass time on a secluded roadway behind the Air Force golf course.

"You'd think if there was any place in the world you didn't have to worry about drunk drivers it would be in a federal prison camp."

The crew had a daily gathering with a van full of lady friends bearing a cooler of beer.

Across the road from the trucks filled with pilfered trash, the van that brought their guests to the rendezvous swayed side-to-side on its springs. Delighted sounds of lovemaking kept rhythm with the rocking van.

Without warning, a SUV skated around a far corner and sped toward the congress of trash haulers. It fish-tailed in their direction, the engine wailing, trying to push the SUV into overdrive. A hundred and fifty yards away, it swerved as if to dodge a roadway obstacle, but too late. The heavy vehicle slammed into a dark lump in the road and the sound of thump-bump alerted the road crew to the vehicle's advance. The SUV twisted erratically, unable to gain control. The trash haulers scattered.

As the SUV came closer, Butterfly took flight. He headed across the roadway. "Help. We'll all be killed," Butterfly cried.

The tires of the SUV screeched, but unable to stop, the vehicle hammered into the hapless Butterfly. His body bounced over the roof and sailed like a Frisbee into the roadside ditch.

The SUV crimped its wheels and steered off the center of the road. It slammed to a dead stop just before crashing into the gully. The left-side door opened and the driver, a woman, wormed out onto the roadway, and standing, reeled as if she were dizzy. It was Dahlia Balyew, the general's wife. She slumped on the ground on all fours, grass-grabbing drunk.

If any of the inmates had looked, they would have seen that she was wearing lime-green panties. But none of them gave a tinker's damn about her. Their attention was drawn to Butterfly. They ran to his side in the ditch. Miraculously, he was still alive.

On all fours, Dahlia vomited. She puked until she couldn't puke any more. Then she puked some more. Puking is like that. Then as she regained some control, she crawled back into the SUV, the engine roared to life, and she sped away.

The Ascendant

Three days later, Butterfly found himself sitting in a straight-backed chair, wearing a restrictive brace on his neck. Everywhere his skin was exposed was littered with bandages.

Wang the nurse stood by, grim-faced, his arms folded across his chest.

A starchy bureaucrat sat behind the desk opposite Butterfly. Twice the young inmate's age, he was playing FreeCell on his computer, waiting for someone to join the meeting. "WARDEN LILLARD" was written on the desk nameplate. His phone crackled "General Balyew" and a no-nonsense war hero marched into the Warden's room.

He shut the door behind him and jump-cut over the genial chit-chat segment the generally leads off a business meeting. Straight to the important part. "The Air Force and the Bureau of Prisons have an unbroken record of cooperation."

"I'd love to help you, General," the Warden said, obviously lying, "but it's difficult to overlook a broken neck."

"I lay on the foreskin of a coma for three days," Butterfly cried. "And then I had to beg that confused young Asian boy for an aspirin. I just cried." Tears the size of horse turds ran down his wounded face.

Wang jumped toward Butterfly as if he was going to strangle the broken inmate. "Who you calling confused? Chump you get no help from Wang you just want to lay out, you lazy buzzard you, Butter-fry."

General Balyew put a restraining grip on Wang's arm and addressed Butterfly. "Listen son, we don't ask and we don't tell."

"Maybe you don't. I do."

"You lazy no good for nothing buzzard, you not hurt you just a waste of good band-aids." Wang was jumping up and down, hopping mad.

Drama wasn't on the General's agenda and his patience was wearing thin. "Shut that dumb buck up, Lillard. For the love of God, man, that was my wife driving."

Warden Lillard turned away from his FreeCell game to give a 'zip it' gesture to Wang.

"The strain to my cervical region is severe and palpable and painful in the extreme," Butterfly wept.

"What's it going to take, son?" the General asked.

Butterfly turned off the tears as if he was cranking down a spigot. He batted his eyelashes at the General. "Aren't you the charmer?"

"How much cash?" the General asked. "Twenty thousand dollars?"

Behind the General's back, Warden Lillard gave Butterfly an upward thumb gesture that told Butterfly the offer was way too low.

"No."

"Thirty. Thirty-five thousand. And you're out tomorrow, a free...er person."

"What about my probation?" Butterfly asked.

"Six months," the Warden said.

"In the name of justice, that's totally unacceptable," Butterfly said.

The General was flushed with the indignity of having to negotiate with an inmate that he figured wasn't even fit to serve his country. "Just keep your gosh-darned mouth shut. I mean about the settlement...cough cough."

"It's confidential," Warden Lillard said.

The General flashed a you-stay-the-hell-out-of-it grimace at the Warden.

"You mock me," Butterfly demanded. "Three year's probation, not a day less. I might need to come back. Three years or I go straight to the newspaper and the BOP and the Air Force. I can just imagine the headlines in my mind's eye. 'Beautiful Inmate crushed like a bug by a drunk general's wife driving a gas guzzling SUV.'"

The General slumped into a chair. Butterfly pulled himself up and stood over him.

"Scratch that," Butterfly said. "I'll make sure it says 'comely inmate crushed.'"

"Give him the three years, gosh darn it," the General said.

"Certified funds, please. I'll pick up my check tomorrow."

"It would only take a shoplifting charge to get Butterfly back to

three hots and a cot as soon as he blew through that thirty-five K. It was just like having keys to the vault if that's the way you roll."

In the parking lot of the FPC, Beale Street and other inmates waved good-bye to Butterfly as he climbed into a taxicab.

"Come back soon," Beale Street told him.

"It ain't all that uncommon for a guy's health to improve when he gets to a federal prison camp. He's got plenty of time to get exercise."

CHAPTER 4

THE CATCH

The wipers on the taxicab flapped back and forth, smearing the windshield and beating a squeaky rhythm.

"Come on, man," I said. "Answer the question. What were you convicted of?"

Putz adjusted the rear-view mirror and gave me a steely look. Ignoring my inquiry, he returned to his soliloquy.

"Some of those guys, man it's like they are in different tribes or something. This card shark we called Rojo. He didn't like me because as far as I was concerned he was a Mexican. But I guess he was a Puerto Rican on a technicality. So, when they ask him his occupation, he told them he was a mechanic which was true, he was a card mechanic, and he thought he'd like a work assignment in the marina. Learning to fix stuff, you know, small motors and crap like that."

The neurons in my brain signaled millions of others to imagine that I was watching Rojo in the barracks myself. He had a crowd of onlookers and was performing sleight of hand tricks for them. He offered his mark a pack of cigarettes, but when the inmate opened his hand, he had a can of mackerel and Rojo had the mark's wristwatch.

"He never set foot inside the marina. That's because if he was a mechanic, and according to the rule, the last thing he was going to see was a motor—no mas motorola para tu, amigo. Pretty soon they put him in charge of landscaping the General's house. They wouldn't let him near a lawn mower. Some other crew did that anyway. Rojo the mechanic couldn't even borrow a rototiller out of the self-help shop.

"They fired us all out of the self-help shop. Put us all on the golf course crew. Rojo had a truck garden going in the woods near the General's house. He kept fresh vegetables on the General's table. The General's wife had some to give away. Things started looking up for Rojo when me and Spock opened business."

Only a low fence marked the border between the golf course and the General's residence.

Gardening was hard work, but Rojo tended the vegetables every day. He chose the location in a clearing that let him keep an eye on the General's house without being seen. From that vantage point he could watch the General's wife Dahlia sunbathe. If she was in the yard, guaranteed, she was wearing a bikini or something scanty. The Latino should have dipped leaves out of the pool himself, but it was more fun to watch her.

Spock and Putz shared golf course tools—rakes, hoes and shovels— with Rojo. The shop assigned them a small two-seated turf truck, a carry-all, with a tiny flatbed and short sideboards. It was just a long golf cart. After dumping the tools, Rojo hefted three clear plastic trash sacks full of garden produce into the bed of the turf truck. He removed the doo-rag from his head and wiped his forehead.

"Rojo, I'm going to kill you," Spock said. He was leaning against a tree, relieving himself. "You...you've been holding out on me."

Through the tree line, Spock ogled Dahlia. She was singing a lilting Germanic melody while cleaning the pool. He froze in his tracks. His fist squeezed around his Johnson like a vise. Sweat beads popped out on his forehead.

Dahlia bent over, way over. She must have been trying to snag a leaf at the end of the reach of her dip net. Lime-green panties.

The Ascendant

"She's winking at you, Spock," Putz said.

"I'm going crazy. I can't sleep," Spock gurgled. "I wake up obsessing."

"Easy pendajo," Rojo told him. "You owe me eighty-five macks. You see to it Spock pays up, puta, or I slice you like a cantaloupe."

Putz tied down his load. "Don't sweat it, Mexican."

"You shut you boca you white-collar gringo punta." Rojo jumped into the turf truck, hit the accelerator and raced a big circle around the garden plot. As he returned to the point of origin, it was clear that he'd acquired a target. He was bearing down on Putz. "Arriba. Arriba. Andele," he shouted.

Putz dodged behind a tree to avoid getting run over. Then another. "Be careful, man, you'll bruise the goods."

Spock still had his best friend in his fist and was staring at the bronzed figure in the General's yard. "Dahlia," he said, "Dahlia, Dahlia." He was transfixed.

P utz and Spock drove several hundred yards away, to the back nine, where a roadway bordered the course. Several khaki-clad inmates patrolled the shoulder of the route through the woods. Two of them were talking on cell phones. Two others lifted the produce bags out of the turf truck and into the back of the crew's pickup truck. Another propped up a hand-lettered sign that read "FRESH PRODUCE."

Across the road was a van. It had a painting on the side of a yellow sunset beyond a couple of orange palm trees. Civilian, and unauthorized fraternizing was going on inside, based on the way it rocked to and fro on its springs.

"Them road crews have it pretty good. Cell phones are contraband but hey, compared to the enterprise we set them up in, phones would be the last thing the hacks would worry about. Anyway, they got them, and since we had strong business ties, they would let me make a call every now and then. I was glad to get a chance to call my BabyDoll or do some of my other business

without a bunch of inquiring minds watching like they did in the barracks."

Rojo grew the veggies and sold them to Spock and Putz, who provided transportation, which Rojo couldn't do himself because of the catch. Spock and Putz marked up the goods and resold them to the road crew, who in turn, purveyed them to the ultimate consumer, a lucky few citizens of Niceville in-the-know to the fresh produce outlet on the secluded road.

One of the inmates tossed a cell phone to Putz and he punched in a number before the phone's owner had a chance to change his mind.

"Ticket agent? I need to buy a one-way ticket to Honolulu." Putz startled. The phone had gone dead.

Putz punched another button and got a dial tone. He entered another number and turned his back to the inmates. "BabyDoll? It's me." After a long pause, he raised his voice. "Say it ain't so. You coming here? For Christmas? For true?"

"At this point in my life, it had never occurred to me. I mean, I never even dreamed that I could achieve dominion over women. The most important thing I could do to help myself was to get my permanent file to say I was an alcoholic. And that was going to be a trick because the file was behind locked doors in the Infirmary."

It don't make any difference what kind of scrape your bunkie gets into, like maybe even out in the yard, you got a special obligation to cover his back. Dickdock was my first bunkie and he made good on his promise to wallpaper my file, him being a medical doctor and all. Opportunity knocked when the warden's secretary started whining about an itch."

An image of the FPC infirmary emerged in my brain. I saw Dickdock and a prison secretary standing together inside one another's space.

"It's awfully uncomfortable," she told him.

She was young, fresh-faced and wore her hair in one of those mall-dos. She was Dickdock's type, legs with feet on the bottom. She was female, Dickdock wasn't. Reaching around her, he pulled paperwork from his pants pocket and stuffed it into a file inside a steelcase cabinet. Now anyone that checked Putz' file would have no doubt, he was a verified alcohol abuser. A piece of paper said so. Paper doesn't lie.

"I better have a look," Dickdock told her.

She brushed at her crotch. Her lip trembled. "It's like a rash. It's uncomfortable."

Dickdock managed to toe the door closed behind him and busied himself to the task of pulling the Secretary's dress above her waist.

"I'm a specialist. Have you been using new soaps?"

"No."

"Taking any new drugs? No?"

"No."

His hands were inside her blouse and around her waist. "Does your husband have any high-risk behaviors?"

"He's an Airman."

In the same moment, while he took her medical history, Dickdock's hands found their way inside the secretary's drawers. He slipped them below her hips like a professional. Not surprising. After years of medical training, such skills had become second nature. She backed up and sat spread-eagle on a desk. Now Dickdock's pants were at half-mast.

"Does he handle jet fuel maybe? Or epoxies? Agent orange?"

"He got a bottle of viagra last week. For Memorial Day."

Dickdock was in like flint and driving for the score. "I could run tests."

"But it's gone."

"The rash?"

"The viagra," she said. She was at ecstasy's door. "Three...day...weekend."

"That's not a rash, that's an abrasion." Dickdock may have had a gambling problem, but he was, nevertheless, a consummate diagnostician.

CHAPTER 5

EPIPHANY

"**T**reatment. What a joke."

Doctor Pfluffer was a woman in her forties, a bored, chain-smoking civil servant who wore comfortable shoes and who had an unending supply of sweaters embroidered with cutesy dog appliqués. Her job in the prison administration was to conduct groups. Groups for drug and alcohol, sex addicts, and chronic pain.

Dickdock and Rojo were in the same drug and alcohol counseling group that Putz was assigned to. It also included a big Cajun kid, Roland, who probably was still in his twenties. He must have been six-foot-eight. He was darkly handsome and muscular, broad in the shoulder and narrow in the hip. Roland had a quick smile. The ladies loved him.

"Roland was a genealogical miscue from God."

A fifty-ish redhead filled out the roster. He was Irish Jimmy, a Yankee stevedore with arms like Popeye. Irish Jimmy had a ruddy, freckled complexion that framed a permanent twinkle in his eye.

In Putz' first group session, Dickdock sat across the circle from him, twisting uncomfortably, trying to obscure the fact that his crotch was crawling. He squirmed like he was trying to draw pictures on the seat of his chair with an itch-a-sketch.

Doctor Pfluffer stubbed out a cigarette as she lit another.

"The way they run the FPC only adds to the nasty taste in my mouth about government-run treatment programs."

"Friends, I hope that you've had a chance to meet our newcomer, Sackett, who might need to be made aware of the aims of the group, the prevailing ethos, as we mental health workers like to call it. It shouldn't take long for Sackett to figure out how to relate in our meetings."

"Everyone calls me Putz," the newbie said.

"So welcome, Sackett. What we have here, is a safe place to go where you won't be coerced and where you can trust people."

"Screw him," Rojo said.

"So then," Dr. Pfluffer said. "Let's pick up from where we left off last time. Why don't you start us off, O'Callaghan?"

Irish Jimmy sat forward in his steel chair. One knee bounced continuously and his words were clipped with a musical brogue. "They call me Irish Jimmy. I haven't had a drink since October. All the stevedores had a big going away party as a send-off to cap fifteen great years as shop steward and let me tell you, that was fifteen years of nothing but party, party, party. Now I'm fifty-three, and I have two ex-wives that I don't regret and all I want is some expensive Cuban cigars, a bottle of Bushmills whiskey and lots of cheap, nasty women. Look at me. How could I have a problem? I'm just the worst drunk on the docks and a no-account father. Now I'm sober and no one is happy."

Dr. Pfluffer nodded approval. "Some members of the group raised concerns about the recent questionnaire. As there was a varied response, it was felt that individual members of the group could contact their respective caseworkers with their individual concerns. How about you now, Thibodeaux?"

Roland spoke through a smile with a thick Cajun accent. "I'm Roland. I'm sitting here with men old enough to be my father and listening to them tell about their craving for booze. Well I drink to erase memories. I hear your penny ante little bellyaches and I just want to upchuck. This here group just brings back the memories of... When I get out, I'll start drinking again. I'll get plastered every night. Just to forget. To forget about the rape when I was twelve. Sold for a carton of Marlboros. That's why I drink."

Again, the Doctor nodded approval. "Many mental health providers feel that expressing distress and or strong emotions can be part of a healing process, not merely something to be pathologized as a symptom of mental illness. We should exercise care to avoid the over-emphasis of medication as a tool for recovery. Ramirez?"

Rojo feigned an eye tic when he spoke to the group. "They call me Rojo. My brother is a big drinker."

Dickdock gave himself over to scratching. "Oh brother," he moaned, digging at his crotch. His neighbors couldn't scoot their chairs away fast enough. They treated the infested Dickdock like he was a Jehovah's Witness.

"He hurt himself all the time," Rojo was saying. "And I afraid he harm his wife and kids, too. He hurt himself many, many times. He starting to see people and talk to them, yes talk to them, si, but there is nobody. He goes somewhere and he doesn't know where he is at all."

Dr. Pfluffer pursed her lips with understanding. "Recovery is a human phenomena experienced in many different contexts. Recovery also entails recovery from being in the mental health system. People with mental health problems still have basic human rights. How about you, Sackett?"

"Screw him," Rojo said.

"Okay, well, they call me Putz and I have been sober since my sentencing, just a few weeks ago. I ain't much of a drinker, never have been, so it was easy for me to quit without drugs or meetings. I definitely have a drinking problem, I'm pretty sure my permanent file lays it all out."

"Screw you."

"Hey Doctor, tell the Mexican he had his turn." The other inmates murmured and chuckled, but Rojo snarled. Dickdock didn't have the ability to pay close attention.

"When I think about real people with real problems like soldiers fighting halfway around the world, or folks with cancers or birth defects or sick babies and that kind of crap, it makes my problems seem pretty small. So, the booze is something I can give up. I can deal with the stress. Life is not really so unfair when you think about it. It's like golf. Play 'em where they lie. I think if we'd all just play them where they lie, we could all come to terms with our problems."

The Doctor was flushed with anger. Her face was stern. "Meet with me at the break, Sackett."

When the break came, it gave the inmates a chance to use the restroom and the Doctor to get her pudgy hands on a package of day-old doughnuts.

Putz took care of business, then strolled to the side of Doctor Pfluffer. "What's the problem, Doc?"

"We're understaffed. Underfunded. Underpaid."

"No. I mean, I got the idea...you wanted to talk to me?"

"Listen, Sackett. Quit being a dope." She stuffed half a doughnut in her mouth and chased it with a gulp of coffee. "You know the drill."

"I don't know the drill."

"Go along to get along."

"Yeah, okay, I do know that drill."

The other half of the doughnut disappeared in one bite. "Good."

"I guess I don't understand where I got off the drill."

"Get Dickdock to explain it." She slapped her hands across one another, pelting Putz in a diaspora of crusty sugar. She flapped her fingers on the patches of fabric between her neck and armpit.

Dickdock had his face against the wall and was digging at his privates as if he were about to explode in an itchgasm.

"He's got his own problems."

"Five minutes," Doctor Pfluffer shouted, then walked away. Putz moseyed over to Dickdock's side.

"What's she talking about, the drill?" he asked.

"You complete the program, and her department hits a trifecta worth about three grand."

"So?"

"So, you pretend like you're sick, she pretends like she's helping you. That's the drill."

"Oh, that drill. Thanks, Bunkie. Is there something I can do for you?"

"I can't think how," Dickdock moaned.

Putz watched the poor doctor dig at his undie bugs, stricken with remorse. The physician could not heal himself. No one could, least of all Putz.

Putz sat on the edge of his 'WATERFRONT' upper berth. Below him, Boss Hack held Dickdock against the lockers. Warden Lillard stood, arms crossed, in the central aisle. His face was standard-issue FPC stern.

"Cuff up," Boss Hack said.

Dickdock managed to get one last scratch at his crotch before Boss Hack cuffed him behind his back. "This is unfair," Dickdock plead. "It's not my fault. I was framed. It was her. She did it."

"He was a whiner, but still I was sorry to see old Dickdock go. Anyone else gets the crabs and they slather him up with that stinking blue oinkment. It's about the only thing inside that ain't grey or khaki. But Dickdock was a doctor. So, warden's rules. No way they let him near the infirmary, not even as a patient.

"Dickdock was right. It was unfair. But everything about incarceration is unfair. Some guys are in prison that aren't guilty of nothing. And then once they get ahold of a guy, it's unfair how they treat him. They turn a regular guy into a thief, then teach him that he's better off to blame everyone else for his troubles. Hell, if Dickdock had been a janitor or a farmer, anything but a doctor, he'd be in the infirmary. Sure as hell not in lockdown.

"Dickdock was probably even blaming me. After all, he was on a mission to refurbish my personal file and he got the crab visitation as collateral damage. It's not like he gave the crabs to himself.

"I knew I was going to miss him. I felt such a sense of loss that I could have cried. I might even miss his constant pissing and moaning. It really hurts to lose anyone when you already got a hole in your heart the size of a pony keg like I had with my BabyDoll.

Boss Hack opened a locker and tossed its contents into a cardboard box. Warden Lillard supervised and scratched his crotch. She stripped the bed sheet, blanket and pillow from the lower bunk. Then, holding Dickdock at the elbow, led him out of the barracks.

"It's not my fault," the prisoner wailed.

The Warden snapped the switch and the barracks were dim. Putz watched the Warden digging at his crotch as he followed Boss Hack and her captive out of the barracks.

The background noise level rose even as the light faded. The shaft of light from the latrine never let the room darken completely. The dorm echoed with loud talk, snores, ripped farts, rap and salsa music. Putz had to tell himself to lie down. Sometimes the stress bothered him less when he was prone.

"Yep. They sent old Dickdock straight to lockdown. No disciplinary hearing, no nothing. And as I mildewed in the dark listening to the rumble of human bowels, I was sad, depressed maybe. They call that feeling 'melon-cholly.' I had suffered a heavy heart before but nothing like this. What I needed was a change of latitude, I needed it bad.

"And that's when I realized that the lower bunk was empty and I could move downstairs. I would still be on the Waterfront, but the lower bunk was a preferred address. I could move out of the skybox. A new home would give me a lift. I hoped."

Putz dropped off the top and onto the floor. He tossed his pillow, sheets, blanket and mattress to the lower bunk and jumped in.

Spock writhed like a snake under a blanket in the next bunk over.

His grunting sounds of self-abuse blended into the cacophony that the officers called quiet time.

A voice bounced around in the echo chamber of the latrine and spooled out into the barracks. "Hey Putz, come in here. You'll want to see this."

"I'm sleeping."

"Your loss." KER-WHOOSH. Anyone that heard the flushing toilet would think a freight train was barreling straight down the other side of the wall.

But the flushing sound cleared his mind, unclogged his brain. He scrambled onto the floor. His mind raced. *What was I thinking?* Just getting rid of Dickdock's mattress wasn't enough. It stood to reason that some souvenirs of Dickdock's tryst with the FPC secretary still inhabited the lower bunk and were on the prowl for a fresh source of tender flesh.

Putz darted into the latrine. He found a bottle of bug poison in a supply closet.

With a chalice of poison, Putz anointed the metal frame of the bunk. Then the walls and even his mattress. The process consumed an entire roll of paper. Now the lower bunk was moist with toxicant. But it was still better than the top bunk.

He rested his head on his pillow. A spare roll of toilet paper was in bed beside him. It looked soft and smooth. He squeezed the roll and he sensed that his anger, the strain, the tension in his arms eased. He took a deep breath, squeezed the toilet paper roll a second time, this time with both hands, and the stress in his shoulders and neck calmed. Just compressing the soft roll, the way it gave way, then relaxing his grip, the way the roll gave back, it seemed to...impart comfort, well-being, reassurance. Squeezing the roll in the dark soothed his anger. He drifted gently to sleep.

In minutes, the overhead lights snapped on again. Boss Hack entered the dorm with another inmate in tow.

He was in his forties, sharp and crisp, with premature silver hair. In the free world he was a GQ fashion plate. He spoke with an erudite, almost Brit accent that Putz guessed was fake. He carried a blanket, pillow, bed sheet and a cardboard box that held his toiletries.

"Right there on the waterfront." Boss Hack showed him the upper berth and his locker assignment. "What did I tell you? Nice, huh?"

"I gave my new bunkie a nickname. Moneybags. And it stuck."

Moneybags stowed his stuff in his locker and as soon as Boss Hack was gone, he undressed for bed.

Then things returned to normal. Loud.

"You want powerhouse?" Spock mumbled, hidden by his blanket. "I'll show you powerhouse. Dahlia, baby."

A voice reverberated from the latrine. "This floor is covered with urine."

Squeezing the toilet paper roll gave Putz some sense of compensation for the ache he suffered, even a sense of power over something, anything, some essence of control. He didn't feel lost any longer. His personal file was going to help him now, not hinder him. He was entitled.

"Holy Saint Michael. There's piss everywhere." KA-WHOOSH. A blast from a commode flushing in the latrine washed the last of the stinking thinking ideas from Putz' brain.

"That's when I had this spiritual flash or what your preachers might call an epiphany. The floor was covered with piss yesterday. It's going to be covered with piss tomorrow. Why gripe about it? It's the drill. It's prison.

"I dissolved right there and then that this place wasn't going to get the best of me. I'd keep my nose clean and from now on, no more whining. I'd play my alcohol abuse scam for all it's worth, build up some cash from the produce scam, and somehow, I didn't know how yet, but I was by everything that is holy going to get that bus ticket to Honolulu and be out by Christmas. I'd meet BabyDoll at the airport. That's the promise I gave my BabyDoll, she wouldn't spend Christmas alone, so that's what I had to do. Making her happy was the only thing that mattered."

CHAPTER 6

BONDS OF LOVE

"**W**hat's this bullshit about a bus ticket to Honolulu?" I asked. "And you never did tell me why they sent you to prison."

"Hold on. I'm getting to that. Getting out of prison ain't rocket surgery, you know. But what is doggoned hard is trying to maintain a relationship when you're inside and the woman of your dreams is on the outside. Like this one guy we called Badaboom. A mafia guy from New Jersey. Or New Hampshire maybe. New someplace, anyway."

Badaboom walked across the parking lot with a rolling gait. He was swarthy with long, thick arms and hands that looked like meat hooks. He was the kind of guy that saw everything, every future move, every tell. With his business associates, anyway, not so much in his personal life.

Across the lot, a long, black stretch limousine drove into the parking lot, a Miami Dolphins sticker pasted on its bumper. A driver opened a backseat door and out popped a bimbo. She was half Badaboom's age. Good genes provided the canvas, but credit for the ornaments belonged to a plastic surgeon. She was perfection. Her long legs looked like Tuscan marble columns, and her décolletage fought for freedom from the low-cut blouse that held plump knockers captive. Trashy and desirable, her lips were full and pouty. Badaboom and his bimbo embraced, then kissed passionately, breaking the vacuum just long enough to climb in the limo.

The chauffeur drove them to an upscale restaurant called The Colosseum, the best Italian eatery in town. It looked out over Choctawhatchee Bay. Their waiter seated them at a large table with several other Mafiosos sporting Hawaiian shirts, Bermuda shorts, black socks and alligator shoes. The men all stood and toasted Badaboom with a glass of vino when he and his bimbo arrived. "Alla tua Salute! To your health!"

A couple of the other diners were inmates; they all escorted flashy gangster debutantes of their own. They dined on spaghetti, lasagna, veal partigiani, tortellini, manicotti, and punctuated their loud chatter and coarse jokes with broad breadstick gestures and clinking glasses of wine.

After the formaggi e frutta, one of the inmates, Rocco, casually told the group, "He's busting my balls." Rocco had a body like a torpedo. Apt. He was a torpedo.

"Who's busting your balls?" Badaboom asked.

"You know, dat guy. Wit the thing. Dat guy wit the thing."

Badaboom sprang from the chair and faked a punch at Rocco. He was as nimble as a gazelle. He laughed like a hyena when Rocco bumped into a waiter who was clearing the plates for the dolce.

"Those wise-guys didn't even eat with the rest of us, except maybe on pork chop night. Don't ask me how they got to go everywhere they went. I didn't see nothing."

In a month, the limousine with the Dolphins sticker drove onto an airport tarmac and alongside a chartered private airplane. Badaboom's bimbo deplaned and flounced into the limo.

"Badaboom had so much stroke and money that some made guy from Miami always sent his driver and a shiny black stretch limo all the way to the FPC just to pick up his girlfriend at the airport when she flew in for visitation."

The Ascendant

The Mafioso idled away their days, congregating beside the swimming pool of a motel out by the highway. While some oiled up and baked in the sun, others busied themselves playing cards, or laughing and teasing one another while watching soap operas on TV.

"Dis one here, she's a ball buster," Rocco said, transfixed by the daytime drama.

"I like dis broad," Badaboom said. "You busting my balls?"

"Busting your balls? Who's busting your balls?"

"Youse."

"I ain't busting your balls. I'm smacking your chops."

"Outside his nickname was 'the Butcher' or something like that so the Warden wouldn't let him work in food service. No kitchen duty for the butcher. He didn't have any work assignment, none at all. The guards treated them guys like celebrities. Didn't any of them do nothing. Hell, they didn't any of them need the 11 cents an hour. Old Badaboom got so lazy he started to get fat and sloppy. I bet he gained fifty pounds."

"I'll show you smack your chops." Badaboom struggled to get up out of the plastic poolside chair.

The other Mafioso cowered as if they feared the big gangster. But they were all laughing. Badaboom was stuck in the chair.

"It's nice to get a visitor. I mean a visitor is a big plus, but the minus side is that every time after they leave, you're got to get a cavity check."

Boss Hack steered Badaboom into a tiny room on the hall between the lounge and the dorm. The windows were hung with Venetian blinds, but so many of the slats were bent and sagging that the view outside was unobstructed. She walked behind the arms-raised Badaboom and patted him down, waist to ankle.

"Okay. Drop 'em."

Badaboom dropped his drawers while Boss Hack walked around the mountain of flesh to face him.

"Lift your testicles."

Badaboom complied.

"Show me the bottoms."

The big Mafioso lifted his nutsack so the little woman could ascertain that no contraband was hidden there.

"Palms."

Badaboom showed palms, then turned and showed the naked bottoms of his feet. He was facing a bench at the window with the gimpy blind.

"Spread 'em."

Badaboom leaned over a bench like 100,000 other inmates before him had done. And like all the others, he put his face into that grimy window while a guard probed his rectum. The superficial purpose of the cavity check was to intercept smuggled contraband. The yardbirds swore that it was to discourage inmates from inviting visitors.

Badaboom reached back for the cheeks of his ass, and spread them wide.

Boss Hack snapped on rubber gloves. The Hack was short and her arm extended from her shoulder to his asshole on a line parallel the floor. Even worse, Boss Hack compensated for her short statue by growing unusually long fingernails. Now her index finger penetrated his poopchute. Badaboom gritted his teeth, sweating out his anger and humiliation.

His nose was against the glass. He could either close his eyes or look outside.

He chose to look, and in the parking lot beside the FPC, he saw his bimbo. She had taken off her spiked heels and she was skipping to the stretch limousine. Instead of hopping inside, she embraced the chauffeur. Badaboom had never really noticed before, but the driver was young and athletic. When he removed his driver's cap, he had a full head of curly blonde hair. He kissed Badaboom's bimbo and she kissed him back in a deep, long, passionate, and by all indications, unusually wet kiss.

"You freaker," Badaboom snarled.

"You probably figured out he didn't really say 'freaker.'"

The limo driver was thrusting his tongue down the bimbo's throat, a throat that was only supposed to be violated by the made man, not a low-ranking associate, all the more maddening since a tongue in the throat is a mere caricature, symbolic of sexual intercourse, so the way the Butcher looked at it, his bimbo was acting out a sexual encounter behind his back right there in front of his eyes at the precise moment Boss Hack's determined and knifelike digit violated his fundamental aperture.

Badaboom never left the lounge that day or the next, or for days after that. He sat by in front of the TV, by himself, sobbing, eating cannolis, watching his daytime serial.

"Badaboom was packing on the weight. He wasn't getting a bit of exercise. But that was just the half of it. His bimbo kept coming for visitation. She started off coming maybe once a month or so. Now she's here twice a week."

The bimbo liked what Florida had to offer. Another day, another cavity check. Boss Hack led Badaboom into the little room and patted him down, waist to ankle.

"Okay. Drop 'em."

Badaboom dropped his drawers while Boss Hack walked around the huge mound of flesh to face him. She poked at his testicles, scrutinized his palms and the bottoms of his feet.

"Spread 'em."

Badaboom leaned, his face in the window, palms on his butt cheeks. Boss Hack snapped on rubber gloves. Badaboom gritted his teeth. A dark anger cascaded over his face when he looked out into the parking lot.

The limo rocked as if someone was screwing inside.

Badaboom and his Mafioso pals grazed on a party plate beside the pool at the motel. They were all as sober as judges, deathly quiet.

"He's busting my balls," Rocco said. The thug was like a puppy, offering his master a squeeze toy. Almost pleading for his capo to quit wallowing in depression.

"Can we get some quiet here?" Badaboom said. He looked sloppy fat, like Jabba the Hutt. When he choked on a bite of cannoli, he tried to stand but he fell back into the plastic deck chair. It folded under his weight like a cheap suit. Two of his pals gave him a helping hand and another slapped his back.

"You got to have less than ten years left to even get in the prison camp. So, it wasn't but another few months after that and Badaboom got his walking papers. He'd paid his debt to society. He was lucky that incarceration didn't give him a genital heart condition.

"The funniest thing about inside is that real free-range criminals, like Badaboom, they had the run of the place but they still worried all the time about getting caught doing something. Pretty much the criminals and the guards treat us white-collar offenders like worms. As if we had everything they ever wanted and just blew it off. The guards know the white-collar inmates are smarter than they are."

Windshield wipers squeaked and Putz slowed their speed.

"You're not a real criminal?" I asked.

Putz inhaled deeply through his nose. "Man, can you smell that barbeque? Whoo eeeeEE."

"What did you do? What were you in for?"

"Listen kid, you don't ask what a guy is in for. I already told you more than I told my bunkies." Putz turned off the wipers. Silence. "They should tell a guy the important ground rules like that in A and O but they won't."

"A and O?"

"**A**dmission and ornamentation. A caseworker oughta tell a guy."

Putz took me back again to his first day on the inside. He'd been shuffled into the office of a caseworker, she looked to Putz to be in her fifties. Behind a desk, she was occupied by a phone call. She was eaten up with that tailored clothes, self-important and self-appointed civil servant look. And the badge of a bureaucrat, a can of diet soda on her desk.

Putz strolled around the office, checking out the diplomas that the caseworker had hung on the wall. One read "MASTER OF SCIENCE IN SOCIOLOGY, OKLAHOMA STATE UNIVERSITY," and it was dated in 1987. When caseworker hung up the phone...

"How about them Pokes?" Putz asked. It was a greeting that he knew was common among OSU Cowboy fans. He wasn't steeped in prison behavior yet, and he hoped he and the caseworker had something in common. He planned on getting a reputation for being friendly.

"Pardon me?"

Putz threw a thumb at the diploma on the wall. "You must have been there during Barry Sanders' heyday."

"The department was chaotic. That name doesn't ring a bell." Her voice was flat, humorless, and she point to a chair where she intended Putz to sit.

"She didn't know who Barry Sanders is. I let that sink in. I asked myself *how in God's little green acre could someone go to Oklahoma State and not know who Barry Sanders is? The best running back of all time?* It didn't make sense. Not a bit. I figured I owed it to myself to put that caseworker to the acid reflux."

"Did you like living in Norman?" Oklahoma State is in Stillwater. Their fiercest rival is in Norman. She would know that if she was legit. The question was an obvious misdirection but Putz couldn't come up with anything better on short notice. Surely, she would know and correct his error. Putz seated himself and propped his feet on the desk.

But the caseworker said, "Norman was fine. Just fine. Nice town. Feet off the desk."

Putz eased his feet to the floor. He wasn't in a hurry. He had to think fast.

"*Bingo* I told myself. *This girlie is lying. Lying through her teeth. She's never been to Oklahoma. That sheepskin was as fake as the sugar in her soda pop.* It didn't take a genius to figure out she got herself this fancy federal job with a phony resume and she was skating on a solid sheet of thin ice."

"All righty then, Sackett. We've got the issue of your alcohol and drug addiction. Then your work assignment. We can go over what I'm sure you're most interested in, your release date, and maybe we'll have time for questions."

"Please, call me Larry."

The caseworker glared. "Your permanent file here is a little ambiguous if you don't mind me saying. Did Judge Weregeld order you into a drug and alcohol program? Sackett?"

"I don't have a drinking problem. I did have a DUI once but that was fifteen years ago."

The caseworker guzzled her diet pop. She never took her eye off of Putz.

"I'm only going to tell you once, Sackett, listen closely to my questions and see if you can't contain your eloquence to a specific answer."

"Heck, I was just a kid." He thought about giving the caseworker a big wakeup call by throwing down a challenge on her diploma, but then he thought better of it. Better to keep his power dry for a time. Even if he got this one fired, they'd just send in a replacement. Someone eager beaver from the JV could be worse. "Sorry. Judge Weregeld suggested that I seek treatment."

"Not an order, just a recommend. Hmmm. I'll incorporate you into drug and alcohol group. Temporarily. This paperwork doesn't seem to call for it. So, one screw up and you're out on your ear."

"I don't think I need treatment."

"This was before I found out drug and alcohol group was a blessing."

"Consider it probationary," the caseworker said. "I'm also going to order a psychiatric examination. I'll get to the bottom of this alcohol thing. Don't think I won't, Sackett." She flipped through pages in the permanent file. "I see you style yourself as some sort of a lumber-jack, Sackett."

Putz didn't answer. He didn't know what she wanted, so he kept his trap shut. Silence.

"I'm going to assign you to work in the self-help shop. Does that suit your skeazy little idea of what you want to with your precious time while you're here at Uncle Sam's expense, Sackett?"

"Whatever you say is fine by me. Can you answer some questions for me? How does this good time deal work? Can a guy get Christmas furlough?"

"We go by the book around here, Sackett. Earn your good time, get a bus ticket home…"

"A bus ticket home?"

"…and that objective is a definite possibility."

Putz jumped to his feet. "No one said nothing about a bus ticket."

"We can quibble details some other time, Sackett," the caseworker was looking at her watch.

"My home is Honolulu."

"Sit down or I'll call a guard. The book says bus ticket."

As Putz sat, the caseworker stood.

"There's a nice bunk waiting for you. You can have the waterfront if you want."

"Sure. Sounds nice."

"Make sure you're in the dorm at four PM for head count. And I'm late for Kiwanis. Stay out of trouble. Mind your guards. Obey all rules. Enjoy your stay. Sackett."

The caseworker shoved a pile of work-assignment paperwork in his hand and walked out of the office.

"My constabulary ain't set up to take crap like that from a man. But the caseworker was female. It was my first day. I was powerless."

CHAPTER 7

FUTILITY

"The caseworker is nothing but a guard that's good at paperwork. Guards. This one guard we called Boss Hack, she couldn't have been much taller than four feet in her stocking feet. She'd usually look the other way if I wasn't creating too much havoc. Boss Hack kept me under surveillance after she found a stash of toilet paper I hid in the General's shed. And sometimes you get caught with contraband on the inside."

Boss Hack opened each locker's combination lock with a passkey. Inmates stood at attention. A white baker's bag sat in Spock's locker.

"What do you suppose is in that bag, Sackett?"

"I don't see nothing in Spock's locker, Boss," Putz said.

"I'm writing up shots if there's contraband in that sack." Boss Hack snagged the sack and peered inside.

Spock ripped the bag away from Boss Hack and smashed its contents in his mouth. With six cookies crammed in his face, he looked like Alvin's sidekick Simon, the tall bespectacled chipmunk, only uglier. "Oatmeal therapy," Spock said, spitting cookie crumbs. "High in fiber."

"Getting shots ain't nothing to laugh about. They write you up and next thing you know you got a disciplinary hearing with a guy called the D H Officer that comes around every couple of weeks or so. Heck, your family can get you in dutch even with the best of intentions."

Then Boss Hack spotted Putz's contact lens case.

"What's this?"

"Contact lenses."

"Contraband. Holy Jesus. Sackett, I got to write this up, and you know how much I hate forms."

"They make you expose yourself to threats almost every day. Don't fart off what I'm telling you, kid. You got to embrace your drug and alcohol program to the hilt."

Putz sat in the most uncomfortable chair in Florida while Doctor Pfluffer paced the room. She was an Old School psychologist. Treatment to her meant she had to rip the scab off of every single one of an inmate's innermost secrets.

"Sometimes, you feel like you have to tell them stuff that ain't true just because it's obvious that they want to hear it. You have to tell them something or they'll send you to lockdown."

"Yes, Doctor, I think you could be right. So sometimes I start having these fantasies about, like you know, something I don't want being told around. It's about members of the same what you might call ornamentation. But that only happens when I drink too much. Which is all the time."

Doctor Pfluffer straightened a photo of a dog on the wall. "What about drugs?"

"I smoke marijuana every day," Putz lied.

Doctor Pfluffer's brow curled with skepticism.

"But then, if you make up crap just to make them happy, you'll never hear the end of it."

It was a different day and Doctor Pfluffer wore a different dog-decorated outfit. She paced the office like a caged cat. "Let's go back to your repressed desires, Sackett."

"I'd rather talk about why I'm hooked on the booze and the weed."

"Have you acted out on this yearning to be with other men?"

"I must have got carried away in the telling about it if I made you think it's a yearning. Because it's not."

"Things can get out of hand and you have to scotch it in the butt."

Another day, another cutesy doggie outfit. Dr. Pfluffer paced.

"Let's say, a man in uniform. An officer in the Air Force perhaps. Are you attracted to a man in uniform?"

"That's a little more pacific than that little thought that maybe only once fleshed out in front of my eyes. When I was plastered."

"I've been dating a Major. Have you applied for a furlough? You might want to join us..."

"No no no. My family is way far away."

Reject. She didn't like being refused. "I'm having a struggle here, Sackett, it's not abundantly clear to me that you have a drug or alcohol addiction."

Putz sat on a chair near his bunk below the Waterfront. He was deep in discussion with his closest associates: Spock, his new bunkie Moneybags, Beale Street, Rojo, Butterfly and Badaboom.

Across the aisle—they called it the street—an older inmate lay on his bed, reading a romance novel. His bed and locker area were messy. The inmates called him Mickey the Snitch. He put down his book and listened in on the discussion at the Waterfront.

"Doctor Pfluffer wants me to play pivot man in a triangle booty shake."

"A manadge a twat?'" Beale Street asked.

"A threesome." Moneybags said.

"What kind of depraved health professional would take that kind of advantage of a desperate soul in critical need of alcohol treatment?" Putz asked.

Beale Street rubbed his chin and looked into the ceiling. "Loss of drug and alcohol. Wow. That's a tough choice. A threesome versus at worst an extra three hundred and sixty-five days," he said. "Might be a fair trade."

"Stand your ground, Putz," Spock said, winking a distorted eyeball from behind the glass insulators he peered through. "She can't handle stress. Irritable bowel." He winked and clicked his teeth. "I sniffed it out."

"If you lose good time, I'll call my lawyers," Moneybags said.

Rojo was less sympathetic. He bent over and pretended to spread his butt cheeks, saying "Hey, puta, take it like an hombre. Hahahaha."

Butterfly was just curious. "Is this Major a pitcher or a catcher?"

"Hey man, just say dah woid, dah guy gets whacked," Badaboom said. "All you gots to do is axe."

"Someone ought to take this matter to Boss Hack." It was Mickey the Snitch. He put his romance novel aside and sat up in his bunk.

Putz knotted his fists and stepped across the street. He glared over Mickey the Snitch. "I don't rat to the bulls nothing. I should kick your fanny for even suggesting that."

The others surrounded Mickey the Snitch and Beale Street pinned Putz' arms back. Dislodged from the conflict, Mickey the Snitch slithered out of the dorm, toward the lounge.

"Why are you guys protecting him? I think he's a stool pigeon," Putz said.

"You're absolutely right. He's the biggest rat fink in the place. But he's no garden variety snitch. He's world class. He snitched his way down from six murders," Butterfly said.

"Yeah," Beale Street said. "He may be a snitch but we always know when."

"He don't know it but he's a double agent. And if you tell him, I'll bust your balls," the Mafioso said.

Boss Hack puzzled over a tape recorder. Mickey the Snitch lifted his shirt tail and hunched over the finger-wave table in her cubicle by the lounge.

"Up the back, Rookie," Mickey the Snitch said. "You never done this before?"

Boss Hack ignored the question. "It's got two hours of juice."

"I guess they got some pretty good stuff on tape. Doctor Pfluffer must have made some immortal proposition to Mickey the Snitch. I never heard exactly."

Boss Hack and Warden Lillard paced circles around Doctor Pfluffer. Cigarette smoke curled into a Klieg lamp that was aimed in her face. Boss Hack showed two flashcards to the doctor, one imprinted with the medical symbol of 'man' and the other with that of 'woman.'

"No. No, I tell you."

Boss Hack introduced a third card. This one was imprinted with a second symbol of 'man.'

"No. Please no."

The fourth card Boss Hack showed the doctor had a crude outline of a dog.

"No. No. No. No. No."

Boss Hack piled the cards together and shook them. They rattled loosely in her hands. "Arf. Arf. Arf. OoooOOOUUUUUUwww."

"Yes," Doctor Pfluffer cried. "Yes. I can't take it anymore. Yes. Yes. Just let me resign. I'll resign. I beg you."

"So, Mickey the Snitch did his thing and the Doctor went packing. Mickey was addicted to snitching I think. A snitchaholic. Sooner or later he would have to be dealt with, but he was a champ in the FPC for a few days. He left some dangling participles though."

The Caseworker walked in slow circles around the seated Putz.

"I felt like my psychotic nature was making progress with Doctor Pfluffer," Putz said.

"She never filed a report," the caseworker said. "There's no document. It didn't happen."

"I still get group...?"

"You don't need group. I'm thinking about pulling the plug."

"In the name of justice...I need group."

The caseworker gave Putz an icy stare. "Your good time is under review."

Putz glanced at the fake diploma on the wall. "You know, I ought to..."

"What?"

"Her being a female...I didn't have a spine. No way I could even stick up for myself. I froze. All I could say was..."

"Nothing." Putz focused his stare on the fake certificate. It seemed to taunt him from its undeserved place on the wall.

"Back to the point, I can't begin to tell you how important it is to know who the snitches are. If Mickey the Snitch wasn't so stinking obvious he would have been dangerous. Like this one time he went after my second bunkie, the guy we called Moneybags."

Wang's storeroom had a dutch door. That's where the inmates gathered once a week to buy merchandise...cigarettes, canned mackerel, candy, and dry goods like spare uniform shirts and underwear. Wang hung out a sign that said "COMMISSARY." Putz and Moneybags stood in line ahead of Mickey the Snitch.

Mickey checked out his purchases: a bar of soap imprinted with "LISA," and a tiny box of laundry detergent. "Six dollars! For a stinking box of Tide? Are you kidding me man?"

"Quit your whining," Putz said. "We're in prison. Some got it worse than you."

"Oh yeah?" Mickey the Snitch backed up and rubbed his back against the gritty wall as if he were a bear. "Has anyone else got chronic skin? Dang it, Dickdock. Where are you when I need you?"

"I have access to a product," Moneybags said, "that improves on Wang's primitive formulations by a factor of ten, at a cost I am sure you will find to be very reasonable."

"How much?" the Snitch asked.

"A mere carton. One bottle of my lotion for one carton of cigarettes."

"You're on."

A few days later, Putz walked into the dorm in his work-assignment garb, a khaki uniform. He noticed that Mickey the Snitch was tidying up at his home. Everything on his side of the street was uncharacteristically neat and clean.

A toilet flushed.

Putz unbuttoned his shirt near his locker. Like the other inmates, Putz liked to ditch his uniform as soon as he got home from work.

"You finished early today," the Snitch said.

"It looks like you had a woman come in to clean up your rat's nest."

"I decided to lay in today. I was sick of it looking nasty."

"Everyone is," Putz said. He continued watching the Snitch out of a corner of his eye. He couldn't put his finger on why, but something was up. He didn't know what it was.

Then a slit-eyed look fell over Putz' face. He did a quick shakedown of his own locker, then skipped out, buttoning his shirt. Mickey had snitched out Moneybags on the skin care product. Putz knew it. He yelled at the Snitch as he left, "You rat."

Mickey the Snitch called behind him, "Go straight on home. Don't stop at that titty bar."

CHAPTER 8

SCAMS

"**I** put two and two together and figured it out. That ratfink Mickey the Snitch had snitched out Moneybags, and since Moneybags was my bunkie, I had a special sacred obligation to come to his aid."

Moneybags stepped off of a blue FPC bus and walked toward the gate along with other khaki-uniformed inmates. He was returning from his work assignment in a warehouse on the base. He wore a windbreaker and he cradled an oversized plastic bottle full of some viscous liquid in his arm. Ahead, he saw that Boss Hack was patting down lined-up inmates, one after the other.

Putz ran nearby. He signaled Moneybags with a waving gesture. He mouthed the words "pat down."

"**I bet I walked past that gate five days a week probably two hundred times and that's the first time I ever seen Boss Hack search out there for contraband.**"

Moneybags nodded understanding, and shoved the contraband bottle inside his windbreaker. Then, cool as a cucumber, he fell in at the rear of the line. When Boss Hack saw Moneybags, she excused the next men and motioned for him to step up.

"Front and center, inmate," she said. "Reach for the sky."

Moneybags assumed the position, feet spread apart. He held his hands, and the bottle, high over his head. Boss Hack patted the

355

rich-boy down, first his legs, then his waist and sides. She totally missed the contraband that he held aloft above her own head.

"That's just how screwed up it is, man. You got to steal crap from the Air Force to have anything clean and decent inside. That's the main thing about minimum security. It stinks, man. Old Moneybags, he was a big shot business tycoon. If you wanted to learn to make money on stuff like corn and wheat and pork rinds, he'd tell you. Heck, he gave stock tips to Boss Hack all the time."

Several years before his incarceration, Moneybags took a wrong turn and found himself on an abandoned industrial site. It was littered with tire casings, busted glass and broken barrels. He stopped to examine a drekky chemical snot that was oozing and burbling out of a crevice in the earth beneath his feet. He rubbed some gunk between his fingers. He smelled it and jerked back.

"He was the best manipulator we had. He pretty much got everything he wanted even though they only let you have a hundred and seventy-five bucks in the bank."

Three months later, he had a solid business up and running. His happiest days were spent inspecting his busy warehouse. It filled with boxes marked "HAIR RESTORATIVE." One halcyon day after another, watching dock workers fill tractor-trailer rigs with boxes of his restorative just as fast as they came out of the packaging machine.

"He put that snot he found in a little flat tin and in no time, he was making a few million every month. The guy was generous with his cash."

Behind a dais, several tuxedo-clad big shots ate rubber chicken in front of a big sign that read "REGINALD P. RAPPAPORT, SWELL GUY OF THE YEAR." Moneybags stepped to the podium with a quick gait. One of the bigger of the big shots reached out to shake his hand, together they grinned into a bank of exploding flashbulbs.

"...and he got tons of awards. They even named a bridge after him."

A big crowd of happy people surrounded a gaggle of glad-handing politicians. Moneybags was the center of attention. He wielded a huge pair of scissors and cut a ribbon near a plaque that read "REGINALD P. RAPPAPORT BRIDGE."

A reporter pushed a microphone in his face. "A man has nothing if he doesn't have a good name," Moneybags said. He wiped a tear from the corner of his eye and the crowd erupted in a collective cheer.

"I sort of liked the guy and he liked me. A rich friend or two wouldn't hurt me once I was back in the free world."

Putz demonstrated a golf swing to Moneybags—grip, address, backswing, and follow through. He used a broom for a prop.

"His connections were always having these charity golf events, so he got a lot of furloughs. If you have Senators as friends, you can get more furloughs than Jimmy Carter has liver pills."

"I carried a bag for all the pros," Putz told his new bunkie. "And the biggest mistake club players make is where they try to strike the ball."

"The only swing thought I've ever entertained is to attempt to pummel it straight down the middle."

Putz shook his head 'no.' "Like you was striking a match. Hit it on the back."

"No matter how careful you are, some of your customers won't read the instructions. And some of them will be G-men. The hair restorative product just wasn't working where the rubber meets the road."

Four male regulators filed court papers at a Court Clerk's office. They stood shoulder to shoulder, each wore a black suit, carried a leather briefcase, and wore dark sunglasses. Each regulator was as bald as doorknob, and all of their scalps were covered with bandages.

"So, with new discoveries under his belt, he put that same goo in a tall skinny bottle that looked like a vibrator and opened a huge market of business with women."

Moneybags strode through a busy warehouse filled with boxes marked "HAIR REMOVER." Dock workers with hand trucks loaded the boxes into tractor-trailer rigs, and if frenetic activity is any indication, the firm was doing land-office business.

"Next he got a wing of a hospital named for himself."

A big crowd of folks surrounded a flock of politicians and Moneybags. He cut a ribbon near a plaque that says "REGINALD P. RAPPAPORT CHILDREN'S HOSPITAL" with gold-plated, giant-sized scissors.

"But Hell hath no fury like a G-woman scorched."

Four tailored female regulators filed court papers at a Court Clerk's office. They stood shoulder to shoulder, each wore a black suit, carried a leather briefcase, and wore dark sunglasses. Bandages covered the legs of each of the regulators. Each of them walked with great discomfort.

"The regulators didn't know it but they did old Moneybags a big favor by closing down his hair businesses. He figured out how to cut that snot with contaminated dry-cleaning fluid, bottled it and sold it to a Russian vodka maker in India."

Moneybags spent his days in a constant state of bliss. He loved nothing better than watching huge cranes lift oceangoing containers and drop them into place on the decks of outbound ships.

"Someone needed to clean up that industrial site, but the government was never pleased with the way Moneybags got her done until he outsourced about a million jobs overseas. That seemed to make 'em happy."

Beneath as sign, "REGINALD P. RAPPAPORT PARK," kids played, frisbees floated, kites soared, and puppies scampered.

"There was something about his bookkeeping though. Who knew you could go to jail for not paying your taxes? Pfffft."

I imagined in my mind's eye what it must been like for a big shot like Moneybag's to surrender to a bunch of bean counters.

The Ascendant

"**E**ven though he always tipped her to good stock deals, that locker-rattling Boss Hack was always on the prowl to catch Moneybags doing business. She wouldn't let him make telephone calls while the market was open. Checked all his mail. All the time threatening him 'if I catch you even reading the business section of the newspaper, you'll go straight to the hole.'"

A toilet flushed as Moneybags walked into the noisy barracks, Mickey the Snitch confronted him, brandishing a half-empty bottle. "This lotion you sold me is allergic."

Moneybags checked his hair in a tiny in-locker mirror. "Caveat emptor, my loquacious lodge-fellow."

"I want half that carton back."

"Gracious heavenly days, Mr. Snitch, you've consumed nearly the entire contents. I'll extend you an offer of one mack for the portion you have remaining. That's my final offer."

Mickey the Snitch rubbed his chin. He had no choice but to take the offer. He was unlikely to get a better one. A can of mackerel was worth more than a half-empty bottle of goop, so the deal was struck. "Do you have visitors today?" he asked with a conspiratorial glance.

"Our transaction is now consummated. Past this, it stretches one's credulity to imagine...that my business...is any of your business."

The next evening, Moneybags and a suited compatriot confabbed in the lounge. His name was Overcomb, a cost accountant with thick glasses and a bad combover.

Inmates milled in the lounge, as ever, making enough noise to muffle their discussion. Overcomb edged his chair closer. He had seen a couple too many Mafioso movies. "We need to talk about that thing."

"To which thing are you making reference?"

"That thing. You know. It's due next month. The thing."

"Taxes?"

Overcomb nodded. "Yeah, the thing."

"You are cognizant of the fact that prison regulations preclude me from conducting business..."

Overcomb grew agitated. "The cash flow just dried up. We got til the middle of next month to pay the thing."

"Tweak a bit here and there. What do I pay you for?"

"You pay me to operate the business. You don't pay me to run up a bunch of personal liability for federal...the thing."

"I'm embarrassed to say," Moneybags looked over his shoulder, then continued in a whisper, "Have you considered utilizing that escrow cash, in the Channel Islands? The sum should be sufficient."

Overcomb handed a cell phone to Moneybags. "They won't release the thing so I can't pay the thing without your say so."

Moneybags looked around for prying eyes before punching a number into the cell phone.

A tiny microphone peeked out from under the coffee table, unnoticed by Moneybags and Overcomb.

The next day, a blue bus drove into the FPC parking lot and opened its door. Outside the bus, Boss Hack ordered an angry Moneybags, "Cuff up."

Putz stood by, unable to help his bunkie.

Moneybags put his hands behind his back and Boss Hack slapped the cuffs on him.

"Appliances don't ride first class."

"I beg your pardon?"

"Spit out the dental work." She held a bag in front of his face until he spat out his dentures.

Now Moneybags' erudite accent was gone. Disappeared. Inexplicable. Without his choppers, Moneybags had an awful speech impediment. He sounded like Freddy Fudd. "I'w make that wotten snitch pay when I get weweesed."

"Okay, Rappaport, load up," the locker-rattler said.

"It's Weginawd P. Wappapowt, to you."

"Is there anything I can do?" Putz asked.

"Caw my warrior."

"What's his name?"

"He's Wennie Witwak. His office is in Maweena Deo Way," then to Boss Hack, "Unhand me, you bwoot."

"Witwak? Maweena…?" Putz needed more information, but Boss Hack was shoving Moneybags into the bus and nothing more was forthcoming. The coach exited the parking lot and turned onto a busy roadway. It passed a large white-on green sign that read "REGINALD P. RAPPAPORT HIGHWAY."

In the name of justice, they send a guy to jail for not paying his taxes, then whack him again when he pays up. Justice is blind. You can quote me on that."

Putz' caseworker and Boss Hack paced rings around a seated Putz. They took turns getting into his face.

"I don't know nothing," he told them.

"Three thousand gallons of paint remover, missing?" the caseworker asked.

Boss Hack jumped onboard. "Maybe you fell asleep."

"I didn't see nothing."

"It seems like everyone assigned to the self-help shop is blind. Well a blind man can't work the self-help shop, Sackett, so you just lost your lazy sleep ins," the caseworker said. "Report to golf course maintenance tomorrow."

"Yes, boss."

"Don't show up one minute late," Boss Hack said. "You're hanging on to your good time by the skin of your teeth, Sackett."

CHAPTER 9

HIJINKS ENSUE

"**Y**our typical inmate don't make a good hand on the golf course. And the brain trust at the FPC thought it was some kind of punishment because golf course work starts at five-thirty. Most of the inmates had never been on a golf course and didn't understand golf has a thing called etiquette. It's just manners. The only manners most of the inmates knew was yelling 'pass the freaking salt' at the top of their lungs."

Spock and Beale Street stood together beside a green with water hoses. A foursome of camo-clad golfers milled around the green as one of them, Major Slaughter, addressed a short putt.

No one spoke quietly inside the FPC, and they really let loose outside. Beale Street was eager for some betting action. "Spock, I bet you a mack this guy misses."

Major Slaughter backed away from his putt. "Quiet, please."

"Hey, dude, leave it up close," Beale Street said.

Spock yelled back at his crewmate. "Hold it down, man, these guys are Building 141." Grrrrooorrrr. His stomach growled loud enough to wake the dead.

"We'd appreciate your silence," the Major said. "Both of you loser convicts."

"Come on man," Beale Street answered. "I got a can of mackerel says you fluff."

Major Slaughter pointed his putter at Spock. "Tell your friend to observe etiquette."

Frap frap. Spock looked down at his stomach. He thought his bowels were making noises again. But the source of the noise was elsewhere. Above them. Behind them.

"Observe etiquette?" Beale Street said. "Who do you think you are, Tiger H. mother freaking..."

FRAP FRAP FRAP. Spock's head bobbled around, hoping to find the source of the sound, a throbbing beat he'd heard before, one he should recognize. And as it got louder, he did recognize it. It was the sound of a helicopter rotor. FRAP FRAP FRAP. It was a growing crescendo, a wall of sound, now seeming to come from directly overhead. But nothing was there.

Dark shadows of helicopter blades blinked over and around the green. All the players looked skyward. Nothing was in the sky but clouds. Not even a bird.

The windshield wipers hummed back and forth.

"What do they expect for twenty bucks a month? You don't have to be good at math to know maybe it's better sometimes to just lay in."

"You gonna tell me what you did?" I asked.

Back and forth, back and forth. The wipers never missed a beat.

"Some jobs pay more. Like eighty a month. Out west there's a prison that milks a big herd of cows, and the scuttlebutt is that driving a milk truck from prison to prison is the best job you can have in whole FPC system. Staying in motels, wearing civilian clothes. But in a regular camp, the tailor probably makes more than anyone else. The Warden didn't like it but he had to let this guy Aldo Gucci run the tailor shop 'cause he was the only inmate that knew how to alter clothes.

"Some guys like being all spiffed up for company. So, the tailor always gets a few extra under the table. If you want to keep any self-esteem, a decent shirt helps, especially if you got visitors.

"The commissary had shirts on back order because every inmate bought one to send home with a Gucci monogram. Aldo was rolling in smokes and mackerel. He was a sweet old guy. I think he was only in prison 'cause some DA someplace was facing re-election. A famous name hanging on a DA's belt is a trophy. The shoe shop is good, too. A boot that don't fit is hell on wheels, so everyone is always offering the shoemaker something and like they say in France, idle hands is a Coupe deVille. And baker is good, too."

The wiper blades flapped back and forth, streaking smears across the windshield.

"I worked around golf my whole life so a five-thirty tee time wasn't no big deal for me."

Putz drove into a copse of trees that was the pivot on a dogleg. It was full of dead timber and fallen limbs. Spock sunk deep in the passenger seat; he used a roll of toilet paper for a pillow. Putz attacked a dead branch with a tree saw.

"You should pace your exertion this early in the day," Spock said.

"I'm just collecting my props." Putz loaded the branches into the back of the turf cart.

"Heck, I used to play hooky to just get to the golf course."

"Too much exercise flattens the villi in your intestine. Proper nutrient absorption isn't a joke, you know."

"Sorry I asked. Holy cow, this tee box is awful." Putz loaded refuse from the bin into a plastic bag. "I'd be embarrassed."

"What are you doing?" Spock emptied his bladder on a thirsty palmetto.

"Two and a half years."

"Get off your feet."

"This is props, man, we need props so we can hide in plain sight." Putz slung the trash bag into the bed of the cart and unzipped his own fly. "Jeezy wheezy. These are the worst tee boxes I ever seen."

"There was only one thing about working on the golf course that was a negative sticking point."

In that moment, Rojo scampered out from a clump of trees. He jumped into the turf cart, slammed on the accelerator, and sped away down the course. Then, fifty yards down range, swinging a wide circle, he headed back, slapping his hind quarters as if he in the home stretch at the Kentucky Derby.

"Arriba. Arriba. Andele." Rojo set a course that threatened to run over Putz. "Bwahahaha."

Putz broke into a run and Rojo whipped his steed harder. "Arriba. Arriba. Andele." Putz dodged behind trees, all the while trying to zip up his pants.

"Arriba. Arriba. Andele." Rojo finally realized that the trees were so tightly bunched that Putz could dodge all day. He laughed again, "bwahahaha," and threw the key to the turf cart into a patch of weeds.

"Seeing those butchered tee boxes was a good observation for me at that point in time because I needed something else other than my BabyDoll and the alcohol group to help occupy my cogitation. Also on the plus side, working on the golf course maintenance gave me some telephonic flexibility."

Peace facilitates trade; usually, Rojo and Putz maintained an uneasy truce. On another day, after offloading produce from the cart, Putz borrowed Rojo's cellphone, then walked away for privacy.

"Union Bus Station? I'd like to purchase a one-way ticket to Honolulu." Putz blinked. The phone had gone dead. He punched in another number.

"BabyDoll. Yeah, it's me, sweetie. Hi. Oh God, it's good to hear your voice.

"Two and a half years. How's school?

"You getting good grades?

"You must have a good professor. Yeah, a dynamic guy, huh?

"Yeah, well they don't make very good money.

"Un huh. A Lexus? That's a lot of car for a college teacher. Professor, right. How did you find out...?

"You're with him now? Oh, caught a ride. I see. To the library. Sure.

"No, I'm not in a hurry. I got plenty of time. In fact, I got nothing but time. Hahaha.

"Oh. Sure. I understand. Yeah, well, I'll call again. Just as soon as I can.

"Look for me at Christmas. I'll be the guy carrying the Christmas tree. Yeah, I love you BabyDoll. Tell me you love...?"

A mechanical click. Putz wanted to throw the cellphone, but instead, he slammed the receiver by punching the keypad.

"College, eh?" Spock asked. "I take it that this BabyDoll person is matriculating?"

"Not right now. She had to answer the phone."

Putz returned Rojo's cellphone. "Tell me where I can borrow some fertilizer."

"Besa mi culo."

"Okay. Tell me where I can steal some fertilizer."

"It's in the shed, puta."

They stopped at a bare patch of ground that was a turf man's worst nightmare. "Park in the shade," Spock said.

"Speaking of women, how's things going with your lover girl?" Putz thought that if he got Spock agitated, maybe he would help with the tee boxes.

"You leave me alone, you human discharge." Spock stared into the sky, muttering. Disquieted. He pulled the lime-green panties out of his pocket.

Putz distributed fertilizer on the ground. "I told you about Baby-Doll. I bet Dahlia has forgot all about you."

"This boneheaded inclination to initiative will cost about a hundred shots if they catch you."

"A little work makes the time goes faster." Putz spread peat moss on the tee box and distributed some seed.

"I've been thinking. About my bowels," Spock said.

"Dear Lord, forgive me if I don't ask."

"Wouldn't you think my age would pretty much rule out ulcerative colitis?"

"Jeez, Spock, I don't even know what that is." Spock could make a guy turn goosey, and Putz wished he was alone to calm his nerves with a few squeezes of toilet paper.

A couple of weeks later, Putz was still on task, distributing peat moss on the tee boxes and seeding bald spots.

Spock seemed to have taken root in the cart. Like a bump on a stump. He froze like a block of ice when he saw Dahlia and her golf foursome approach in their golf carts. Putz was caught unawares, and startled when he heard a woman giggle.

"Scramble, man, you're busted now," Spock said.

Putz scurried to gather up what was left of a bale of peat. He hid it behind the cart as the ladies readied to tee off. As Dahlia selected her club, Spock stiffened involuntarily and his foot hit the accelerator. The engine roared to life.

"Quiet, please," Dahlia said. Her Germanic accent demanded compliance.

Putz kicked Spock's foot off of the pedal and the engine died.

"Have you girls noticed how nice these tee boxes are starting to look?" Dahlia asked her friends.

"This is the way tees are supposed to be maintained," a major's wife said.

"I wish I knew who to thank," Dahlia said.

WHACK. One of the ladies smacked a drive. It hugged the right side of the track, seemed to climb effortlessly above the trees, then curled back left, bounding to the middle of the fairway. "You're up, Dahlia."

Dahlia selected a club, walked onto the tee and, and fanny aimed in the direction of Putz and Spock, bent over to tee her ball. A spectacular view of a lime-green panty-clad patoot saluted the maintenance men.

Spock's head nearly exploded. "Jesus, Mary and Joseph. I'm going to have an aneurism." Drool oozed down his chin.

Dahlia swung, made nice contact, and watched while the last two ladies teed their balls and hit. Then they bagged their drivers and before driving away, Dahlia deposited a white paper sack beside the tee. Then they were away.

"Hahaha. Littering. She wants to show me her contempt for authority. That minx," Spock said, mopping his brow.

"You're nuts. It's a gift. She left us a present. A thank you," Putz said.

Putz drove alongside and picked up the white paper sack. He reached inside to discover its contents. Cookies. "Oatmeal. It's her way of telling us 'thank you' for the tee boxes."

"Give me one of those," Spock demanded.

Putz extended the bag to his crewmate and as a reward, Spock grabbed it away.

"These are for me. She knows the way to a man's heart is through his alimentary canal." Spock put the sack of cookies under his seat, out of Putz' reach. "God, what a woman."

"Keep 'em," Putz said. He didn't like oatmeal cookie powder all that much, and that's all that what would be left if he put up a struggle with Spock. Besides, cookies only provide temporary solace. They don't have the power to soothe a savage breast like a nice plump roll of toilet paper.

With the last bit of air in his lungs, Spock answered, "Jesus, Mary and Joseph. She does love me. This is as real as it gets."

▌▌ forty-seven, forty-eight, forty-nine," Boss Hack counted
●●● them off that evening. "Okay, count's right," and left the barracks.

The Waterfront bunk had just one occupant. Putz was again without a bunkie. As soon as Boss Hack was gone, all the inmates changed out of their khaki uniforms and into sweats or gym pants.

Rojo confronted Spock, "Pay up your debts, Spock. You owe me sixty macks."

"Help yourself, Rojo," Spock said, shaking cookie crumbs out of his uniform. "Take sixty-five if you want, you earned it. There's a couple packs of smokes in there too. You want them, too?"

Rojo's brow scrunched in suspicion. "You sick man?"

"I haven't felt this good since a hot oil enema restored my bacterial bloom."

"Que pasa, Putz?" All the inmates were curious. "What's come over this crazyman?"

"It's my new 'work is its own reward' program," Putz said. He forced a couple of tolls of toilet paper into empty spaces in his locker. "A twelve step. Under my tutelage, Spock has found the meaning of life."

"I'll bite," Butterfly said. "Okay, Spock, what's the meaning of life?"

"Up yours," Spock said. "Figure it out for yourself."

CHAPTER 10

FELONY

"So, three days before Christmas, me and old Spock were crewed with Irish Jimmy and Roland the Cajun kid. A washed- out sand trap along the 14th fairway needed repair. It was bright and early..."

"Holy Saint Michael," Irish Jimmy said, inhaling through his nose. "Where am I getting that smell? Cigar smoke. What I wouldn't give for a great big fat cigar."

Putz wiped his sweaty brow. "Borrow me your phone," he said to Irish Jimmy. "Do you mind?" He punched in a number.

"Union Bus Station? This is Mr. Sackett and I want to speak to your manager." A mechanical click; the call was over. Putz scowled. Irish Jimmy was still sniffing the wind. Putz entered another number, lots of digits so the number had to be long distance. He listened. No answer. He snapped the phone closed.

With no warning, a couple of golf carts skidded to a stop nearby. Together, they carried four golfers. Soldiers. Each of them wore camouflage golf gear littered with ribbons, stripes, medals and pins. Officers. They all puffed on big stogies.

Irish Jimmy inhaled the second-hand smoke deeply, through his nose. He was taken up in rapture, his voice dripping with such reverence that it reminded Putz of a Methodist preacher speaking the name of the Almighty from the pulpit.

"Hey convicts, we're acting on intelligence." It was Major Slaughter. "Looks like someone's selling produce back here."

"Arturo Fuente," Irish Jimmy said in a rhapsody.

"We can fix you up, but cash don't do us much good," Putz told the Major. "It's contraband."

"Putz, deez guys are smoking Arturo Fuentes."

"We'll load you down for a dozen of those CEE-gars," Putz told the Major.

"Five."

"Eight."

"Six."

Putz nodded his acceptance and with a 'thumbs up' and loaded a garbage bag full of the best home-grown produce ever raised in Florida into the back of the Major's cart. And thrusting his palm toward Major Slaughter, said, "That'll be seis Arturo Fuentes, El Major-o."

"Come and get them."

"What? Where?"

"Building 141," the Major said. The golfers laughed like devils, then jetted away, leaving Putz with nothing in his hand but his ying-yang.

"A woman is just a woman but a good cigar is a smoke. If that Rambo major thought he was going to stiff the Putz, he had another think coming, I tell you."

CHAPTER 11

PENETRATING THE INNER SANCTUM

"**B**efore noon, everyone in minimum security would know that I'd been disrespected by Major Slaughter. By evening I'd be a laughing horse. It's prison, and in prison, even the walls have ears, even if there's no wall."

"You have to get the man his cigars," Roland said.

"I don't think they'll let me order them at the commissary."

"Even if you could, you have to get the purloined cigars. Replacements won't do. If you want respect, you have to get the originals. From the source," Spock said. "But then, you'd have to be a hero. Putz."

"Spock, you're a flake," Putz said. But even a flake can be right part of the time. Irish Jimmy was a friend. That venomous Major had swindled a good guy that wasn't asking for anything for himself but a good smoke. A lot of guys would slough off the idea of his buddy being disrespected. Not Putz. Spock was right. It was important. If he let the matter hang, the inmates would treat him like a punk, and worse, so would the guards.

"I'm going after those cigars," Putz said. They were nearing a heavy wooded patch near a lake.

"Stop," Spock shouted. "Emergency." He sprinted into the bushes and squatted, his pants around his ankles.

"You okay?"

"Processed oatmeal," Spock wailed. "Instant."

"Dude, if you poop out something long and pink you need to swallow it quick. It's your tongue," Putz said.

"I can die now. The legacy is intact."

"Hurry it up. I'm on a mission."

"I may die, but at least there's someone to carry on the family name. My sister-in-law had a boy. A son to carry on the family name."

"Glowczyzna. I get it, man, it just wouldn't be right to let a heritage like that die off."

"True," Spock might have said, his vocalization sounded more like "t'roOOO-ah," followed by a whimper.

"No other men in your family?"

"There's an uncle. Casimir. UuuunnNHHh, oh Lord. Well, we call him 'uncle.'"

"How's that?" Immediately, Putz crunched his face into that 'I should have known better than to ask' face.

"Hermaphrodite."

Putz couldn't extract himself from the turf cart fast enough. He was pissed. "Now daggonit Spock that's just bald-faced horse hockey and you know it. Can't I go get some cigars without you shaking a morphadite out of your family gene pool? Crap."

"UuuunnNHHh...oh the humanity. I'm melting."

"Well hurry it up. I got places to go." Putz grabbed at Spock's roll of toilet paper.

Spock snatched it away. "That's my roll. I'm taking my ass wipe and going home. You get the cigars yourself."

From across the lake, the maintenance men heard the piercing scream of a woman's voice. "EEEEK! EEEEK!"

It was Dahlia. Her voice cried out again, unquieting the peaceful lake and maintenance men on the far side.

"Look," Putz shouted at Spock. "A gator."

Dahlia was alone on a tee adjoining the lake. Alone except for a half a bottle of vodka in her hand. An alligator swam in her direction. It slithered ever closer. "EEEEK! EEEEK!" But she never dropped the bottle.

The gator pulled itself onto the bank.

Putz jumped into the turf cart and jammed his foot on the accelerator. He roared off toward the tee box. Still squatting, Spock peeked through the underbrush.

"Stay out of it, Putz. This is my business."

Putz slid to a stop. He leaped from the vehicle, dashed to the back of Dahlia's golf cart, and grabbed a club from her bag.

He took a quick glance at the clubhead. It was marked with a "5." Putz pursed his lips and shook his head 'no.' "Five iron? Nah. Six is plenty." He returned the club to the bag, and withdrew the "6."

Now Spock scurried toward the action, trying to run, cinching up his belt, all the while bobbling a roll of toilet paper, its tail flagging behind, reeling longer with every stride.

As Dahlia's caterwauling intensified, the alligator stalked closer, its teeth menacing, its mouth gaping open and snapping shut.

"EEEEK! EEEEK!" The mouth of the alligator again yawned wide, showing a pink gullet that darkened to a cavern beyond his sharp teeth.

Putz scootched warily toward the oncoming lizard, between the beauty and the beasty. And with the smoothest of takeaways, lofted the six iron in a perfect-form backswing.

"That whole year was like a filament of my imagination. But for a moment there, I felt like a real man again, alive in my own skin."

KA-BLOOIE. The alligator exploded in a spray of blood and gore.

Putz jerked around. Dahlia held a pump shotgun at crotch level. She pumped the gun again and pulled the trigger. KA-BLOOIE. The gun fired again. Pump, KA-BLOOIE, pump, KA-BLOOIE, pump, KA-BLOOIE. Hunks of alligator flesh, blood and gristle splattered across the tee.

"You've killed an endangered species," Putz shouted.

"Don't take another step," Dahlia said, and Putz complied. She was boozy and her shotgun was now pointed directly at his chest. She took a step in his direction, another and another, each step slower than the last. Now the barrel was under Putz' chin. And Dahlia snatched his FPC cap. "My trophy. I'll wear it in remembrance."

"That's uniform. I can't go back without it," Putz pleaded.

"Then you have a problem, inmate," Dahlia said. "Go away now. I have a round of golf to finish." She crawled into her cart and drove away.

Putz remembered his quest. He would by everything holy get those cigars, but he didn't need Spock hanging on, especially if the fool was going to be spraying poop like a fire hose. But he couldn't leave him. The derelict needed a keeper.

Putz dropped him off with Rojo, then sped on, to the course maintenance shed. In a trash bin, he found an empty pack of Camel cigarettes. He picked up a roll of clear plastic refuse bags. The cart already held two bags of trash. He jettisoned surplus toilet paper.

Now he was off again, across country, past the clubhouse, steering a course around the driving range, fearing he might attract too much attention. He continued past the parking lot and dodged traffic on a busy road. Ahead of him was an avenue that led to a well-fortified gateway into Eglin Air Force Base.

He turned onto the boulevard. The distance between Putz and the gate was still a quarter of a mile. Ahead, he saw a long line of vehicles backed up, waiting to enter the gate. Snappy-uniformed guards searching the first vehicle, a limousine with flags waving from the front-fender aerials. All the doors were wide open. The trunk was sprung and the contents of suitcases spread across the lawn. The well-dressed passengers of the motorcar, four women, stood spread-eagle with their hands on the car's roof. The guards molesting them, taking turns, groping their breasts, reaching up their dresses from behind, probing their crotches. The prettiest ones, those posing the greatest hazard to national security, were directed to the side for follow-up gropes. Dozens of cars waited patiently for a turn. Putz eased it up and over the curb and drove toward the gate on the grassy lawn beside the road. Nearing the gate, he slowed to a crawl. He caught the attention of one of the armed molesters, thumbed at the trash bags in the bed of the cart, and flashing the empty pack of Camels in his palm as if it were a badge, got a nod. He resumed speed and breezed past the gate.

"A guy in khaki with a bag of trash is like a stealth bomber."

Putz was on the biggest and most secure air force base in the world. He had no idea how he would complete his mission of getting cigars for his pal, or how he would locate Building 141. When he ran into a group of airmen walking, he stopped and pretended to pick up litter. He was unseen, hiding in plain sight.

He drove past maintenance hangars and air traffic towers, on-base housing complexes and parade grounds. The smartest thing to have done would have been to ask for directions, but being a male, that course of action was entirely out of the question. Moreover, he would not breach the hiding-in-the-open protocol.

Arrows on the signboards directed travelers in all which ways to dozens of buildings and facilities, each marker painted with an unintelligible alphabet soup of military acronyms. Then he spotted a cluster of office buildings almost at the horizon. Promising. Ignoring the garbled signs, he drove in that direction.

Nearing the complex, he saw that several smaller campuses were set off from the center giving the footprint of the complex the shape of a five-pointed star. Ahead he found another signboard. He stopped to study this one closely and found what he was looking for, an entry that said "BUILDING 141 ➡."

He turned the nose of the cart to follow the arrow, maybe the distance of a good driver-nine-iron. He approached one of the smaller campuses, a cluster of two-story buildings.

The sun seemed to dim near this point on the star. A windsock hung as limp as a dishrag from a pole beside the road. Then the earth was overtaken by a frightful sound. He was ill at ease, filled with dread. Fwap fwap fwap. Close by and unmistakable. The beating noise of the blades of a helicopter. FWAP FWAP FWAP. The throbbing rotor-sound grew louder, now it was thudding above him, assaulting his ears as if it were directly overhead, on top of him. A twisting, strobing shadow overtook the cart, then moved on.

Putz looked skyward. Nothing but thin, puffless clouds. Not even a bird. His body shivered, but he pushed ahead, his cart's snout in the direction indicated by arrow on the roadside notice.

He progressed down a lane, stopping at trash bins, pretending to pick up trash, under the radar of the groups of Airmen that filed along on sidewalks. A building loomed ahead. It stood out from the others in its splendid gloom. Ominous and dark, it reminded Putz of Darth Vader.

Building 141. Putz slowed, approaching the edifice with caution. He pulled into a lot and parked alongside a dumpster. He snagged a roll of trash bags from the bed of the turf truck and entered the building. A sign over the door read "BUILDING 141—SPECIAL OPERATIONS."

Inside the entrance, two marshals operated a metal detector. Behind them, the motto of Spec Ops emblazoned the wall in giant letters, warning all who entered that "IF I CAN SEE YOU, I CAN KILL YOU. IF YOU RUN, YOU'LL DIE TIRED."

Putz gripped the roll of trash bags in his armpit. He flashed the pack of Camels at the marshals, who nodded and looked away. He stepped around the metal detector and into a lobby.

A quick scan of a directory gave Putz the information he needed. "MAJ SLAUGHTER SPEC OPS A-27".

Putz entered a corridor designated "A" and worked his way, careful not to hurry, toward the far end. Light in the hallway was dim; it extended ahead as if it were a tunnel. He emptied trash from each room, here and there leaving a loaded trash bag in the hallway. Like a trail of breadcrumbs, the refuse tracked his progress. A-24. A-25. A-26. He drew near and entered a room designated "A-27."

Inside, Major Slaughter sat behind a desk. It was uncluttered and polished to a sheen. His walls almost sagged under the weight of certificates, commendations, awards and military paraphernalia.

The Major was sharpening a knife. It had a long, shiny blade with a deep bloodline. The Major's eyes gleamed with a predatory lust.

The desk was in the middle of the room, and behind it a credenza against the back wall. On top was a humidor, and on one end, on the floor, a trash can.

Putz walked past the Major's desk as if he owned the place. "Escusa, senor."

Putz opened the lip of the humidor and dumped all of the cigars, dozens and dozens, into a plastic bag. Then he dumped the contents of the Major's trash can on top.

"Gracias, senor. Buenos."

"Freak off," the Major said, testing the sharpness of his blade on a fingernail.

Putz exited the room. Major Slaughter never looked up.

In the corridor now, Putz backtracked, picking up the trail of trash bags that evidenced his journey into Building 141.

CHAPTER 12

BLIND JUSTICE

"So, I got a ton of cigars and a disciplinary hearing in two weeks if I don't get out in three days with a bus ticket to Honolulu. And no FPC cap on my head which is automatic shots. I never felt so all alone. I was as low as whale poop in bottom of the Mariana trench."

From the nearby airbase, Putz heard sonic boons BOOM BOOM BOOM.

CRACK CRACK CRACK. A wooden gavel slammed on a judge's bench and the sound echoed around a cavernous courtroom. The sonic booms triggered a memory that he had tried to bury. He couldn't repress it now. A wave of reminiscences washed over him. He remembered the last day he saw his BabyDoll, the day of his sentencing hearing.

He wore a Hawaiian shirt, that part of the memory was vivid, and he remembered too that he turned to BabyDoll with a smile and a 'keep your chin up' gesture. That part was seared. Seared. Blonde and bouncy, she sat in the otherwise empty gallery. She was younger than Putz, over-endowed and was cuddling a teddy bear for bravery. And fussing with a hemline that was hardly long enough to mask her most outstanding feature, what had first captivated Putz' interest in her. She had a nice round fanny.

A baby-faced lawyer sat beside Putz, his name was Smucker. His prosecutor sat behind a matching table across the well of the court.

Above them on a platform at the front of the courtroom, a clerk, a bailiff, and a court reporter flanked a stern judge. The jurist was female, probably in her fifties. Her courtroom was as cold and uninviting as an operating theater. It had none of the warm wooden panels or rich appointments that John Grisham novels suggest are ubiquitous in American jurisprudence. The plaque on her bench read "JUDGE WEREGELD."

And the judge was talking. "Larry Joe Sackett, you've been charged with an offense under section eighteen fifty-two of title eighteen of the United States Code."

Putz stood. "Guilty, your honor."

"Hold your horses, cowboy. First, I get to ask you 'how do you plead.' Ahem. How do you plead?"

"Guilty."

"Recommendation?"

The prosecutor rose to his feet. "The government asks for restitution, your honor, a fine of a thousand dollars, and incarceration. We have a plea agreement, your honor, and we're dismissing charges against the defendant's co-conspirator."

BabyDoll giggled and gave a cutesy little wave to Judge Weregeld.

"Incarceration is to take place in a federal prison camp," the prosecutor continued, "pursuant to the plea agreement. We'd suggest Eglin Air Force Base in Florida. Mitigating factors would argue for eighteen months. That's the lower end of the DOJ sentencing guidelines."

"I'll accept your recommendation on the camp, but the defendant's behavior was wanton and willful. Defense counsel, do you have anything to say?"

Smucker shrugged.

The Ascendant

Judge Weregeld peered over her glasses. "Is there any reason I shouldn't enhance the sentence? I'm leaning toward thirty months."

"He was under the influence, your honor," Smucker said. "Everyone knows a drunk can't form the requisite intent."

"He was?" the prosecutor asked.

"No, I wasn't," Putz said.

BabyDoll jumped to her feet. She nearly fell off of her high-spiked heels. "He was as sober as a judge."

"Alcohol or drugs?"

"No," Putz insisted.

"He doesn't even drink," BabyDoll cried.

CRACK CRACK CRACK. The gavel slammed again against the judge's bench. "Two years! Can I have quiet now?"

"He won't be with me for Christmas," BabyDoll plead. "Dahlin' you've got to be out for Christmas."

CRACK CRACK CRACK "Two and a half years. Mister big shot defense attorney, you tell that client of yours he better learn to keep his mouth shut. Am I clear?"

Schmuck nodded.

"You better seek drug and alcohol treatment when you get settled in your new home, buster," the judge said. "And I'm not listening to any phony baloney give me-time-to-wind-up-my-affairs plea, either. Surrender yourself three days from today. February 10th. At two o'clock p.m. at the Federal Prison Camp at Eglin Air Force Base, Florida. Now let me tell you something, son. I'm probably wasting my breath because you don't look like the kind that knows how to listen. But you'll improve your chances if you take my counsel to heart. You probably don't believe it but I never want to see or hear from you again."

"Thank you, your honor. Just what is it you want to tell me?"

"Learn to keep your mouth shut, you dope. Two and a half years. Do you have more smart aleck remarks? 'Cause I can go higher."

"Thank you, your honor," Smucker said. His voice was inaudible. The judge's ringing pronouncement reverberated in the near-empty chamber. Finally, it died away. "Court's dismissed."

BabyDoll boohoo-ed into Putz's shirt-tail.

As the judge swooped out of the courtroom, her bailiff cried out "all rise."

The lovers embraced as if they would never have the chance to touch one another again, the bitterness bettered by the sweetness.

"He was cold sober," BabyDoll blubbered to Smucker.

"Two and a half years. For cutting down a tree?" Putz asked.

"The devil's in the details, pal. It was a national forest," Smucker said.

"It's not Christmas without a tree. You promised me...I'd...that I'd... never be alone at Christmas." BabyDoll buried her face in Schmuck's shoulder.

"He'll get some good time. I'm pretty sure. He might."

"I might?"

"You bet your life you might. Then they let you out to a halfway house."

"Dahlin', I'll wait for you." But the waterworks seemed to have been cut off at the spigot. "I'll wait til Christmas. Not a day longer."

"So, now it was a week before Christmas, and my BabyDoll was on her way. I didn't know if I was even going to get to see her because of the disciplinary problem hanging over my head and getting worse all the time. And that bus ticket to Honolulu."

CHAPTER 13

ASCENDANCY OVER WOMEN

It was early afternoon and returning to the course, Putz was bushed. But as he shook the old memories, he spotted Irish Jimmy on the 18th fairway and delivered the Arturo Fuentes. He was nearly run down by Dahlia. "Hey. I want my cap," Putz shouted as she sped by.

"Idzzzz mine," she shouted back, her tongue thick with vodka. She put pedal to metal and Putz took chase. Across fairways and around lakes, sand traps and greens. Before long, her evasive maneuvers led her near Rojo's garden.

"EEEEK! EEEEK!" Dahlia screamed.

Spock saw what he couldn't unsee. His worst fear. In his mind, Putz was chasing Dahlia to have his filthy disgusting perverted way with the temple that was her golden body. Dahlia. The woman of his dreams. A deity. The goddess atop the pedestal. The divine in a vesture of lime-green panties, who would be polluted by the mere touch of the profane Putz, who had once been his friend, but in this moment, his mortal enemy. "Son of...Jesus Mary and Joseph. I'll kill the porch climbing slug in a ditch."

Spock and Rojo loaded into a cart and roared after Putz in hot pursuit. "Arriba. Arriba. Andele," Rojo shouted. "I'll kill you with my bare hands," Spock added.

Rojo's steed had superior power. As he gained ground, Putz' cart began to sputter. "Out of gas," Putz banged his fists on the wheel.

Hearing the shouts of the Latino and the crazy man behind him, Putz broke off his pursuit of Dahlia and rolled to a stop in a clutch of trees.

"Coward. Face me," Spock shouted. "That's my woman."

"Arriba. Arriba. Andele."

Hammer down, Rojo chased Putz into the woods. Running, dodging, evading, the prey broke out of the timber and into another fairway. No trees guarded him.

Over his shoulder, Putz could see that the lunatics were ever closer, now drawing down on him. His muscles burned with exhaustion. He gulped for air like a landed carp.

He counted his options and they were non-existent. So, he reversed field. He ran headlong into the face of the oncoming cart. He launched himself fist forward at the adversary in the passenger's seat, Spock. Like Superman, Putz flew parallel to the ground. And as he slammed into Spock, face-to-face, the steering wheel of the cart spun wildly. It tipped on two wheels. Spock and Putz spilled off in a heap.

Without their weight, the turf cart twisted and turned further. Rojo had no control.

"Ayuda me Jesus," Rojo cried out.

Putz and Spock wrestled one another to the ground. Both of Putz' hands gripped Spock around his turkey-like neck. But over their shouted threats to one another, they heard Rojo's death rattle. "OoooOOOOOooooo..."

The combatants stopped their battle, disengaged their bodies, and approached the wreckage. They found Rojo underneath the upturned cart. His tongue hung out, his mouth drooled a trickle of blood.

Spock felt Rojo's neck. "No pulse." Rojo was as dead as a man with two doctors.

"Cerebral hemorrhoid," Putz said. His mouth formed a shape to rip off a spiel of profanity.

"I don't mind telling you, I said a ton of explicatives."

"Why were you doing trying to run me down?"

"What are you doing running after my woman?"

"She's the General's wife, knucklehead. She's not your woman."

"She gave me panties."

"Rojo stole those, chump."

"Liar!" Spock leapt for the throat of his mortal enemy and again they wrestled to the ground. Putz gained the upper hand with a choke hold.

"She means nothing to me. I need your help."

"What do you want?" Spock squeaked.

Putz eased off and gave himself a moment to think.

"Help me load the Mexican." Together, the maintenance men righted the cart. They loaded Rojo's lifeless body into the bed.

"Oh, Lordy," Spock said. "My gastrointestinal tract can't take this stress."

"Just keep your mouth shut. We can't stop now."

Putz drove the turf cart back to the far end of the course. A couple of hundred yards away, a road crew malingered beyond the fence. Spock rode all the way in a glassy catatonia, as immobilized as the passenger in the bed of the cart. "Get off your pampered duff and help me lift him," he told Spock as he dismounted the cart.

"We could stuff him in a storm drain," Spock said. "Or throw him in the lake. Let the alligators eat him."

"They won't eat his clothes."

"Yeah, they probably know better than to eat Puerto Ricans anyway. Gad, I'm bloating just thinking about it."

"We're going to hide him in plain sight."

Putz and Spock hoisted Rojo's lifeless body over the fence, then Putz dragged the corpse to the middle of the road, leaving it crosswise. He thought to steal Rojo's cap. That would solve one problem, he thought, but if Rojo's body didn't have a cap, it might arouse suspicion. And the deceased has written "Rojo" under the bill. Wearing Rojo's hat could only draw attention. So, after securing Rojo's hat on his head, he returned, jumped the fence and slid under the wheel beside Spock.

Before making their getaway, the scream of an engine came from the far end of the road. They turned to see an SUV weaving down the roadway at high speed. Without slowing at all, it ran over Rojo's body with a bump-thump, then it fishtailed erratically, past the squashed body in the road.

A couple of hundred yards away, inmates from the road crew scattered as the SUV approached.

Butterfly fled across the roadway. "Help, we'll all be killed," he screamed, distant and in vain.

Tires screeched. The SUV hammered into the running Butterfly. His body bounced up and over the fender, windshield and roof and rolled into the ditch. Skidding to a stop, the SUV ejected its driver. As the inmates rushed to Butterfly's side, the driver slumped out onto the roadway on all fours. The unmistakable sounds of retching fell on the ears of the maintenance men.

The driver wore lime-colored panties.

"Dahlia," Spock wailed.

She gained control, got back in the SUV, and drove away.

"Hold on tight, Spock, we're making tracks, and if you even think about mentioning your bowels, I'm going to kick your whoosey whatsey up between your shoulder blades." Putz pointed the nose of the cart in the direction of the garden in the woods, the patch below the storage shed and swimming pool, the residence of the General and his homicidal wife.

When they got close, still rolling, Putz jumped out of the cart. "Get back to the barracks. Be there for head count," he told Spock. "And keep your mouth shut. You hear me?"

Spock nodded as Putz ran out of the woods, up a low grade, into the teeth of perdition, Dahlia's house.

The Ascendant

The atmosphere inside the General's house was noir. Putz found Dahlia in the great room. A single shaft of light stabbed across and down from above, and in it, dust glittered as if loitering on the beam of light. Swanky saxophone music tumbled into the space from another room.

The General's wife had changed out of her golf togs. Now she wore a floor-length, cool white satin dressing gown that was open to her navel, alluring, dressed to the nines.

When he could rip his eyes away from her, Putz saw that his baseball cap rested on a sofa table beyond her.

She stood beside a bureau with an open drawer. Putz could see that the storage space contained a pistol, one that appeared to be nickel-plated with pearl grips. Dahlia left the drawer open long enough to make certain that Putz saw the weapon, then eased it closed. She glided across the great room and mixed a cocktail. She downed it in a moment. Standing now in front of the mantle of a huge fireplace, her gown seemed to defrost, melting to opacity.

"I suppose you think you can break in here and have your way," she said.

"I thought maybe I could borrow back my baseball cap."

"I won't call the guards. You're safe here. Sit. You look exhausted."

"I saw what happened by the road. I ain't going to be the fall guy for nothing."

"Vodka makes me do foolish things. Let me fix you a drink."

"No thanks. It's an alcohol group policy. They're funny about that."

"I see. You wouldn't be caught dead having anything to do with a tired old sack of bones like me." Her tongue was thick with booze and her Euro accent more pronounced. Dahlia sat her empty glass on the mantle, and leaned back, languorously. One hand felt inside the neck of her garment, the other rubbed her thigh. Her nipples went erect and out-thrusted. Now a pair of eye-pleasing half-moon bumps appeared on the satin gown, light above and dark below, complimentary dualities, fire and ice.

"No one ever called you a sack of bones."

"Why didn't you get me a Gucci blouse?"

"Why do you torment my pal Spock? Listen, that ball cap has a gallon of my DNA in it so just let me have it and I'm adios."

"You can't leave. Have a drink. I think I might have killed a man."

"Far be it from me to be a stickler for numbers, but I can see where the brain thrust of the long arm of the law around here might figure you killed two."

"One. Two. What's the difference?"

"My best friends are killers. They think it makes a difference."

"You're nothing but a coward."

"Yeah? Well you're a...lousy cookie maker."

"You sad demented loser. I guess you prefer to punk for Black Bubba."

A glassy stare overtook Putz' face. He didn't like being called a loser or a punk. He stepped closer to Dahlia. Closer. Now he was in her space.

"That's my friends you're talking about."

"Did you see me run over that man?"

Putz spotted a telephone. "I think I'll call the police."

Dahlia leaned toward him on the sofa table, and for a slim moment, Putz thought she was going to give him his cap. Instead, she pulled the pistol from the drawer.

He had nothing to lose. Putz walked toward Dahlia, slowly. Her hand shook. She had no intention of pulling the trigger. She knew, Putz knew. He grabbed the gun and Dahlia struggled, but she gave it up, far too easily. He twisted the pistol out of her grasp.

"You saw." She had a mocking smile. "You have nothing. You will never tell."

Putz' face grimaced with anger. Not hatred. He was angry that he was having so much trouble getting his walking papers, he was angry that Rojo chased him in the turf cart, and angry that he had to fight Spock. Most of all, he was furious that that he felt sorry for the woman with the lustrous locks of hair falling over her shoulder, and spilling across her pouty breasts. The woman in possession of his baseball cap. He knew she was the SUV driver and he knew that she was drunk. They both knew. Unseen by the crying woman, Putz emptied the bullets from the weapon and put them in his pocket.

Dahlia fell to the floor in a heap, sobbing into her hands. "Shoot me. Put me out of this miserable life."

Putz pointed the pistol at Dahlia. "So. This is what you want." CLICK.

Dahlia screamed.

CLICK CLICK. She fell silent.

"Take me, you animal."

Putz threw the gun aside, then dragged Dahlia to her feet. He slapped her across the face.

"You'll take me...if you're a man."

"And my kiss will dissolve the silence that makes you mine," Putz said.

Putz and Dahlia gave themselves to one another with wild abandon. On the floor of the great room, against the wall, on the couch, the mantel and desk. A bullet fell out of Putz' pocket and onto the floor. Then another. Before darkness overtook them, all the bullets had spilled from his pocket and into the lush pile of carpet in the great room.

Dahlia lit two cigarettes and gave one to Putz.

"I can't go on without you. When can I see you again?"

"Check with my appointment secretary."

"Don't be like that. Don't be like...the others."

Dahlia used her cold sexuality to define herself, a weapon she hoped could free her from an unbearable existence. She manipulated, seduced and destroyed, but in the end, it was Dahlia that was ruined, by her own hand, driven by craven passion. She fell into the pit with her victims, herself the most wretched of the fatalities she left in her own wake.

"That cold, heartless Jezebel. She'd never given herself to a man. Not really, not until…that day. She was like a black widow spider. She thought it was amusing, to set a trap to devour me, but her lust put her in the snare. And in my act of taking, I gained…my ascendancy."

"I'm out of here," Putz said.

"I can't live like this. My marriage is a prison. It has no love. I'm shackled to a loveless existence. What's your name? You haven't even told me your name. Please, tell me. Don't do this to me." Dahlia was a broken woman, sobbing inconsolably, heartsick.

Putz yanked on his baseball cap. "I am man. You are woman." Dust swirled in the shaft of light that fractured the great room. Putz was gone.

CHAPTER 14

WALKING PAPERS

"I made it back to the FPC ahead of head count. I was exhausted from the fighting and running and...the rest. I almost got ran over by a turnpike bus as it turned into the parking lot."

A sign in the destination window of the big sleek motorcoach read "HONOLULU, HAWAII." It stopped near Putz, pulling alongside with a whoosh of its brakes.

The door opened and out jumped Moneybags. "Putz."

"Moneybags. Good to see you, bunkie."

"It's good to be seen."

"What happened to lock down?"

"They sent me back. The IRS couldn't negotiate my check. They had no cause, no reason to discipline me."

"It bounced?"

"Like a crème brûlée. That hot check proves my innocence."

Putz pumped his bunkie's hand and slapped him on the back. "I couldn't find your lawyer."

Moneybags shrugged. "Not to worry. I shot a seventy-three on furlough. They put my name on an enormous crystal vase. I owe it all to your coaching."

"The bus?"

393

"There's no task too daunting if it facilitates my bunkie." And as he said it, he handed Putz a ticket, destination: Honolulu, Hawaii. "We bought the bus line out of bankruptcy."

Putz marched into the office like he owned the place. He hovered over the caseworker.

"Here's my bus ticket. I want those walking papers and I want them now."

"I don't have you on my appointment calendar," she said.

"I don't have time for that."

"These things take time, Sackett."

"Listen, lady, you're out of time. I'm making a call to my BabyDoll, and I'm going to use your phone. And if you try to throw up any barricades or if the paperwork ain't done when I'm finished, I'm calling the Warden. If I have to call him, I'm telling him about that fake sheepskin you got hanging on the wall. We'll see how long it takes YOU to get YOUR walking papers and if anyone has to wait in line for an appointment."

"You wouldn't."

"Yeah, believe me, I would. I'm so torqued that I can't wait to watch you squirm with an Alcatraz hanging around your neck like me which from now on you'll refer to as Mr. Sackett. But it's up to you. Is it going to be my way? Or the highway?"

His barrack's mates gathered in the parking lot to wish Putz a fond farewell. Once on board the bus, destination Honolulu, Hawaii, he opened a window and waved goodbye to his friends.

As the bus pulled out of the prison parking lot, Beale Street told Moneybags, "He'll be back."

"I rather doubt it," Moneybags said. "And I'm willing to wager a case of hair restorative that he won't."

"So, the way I got it fingered, I tampered with evidence of a crime which I could only hope would be a federal offense, and on top of that I extorted a federal agent, either of which would have put me in lock down til the end of whenever hell freezes over."

The bus rolled out of the FPC's parking and onto a roadway. It passed a large white-on-green highway sign that designated the thoroughfare as "REGINALD P. RAPPAPORT HIGHWAY."

Putz checked arrival times on an overhead monitor. Niceville had a modern, bustling airport that adjoined Eglin Air Force Base. He had arrived well before BabyDoll's scheduled arrival time and he was happy that he had. Scores of eager beach-bound travelers crowded the baggage carousels. Standing room only. Christmas was a busy season on the Redneck Riviera.

Putz had a three-foot-tall plastic Christmas tree tucked in his armpit and a wide grin on his face. He stopped at every monitor he passed to double-check arrivals.

The free world was grand. No one was farting. The speakers in the terminal weren't blasting rap music; they were playing cheerful Christmas tunes. The sun was shining, birds were singing, and God was in His heaven. The ordeal was over, but incarceration had been nothing compared to the hell of separation from his BabyDoll. Everything was perfect until he noticed the flashing banner on an arrival monitor. Delayed. Delayed. Delayed. It was BabyDoll's flight.

"Oh jeez. Late. She won't like that." Nearing a bar, he hesitated, then looked in. The dark quiet appealed to him. It held only a couple of patrons. He checked his watch. He was tense. He wished he had a roll of toilet paper to squeeze. He licked his lips.

"Because of my alcohol problem scam, part of my probation was no booze. Heck, except for maybe a couple of icy cold brews every now and then, booze hadn't even touched my lips for ten years."

Putz seated himself at the bar. He pulled out an adjacent stool and let his plastic Christmas tree join him. He hadn't had the luxury of a quiet place since he walked into the FPC. He would have liked the Christmas decorations on the backbar but he couldn't let himself look up.

"What will you have?"

"Ginger ale." Putz stirred the ice in his drink with his finger. The cubes tinkled against the glass. He stared into his glass. The ice tinkled again. A torrent of old memories tumbled into his brain.

It happened three years ago, at a time when Putz was flush with cash. The golf season had been good to him. He'd been carrying the bag for a guy that had won a couple of tournaments.

He'd booked a rustic cabin high in the mountains. He had two weeks of BabyDoll and snow and skiing to enjoy. She loved frolicking in the powdery white stuff and letting the cold turn her round cheeks cherry-red, then shooting schnapps and snuggling with her afterward. Putz was cleaning up the kitchen when he heard bells, a tiny jingling.

He looked around to see BabyDoll standing in the door of the cabin. She had a small fir tree in one hand and a tree saw in the other. A gust of wind and snow blew in behind her and the tinkling bells jingled again.

"Look. I cut it myself."

Putz slammed the glass of ginger ale to the bar with a crash. When the bartender looked his way, Putz told him "Whiskey. Make it a double."

He tried his best to drown his memories for two hours.

"Hey, pal, I think your plane has arrived," the bartender told him.

Thank goodness, the guy took notice. He deserved a nice tip. Putz gave him what amounted to a week's pay at the FPC.

With his Christmas tree under his arm, Putz waded through a gaggle of eager greeters and kinfolks. The men wore Bermuda shorts, sandals and black socks. Weary travelers dribbled out of a restricted area and to the baggage carousel. No BabyDoll. A pin-striped corporate type checked his wristwatch. A family, the mother trying to rein in the kids, their father shouting at them to walk. An elderly couple. Many more like them. Still no BabyDoll.

She was the last of the deplaning passengers. Putz waved a greeting. He thought his heart would explode. It seemed like it took her forever to cross the restricted area. Finally, she was outside the area set off by warning signs.

He reached out. He needed a kiss. A hug. A kind embrace from another human being. He hadn't been able to caress her since a time he wanted to forget. He reached out for her, but she pushed him back with a stiff-arm, right to the heart.

"I am so mad," she said. Her eyes were a-flutter. "First they cancel my flight. So what if an engine falls off or some lame excuse. I stand in line for a total hour to get a crappy little piece of paper and then have to run like crazy to change terminals and then I snag my hose. Oooooo those muddy funsters are awful darn lucky. I ran like a madwoman or I would have missed the plane to Niceville completely."

BabyDoll spotted the plastic Christmas tree. "Eeuuww. What is that?"

"It's a Christmas tree. I promised you a Christmas tree." His body ached for intimacy, for tenderness, an affectionate caress from another human being.

The eyelid flutter went into double-time. "I am so going to sue their hineys off. Then to top it all off, I'm sitting next to this wild-eyed raving lunatic who is like playing with himself. 'Dahlia. Dahlia.' Then he's mumbling the whole way about spilling blood and chasing men on all fours. Some sickos need to be put in jail."

"You had it pretty bad I guess."

"Eeuuww. That tree's disgusting. What makes it stink?"

"I wish you wouldn't whine."

"If that wasn't bad enough, then I find out you don't get a meal voucher unless you ask for it for their crappy airplane food if you can call it food. Peeuuww. The smell of that tree makes me want to retch."

"I bought it for you." Putz tried to kiss BabyDoll again, to hold her in his arms, to be embraced, but again she pushed him away.

"Eee-yuck. What do you want me to do with it?"

B abyDoll handed a boarding pass to a stewardess stationed at the terminal end of the skywalk. She hobbled forward, as if one of her shoes had a broken heel. Behind her, the large end of the plastic Christmas tree stuck out of her ass from below the hem of her dress. She clomped down the narrow passageway, away to board her departing plane.

CHAPTER 15

I ENTER THE FPC

The windshield wipers beat back and forth and I did a slow burn. That last bit of detail hit me across the face the same as when Fonzie jumped the shark. Or when Keanu Reeves made the bus jump the gap in the bridge in *Speed*.

"Buh-loney," I said. Nothing this asshole said was true. That's why it seemed like I had been watching it. Old TV sitcoms. I'd been watching *Gilligan's Island* reruns for the last couple of hours.

"If I'm lying I'm dying," Putz said.

"Nice try, asshole, but the golf clubs aren't for sale."

"Okay. Okay. I'll tell the story again, but this time, I'll take the Christmas tree out of her ass. You like that better?"

"Just take me to the camp. And keep your trap shut, I got some things to think about."

"I didn't get to finish telling you about Aldo Gucci. Sheesh. Some people."

I noticed that the cab passed a sign on the highway that led to the FPC. It read "REGINALD P. RAPPAPORT HIGHWAY." Didn't prove a thing. It was only natural for Putz to know that name. Big deal.

Putz steered the cab into the parking lot of the FPC. He drove past an empty gatehouse and parked near the front door. He sprung the lock and I collected my leather grip and hard-case golf bag from the trunk.

"My offer is still good. A hundred twenty-five for those Callaways."

"These cost me a grand." I shoved a wad of cash into Putz' hand for the fare.

The cabbie shrugged. "Suit yourself, big tipper. It's that middle door."

I carried my grip and clubs toward the front door to the facility. *I'll be damned if I look back at that asshole,* I told myself. I was sick of the guy and his bullshit big house stories. *He must take me for an idiot.*

Inside, a secretary sat behind a desk, reading a movie magazine, chewing gum. She was coiffed in one of those Woody Woodpecker mall-dos. She gave me the once over. "Something I can do for you?"

"Conrad B. DuRoy reporting for service." I saluted. I might as well act like I wasn't intimidated. Besides, my classy looks figured to put me in the top five percent of guys in this place, and experience told me these semi-pretty girls were pretty easy to convert to resources. "You can call me Conn," I said with a wink.

The secretary let her eyes measure me a second time. Up and down. A Mona Lisa smile curled her lips. "I figure you for about...an eight."

I always figured myself a solid nine, but decided to take eight as a compliment.

"Sit in here. You can put those articles on the table." The order came from behind me, from a short woman who sat behind a table in an adjoining room. When she stood, I was surprised to see how short she really was. The top of her head didn't reach to my underarms. She wore a shiny badge on her belt.

"Sure...uh?" I looked the room over for a name.

"I'm Miss Hack. The inmates call me Boss Hack. And it's my job to tell you what to do, and it's your job to do what I tell you to."

The Ascendant

I lifted the grip and golf bag onto to her table, then watched as Boss Hack dumped the grip's contents in a box, one item at a time. She stood the golf clubs in a corner. The only items left on the table were a toothbrush, a razor, sneakers, one T-shirt and a pair of pants.

"You can ship that other stuff home if you got a cardboard box," she said.

"Can I buy one in the commissary?"

"If you want a cardboard box, you bring your own cardboard box, DuRoy."

"I'll know next time."

"No one likes a smart ass, DuRoy. Stay here, I'll be back."

Boss Hack carried my boxed valuables out of the cubicle. She only left those meager things she'd set aside on the table. She came back minutes later to gather up the bag of golf clubs. Because of her short stature, picking them up was a struggle.

"Be careful with those clubs," he told her. "They're almost new."

Boss Hack returned a sneering look of disgust. "Wise up, chump." She tried to shoulder the bag but the base drug the floor. She battled the bag and heavy clubs out of the room.

It must have taken her five minutes to return. She didn't utter a sound or make eye contact as she walked behind me and pushed my arms to the sky. She patted me down, waist to ankle.

"Okay, sunshine. Drop those drawers." I slowly unbuckled my belt.

"Come on. Come on. We don't have all day, DuRoy. Skivvies too. Shoes too."

I dropped my drawers, then the underwear, as Boss Hack circled to face me.

"Lift your testicles."

I complied. The ceiling had that sprayed on popcorn texture crap.

"Now show me the bottoms."

My brow knitted in confusion. *The bottom of what?* I adjusted my grip on my nuts and twisted until they hurt.

"Not your nuts, dumbass, your feet."

I turned to the wall, and leaning on a waist-high bench, showed the guard the naked bottoms of my feet.

"Palms...okay bend over and spread 'em."

I leaned over the bench, palms to the wall. I distracted my concern for my asshole by looking out the window through a misshapen Venetian blind. I thought maybe that would help me endure the indignity of the inspection, and perhaps it would end sooner. SCHWACK. SCHWACK. I heard a sound I'd heard before, the sound of someone snapping on rubber gloves.

In the parking lot beyond the window, I saw Putz. He was standing by his cab, grinning like an opossum, with my golf clubs slung over his shoulder.

The cabbie's voice was muffled by the glass but his words had no trouble carrying through the window to my ears. "Hey pal, lucky me, I got 'em for seventy-five." Putz clicked his heels, saluted, then threw the bag of fancy new golf clubs in his trunk. The taxi took off in a puff of pollutants.

My face curled into a wince. The finger that was probing my asshole seemed to have a long and sharpened fingernail.

Groaning, I asked my tormentor, "Is that Putz as big a liar as I think he is?"

The probing finger came up empty. SNAP SNAP. Boss Hack removed the rubber gloves. "Dress and make sure you make head count at four."

I stepped out of the examination room and past the secretary. Except for a toothbrush and razor, I was wearing all my worldly possessions.

The secretary gazed at me over her glasses, her lip curled to warn me that I was no longer a human. "That didn't take long," she said.

"It's not every asshole can sing country western," I said, blushing bright red.

The secretary reached into her middle drawer and pulled out a dog-eared list. Centered, underlined, in caps, the title read "OLDIES." She ran her finger down the page.

"Whoa. Number fourteen. Haven't heard that one since last August. And I had you pegged as an eight. Report to A and O, DuRoy."

She thumbed me toward another office. It was bigger than Boss Hack's tiny room, an inner office with no windows.

The caseworker pointed to a chair and I sat. Another woman. Her desk was littered with doughnut carcasses. While she occupied herself with paperwork, I let my eyes roam the room. File cabinets. Case files. Racks. Trays. Pink message slips, yellow sticky notes. A diploma on the wall. I was nervous, and I caught myself humming "Cocaine Blues" under my breath.

My eyes strained to read the diploma: "MASTER OF SCIENCE IN SOCIOLOGY, OKLAHOMA STATE UNIVERSITY."

I heard my heartbeat. Thumpthump. "1987." Thumpthump.

"All righty then, DuRoy. Since there are no issues of substance abuse, let me first share the good news. I've set aside a nice waterfront bunk just for you."

Waterfront. My heartbeat accelerated its pace and volume. I heard and felt my pulse in my eardrums. Thumpthump. Thumpthump.

"Oh, no need. Nothing special for me," I said. My throat was tight and my voice was thin. Thumpthump. Thumpthump.

"Okay then. We'll take just a minute to discuss your work assignment, and then move on to what I'm guessing you're most interested in, pinpointing your release date. Do you have anything to say?"

"Pardon me," I strained to say. Thumpthump. Thumpthump. Thumpthump. Thumpthump. My heartbeat quickened, doubling its pace. My jugular veins throbbed and blood pounded at my temples. I had despised and rejected the counsel of a learned man, a man of sorrows, a man acquainted with grief. It was as if I had hidden his face, despised him, esteemed him not. I swallowed hard, struggling to force a tiny wad of saliva down my parched throat.

"Do you have anything to say?"

"I do."

"We don't have all day. Spit it out."

"I smoke marijuana every day."

THE END

www.ingramcontent.com/pod-product-compliance
Lightning Source LLC
Chambersburg PA
CBHW030336120726
47901CB00007B/1811